SHATTERBONES

ROBERT BROWN

SEVERED PRESS
HOBART TASMANIA

SHATTERBONES

ISBN: 978-1-925493-68-9

This book is dedicated to my amazing wife and partner of seventeen years. You are my one blade of grass.

CHAPTER ONE
BLUE HAZE

Link-In Initiated

12:37PM
Washington D.C.

The distinct popping sound of gunfire can be heard echoing through the armored and reinforced interior of Air Force One. Four Secret Service agents rush up the stairs into the president's traveling office at the top of the jet's cabin.

The president is pushed through the communications room and into a corner of the lounge just outside the cockpit door. The agents take positions around the room hoping to save the president's life. Two other people in the office follow protocol and crouch to the sides of the aircraft to stay out of the agents' line of fire to the stairs. The third man, General McKinnon, draws his own weapon and takes position in line next to the agents. They all await the approaching threat to enter or for the all clear to be given.

"What's happening out there? Is it terrorists? Did someone sneak on board with the press pool?"

A violent shudder reverberates through the 747 followed by the sudden loss of gravity as the plane begins to quickly descend toward the earth. Shouted warnings are given over the intercom as the president and his men are thrown against the ceiling of the craft.

"Massive depressurization detected. We are making an emergency descent to eight thousand feet."

Immediately after the aircraft begins its controlled fall, the noise of gunfire ends and the clamor of screams and shouting echo up the stairwell to the men. The president watches lead agent Barlow holding his hand to his ear, getting filled in on his earpiece even as he works to steady himself on the ceiling and readies for the gravity to return.

A chill runs along the president's spine when he sees the fear etched on the face of this man he thought was made of stone.

"It's still heading to the president. We have to move him into the cockpit!"

1

"Get ready, Mr. President. The pilot is leveling the plane and will open the cockpit door. As soon as you are inside, they will lock that door, strap you in and we'll continue our descent."

"How many of you are coming with me?"

"Mr. President, someone is back there tearing the plane apart and killing everyone. If it makes it past us and into the cockpit…"

His words are interrupted by the odd sensation caused as the aircraft slowly levels and the men awkwardly drift to the ground. As soon as they touch, a somewhat familiar face appears at the top of the stairs and the men begin firing at the target.

The approaching man's movements are blurred with speed. Few rounds are able to be fired from the firearms defending the president, fewer still find purchase in the flesh of this attacker and none are causing him to slow down. He grabs an agent with one hand and tosses him against the back wall with an impossible force. A horrendous cracking sound is emitted as his body hits the solid surface.

After placing his remaining bullets center mass into the assailant's chest, a second agent is folded backward and in half by the massive arms of the pale white attacker. As the seconds tick on, the president watches as one by one, each of the men defending him die. The cockpit door behind him opens and a co-pilot attempts to pull the president to safety, but the president grabs onto the door frame to keep from being pulled in and watches the creature approach him.

His mind is locked in turmoil as he looks at the pale white body stepping forward. The towering and muscular man before him has the president's face but the first lady's eyes and is familiar while at the same time completely unknown.

With bodies littered around the galley and office of the upper deck, the president stands face to face with the blood-stained head and body of someone he now admits to himself that he knows.

Hello, Father, are the final words the president hears before his death. Moments later, Air Force One begins an uncontrolled spiral and a pale, muscular man climbs out of the shattered cockpit windscreen and jumps clear of the plane as it falls to the ground below.

11:37AM
Chicago, Illinois

Imelda Bautista passes a bowl of Pork Adobo to a festival attendee when the light in the sky turns an unusual blue. The festival is filled with strange sights, sounds, and smells, so the blue-tinged light is less noticed by people here than it is in other parts of the globe. The delicious aroma's wafting through the air help to distract people from visual sensory clues and signify yet another marvelous food festival is being held in Chicago. This time, it is the annual Albany Park World Fest which features specialty dishes from around the world.

Imelda remembers the tales her grandparents told her in the Philippines and becomes rigid with fear. Blue light in the day signifies the arrival of the Aswang. Her parents and grandparents were not superstitious people; in fact, they were not religious at all, which is extremely unusual in the highly spiritual and largely Catholic country. Her parents were scientists, like her grandparents before them, and they looked at the world with a skeptical wonder.

She remembers her grandmother explaining one day, *The folk tales and stories are all there to make sure you follow the rules, Imelda. Every one of them is made up except for one. The Aswang are real. We know because years ago, your grandfather fought one during the war. They show up during the blue light. If the world turns blue, you must leave where you are and find safety.*

Imelda's husband is from Bohol Island in the Visayan region of the Philippines, the same area Imelda is from. While he doesn't know her family history or the tales of the Aswang and the blue light, he knows his wife. She is a no-nonsense woman that is the love of his life and has kept him in check from the first day they were married. Depending on the tone she uses, if she says to do something, he knows how quickly he should get it done.

She turns to him with a face drained of color and tells him firmly, "The Aswang are coming, we have to run." Looking into her eye's, Arvin knows not to hesitate. He drops his pan, grabs her hand and starts running out of the festival with her in tow behind him. Weaving between the booths and around the attendees that make up the thick crowd, they glance behind them as they hear the first screams.

The shrieks and yells start erupting all around them as they see people's children collapse to the ground. The Bautistas continue their run to the exit and nearly collide with a mounted police officer riding his horse at a gallop to find out what the commotion is about. He has to turn his mount away and head around a small wall as the flow of people running from the festival grounds intensifies.

Here and there in the crowd, there are flashes of movement, something fast moving through or over the throng. A blur of speed and then someone gets knocked down. Arvin and Imelda make it another half block before stopping at a large tree to find a safe way to escape. Looking back the way they came, they see the police officer struggling to hold on to his horse as it rears up over the surging mob. Something, a fast and terrifying shadow flies at him knocking him off of his horse. The Bautistas continue their run from the festival grounds, not knowing where they can go that is safe.

Only three blocks away from the festival, Arvin stumbles forward and falls in an awkward stop. A horrendous roar from around the corner just ahead of them forces a perilous choice for survival. While Imelda grabs hold of his arm to attempt reversing their course, Arvin is pulling against her tug to move toward a small pizza shop near them.

"We can't go back Imelda, look." His arm thrust out pointing to the three white creatures bounding toward them.

They reach the door, but it is locked. A sign in the window proclaims the owners can be found at the food festival in booth number twenty-three. Arvin pulls Imelda into a crouched embrace, huddling for impact from one of their approaching attackers.

Daring a glimpse at his certain death, Arvin looks to the street where the three Aswang are nearly by him and his wife, but the runners' focus is up the street instead of on the couple. Another immense roar echoes from the intersection. Turning his gaze farther, Arvin sees a gigantic monster being attacked by some of the pale creatures that have just passed by. It is easily twelve feet tall, nearly as wide and is swinging a motorcycle around as a club.

The three new man-like creatures join in their comrades attack on this grotesque troll-like monster and enrage it even more. It swings the motorcycle around at them and succeeds in smashing one into the ground with the bike. The strength and motion of the swing causes the pale creature and the motorcycle to disintegrate into each other. The monster grabs another Aswang off its back, bites of its head and tosses the body away.

The remaining pale-bodied mutants jump clear and stand surrounding the hulking brute as it increases in size. Frozen in place with fear and curiosity, Imelda and Arvin look on as several more of the pale creatures emerge from the surrounding streets to surround the giant beast. When the attack begins, the couple realize too late that they should have used the moment of calm to escape.

In desperation, the growing behemoth picks up a small car, swings it at two of his attackers and then tosses it at another one leaping through the air. The vehicle misses its intended target but continues through the air until it bounces off a tree and crashes down onto the Bautistas, ending their flight to safety.

10:37AM
Frederick, Colorado

The curtain above the sink is fluttering in a light morning breeze. Even with the wind blowing across her face, small beads of perspiration form on Laura Martinez' forehead while she washes the pans from breakfast. The air is hotter than usual, and she isn't looking forward to another day full of housework in oppressive heat.

The summer temperatures don't usually get too high and when they do, they don't last long, so Laura and Jeff, her husband, decided against installing an air conditioner at the ranch.

"I'll be damned if I'm going to go through another summer like this," she whispers to herself.

This house was her childhood home and that also played a role in their decision not to make major changes to the house. The temperatures were never this oppressive when she was growing up, or at least she didn't recall them as such, so it is primarily her influence that guided them in the decision. Only the last two summers have been difficult with the heat, but increasingly so.

They moved in four years ago after her father, Clay, had to give up farming. He was in an accident with a drunk that was driving a state road grading tractor on a main highway. Her father's leg and arm injuries were serious enough to make continued farming too painful, and the settlement from the state was enough to allow her parents to quit altogether and travel. She doubted her father would have left the farm even with his injuries, but the emotional suffering and shame he felt after the crash was too much for him to stay around his daughter.

At the time the accident occurred, Laura and Jeff were already looking for a small farm they could buy and raise their three children. Their daughters, Julie and Samantha, were in the truck with Laura's father when the drunk guided his tractor over the median, knocked their truck into a ditch on the other side and came crashing down to rest on top of her father's vehicle and its occupants.

Julie was killed instantly, and Samantha suffered severe brain damage that will prevent her from ever leaving the hospital. Clay wasn't to blame in any respect for the accident. The girls were all strapped in, and he was even driving below the speed limit as he normally does in his non-rushed manner. He still feels responsible for their family loss.

I insisted that I take the girls shopping, he told Laura during an emotional family grief counseling session. The counselor later told Jeff and Laura that Clay had internalized his own version of the events which he was able to reconstruct from the patchwork of memories he had before the crash. *It might take years for him to accept that it was the girls who insisted he take them on a drive. He may never fully accept the truth that he has no guilt in the crash.*

The light at the sink changes to a strange color, causing Laura to squint at her hands then up to the bulbs in the ceiling. The light, of course, is off. *It's daytime,* she chides herself and cranes her head forward to peer out the window at the unusual blue hue in the sky. The colorful interruption has given her the opportunity to glance at the clock and realize her son and husband are still not back. Drying the last pan, she heads to the backdoor on her way to admonish her two favorite men for allowing the time to fly by and not come in for Carl's schoolwork.

Too often, Jeff and Carl would get embroiled in animated discussions about the latest TV show or movie they had seen and the time of finishing the morning routine's would drag on past the time to get to his studies.

While always portraying outward annoyance at their careless lack of time management, inwardly she loved their bond. Carl has a mild Autism that wasn't an issue with schooling early on, but after the accident and loss of his sisters, he stopped caring how he behaved. Carl's reaction was severe enough that they decided it best to keep him home for his education until he and his parents could come to terms with their loss.

With three years under their belts, they doubt they will have him return to public school. Besides the obvious benefit of having increased stability, Jeff and his son formed a tight bond of emotional recovery. They do everything together, and Laura gained strength herself from seeing their close interactions over the years.

Dust and heated air hit her when she steps through the back door. Their three horses are kicking up a storm in the pen across the yard, and the cows are all running in the distance. Something is wrong with them, but the unusual light seems a plausible explanation and right now, Laura is mainly concerned with getting her husband and son back on track with his morning lessons.

"Jeff, Carl, it's time for school!" Walking toward the barn, Laura is getting aggravated that they won't at least acknowledge her statement with a reply. "Boys, you can finish up your conversation inside, your geometry lesson won't be any…"

She stops in a moment of panic when she sees a pair of legs sticking out from behind an interior wall. Her panic turns to anger when one of the legs twitches, and she is sure her two favorite men are once again playing a horrible prank on her.

"If you two think you're going to scare me again, you're wrong."

Walking beyond the wall, she freezes with fear at the scene. She understands this is not an elaborate joke, but her fight or flight response has locked her feet in place thinking she should fight to save what is left of the man on the ground. In her moment of terror, a familiar yet distorted face turns to look at her. She screams and runs in terror from the body on the ground and the creature that was feeding on it. Dirt is kicked up from the floor both by her feet as she runs and by the monster chasing her on all fours as it tears out of the barn section she just left. She makes it to the door when a large hand slaps down on her back, slamming her into the ground. Her screams of fear and agony echo into the morning air while the horses break out of the pen and run to freedom and safety.

CHAPTER TWO
THE CAVANAUGHS

9:37AM
Eugene, Oregon

Pleasant visions of cruising in a boat on the lake dance in Greg Cavanaugh's mind. He has been planning on buying a speedboat for years. The decision was made to finally get one as a victory gift to himself for winning the congressional seat to the U.S. House of Representatives. He won the 4th seat last November and hasn't had the time to buy his present yet but made an appointment to see the boat seller tomorrow.

With eyes closed, sitting in the lounge chair, he imagines that the light breeze flowing over him is instead the wind as his boat speeds over the lakes waters. Even the drips hitting his face make him imagine the watery spray of waves. *Drips?*

Greg opens his eyes to Evelyn standing above him. His wife was letting the condensed water from a cold glass of ice tea drip onto his forehead.

"You were thinking about that boat again, weren't you?"

"Guilty as charged. Thanks for the tea."

"And why do you assume this is your glass?"

"Because you always put lemon in yours." He smiles and pats the chair next to him. "Evelyn, sit down."

She hands him his glass and struggles to lower herself into the seat next to her husband of fourteen years. The difficulty in sitting is due to her wish coming true as well. Greg wanted his boat, and Evelyn wanted another baby. They had been trying for eight years to have another child after their son, Lloyd, turned four, but the stresses caused by their lifestyles prevented her from getting pregnant again, that is until victory night after the election.

She smiles at him and rubs her belly happily while giving him a beaming smile with eyes full of joy.

"What can I do for you, Representative Cavanaugh?"

"Close your eyes, Evelyn. Close your eyes and listen."

She leans back and listens to the mid-morning world. The leaves in the trees around them are lightly tapping each other and a sprinkler is spraying water in the distance, but she hears nothing else.

"Do you hear it?"

"What am I supposed to hear?"

"You can hear the wind. I swear I could hear a cloud float by earlier."

Her head cocks to the side slightly and her expression changes to one of concern like the heat of the day or the stress of the bills he has been working on are getting to him.

"I'm talking about Lloyd."

She gives a nod of understanding. Their son is away at summer camp. Normally, their backyard is a battlefield of terror that only twelve- and thirteen-year-old boys know how to conjure. Their son is especially fond of history, and he and his friends are part of a medieval reenactment group. They are often charging around the yard with swords and in knight and ruffian garb.

"It is peaceful now that you mention it. I was surprised not to find you in the study."

"We have a week with him at the camp, and I intend to enjoy every minute of it. I don't know when I'll be able to spend time the backyard again without dodging axes and swords."

"Well you've earned it mister."

"We've earned it," he says leaning forward and giving her a kiss. "I won't be able to stay out here long if this heat keeps up, though. It feels like it's in the mid-eighties already, and it's not even ten o'clock. What did the weather people say today was going to be like?"

"I don't know. They were saying something about it on the T.V. when I came out but I wasn't listening. You're right, though, if this keeps up it will be a scorcher."

"Even with the heat, it's a beautiful morning. What is this?"

Greg stands up and looks around as the color washes out of the surrounding trees and the world fades to blue.

"Evelyn, what's going on, are you okay?"

Hunched over her knees, Evelyn is holding onto her stomach.

"I'm fine, the baby just started kicking really hard. I think something's wrong, everything looks odd."

"If you mean the washed out blue, I see it too."

"Oh good. I don't want anything to go wrong. Could you help me up? I want to go inside."

Halfway back to the house, a strange howling noise echoes through the air making the hair stand up on Evelyn's neck. They stop, look at each and he is nodding at her.

"I heard it too," he says while pulling his phone out of his pocket to make a call.

"Was that a scream?" she asks gripping his arm as he dials 911.

The Cavanaugh's live on the outskirts of Springfield, Oregon on a quiet street called Clearwater Lane just north of a section of the Willamette River. The house is removed from the regular congested sections of suburbia where house after house sit in close proximity to each other.

The homes out here are all on their own five- or ten-acre lots, and the various owners take pride and care in what they own. Criminal activity doesn't occur in this part of the city. It is too heavily patrolled by the private security the local landowners hired to protect their property and lifestyles.

"I got put on hold," he says, looking angrily at his phone as if he can force the police to pick it up.

Another sound echoes through the sky making them both start moving their feet.

"That was a gunshot," they say in unison and run to open the back door of the house.

The next ten minutes are spent in frantic and useless phone dialing. They never reached the police. Their cell phones went from constant ringing, to messages that the system was overwhelmed, to steady busy tones. Even the landline they have in the house was no good to them. Every number they had to dial was for a cell phone on the other end or other messages and busy signals. No calls were going out over the airwaves.

"I have one more number I can call, Evelyn, I'm heading to my study. You keep trying our phones, maybe you'll get through."

Returning to the kitchen a few moments later, Greg pauses at the kitchen entryway and looks at his wife. She is drinking a glass of water which is shaking in time with her hand. Turning her head toward him, her tear-soaked eyes are red, but instead of sorrow, they now express anger.

"I haven't gotten through. Not one damn phone number I called is connecting."

Stepping forward and grabbing hold of her hands, Greg smiles.

"My number worked." Her eyes light up but he shakes his head to prevent her from asking anything. "I don't know about Lloyd; in fact, I don't know anything."

"You don't know anything? Who the hell did you call?"

"After I was sworn in, they gave me a package to be used during emergencies. It had a number on the front that I was supposed to call if there was ever an attack or normal communications went down. They barely let me ask any questions, so I don't know what is going on. They asked who I was and my authorization code, how many people were here and what our current situation was."

"Our current situation? Compared to what?"

"That's what I asked. They asked if we were currently under attack or in immediate danger. I told them about the gunshots and the screams, that Lloyd is at a summer camp and we're the only ones here. After I gave them the camp's address, they said they would try to get someone out here right away and hung up. When I dialed back, I got a message telling me our call has been received and help is on the way."

The surface of the water in Evelyn's glass ripples, and the windows shake as well with the clap of sound that hits the house. Both rush to the back door and run out into the yard to try and see from which direction the explosions sound came.

Returning to the backyard reminds them both why they retreated inside in the first place. The muted sound of a distant explosion was enough to breach the sound dampening construction of their home. The now regular crackle of gunfire in the distance reaches their ears to remind them something terrible is happening in Springfield today.

"We shouldn't be out here. We can't even see anything from back here, our yard is too secluded by trees."

"What do you think it was?"

"There's too many possibilities for me to know for sure. I might be able to see something from the roof, but I need to get you back inside first."

Another sound of an echoing crash reaches them before they return to the house.

"We have to get back inside!"

Before reaching the backdoor, a police officer rounds the corner of their house followed by several stiff-looking armed men in suits that Greg thinks belong back in Washington D.C.

"Representative Cavanaugh?" the leading man asks.

"Yes, that's me. What's going on? Did you hear the explosions?"

"Sir, we have been sent to take you and your wife to safety. Where is your son?"

"Lloyd's at summer camp." Evelyn's motherly anxiety is etched on her expression and the wavering sound of her voice tells Greg she had momentarily forgotten about her son's absence with the other dangers around them.

Over the last six months, she had gotten used to seeing Washington security work, or at least she thought she had. This is something different, though, and the appearance of these men at her home amongst the sounds of what seem like distant warfare is making her tremble with fear.

"Sir, ma'am, we have to make sure your son isn't here. Are you certain he is not in the house?"

11

"No. He's at summer camp like my wife said. I told them where he was when I called. What's going on?"

"Are there any other children or adolescents in the house?"

"No!" Greg yells at the man for ignoring his questions. "Now tell me what the hell is going on! What is happening out there?"

"Sir, I am Agent Everett, and we're with Homeland Security," he says showing his identity badge. "I have to ask you to step into your house, and we can answer the rest of your questions inside. It isn't safe out here; we don't know how many of them live in this area."

Greg and Evelyn are ushered nervously into their house followed by four men in suits with guns drawn.

Agent Everett turns to dismiss the police officer.

"Thank you for your cooperation in getting us here, Officer. I'm sure you will have plenty to do today, and we shouldn't keep you from your duties any longer than we already have."

The dismissal is polite enough, but you could hear the strain in Everett's voice as he spoke.

"Representative Cavanaugh, I have a phone number you're supposed to call to be filled in, do you have a phone?"

"Yes, right here," he says showing his smartphone.

"Only land lines will be working now, I'm afraid. There is a national emergency going on, the cell phone lines have been shut down to prevent panic from spreading."

"If you think shutting down phone lines will prevent panic, you're kidding yourself."

"I don't make the rules, sir. I'm just repeating what we were told. Do you have a land line?"

"Yes, it's in here."

The distant sounds of more yelling and gunfire drift in through the open back door until the final man pulls it closed. Evelyn paces back and forth while her husband dials the number Agent Everett gave him. Earlier, her demeanor changed from fearful to anxious, now she looks more resolute, almost determined to take on whatever comes their way as she rubs her swollen belly.

The conversation is brief, and Evelyn watches as her husband shrinks into the chair with every nod and acknowledgment he utters at the phone. When he is done, he lifts the receiver to Agent Everett who takes it from him.

"They need to give you instructions," he says in a depressed and hollow tone.

Standing to face his wife, Evelyn is shocked to see her husband look aged and defeated from the call. The only other time she saw him like this was after he learned of his father's death.

"What is happening?"

"They will take us to a secure location."

"Who is picking up Lloyd? Are they sending someone to pick him up?"

He looks at her and shakes his head.

"They brought all of these men with them because of Lloyd."

Evelyn doesn't understand and puts her hand to her mouth in a mix of concern and shock. What could her twelve-year-old son have done to bring Homeland Security to their home with guns drawn?

"This is a mistake, right? I mean Lloyd has never done anything wrong. He didn't access some of your work on your computer before he left, did he?"

Greg grabs his wife into a hug. The type of hug no mother wants to feel when discussing a child. It is a hug of desperation, a grip of despair.

"It isn't about the computer. It has to do with the shootings and screams outside."

CHAPTER THREE
THE TAYLORS

9:37AM
Santiam Forest, Oregon

"Mmmm, that smells good." The aroma of bacon and eggs wafts into the tent when Robert opens the zipper.

"Hey, sleepy head, everyone else is outside eating already, but I thought I would let you sleep in."

Rolling over with a stretch and a groan, she smiles at her husband and whispers, "Thank you."

"Tell me what you'd like to eat and I'll get started on it." He smiles while reaching for the tube of sun block he came in to get. "If you're going hiking with us, you need to get moving, Tanya. The kids are finishing their food, and I just came to get their sun block on and we can go."

"I can finish whatever's left if it will save us time."

"I'll have to make more for you. There won't be anything left when they're done."

"Okay. I'll take some scrambled eggs and bacon and I'll be out in a few."

"Love you." He smiles and leaves the tent.

"I love you too," she calls out to his retreating shadow.

Nothing is easy when you have kids. That isn't to imply that it should be avoided or isn't worthwhile, because it is. It is just a fact that everything is difficult when you have children. Like bathing a cat, or holding on to a lively puppy, children manage to wiggle away and run in the least convenient direction. This trip was different, however. Either the kids were all genuinely excited about going camping or the stars were magically aligned to get them out of the house when they needed to go. Even the morning ritual of getting them all ready for the hike went smooth.

"We're all going to need this if the heat keeps increasing." Robert hands the sun block to his oldest daughter, Cora, while squinting at the sun in the sky.

"If you let me have my tablet, I can look at the weather forecast." The pleading tone in her statement makes him smile and shake his head.

14

"No internet until tonight. Please help the others put the sun block on, I'm going to make your mom some breakfast."

"Is she coming with us?" Elizabeth asks excitedly.

"Of course she is. You don't think I can handle all of you on my own, do you?"

The kids all jump up and down cheering their mom's inclusion into this hiking trip. The soft sounds of nature in the morning have all vanished into the din of exuberant noise the five children produce.

When Tanya emerges from her tent, she is bombarded by the rushed hugs of her kids all wanting to be the first to say good morning. She struggles to wade through the flood of children pressed around her in order to make it to the picnic table where Robert is making the eggs and smiling at her.

"Dad told us we had to let you sleep!" one of them states accusingly of their father with a round of agreement coming from the others.

"And I'm glad you listened to him." She groans a bit while picking up their youngest, Gabriel. "I was up late finishing an assignment."

Tanya is taking online classes for a masters in nursing administration.

"Now I know why you grabbed the sunblock from the tent, it's already baking out here."

"Dad won't let me look at the weather forecast!" Cora complains

While Tanya eats, the kids explore the campsite they didn't get to see last night during their arrival. Robert keeps an eye on the kids over Tanya's shoulder as they sit across from each other at the table and enjoy being out of the city for a while.

"How did you get them ready so quickly?"

"They've been up for a while, but honestly, it wasn't all me. I didn't have to struggle with them to get dressed and ready. I'm as surprised as you are that they are ready to go. Cora has been helping out a lot also."

"How are you feeling? You were up as late as me, and I'm sure you woke up when they did."

"I'm all right. It felt a bit strange waking up with the sun this morning, but the newness of the area is keeping me fresh. I'll sleep like a log tonight, but right now, I'm ready to get on the trails."

"I don't know how you do it."

"Denial. I keep my mind and body in complete denial on the amount of sleep they actually need."

*

Hiking feels great. The family is following a series of well-made trails through the mountain terrain, but it still feels like each of them are getting lost in the wilderness. At least they are losing the regimentation of living in the city. The feeling of solitude is amplified by the fact that the trails are largely empty today. In the ninety minutes they have been hiking, only three other groups passed them on the trails, two couples and a family with a teenage boy. On normal hiking outings, they are passed on regular intervals by other hikers that aren't slowed down by five children the way Robert and Tanya are.

Cora stops on the trail and kneels down ahead of everyone. "Mom, Dad, I don't feel so good. I think I'm starting to see things."

Gazing around at the sky, the trees and flowers along the trail, everyone is bewildered. "It's not just you, Cora, I see it too, everything has a blue tint to it."

"Robert, listen."

"I know. Something's wrong."

The world falls into silence with the arrival of the blue tint. The birds, the insects, even the wind seem to have vanished from the planet and the dead silence filling their ears causes the hair on their necks to stand on end.

This silence, like all horrific periods of calm, is broken by a piercing scream in the distance. It isn't a singular scream, however, it is the repeated and broken crying out of someone in painful agony. The distant screamer continues their cries of pain, and the world around them explodes into a terrifying symphony of sounds. A rushing din fills the air of what seems like every bird in the area taking to the skies. They are cawing and chirping their displeasure at what is occurring in the world. Squirrels and chipmunks also start crying out, and even the dragonflies and other buzzing insects of the world erratically take flight around them.

Robert draws his handgun and looks over to Tanya to see she already had hers out and ready. The next sound fills his heart with pain and fear. Having been distracted by the reaction of the wildlife to the blue light and the explosion of noise responding to the distant scream, he failed to notice his own daughter collapsed on the trail in front of them. Elizabeth, their second oldest and Cora's best friend, is at her side screaming for her parents to do something. Her concern turns to fear, and she jumps up and backs away from her sister when the first sound of cracking emanates from Cora's body.

Cora's own agonized screaming accompanied by the sound of her breaking bones fills their ears. Their daughter is writhing on the ground in front of them and appears to be wrestling with an invisible attacker. An attacker that is snapping all of her bones. Her arms, legs and fingers are all bending by themselves in unnatural directions as they all watch helplessly. Each new bend is accompanied by the popping sounds of the bones beneath the skin breaking and renewed cries of agony from her.

Behind Robert and Tanya, their other kids are screaming and crying, and Robert grabs onto Elizabeth to prevent her from running back to Cora's side. Mere seconds pass as the frequency of her bones breaking intensifies into a crackling sound. It is more like the loud crumpling of a newspaper rather than solid bones.

Her body begins straightening out, twisting itself back into a form similar to her original shape, but longer and more muscular.

With one final popping sound, as if everything just snapped back into place, her head pivots toward her family, and she jumps to her feet facing them. Her clothes are ripped and dangling off of her in places both from her increased size and the violent thrashing against the ground. Their twelve-year-old daughter is easily a foot taller than she was a few seconds earlier. She looks more like a steroid-bulked Olympic runner than the lithe little girl who was with them less than twenty seconds ago.

Robert watched it happening, and he still doesn't believe what he is seeing. Still, worse than their daughter transforming into a young adult in front of them, is the look in her eyes. There is a fierceness in them, and she seems to be looking at them not as her family, but as something else. What that something else is becomes apparent when she opens her mouth to scream at them and they see her teeth. Her canine teeth have reformed with the growth of her body and resemble the often laughed at image we know only from exaggerated movies. She has the teeth of a vampire.

Tanya steps to Robert's immediate left and the rest of their children crowd in behind them as they look at the person or creature Cora has become. Her face is smeared with dirt, and fresh tears continue to pour from her eyes. She smells the air between her and her family, and it looks as though her ears twitch before she abruptly turns her back to them and crouches down in a defensive pose against an attacker no one else can see.

Looking beyond her on the trail in the direction they were heading, they see what appears to be a man running, but moving unnaturally fast. Cora turns back to her family one more time before uttering one word, "go" and then runs to a collision course with the man heading their way.

Tanya grabs Gabriel, Robert picks up Emma, and they turn to run, but the parents' eyes linger in the opposite direction of their body's movement to see what will unfold. Cora impacts with the man and begins a furious struggle with each being slammed against the rocks on the ground and the trees next to the trail.

The shrunken fit of the clothes on their daughter's attacker tells them it is most likely the teenage boy that had passed with his family earlier in the day. He is much larger than Cora, and Robert realizes she is not the focus of his attack when he finally bests her in fighting. He knocks her at least twenty feet away and into a tree. His head snaps in the family's direction up the trail and his eyes lock on Robert's.

"Tanya!" he yells to get her attention at the attacker's approach.

They are handicapped in defense while having young children. Even against a normal attacker or pursuer, they wouldn't stand a chance of escape or evasion. Their only prospect to defend themselves and their children against animals of the human or wild kind might not make a difference against this fast-moving threat of distorted humanity approaching them. Still, Robert raises his gun and fires at the running bulk heading toward them while lowering his daughter Emma to the ground with his left hand. Tanya steps up beside him, and they count the short seconds they have before the man reaches them while firing every loaded round they have.

He is hit multiple times in his approach and begins to turn away from them, but his momentum causes his body to fall and roll at them anyway. When he stops, he twists his body like a cat and crouches on his hands and feet as if ready to pounce. Robert is fumbling with a new magazine to reload his gun when Tanya pulls her trigger and starts putting bullets into the skull of this boy turned monster.

Instead of falling dead, he starts backing away as if in pain rather than mortally wounded. He doesn't travel far before he is grabbed from behind by Cora who once again yells for her parents to "Go" before ripping into the neck of the wounded man.

They both hesitate to leave without their eldest child. Even with the horrific scene of her devouring their potential attacker and her distorted transformation, she is their child, she is a part of them. Tanya steps forward with her hand out and whispers Cora's name.

The immediate look returned can only be described as animalistic and fierce. Robert grabs his wife's arm and pulls her back to him as if she were attempting to grab a steak from a starving wolf. Cora pauses and has a small convulsion before telling them all they need to know.

"Leave me here, a part of me wants to do this to you." Tears stream from her face as she forces the words out.

Tanya shakes and sobs as she gathers up her other children and turns them down the path toward their campsite.

"Goodbye, Cora. I love you."

Robert leans down, picks Emma back up and turns away from his daughter's gruesome feast. He only makes it ten feet before Cora lands in front of him, having jumped over his head from her place on the trail where she left her fresh kill. He freezes in fear for a moment, but she steps in and pulls him into an embrace and rubs her face against his chest smearing his shirt with the dirt, tears and blood of her ordeal.

Releasing him and Emma from what he believes would be the final act of tenderness and emotion he will receive from his daughter, she smiles briefly before frowning and crying anew. "There will be more. Just like me, just like him. You have to get prepared."

With those words, she jumps away from her father and returns to the body of the boy, and Robert runs to catch up with his wife on the trail.

Along the trail, the deadly truth of Cora's statement plays out before they make it back to camp. At first, they pass the body of an elderly man lying in the bushes. His skin is pale white, and his eyes are stretched wide in a gaze at the unusual blue-hued landscape. He is obviously dead and most likely drained of blood if other children are changing the way their daughter has. There is a fleeting moment of normalcy with Tanya's desire to check on the man's condition, but that moment passes as soon as they hear movement on the trail up ahead and see another two bodies.

Another girl, similar to Cora, is leaning over an elderly woman, probably the old man's hiking companion. She is latched onto the woman's neck.

The trail is narrow, and they are forced to walk into the bushes to edge around this girl with her prey, guns out and ready for her to pounce. Robert hands Emma to his wife and stands between his family and the girl as they pass, waiting for her to move. He has his gun trained on the girls head, but knows he has little chance of stopping her if she can move like that boy or his daughter did.

Back on the trail, Robert tentatively walks backward, keeping his eye on this threat to their rear, and the girl finally takes physical notice of them with her head popping up to stare directly at the armed father. He steadies his gun's aim, but true to his fear, the girl jumps at him and knocks his arm to the side, making the single shot he manages to fire to go wide. The speed they have is incredible.

Instead of biting him or knocking him down, she sniffs at his shirt and pierces his eyes with her stare. Her head pivots and shifts as she smells him, but her eyes never move away from his. His hand is shaking, still holding onto the gun she pushed away. He wants to pull it up and aim it, but he knows he won't have the speed to shoot her.

"You don't need to shoot me," she exclaims stepping back away from him and seemingly reading his mind. "Not that you could if you tried."

"Can my family and I leave?"

A noise on the hillside in the sun makes the girl slink back away from him.

"You need to mark them all if you want them to live," she cries out while backing away to her previous victim.

Robert watches as the old woman's body is dragged out of sight down the trail. When he turns, he sees Cora standing between him and his wife. Cora has grown taller again and has something sticking out of her back under her shirt. A deep womanly voice of confidence echoes from her throat. "That girl was right. I need to mark you all."

She walks up to her father and now stands almost face to face to his six-foot height. She pulls his head a little lower to hers and begins crying again. At least it seems like tears at first, but they are thicker like gelatin. She rubs them on his face then bears her teeth, her new fangs, and rakes them up his forehead giving him two small cuts.

With a small bittersweet smile, she turns from him and does the same with her mother and her brothers and sisters. Giving an unusually tender hug to Gabriel, she hands him back to Tanya and faces her parents. "I don't know exactly what is happening, but I am beginning to. This isn't just here, I think it is everywhere. You should stay at the campsite. Don't go home, I can't protect you there. I will tell you what is happening when I find out more."

Robert's body is numb and weak when he emerges from the forest. Tanya exclaims the same feeling of exhaustion. Besides the inexplicable occurrence of the blue light, transformations, and murders, they have been carrying their youngest children for most of the day. Tanya and Robert hold on to each other and pull their children in close as they walk past additional scenes of death and other small groups of people huddled in fear and confusion.

The group walks through the campsite parking area and to their tent and camper. Along the way, bodies in various conditions of injury are pulled away from them and their path as the mutated children smell the air around the family and give them a wide berth.

Tanya ushers her children into the camper and Robert follows, shivering with fear and uncertainty as he heads to the back cabinet to get the bigger guns and start loading them.

CHAPTER FOUR
EXODUS

Springfield, Oregon

With no belongings in hand, Evelyn and Greg are rushed out of their house toward the waiting SUVs in their circular driveway. Their government saviors arrived in vehicles that look somewhat worse for wear. A crushed grill, shattered windshield, and smeared blood on the front of one of the vehicles makes the two hesitate and slow their approach. Staring at Agent Everett, Greg pulls his wife in close and turns his concerned expression to the men at his side.

"It's a warzone out there, sir," he states before Greg can utter his question at the scene. "It isn't pretty, but we have to get you to the airport."

The two climb into the backseat of the undamaged vehicle and watch as the first one speeds off ahead of them with their own cars tires spinning out before locking into the gravel to keep pace with the lead SUV.

The Cavanaughs haven't gone through all of the required training protocols as some of the senior members of government have. Emergency evacuations of all government personnel during regional crises was a regularly practiced drill for the DHS. A crisis on a national scale such as this was theorized but never implemented in practice or pamphlet form. The hope was that individual offices would implement their own protocols to gather as many members of the government as possible and take them to their respective safe locations.

"This isn't the quickest way to the airport" Greg offers as the vehicles turn west on Main Street.

"We tried coming down the freeway to get to you, sir, it's not an option."

"Is it that bad?"

"What did they tell you on the phone, sir?"

"Not a damn thing, they only…"

"Holy shit!"

A jolt slams everyone to the left side of the cab when the driver turns the wheel sharply to avoid hitting the lead vehicle.

A man has jumped onto the SUV in front of them and is pounding and scratching at the roof, trying to gain entry. As the vehicle they are in passes the swerving SUV in distress, flashes of light erupt from the gun barrels of the men inside pouring lead into the pale white attacker above them.

The expected outcome of the man falling dead and rolling off of the vehicle doesn't occur. Instead, he hops to his feet in a crouch and makes an impossible jump to the low roof of the next building they pass.

"What the hell was that? How did that man jump that far?"

"That is what we are up against out here, and it wasn't a man, that was a teenager."

Even through the increasing stress and with the shock of seeing the attack, Evelyn is able to laugh at the ridiculous notion that the man attacking the other vehicle was anything other than a full-grown man.

"We asked about the location of your son for a reason, ma'am. What we have been told so far is that children are mutating rapidly into adults and attacking other people."

"And you think my son is involved in this?"

The man in the passenger seat undoes his seatbelt and turns back to the pair and yells, "Listen, lady, maybe you should be thanking us for saving your ass instead of running home to protect our own families. I have a wife that's out there with my son and daughter, and I'm stuck here trying to get you to safety. I don't know if my kids have turned into one of those creatures like others have or not."

Something crashes into the passenger side of their SUV, knocking the argumentative agent's head into the door frame. His limp body slams into the driver and shattered glass from the side windows fly around the compartment. The impact pushes their vehicle sideways for a few seconds, and the SUV's squealing tires skid across the street until they get enough purchase to begin moving beyond whatever has hit them.

The driver's left hand is turning white with strain as he attempts to keep the vehicle in control while shoving his unconscious partner away from him. The vehicle rocks several times to each side, threatening to overturn before the driver is finally able to regain control.

Ultimately, his skill behind the wheel has them speeding away from the danger.

All of the passengers turn around to peer out the rear window as the giant creature that rammed into them continues its course and steps into the path of the second SUV, ending that groups attempted escape of the returned rooftop terror. The rear end of the crashed vehicle lifts from the ground slightly as the larger monster crushes the front end before its own injuries cause it to collapse to the pavement and roll away.

"What the hell is that?"

A second large hulking creature steps out from the same side road as the first one and heads toward the wrecked SUV.

The straight stretch of road they are on doesn't save their senses from witnessing the assault and final stand of the men behind them. The giant creature rips the passenger door open and pulls out the man from inside, seeming impervious to the bullets that man and the others are firing at the new threat. His head disappears into the gaping mouth of the tremendous creature, and they watch as it is pulled cleanly off. A curve in the road ends their view of the horrific scene they are speeding away from, but the images are still burned into their minds.

The numbed passengers silently turn to face the oncoming road in this new devastated landscape. Wrecked cars, bodies and some form of destruction are noticeable on almost every street they pass. The driver expertly swerves their own damaged vehicle through the wreckage on the road.

"We're good, Everett," the driver calls back.

"What does he mean we're good?"

"The bridge ahead is clear. We didn't know if we could make it across the bridge into Eugene to get you to the airport, sir." The driver shakes his head to stop the question he believes the representative is going to ask. "I didn't think it was necessary to worry you and your wife that the bridge might be out, and honestly, we didn't have the time to lay out our plan."

"You need to warn us about the possibilities in case we have to leave the vehicle and run for it."

"With all due respect, sir, you live here as well as we do and know the way to the airport. Any potential roadblocks that existed before are still there and in all seriousness, if we have to leave this vehicle before we get you to the plane, we aren't going to make it."

"Like a plane is going to help you!" Weak-sounding sarcasm is coming from the recovering agent in the front. His words are filled with depression and anger.

"What is your problem?" Evelyn asks.

"You know what my problem is. My family is out there, and in a few blocks, I'm getting out to go help them. I'm not in the Secret Service and you aren't the president or his wife. All I care about right now is getting back to my family. As for you two going up in a plane, we aren't even sure if aircraft will stay in the air anymore."

Agent Everett shakes his head and turns to Greg and Evelyn. "Planes have been falling from the skies since this blue light arrived. It is possible that it's affecting them structurally in some way, but more likely, it is children that have mutated while onboard planes that have brought them down."

"How many planes have crashed?"

"I don't have an exact number. I believe there are about three to four thousand planes in the air at any given time. We can assume any flight that had a child onboard who changed will crash so it is likely in the thousands."

"Thousands?"

"Yes, thousands. And those thunderous sounds you asked me about earlier were most likely planes crashing around Eugene and Springfield. Although I haven't seen any come down, I don't know of anything else in this area that could produce such a tremendous explosion."

"We might have one up ahead," the driver mentions, indicating a huge column of black smoke off to the left.

They all crane their necks to look at the flaming debris among the remnants of houses as they drive by. A piece of a wing sticking out of a flaming building three blocks away confirms the tale of devastation. A medium-sized commercial plane went down on the subdivision, and it wasn't a controlled crash. The breadth and depth of the destruction makes it look like the plane started rolling before or after it hit.

There are no firefighters or fire trucks battling the blaze and no police in the area cordoning off a safe zone around the accident. Anyone that survived when the plane crashed and caused the spreading fires are left to fend for themselves in the chaos the city has found itself in.

"I wish we could stop, I feel like we should help."

"We should, but we can't. You can see there is nobody standing around out there trying to help. Everyone is running for their lives like we are or they're in hiding."

Two minutes later, the SUV pulls over and the man riding shotgun gets out. He shakes glass from his jacket and pants and without a word or acknowledgment that the others exist, he runs across the road and disappears around the corner of a house on his attempt to make it home. The SUV continues on.

"That's the third plane crash we've seen," Evelyn states as they move beyond their view of another smoldering crater of wreckage in a field. "I can't imagine what is happening around the country right now if this many planes have crashed just here in Eugene."

"Be thankful we aren't trying to take you to Portland International," the driver offers. "The area around major airports will have the most concentrated crash sites. Everett, we'll be there soon, you should start to fill them in."

Nodding silently at the suggestion, he scans out the windows in all directions before beginning.

"We have a pilot and a group of armed DHS officers waiting on you with a small government jet. We need to get you to the Salem Airport and then to a secure facility in the capital where you will ride out this storm with other officials.

"When we spoke with the pilot before leaving your house, he said things weren't that bad at the airport, but he could hear approaching gunfire in the distance, so we might have to jump out and run to the plane. If we have to run, our people will be firing their weapons in our direction, but they will be shooting at targets behind us. DO NOT FREEZE! These mutants are fast, and if you stop, you will probably die. Got it?"

Greg and Evelyn both nod. Greg was in the military, but never faced any actual combat. He understands first hand from speaking with those that had been in various battles, how terrifying the first firefight can be. People like him, civilians, often freeze when bullets start flying around them instead of moving to safety.

"I'm going to drive us in fast and stop as close to the plane as I can without blocking the wings so we shouldn't have to go too far. Just keep your eyes on the door of the plane and run at it. No matter what you hear, keep running and get in that plane."

"What if they aren't there anymore?"

"They wouldn't leave without you."

"That's not what I meant. What if they've been killed?"

"Then we'll do our best to get you to Salem by car."

The guarded entry to the private plane hangars is abandoned as they drive through the already-broken gate. On the other side of the car, a small plane lands on the shorter runway.

"At least we know planes can still fly if that one is coming in safely."

"There's one of them to the left, sir!"

Two people are next to a building. One man is hunched over the body of the other in what appears to be an effort to resuscitate at first. As they continue by, the kneeling Samaritan lifts its head and turns its gaze to their vehicle showing a bloody face from its attack on the victim it captured.

"Our plane should be on the ready lane just opposite this hangar. Get set to make a run for it."

Rounding the building, the plane is exactly where they hoped it would be. The men guarding it are in place and ready for Representative Cavanaugh's arrival. The mutated children are there as well; two of them, hopping between the armed men firing at them. The bullets fly as they attempt to stop their continuing attack.

Of the nine men guarding the plane, two are on the ground. One lying still in a twisted heap and the other struggling to crawl away, pulling his legs behind him. The mutants seem to be toying with the men like cats. Landing next to one, grabbing and quickly tossing them five or ten feet and jumping away before they can be shot by the other men.

When the SUV pulls up, the driver and Agent Everett step out with their guns firing before their feet hit the ground. What looked like wild shots all missing the mutants as they drove up was actually multiple direct hits to their bodies that weren't doing much to slow them down.

"Run to the plane!" Everett yells while grabbing Evelyn out of the SUV.

Evelyn bolts for the door of the plane and watches a man raise his gun to her face as she approaches.

Keep running. Don't stop. She tells herself as she moves directly toward the flashes of the firing weapon. A mutant leaps over her and lands by the man making the shots, grabbing him and tossing his body away. The man's back hits the plane's wing, and his brief silence of shock is ended when he hits the pavement and starts screaming in pain. The mutated attacker spins his gaze to Evelyn but then leaps to the source of the next set of bullets that hit it in the chest.

Evelyn trips over the final step and falls into the plane and screams in terror when a body lands on top of her, sure it is the mutant that eyed her seconds earlier. Instead, she is pulled up by her husband who fell in after her and landed on her back.

"Go, go, go!" a man in the cabin yells to the front of the plane and the engines pitch grows higher as the plane begins to roll. "You need to get out of the doorway," the man yells while roughly pulling and then shoving the two away from the entrance.

Two men jump into the plane followed by a mutant that lands in the doorway as well. The smaller doorway frame forces the mutant to stand still long enough for the men inside to make several shots directly to the mutants head, causing it to fall back out.

"Did you kill it?" Greg asks.

"No, it's just running away."

"How the hell are we supposed to survive this if bullets to the head don't even work?"

The man turns to look at Greg and shakes his head with an expression of defeat before returning his gun's aim to the doorway at the arrival of a new shadow. Lead agent Everett made it and smiles at them from the doorway as the jet continues its taxiing to the runway.

"The two that hit us are down, but there is another heading our way. Everyone get in position to take my place when my gun is empty."

"Try to shoot it in the head! It makes them run away."

Yelling back into the cabin to express his frustration he says, "I have been trying to shoot them in the head."

The pilot makes a sudden turn with the plane, throwing everyone off balance. Everett regains his footing and turns back to the doors opening but too late to stop a mutant from landing on the door frame and grabbing him by the head. With a quick yank and twist, Everett's body is pulled out the opening and thrown to the rear of the plane. His right leg gets sucked into one of the small jets on the back of the Beechcraft Hawker. Bullets fly from the other officers in the cabin, but the damage is done. Everett is gone, and the plane won't fly. The mutant falls out of the door with multiple hits to the head and runs away from the craft.

"There's a plane that just landed on the runway. If they have any fuel left, that's the only way we'll get out of here," the pilot calls back to the others as he stops the jet.

"Are there any more guns on this plane? I don't think my wife or I will last out there without one."

Opening up a locker on the back wall, there are a few handguns and some short barreled AR-15's. The officer pulls the charging handle on each rifle as he hands one each to Greg, Evelyn, and the pilot.

"I've already switched them to fire on the dial here. Don't switch them to full-auto, you won't hit anything and will just waste your ammo. Here's a Glock for each of you and extra magazines for the guns. The same rules apply as before. Once we get out that door, make a straight run for the other plane and don't stop to shoot unless you have to."

The remaining DHS officers climb out of the jet first. Two run toward the taxiing plane heading toward them on the runway and the other runs to the motionless body of agent Everett. Greg jumps down next and helps Evelyn hop down to the pavement. The extra weight and bulk of her pregnant belly already made this morning a difficult one, having to all out run nearly a hundred yards to an approaching aircraft will push her to the limit of her physical condition.

On their run to the new plane, a few gunshots erupt from behind them, and they know another mutant is on its way. The two DHS officers at the second plane are waving at them and readying their weapons but not firing often, so the threat must not be that close yet. The pilot has passed them during the run and is in the lead but can't help himself and turns his head to look at the threat behind them while running along. His turning head throws him off balance and causes him to fall, painfully cracking his head on the ground while Greg and Evelyn pass him by.

They have twenty yards to go, and the kneeling men start shooting at the unseen approaching danger. Greg is right behind Evelyn. The fear inside him is urging him to bypass his wife and make it to the plane in front of her, but he holds the apprehension at bay and awaits the inevitable impact of the creature hitting him from behind.

Greg watches the direction of the firearms aim in front of him shift closer and closer to his own body, signaling the fast approach of the demon running behind him. With a shadow over his head, he watches with dread that the creature chose to attack Evelyn first. *Does it know I won't leave her behind or is it just attempting to block our escape to the plane?* he thinks as he watches his wife impact hard with the ground before her. It struggles to gain its balance while standing on Evelyn's back and turning to reach for Greg. Greg jumps to the side trying to clear the reaching arms of this pale muscular man while also allowing the men in front of them a clearer shot at the creature. Greg also needs to get a better angle for himself to start firing on the beast without sending his bullets into the plane they need to escape.

The firing men are able to plant several bullets into the head of the creature, causing it to leap off and away from Evelyn. This time, the monster wasn't as lucky as the others had been. The bullets are doing more damage, and it collapses and starts twitching on the ground fifteen feet away. The DHS officers continue firing bullets into the mutant's body and yell for the others to get on the plane. Greg helps his wife as she struggles against pain to get up.

Her face is bloodied from the impact with the ground, but it is her stomach she is cradling with her arms and she doubles over in pain when she tries to walk. Greg lifts her up and carries her to the plane.

"Greg, something's wrong. I think I hurt the baby," she cries before passing out.

In the current lull, one of the DHS agents is running to the pilot that fell down behind them. He was attacked by the mutant while on the ground and is pulling himself along to reach the plane as well. It appears the mutant broke the pilot's leg instead of killing him, perhaps to keep him from getting away.

A loud bellowing yell coming from the airport hangers makes them all turn around to see one of the behemoth creatures that attacked their SUVs in the drive to the airport has arrived and is heading toward them.

"Get on the plane now!" Greg yells to the DHS men still on the ground.

A yellow airport fire engine races around one of the far buildings and heads full speed at the hulking monster running toward the plane. The driver of the truck starts honking the horn and turns on the sirens, getting the creatures attention. As the monstrous beast begins turning its body to look at the noisy vehicle, the truck crashes into it. The front of the truck is totaled on impact, but the creature is destroyed as well. Its limp body bursts open and splays out on the runway when it impacts the ground.

The driver climbs out through the partially collapsed windscreen now absent all glass and begins running toward the plane as well.

"Will this plane be able to carry everyone out there?" one of the men asks the pilot.

"She's made to carry six passengers with a bunch of luggage so we should be fine. I was only coming to Eugene for a quick meeting and was going to head back home tonight so I don't have any luggage in the hold."

"What the hell is going on out there? The people in the towers have been so busy dealing with all of the planes falling out of the skies, no one has had time to tell me anything."

"This blue light is making children mutate. They are growing to adult size, their skin bleaches white, and they are incredibly fast and strong. Look, as soon as that firefighter gets on board, you get us out of here. You can't wait for anyone else or we'll lose our only way to escape."

"I'm ready to take off as soon as he's aboard. I saw your group get attacked by those naked men, you say were teenagers, but what the hell was that thing the fire truck hit?"

"I don't know. Two of them attacked us on the road while getting here. They were just as big as that one, but I have no clue what they are or what they used to be."

"What the hell is Washington going to do about this? Are they sending help to Oregon?"

"This thing is worldwide, not just in Oregon."

"Well, the president has to do something about it!"

"Mister, we were ordered to gather every living member of the government and take them to safe locations. The president is dead."

The final member of the Eugene exodus climbs on board, and the pilot takes the plane down the runway and up into the air before any other threats appear on the ground around them.

CHAPTER FIVE
FLIGHT TIME

Oregon

The passengers on the plane express the fragility of the human condition and the destructive power of war and conflict. There is blood on the seats and smeared across one of the windows. Two of the men look shell-shocked and are staring wide-eyed, silently into some image only they can see. The injured pilot and Evelyn are both moaning and crying from their own severe levels of pain and sadness. Only the new pilot, Greg, and the firefighter have retained their senses to some degree, but it is largely for the benefit of the others in their care that they haven't succumbed to their own version of stress-related shock.

The pilot from the DHS jet is having his leg wrapped by the firefighter. Greg thought the pilot had his leg broken by the mutant when he was attacked, but apparently he was shot in the leg by one of the DHS officers as they attempted to shoot the mutant that was attacking him. His leg is in fact broken, but the cause is the bullet that hit the bone and shattered it.

Unable to stop the flow of blood, the firefighter had to resort to the less desirable act of drawing a belt in a tight tourniquet above the wound to end the blood loss. Most likely the pilot will lose his leg when they make it to a hospital, if they can make it to a hospital in time. His blood loss has slowed, but not completely stopped so he may not live to make it to safety.

The firefighter's own arm was cut when the behemoth creature crashed into the fire truck. It is a painful wound and a deep gash, but manageable in terms of injury. He rips a piece from his T-shirt and has Greg help him wrap it around the wound to stop the blood and keep it from tearing open more until it can receive stitches.

The most difficult and troubling aspect of the injuries and pain in the plane's cabin are those of Evelyn. She is having severe abdominal pain and has started bleeding vaginally. Her sobbing tears are interrupted for just a moment when she turns to her husband and again says, "I think I lost the baby."

Time would tell if the injuries from her fall and getting slammed to the ground by the mutant have caused her pregnancy to be aborted or if the bleeding is caused by some other equally serious or deadly internal injury. Greg does his best to clean the blood from Evelyn's injured face with a strip of shirt and water from a bottle. She has a small split on her forehead and has a broken nose.

Making it to the safety of the secure location is the key to survival. If the whole world has become this nightmare of destruction, there is little chance for any healthy and robust individual surviving for more than a few days if things don't change. If everything remains as it is right now, those with injuries as minor as a cut could die from infection without having free access to the medicines modern society has come to rely on. The concerns of their future and safety are playing on the mind of the pilot flying them to some unknown land of safety.

"You say there is a secure location you're taking those two people," the pilot calls back from behind the yoke.

He is met with an acknowledging look from one of the DHS officers, but not a reply.

"Hey man, focus, I asked you a question. You said you're taking that man and woman to a secure location in Salem, right?"

Shaking his head to remove the cobwebs of thought he was lost in, the man fully returns to the present. "Yeah… Yes. He is Representative Cavanaugh, and she is his wife. We are supposed to make sure all government personnel are taken to secure locations to ensure the survival of the government in some form."

"And you know the location of this secure facility?"

"Yes, both of us do," he says nudging the other officer who nods his head in reply to the bump.

"I agreed to fly you out to Salem and that's where we're headed, but what guarantee do I have, do the firefighter and I have, that we'll be let into this secure location if we get you there?"

"There's no guarantee I could give you. I don't even know if Frank or I will be allowed in once we arrive. They could very easily send us out to try and get someone else and prevent any non-essential personnel from coming in.

"There is a chance that a skilled pilot and trained firefighter with EMT classification would be welcomed in any shelter, however." Looking back to the pale and passed out form of the DHS pilot, the man comments, "I don't think our current pilot is going to make it based on our flight time and his condition so his misfortune is a possible benefit to you."

Looking from the still body of the injured pilot to the firefighter, he asks "What is your name, G.I. Joe?"

"Just Ronald."

"Just Ronald? What was that crazy thing you did with your firetruck?"

"I'm Ronald Fulton. Everyone in my group was killed or dragged away by those jumping psychos you say are mutants. Me and Kenny made it out of the hangar on the truck you saw me driving, but Kenny was pulled off before I came around the building. We were just trying to make it to this plane like you were. When I saw that giant blob looking thing, I knew the plane wouldn't make it anywhere if that monster was still running around so I stepped on the gas and hoped for the best. I didn't have time to think it through, I just did what I had to, to make sure I could get out of there."

"Well, Ronald, I'm Craig Miller and this is agent Frank Barlow. We're DHS if you haven't already gathered. I'm sure there is a new shortage of any people with medical training with the current level of destruction. You might be able to walk into the shelter and become king."

"That brings me to my second point." The pilot brings the conversation back to him. "Being let into this secure location depends on us being able to get there safely. A lot of people live in the Salem/Kaiser area and the road to this place could be just as bad as the area we left? Where is this facility and how do we get there?"

Frank and Craig look at each other in silence.

"Listen up, assholes. I saved your lives getting you off the ground back there, so you owe me. I don't care how secret this place is supposed to be, you need to tell all of us how to get there."

"He's right," Greg adds. "Seven of your men came to our house, and there were another nine at the airport waiting for us but now there is just the two of you. We all need to know how to get there, and I mean exactly how to get to this place. There aren't great odds that any of us, let alone you two, will survive the trip. If you both die or we all get separated, we still need to know how to reach the facility if we manage to survive the trip."

Nodding, Craig replies, "It's on the Willamette University campus, at Ford Hall. They finished the building in 2009 and a secure shelter was built underneath. It's two or three stories underground, possibly more."

"Good. Now what do we do if we can't land at Salem airport? Do you have a secondary location to take these two? If you do, it better be within a few miles of Salem because I won't have the fuel remaining to take this loaded plane even as far as Portland."

"Portland does have the secondary site, but I wouldn't want to go there even if you did have the fuel. If Salem is overrun, then Portland will be worse. You're the pilot, you must know the area, right? If we can't land in Salem, then the choice is yours to go wherever you think we can safely set down this plane."

*

The flight over McNary Field Airport in Salem was disappointing to say the least. Two of the behemoths were patrolling the runways amidst a collection of destroyed planes and vehicles. Several jets littered the ground that resembled the plane in which the Cavanaughs were supposed to make their escape from Eugene. They could be the private jets of any wealthy person, but with the government's history of purchasing many identical items at once in an attempt to save funds, the likelihood is those wrecked craft below belonged to other senators or representatives that were headed to Ford Hall's shelter.

"I hope some of them made it."

The sentiment is shared, but the reality of that happening is less likely.

"I'm going to fly over Salem and Kaiser to see what things look like on the streets. If it isn't as bad as the airport, we might be able to land outside of these cities somewhere and make our way in."

The amount of fires that could be seen blazing around the adjacent cities expressed the tale of destruction below them without the visual flyby the pilot wanted; no one questioned him, however. Whether he needed to be sure about what was down there or he needed time to figure out where to go next, no one pressed him to move on.

Salem's streets do not look like Eugene's in one very large respect: Salem is filled with the behemoth monsters and has much more destruction. The fast, pale mutants are on the streets as well jumping around while chasing down prey. The larger lumbering brutes seem to wander aimlessly destroying everything in their path.

"Hey look at this," the pilot says as he starts circling the plane in a spot over the city. "One of those giants is in a park getting attacked by the pale mutants."

The group watches out the window as three of the pale mutants jump on and attack the large creature. They are flung about by the monstrous brute as wildly and easily as they were throwing the agents at the airport. The group collectively recoils as one of the pale mutants is torn in half by the beast, each piece casually cast aside.

"Well, pilot, like I said before, it's your call on finding a safe place to put us down."

"John Rutledge. That's my name."

The plane takes a sharp turn and starts ascending.

"You know where we're headed?" Ronald asks.

"We're extremely low on fuel. Ten to fifteen minutes of flight time left. I'm taking us to the Santiam Forest in the mountains. If they are mutated children like you say, there will be fewer of these things in the mountains than in the towns. I will follow Highway 22 to make sure we have a place to land when we run out of fuel."

"Follow 22 and landing without fuel, shouldn't we put down earlier? My wife needs a doctor."

"Greg, Mr. Cavanaugh, I'm sorry, I truly am. I flew around Salem and Kaiser to look at the hospital areas hoping we could bring your wife to safety. There is no way we can land in or near a city with all of those things down there. How can we get her to safety when she probably can't walk let alone run right now? I'll follow Highway 22, toward the mountains and put the plane down when we have too."

"Shouldn't you take us to the next nearest airport or runway, even if it's a small strip somewhere?"

"Our nation's highways were built with the prospect of military transport and travel or planes needing to make emergency landings occasionally. Built into every highway in the USA, there are level, one-mile sections for planes to land. As long as I keep us close to that highway, we will have a safe place to put the plane down provided there aren't any of those things or accidents on the road at the time.

"What I will try to do is take us down close enough to a small town so we can find a vehicle, but not so close enough to be immediately overrun. I'm hoping we can make it as far as Mill City or Gates, they are both just outside the forest on the highway."

"Taking a vehicle from a small town local isn't going to be easy or painless. Especially since we'll need a truck to carry all seven of us," Frank says.

"Six of us," Ronald replies. "This man is dead."

"Do any of you know his name?"

Ronald goes through his pockets and pulls out his wallet. There is a picture of the pilot standing next to what must be his wife. They are smiling and posing next to each other at some event or party. The picture is passed around to the others.

"His name was Terry Bradford."

Greg grabs the picture last, writes the man's name on the back, and puts it in his pocket. Evelyn begins to moan again and pulls Greg's head to hers. Crying into his ears in an attempt to whisper but everyone can hear.

"They killed our baby, Greg. Those monsters killed both of our babies."

She has miscarried their child.

CHAPTER SIX
LEISURELY STROLL

Oregon

The scenery over the countryside appeared serene from the air compared to the mayhem people were most likely dealing with down there. Wrecked vehicles on the road below looked like they were simply parked at odd angles rather than betraying their devastating ends. The group witnessed what appeared to be a new game being played on the roads. A cross between the hundred yard dash, leap frog, and tackle football played out over and over again.

Regardless the distance from the city, this same deadly game was replayed below them. What hope of finding a safe place to survive is there when the children of the world have violently turned on their parents and society. There might have been a small hope of containment had this event occurred during the school year. Maybe then, with most children relegated to specific locations and buildings, government and military forces could have quarantined those areas with the most mutated children. Maybe, but not likely. They are too strong, too fast for containment without foreknowledge to be possible.

"We're getting close," John announces to the others from the front. "The next town coming up is Mill City, and I'm going to set the plane down right after we pass it. The road starts curving as it heads into the mountain pass, and we won't make it to another straight stretch with the fuel we have remaining.

"I'll circle the area once to check the roadway and the town's condition before I set us down, but won't be able to take us anywhere else if the area looks bad."

Mill City has one fire and a few wrecked cars that can be seen from the air, but the truly hopeful sign is two large groups of people moving through the streets below. They are traveling too slowly to be mutants and seem to be organized in defensive circles.

"At least the people in this town have banded together in order to survive," Greg says.

"The sentiment is nice, but there had to be a small number of mutations in this town for them to survive in the open like they are. That and a hell of a lot of guns."

"I'm going to land now. We can find out how safe this town is once we're down there. If it's good, maybe we'll be able to stay in this area with someone."

With the relative calm of Mill City, the pilot circles the highway and lands facing west so they will be closest to the town when they stop. The plane is taxied into an empty lot next to the road, and they climb out with guns ready for the next attack. Instead of a silent attacker jumping at them, the sound of a vehicle coming up the road greets them.

A truck swerves into the lot they are in and skids to a halt in the dirt and gravel.

"Can you take me with you?" the man yells jumping from his truck and running to the plane's open door.

"It's out of fuel, we can't take it anywhere right now."

"Damn it! God damn it! You people have no idea what kind of shit storm you just landed in."

"If you mean the children mutating, it's happening everywhere. This is worldwide."

"No. It can't be."

"It is. We just came from Eugene and flew over Salem. Right now, those cities are being destroyed. Look, mister, we flew over Mill City and saw the people there all gathered together in groups to fight. That isn't happening any other place yet and looks to be our best bet for survival. Can you drive us down there?"

"Look, I was headed to the forest to a camping spot I know and stopped here thinking you could get me somewhere farther away to safety. If you want to come with me you can, but I'm not going back to Mill City, I just made it out."

"You don't seem to understand how dangerous these things are. I just told you they destroyed Eugene and Salem. Those Mill City defensive groups are our best bet to survive the mutants."

"They aren't defensive groups, those people are being herded. They were captured by the mutants and are being herded like cattle. If you want to head there, go ahead, but you'll be rounded up and kept for feeding. I'm heading to the forest right now. If you want to go with me, get in."

The man jumps in, starts up his truck and throws his hands up in the cabin before yelling, "Are you coming or not?"

Frank gets in the cab with the driver while Greg helps Evelyn climb into the truck bed after the others. As soon as everyone is in, the trucks wheels start spinning in the dirt and the truck takes a left on the road toward Mill City.

"Hey, what are you doing, the forest is the other way."

The driver pulls a pistol on Frank. "I'm sorry man, I really am. They have my sister back there. They told me I could go out to your plane, and if I brought people back, they would let me have her and we could leave!"

As soon as the truck turned left, the others knew something was wrong as well. Two handguns and a rifle are pointed at the driver's head through the rear window of the truck but with the driver's gun on Frank and the truck gaining speed, shooting him could kill them all.

Frank tries to knock the man's gun away, but fails. Frank's head jerks to the right with the explosion of bullet and blood right before three triggers are pulled sending bullets into the head and back of the driver.

The truck swerves to the right and violently bounces in the small ditch next to a steep hill which brings the truck to a standstill while almost turning over. Agent Miller jumps out of the back and pulls the driver's body out of the truck. He picks up the man's gun and climbs into the driver's seat in an effort to back the truck off the incline and get them headed to the forest.

"What the hell is going on? Why was he taking us into Mill City?" Ronald calls through the shot-out rear window.

"I don't know and we aren't waiting for anyone else to come along to find out!" Craig yells back.

He gets the truck turned around and ready to speed off to the east. He can't see to drive because of the gore from the driver's head plastered on the bullet shattered windshield in front of him. He doesn't want to use any more ammo or make the extra noise but is forced to shoot at the windshield several times to break it enough in order to kick it out.

Once the glass is gone, he puts the truck in drive and speeds them east to the forest. They still have to drive through the town of Gates, which is just up the road before they are into the non-populated portion of the highway.

"We aren't clear yet, so get your guns ready!" he calls back. "Anything could come out of the town up ahead to try and stop us."

"Or anyone," Greg says quietly but is still heard.

The town of Gates flies by in less than a minute at the speed Craig is driving. It is fortunate that no wrecks or roadblocks were set up along the route; he likely would not have been able to stop.

The only sign of life they witnessed was a lone figure disappearing in the distance, a man or woman, that walked out into the road after they passed. It could have been a regular person or one of the mutant kids, but at their speed, even a mutant couldn't catch them.

"Shit...shit, shit!" Craig yells from behind the wheel. "This truck is on empty, we won't be going very far."

"Even on empty, most vehicles can make it thirty or more miles," Ronald offers.

"Yeah, but I don't know how long that guy had it on empty. We're going to have to find a safe place to go soon. I think we should follow the next road that can take us into the hills."

The next road they come to is one they quickly pass due to the houses in the area. They can't risk a chance on running into a mutant and any house or community could mean kids.

They find their first non-occupied road just past the Big Cliff Dam. It's a small dirt road that runs adjacent to a dry creek bed.

"This looks like our best bet," he says as he drives the truck up the dusty lane. *I hope this takes us somewhere we can survive,* he thinks to himself.

They drive slowly along the road for a couple of miles seeing nothing but hill-covered trees.

"How long do you think we'll be able to survive on our own in the forest with no supplies?" Ronald asks.

"I'm perfectly willing to let you head back to one of those towns after I get these people somewhere safe," he snaps back.

"Don't jump all over me. I'm just thinking beyond the moment. We'll have to find shelter if we want to make it through this…this…"

"Clusterfuck," John adds.

Ronald nods. "Exactly! I haven't seen anything along this road, and Mrs. Cavanaugh isn't looking good."

The sputtering truck engine makes up their minds for them on where they should go. They are out of gas and will have to look for a place to stay, along this road or in trees and hills.

The group gathers around the bed of the dead truck. Evelyn looks pale, but says she is no longer having severe cramps.

"We can't wander off into the forest or we'll get lost, and there isn't anything behind us for miles so our choices are pretty basic. We can keep walking up this road or make a camp near the truck in the woods here."

"I'm feeling better, but not well enough to keep wandering without hope of a fixed destination," Evelyn offers.

"Unless we find a map of the area in this man's truck that shows a resort hotel just up the road, I think we should make a camp here and keep going up the road tomorrow morning."

Shared looks and nods are given by everyone.

"We also have to take care of Frank's body," Craig says motioning with his head to the truck's passenger seat.

With heads hung, they remove him from the truck and lay him on the road as gently as possible.

"I don't think we should just leave him here, but I'm not sure what to do with him. Any suggestions?"

"There isn't a shovel in the truck, and we also don't have any food," Ronald says. "As cold as this will sound, I think we should leave him here. We need to conserve our energy because we don't know when we'll eat again and trying to bury him or take him somewhere else will cost us too much."

"What about predators?" Greg asks.

"If a wolf or bear is in the area, it's better for them to take Frank's body than to come after one of us," Craig says grimly. "At least it will be a better end than those poor people who will be rotting in the city streets around the world."

The group awkwardly look at each other while absorbing what he just said.

"All right, I'll check out this side of the road for a decent campsite," Ronald says and walks off.

"I need to relieve myself, so Greg and I can check this side," Evelyn offers.

"I'll carry Frank's body to the base of those trees over there if you can help me," he says to John.

Before they can head into the trees, a shadow quickly passes over them, and they get a glimpse of something large moving through the air before the trees obscure their view.

"What the hell was that, was that a plane?"

"I don't hear an engine, but it could have been some kind of drone," the pilot offers.

The hair stands up on Greg and Evelyn's necks.

"This doesn't feel right," Ronald exclaims in solidarity to the others feelings.

Then the flying shadow returns, moving over them once again, then another time before landing in the road below them.

"Please don't shoot at me," the topless winged woman before them exclaims to the groups raised and shivering firearms. Pointing to the trees, she says, "If you shoot, they will attack you, and I don't want you to be harmed."

In the woods, three people step into view. The pale white skin and naked bodies show them for the mutants they are. Only one of them retains pieces of the clothes she wore before she mutated. The other two are completely bare.

"Please excuse our lack of clothing," the winged woman continues to the shocked group. "When we changed, many of us were wearing clothes that would no longer fit once we grew."

Greg, Ronald, and the others look at each other nervously but none of them lower their weapons.

"Please," the winged woman says again. "Please lower all of your guns. You know what we are capable of in spite of your weapons. If we meant you harm, we simply would have attacked."

Agent Craig Miller and John Rutledge the pilot stand shivering but firm for a few moments more, but finally recognize the impossible position they are in and lower their firearms, the others follow their lead.

"Ma'am, do you need a doctor?" The tone the winged woman expresses to Evelyn is gentle and with sincere concern.

Evelyn is leaning into her husband while standing weakly in his arms. From outward appearances, her blood-stained clothing imply a severe injury.

Lifting her head in defiant anger at the beasts that caused her to lose her child, Evelyn asks, "What are you?"

"I am a twelve-year-old girl," she says holding her hands out in a placating manner and her large wings spread out behind her as well. "At least I was a twelve year old this morning. My name is Cora. I don't have the words to explain it all to you, but my mom or dad might be able to tell you more."

The innocence of Cora's words and expression of them brings tears to Evelyn's eyes. Her anger at today's events are replaced by a motherly instinct to care for this lost girl. Cora's body is an adult's, but her words and mannerisms reveal who she is inside the six-foot frame. "Your parents are out here?"

"Wait. Why are we listening to her? What are we doing?" Agent Miller says. "Look at her. Look at her breasts. That's no twelve-year-old girl and no type of mutant we have seen. How can we trust her?"

Cora crosses her arms in front of herself in embarrassment. "I didn't have these this morning. I haven't figured out how to cover myself without binding my wings." Her wings spread out and flap strongly behind her blasting wind at the group. "Aren't they amazing?" Her face lights up in pure excitement when she causes the group members to take a step back with the blast. She is in oblivious disconnect to the terror such an action produces in the people before her.

"You're going to kill us aren't you?" Ronald yells at her. "Why don't you just do it instead of toying with us like this?"

A frown replaces Cora's smile, and she looks at the expressions on the faces of the people before her. She returns her arms to cover her breasts and lowers her head in embarrassment. "I... I'm sorry. I didn't mean to scare you, and we aren't here to hurt or kill you, we are here to help. It isn't safe to be alone in the woods under normal circumstances, and I am worried about your injuries."

"I'm sorry for his interruption, Cora," Evelyn says, looking at Ronald with anger and nodding her head toward the mutants standing in the trees. "Your wings are amazing and you are beautiful. You shouldn't be ashamed of how you look. I had a miscarriage earlier, that is why my clothes have blood on them."

"What is a miscarriage?"

"I was carrying a baby, I was pregnant and the baby is gone."

"Was it because of us?"

"It was because of people like you. We barely made it out alive and many people died in order to get us here."

"I'm so sorry."

"If you don't mean us harm and would like to help, I would like to see a doctor and Ronald has a shoulder injury that needs to be looked at. Did you say your parents are out here somewhere?"

"Yes, they are at our campsite. We were hiking earlier when my bones broke and my body grew." She winced slightly when she mentioned her bones breaking as did the mutants standing nearby. "They are still at the camp as well as a bunch of other people and families."

"We didn't know any of you could still speak," Greg says. "In fact, every one of you we have met so far has tried to kill us. What's different about you and why should we trust you?"

Evelyn grabs her husband's arm and squeezes it. "What are you doing?" she whispers.

"I'm being honest," he states loudly back to her for everyone to hear. "Like Ronald said, if you are going to kill us, then get it over with. I don't want to be played with like some cat's toy. I have seen far too many people murdered by you mutants today to simply take you at your word right now."

"I'm sorry for what you went through, mister. Our urges are hard to overcome when we first change. I have never felt so hungry and unable to control myself like I did after I went through the change. We have all done horrible things today, but we aren't planning on killing you and won't hurt you if you don't try to hurt us."

"So what do you want?"

"I want you to come with us to the campsite."

"Do we have a choice?"

Her wings tuck in behind her and she walks up to Greg and gets uncomfortably close for his liking. Whatever her age was this morning, her body is that of a beautiful young woman and even with the strange wings protruding from her back, this half-nude woman is attractive. She sniffs the air between them and places her right palm against Greg's forehead then closes her eyes.

Three seconds later, she withdraws her hand, glances at Evelyn, turns and walks away. "No, Representative Cavanaugh, you do not have a choice." Her words and tone sound far more mature than the youthful way she opined before. "Thank you for sharing your thoughts with me. If I leave you out here, you will die, and there has been enough death for today. Because you are with the government, you will be valuable in preventing a global war that would wipe out all the versions of humanity that are remaining. You will accompany us back to the camp where my parents and siblings are. Then we will work to ensure your continued safety until you can be reunited with the government that wishes your return."

She stretches her wings out and gives two great flaps to get herself airborne.

"It is a long way up the hills to the camp. You should let the others carry you," she calls down from above.

"And what about our guns?" Agent Miller calls out.

"Take them with you, you still may need them although they won't do much against us. There are other things in the world that are dangerous besides those of us you call mutants."

With those final words, she flies off and several more tall mutants step out of the woods joining the others that were standing in wait. They turn their pale backs to the group members in an offer for them to climb on.

"Do any of you speak?" Evelyn asks a tall mutant that approaches her.

"Yes, we can all still speak, but we are subordinate to Cora."

"And can you read minds as well?" Agent Miller asks.

"No, only some of those with wings can read thoughts and memories."

Miller grips his gun tighter and in a flash, one of the mutants has him pressed up against a tree with his right arm and gun stretched out away from him.

"She said we wouldn't be harmed," Greg yells while backing away.

"She said you wouldn't be harmed if you don't try to harm us. This man was going to shoot me. We cannot read minds, but we can sense tension and danger," he says, looking directly into Miller's eyes. "If you try that again, you won't be able to use that arm." The mutant releases him and allows him to keep his gun.

CHAPTER SEVEN
CAPTIVITY?

Oregon

The vampires exit the tree line and lower everyone but Evelyn to the ground. The foreboding feeling many of them were having during the unwanted trip here dissipates into confusion as they look at the group ahead in the camp. Other than the tall, pale creatures walking calmly around the grounds, the site looks like any normal campground. Tents and campers abound and several families, including young children, are walking around freely.

Cora walks up to them as they arrive. Her approach is slightly less alarming this time as she has managed to cover her breasts with a shirt that must be cut open on the back to allow for her wings.

"Welcome to our camp. My dad made this for me." She smiles while pointing at the shirt, knowing what their thoughts are. "Please, come meet my family, they are over here."

"I didn't know any children survived the change," Miller says.

"Survived? Interesting choice of a word." She glances back at him with a sadness in her eyes while she walks. "I guess our childhoods did die today. This transition is more difficult for the others than for those like me. I am able to absorb some of the thoughts and experiences other people like yourselves have had. You can imagine how comforting such knowledge is. It allows me to understand the transition into adulthood in a way none of them ever will."

"Them, you mean the ones without wings?"

"Yes, and even some with wings. I have only met a few, but not all of them can read minds."

"And are there many others out there like you?"

"Yes, I'm sure there are. Most children changed into the regular walking adults, but there are probably many out there like me as well. At least it feels like there should be many more."

"What about the tall, fat monsters?" Ronald asks. "The ones that look like…like mountain trolls?"

"I haven't come across anything like what you are describing. May I look?" She stops and holds up the palm of her hand.

Hesitantly, he walks forward and allows her to place her palm on his forehead.

"Think about what you saw and I should see it." She pulls her hand away and crosses her arms in front of her chest again in embarrassment.

"I...I'm sorry. It's difficult having you so close to me for some reason. I didn't mean to think about you in that way."

"It's all right. It is neither of our faults. This transformation has caused changes in me beyond my wings. I am secreting pheromones that cause the others to follow me. I can't control it yet. I guess it affects non-mutated people differently."

Cautiously uncrossing her arms, she steps up to Roland again, smiles and places her palm on his forehead.

"Oh my. I haven't seen anything like that up here," she says and pulls her hand away. "I hope we don't encounter any of them in the woods. Mountain troll is a good description.

"My parents are in front of this camper," she says with an outstretched arm while walking around the front. "My mother is a nurse and will be able to help you with your shoulder, Ronald. Mrs. Cavanaugh, my mother will hopefully be able to help you with anything you need as well. Mom, Dad, this is Representative Cavanaugh, his wife, and the others in their group. This man has a cut on his shoulder that needs to be looked at and Mrs. Cavanaugh has had...um, she's had a miscarriage, Mom."

Tanya stands and nods at her daughter. "Ronald? I assume you will survive a while longer since you are up and about so I'll look at you later." Turning to the vampire carrying Evelyn, "Please follow me with Mrs. Cavanaugh. I'm just taking your wife to lie down in our camper, you are free to come with if you want."

"Thank you, I will." Turning back to the others as he walks away, he says, "I'll make sure she is all right and come back out."

Robert glances at each of the new arrivals before standing up and stretching out his hand to them. "I'm not sure how appropriate this is, but welcome to our camp."

Agent Miller takes Robert's hand in his and shakes it.

"Thank you, I guess."

"I imagine you have a lot of questions. I know I have a bunch for you and your group. Do you mind me asking first, how far is this thing spread? There's nothing on the radio. The phones aren't getting any service. All we know is what's been happening in the forest."

"This is global."

Shocked, Robert takes a step to steady himself. "Global, are you sure?"

"Yes. Although we didn't know any children survived or remained unchanged until now. We haven't seen any children since...well, we haven't seen any at all today."

"We protect them," Cora says from the side. "If there are any small children in an area, those of us that have changed take them to a safe place to hide. It's instinctual."

Robert nods and tries to fill in the rest. "All of the children that changed here are between ten to fourteen years old. If it is the same everywhere else, then the transformation must have something to do with the hormonal changes in the body, so only those in puberty go through The Shattering."

"The Shattering?" Miller asks. He notices Cora recoil a bit at the phrase.

"I assume none of you have watched a child go through the transformation, let alone your own."

Heads shake among the group.

"The Shattering is the only way I know how to describe it. It begins with their bones breaking. Just snapping on their own. Right in front of our eyes, we had to watch as my little girl's body was twisted and broken. She wasn't more than six feet in front of me, and it looked like she was being crushed by some unseen force. Her bones started breaking more rapidly and on top of her screaming, we could hear her bones all shatter. The sound was like a crackling fire or twisting a roll of bubble wrap and having the bubbles all burst at once.

"Then she stretched and grew right in front of us. When she stood up, she was the woman you see before us now. Except for the wings. The wings she started to grow after she protected us, and I believe she is still growing taller."

"She didn't attack you?"

"Not all of us will attack our own family," Cora says stepping forward and reminding everyone she is still here. "I don't know why, but some will drink from their own parents while others will avoid them and seek out others to drink. Others like you."

"Drink from us?"

"We aren't mindless beasts," she states angrily. "I can sense what you are thinking even if I can't see it for myself. We can still talk, we are still the children...the people we were before, but the change makes us hungry. If they don't replenish their nutrients by drinking blood shortly after they shatter, they become desperate and dangerous. They will attack any living person they find and often drain them, causing them to die."

"They. You keep saying they as if you aren't one of them. And drinking blood? Is that what this is all about?"

"I am not one of them, I'm something else. Yes, we all need to drink blood, at least right after the change we do. I'm not certain how much or even if we will need to keep feeding now that the change is complete.For me, I don't crave regular human blood. I feed on the Shattered Ones."

"You mean you are vampires?" Ronald asks while looking around at the pale, partially clothed bodies walking amongst the groups of people in nearby camps.

"Yes, I guess that is what we are." And she smiles innocently, but it looks wicked in the dimming light of the day.

"How can you smile about being a vampire?"

"I think it's better than being a werewolf. Oh wow! I wonder if some people turned into werewolves?"

"That's ridiculous," Agent Miller says.

"It might not be," Robert offers. "There are stories of werewolves and vampires from our past. Maybe something like this has happened before and those weren't just fairytales like we thought."

"That would explain the mountain trolls," Ronald offers. "This blue light could be causing all types of different mutations."

Greg walks back to the group in a dazed manner looking around at the people in the camp and back to the camper he just left. Grabbing Robert's arm when he reaches his group and trying to whisper, "It seems pretty calm here, so I'm not sure if you realize what's happening out there. These mutated children are killing people, thousands of people are dead, maybe millions. Do you understand how dangerous they can be?"

"I think it would be best if you all followed me. I'll show you what we've been through and explain while we walk. The campground is half-full right now, but this morning, there were no open spaces."

"If the mutants here let people go home, none of them will make it, it's too dangerous out there."

"No one left for home." The sadness in his voice tells the same story the group experienced during their escape. "Take a look over there."

At the edge of the camp, near some newly uprooted trees, lies a large mound of fresh dirt and several lifeless bodies as well. Three mutants are moving the deceased into their final resting place.

"We witnessed the attacks firsthand. I saw several of these mutants feeding on people right after the change, and my family was nearly attacked by one as well. I know how dangerous they can be."

"Then how the hell can you calmly sit here with your children, with other people's children walking around? They could be killed at any moment!"

"My daughter saved us. I could see the hunger in her eyes right after she changed, but instead of attacking, she defended us from a mutant boy who was coming to kill us. He was larger than her and managed to throw her against a tree to continue his attack. We had firearms, but they only slowed him down. If it wasn't for her, at least my wife and I would be dead right now.

"I know how terrifying being attacked is, but mine isn't the only family that survived The Shattering today. All of the other people you saw when you arrived were protected by their own children and some were even protected by our daughter or others when one of the children changed and wanted to attack."

"But they're murderers!" Miller yells, drawing the attention of the vampires on burial detail who hang their heads at the words.

"Look at them. They aren't burying the dead because they were told to, they are doing it because they regret what happened here today. They are embarrassed and remorseful. Did their actions cause people to die today? Yes, but you don't charge a pack of lions with murder when they kill another animal for food."

"Yeah, well, the food doesn't normally walk around calmly amongst the lions either," Miller snaps back. "The prey hides and avoids the predators."

Robert turns to face Miller. "If the prey doesn't spend time with the predator then why are you here?"

"We had no choice."

"And neither do we. I understand there are mutants out there that will kill us and there are mutants right here that protect us. Think about how your day has gone up until you met my daughter and decide where you would rather be right now. If this is global like you said it is, this is the safest place for all of us, at least for the time being. Now if you folks are hungry, follow me back to my campsite, and I will get you something to eat and drink."

They all fall silently in step behind Robert after he walks a few paces away.

"Agent Miller, you were charged with bringing me and my wife to safety today and if it makes you feel any better, I think you succeeded. The world has changed more than we could possibly understand right now, and being among these people and mutants is our best opportunity of figuring out what happened, why it happened, and if there is any damned thing we can do about it."

CHAPTER EIGHT
THE PRESIDENT OF THE UNITED STATES

Undisclosed Location

"Turn the TV up, it looks like they might finally be telling us something," Charles says from the corner of the crowded warehouse where he and many other people are huddled in fear.

With the volume bar going up, people start hearing the message "…of the press, the President of the United States."

Gasps of concern echo through the room as the man who walks up to the podium is not who they thought would be standing there.

"My fellow Americans, I know I am not who you expected to be addressing you tonight. For those of you watching or listening, you are all aware of the horrific attacks and destruction we witnessed today. None of us, even in the government, have made it through this day without tremendous loss and suffering. My name is George Connelly, and until this morning, I was the Secretary of the Treasury. The fact that I am now addressing you as the President of the United States is a testament to our losses. I was fifth in the line of succession, and I am telling you this to implore your understanding that our government is struggling to come to terms with what has happened to the same extent that all of you are.

"I am working with my military advisors to address how to appropriately deal with and contain this situation which is made more difficult with the understanding that these attackers are our own children and are not committing these attacks out of ill will or malice. Our best and brightest scientists are working to understand what is going on in an attempt to help us gain a foothold on the problem.

"What I want you to know is this, we are working to address this situation and have had success in containing the threat of the mutated children in several areas, but are seriously undermanned due to the extreme strength and speed they show. If you have safe haven now, stay where you are until you hear more from authorities in your area, either in an address like this or preferably by loudspeaker when we clear safe zones in which people can live.

"Try to remain calm and keep each other safe. I will address the nation again tomorrow night at 7PM. Please let anyone you know what you have heard tonight. Remember who we are as a people and what our nation stands for, and know that while it may be tempting for some to go out and seek revenge for what has happened today, understand that the threat is not over and your survival depends on you remaining in secure buildings and in large groups.

"May you all continue to be safe and know that we will overcome this disaster just as we have overcome all others. Thank you and goodnight."

Walking away from the podium, the exhausted man exits the room followed by dozens of guards and advisors before the screen goes back to the emergency broadcast picture.

Collapsing into a chair, President Connelly looks at the multitude of people before him. "Tell me someone knows what is going on. Any of you that need more time to figure this out, just leave, you are no good to any of us. If the next few days are as bad as today, this country will no longer exist. We need to be on top of this now."

"Mr. President, there is just too much going on…"

"Shut up and get out." His finger points at the former president's chief advisor. "I am serious, get out. You are fired. Anyone else that is unable to give me some information about this, leave right now. This is no longer time for your political games and second guessing, this is time for information, calculation and action. If you can't be a part of that then you are not needed or wanted here by me."

Several members of the former president's staff and various other advisors walk out of the room and Connelly looks at the few remaining besides the secret service officers. Two men in uniform, one in a suit, and another man more casually dressed remain. "Tell me what you know."

The two members of the joints chiefs of staff step forward and start speaking, but the man in slacks without a tie burst in front of them and cuts them off. "Mr. President, we need to find Dr. Usachova. I am with NOAA, and Dr. Usachova has information about what is going on. She should be able to tell us how to stop or deal with it."

"So you're Noah or you're with Noah? Who the hell is Noah?"

"I'm sorry, sir, I am Peter Sergeant, of the National Oceanic and Atmospheric Administration. N.O.A.A. Dr. Usachova gave a presentation a month ago about the mutative effects certain cosmic particles could have on the planet. She is our best hope at understanding what is happening and how many more changes we might have in store for us."

"Where is this doctor?"

"She's in Boston, sir. I am trying to track down her last location."

"Damn it! Somewhere in Massachusetts doesn't help us out much, does it? We don't even know if she's alive! Don't you have someone with this information in your department?"

"We specialize in the atmosphere, sir, not cosmic particles or radiation. Alfred Gorman, the director of NASA, or his deputy, are the only ones with direct knowledge of her presentation that I am aware of. It was classified and given specifically for them. Doctor Gorman urged me to come to you with this information."

"Well, let's get Alfred and his deputy in here. You know where they are, correct?"

"Yes, sir, they are both dead."

Slouching back into his chair, Connelly nods to one of his aids. "Get it done. Find this Dr. Usachova and have her protected at all costs."

Turning to the others after Peter Sergeant leaves, "What about you? You two have the uniforms and know how to win wars. Do you know how to stop what is going on out there without killing all of our children to get it done?"

"Mr. President, there are historical precedents that have occurred which should help us defend ourselves from the mutated children. Things that seemed to work when this has happened before."

Standing up and shouting at the men, "When this has happened before! I don't remember ever hearing about groups of children mutating and attacking humanity. Is this some type of chemical attack?"

The chairman of the joint chiefs stands at attention and attempts to deliver the news of what they know with force and purpose, but even he is having a difficult time accepting the possibilities of what they are facing.

"Sir, what I am going to tell you will sound insane, but I was privy to the classified briefing Dr. Usachova presented and our military research arm came up with possible episodes in historical writings that aligned with what the doctor was proposing.

"I completely concur that she is vital to us understanding what may happen in the future, but we already know what has happened in the past when this mutation arrived. The cosmic particles that have breached the entire planet this time have gained entry in historical times at various locations. There are examples from ancient Greece, Rome and even Mesopotamia. I think the most recent example you might be familiar with is Transylvania, sir."

"Bullshit. This is bullshit. You are not telling me what I think you are."

"Sir, I know about your escape from Philadelphia this afternoon. You have observed what others have, and you know as well as I do what we are facing. Specifically with the children that change into tall, pale adults, we are dealing with a mutation that appears to turn our children into vampires."

The president walks up to the chairman and stares him down. "You've lost your mind, General." Turning to the man at the general's side,

"Admiral Pembroke, right? Tell me you don't buy into this mystical horseshit and can tell me what the hell is going on."

"Mr. President, all of our information, the reports we have from our intelligence and research divisions, the records search of historical archives, they all point to what General Gutfeld is saying. This mutation is causing them to grow disproportionally fast and strong. They also appear to be craving blood. Whether this is a response to the accelerated body growth needing to replace lost or depleted nutrients or a secondary driver of their transformation, we don't yet know. All of these things added together point to what we historically know as vampirism…sir."

Shaking his head, the president turns to the only remaining person in the room, Peter Archibald, the Director of Homeland Security. "Is the blue haze out there causing hallucinations?"

"Sir, I'm afraid everything they are telling you is accurate."

"So what are we supposed to do, start shooting all of them with silver bullets?"

"Silver bullets is a possibility sir, but many stories relate that specifically with werewolves," the general replies with a serious tone. "What we are preparing to use is garlic and fire."

"Is this the best you men can come up with? You are supposed to be the best the military has to offer and with all of our weapons, with all of our research and knowhow you expect me to tell the American people tomorrow that they are facing a mythical monster and their trusted government is planning on using smelly vegetables and flaming torches as the primary weapons in this fight? Should we head to the farms and stock up on pitchforks as well?"

Ignoring the sarcasm in the president's shouted words, the general continues. "Using garlic will hopefully work as a deterrent, sir. We are preparing to deploy garlic sprays and powders to see if we can use them to push the mutated children out of certain areas. This will enable us to create safe zones to which we can take the population. Traditional firepower is non-effective. Our bullets only slow them down and often not fast enough to make a difference I'm afraid.

"Reports we have suggest even bullets to the brain won't kill them and haven't prevented the mutated children from taking down their prey. And once they drink the blood of their victims, they fully regenerate. The only thing in literature that works to completely kill a vampire is fire, sunlight, and a wooden stake through the heart. We know, because of their activities today, that sunlight doesn't harm or bother them. I also doubt a wooden stake will have a greater impact than several lead bullets through the heart, but we will test that hypothesis as well when we are able to capture one of them. Because garlic is just a potential deterrent, fire is the only weapon we have that has any real chance of working at this point."

"So you haven't tested using fire yet?"

"No, sir, up to this point, we haven't had the ability to make any organized response, at least none that have turned out successful. With the amount of people we lost and the absence of recent communications, I wasn't sure we were going to make it. As you know, even on our military bases, we have been struggling to survive. Only in the last two hours has the destruction and fighting slowed and it isn't because of any winning strategy or success on our part. The children have stopped mutating, and those that mutated earlier are no longer physically attacking adults."

"So what are they doing? Are they withdrawing, what are the plans for a counter attack?"

"Mr. President, from all satellite and visual information we have gathered, they have won."

The president steps back and eyes these two men with shock and anger.

"The mutants are gathering the survivors into mass groups in all locations they have under their control. As you know, Mr. President, that is the entire nation. I'm sure there are random locations where people are still freely roaming or rather have eluded capture by the mutants so far, but all the data that we have shows the war is now over and the mutants are in control."

"Our armed forces…"

"They are largely gone, sir, and those bases still intact will be overrun shortly due to the completely ineffective nature of our weaponry. Our only remaining effective forces are those on our ships, submarines, and remote bases. We have some Air Force personnel that have survived the day by remaining airborne, but as I said, there are only a few bases that are not already under mutant control. When our pilots are forced to land after our airborne refueling platforms run dry, they too will be captured or killed depending on how we frame the situation for them before they land."

"How we frame their situations?"

"Sir, as I said, at this point, they have won. Unless the children that have mutated return to their former selves or die due to complications from their mutations, there is no way for us to take back our country or the world without potentially ending the existence of the human race. We would have to kill all of them to stop what is going on, and I frankly cannot see a way to do that with the strength, speed, and regenerative abilities they have."

"What are you suggesting, General?"

"No matter what these people, these mutations, have done, they are our children. Without our children, we will cease to exist as a species. Right now, we might have the ability to find a way to coexist. Those with vampiric mutations have stopped attacking people and have been gathering humans together. Some reports suggest they have been protecting their groups, particularly against the larger, bulkier mutants."

"Admiral, talk to me. Are you suggesting as the general is that humanity's day is over and we should surrender to our enemy?"

"Mr. President, I think fire is our one possible way to overcome the mutants. We have a group preparing to launch an offensive against the mutants controlling the area around the capital. If fire shows any ability to damage or kill the mutants, we can use it to stop them. General Gutfeld's greater point about the survival of our species is a valid one. If we are successful in wiping out the mutants, we will be erasing our future. No matter the outcome, sir, humanities time on this planet appears to be at an end."

The room they are standing in remains silent. The president is staring at a portrait of a graduating class hanging on the wall of this school's shelter. The two men stand stiffly, waiting for their president's orders and reply.

President Connelly slowly turns and faces them. "This is it then." He walks over to a desk and sits on it. "I won't give up our nation without a fight. Even if it's true, as you say, that the fight is already over, we need to know if fire is an effective means of stopping them. I won't let my fellow countrymen be rounded up into groups like cattle so those monsters can use them for food.

"They may be our children and perhaps they control most of our nation's lands now, but if we can push them back with fire, then we can reclaim territories and find a way for humanity to survive."

"Sir, we need your order to start using flame throwers and firebombs. This will potentially destroy all of the buildings in the capital as well as be a direct attack on U.S. citizens on American soil."

"Are there other locations set up to test the fire other than Washington?"

"With our current situation, strategically, Washington D.C. isn't any more significant than Detroit, but it would be a great psychological victory for our people to know we can retake the capital."

"Then do it. Send in who you can with whatever you think will work. If you can push the mutants out through fear, perfect. If it comes to force, kill every last one of them if you think it will help us ultimately win this war."

Homeland Security Director Archibald finally steps forward to give his input. "Mr. President, I don't advise moving on Washington. Not until we know if the weapons we try will be successful. There is too much at risk.

"If we fail with the first attack, especially on the capital, it will be a devastating blow to the morale of the other survivors out there. Secondly, there are two major groups in the D.C. area that will come back to haunt you if you are successful and kill them all. The children of Washington's elites will be one of the major groups of mutants in that area as well as the predominantly African American population of the surrounding areas. Taking out Washington D.C. will turn the surviving leadership as well as the black peoples of this nation against you."

"Our nation...the entire human race might be on the verge of extinction, and you are talking to me about race relations and protecting some senators mutated vampire child? What the hell is wrong with you?"

"With all due respect, sir, the world may not come to an end. If it doesn't, then what you do during this crisis will be heavily scrutinized in the aftermath."

The president looks between the three men for a few seconds and clenches his teeth together in determination not to yell. "I take it you haven't been exposed to anything outside yet, am I right?"

"I have not been exposed to any of the mutated children yet."

"Well, let me enlighten you. I watched as my neighbor was ripped apart while we made our escape this morning. He was killed by what I can only guess was his own son. That boy of his turned into one of those gargantuan monsters. If you saw what was going on out there, you wouldn't... Just get out of here. Get out!

"I want you two to know exactly where I am coming from. My son, my daughter-in-law and their children live and work in the Washington D.C. area. I understand more acutely than most what losing lives in our capital will mean. With that said, if you think clearing the capital will help save the lives of our people or help them hang on until we are able to rescue them, then you do every damn thing possible to clear out that area. Even if you have to burn down every building but the White House to do it. Do you understand?"

"Yes, sir."

CHAPTER NINE
HELLFIRE AND DAMNATION

Washington D.C.

At 3:00AM, the first missiles rain down on the Palisades and Foxhall Crescent suburbs west of downtown Washington D.C. For twenty minutes, bombs and missiles will pummel the area through which the landing troops will tread. The residential area should be effectively leveled by the precision and devastating effect of the ordnance being dropped.

It isn't the random bombing that occurred in battlefields past; this is the focused destruction of every standing residence in a forty-block area leading up to the main targeted location. Thousands of troops are preparing to arrive at their goal to ensure the greatest chance of defeating the mutant threat.

At 3:23AM, the troops are unloading on the banks and climbing up to Canal Road. From the Potomac River onto the banks of the capital, the ships firing and the soldiers and sailors advancing are carrying the weight of the nation's survival on their shoulders. As regular ordnance rains down on the lands before them, gasoline bombs of varying magnitudes erase the darkness of the night and the report of each explosion is felt for miles.

The campus of George Washington University is the targeted first stop of this campaign. Satellite imagery shows thousands of people gathered on the campus as is the case with many locations around D.C. The absence of major memorials, museums, and government buildings was an important determining factor in choosing the invasion from this part of the river. The primary rationale was the single-family-home design of the locale. Fewer multiple family residences meant fewer possible civilian casualties of individuals that have successfully hidden from the mutants that have taken over.

The advancing troops shoot flames into the night air at the dark trees before them as they proceed without assault. Four thousand troops have been assembled and advanced onto our own shores and are working their way toward an American suburban battlefield without normal firearms at the ready. Most instead have hoses and nozzles attached to the tanks of accelerant on their backs. Thousands of soldiers walking through the night with dragons of Hell belching their flame at the darkness through which they walk.

Those with regular weaponry have irregular ammunition. Flamethrower rounds are loaded into their shotguns instead of the usual lead slugs or buckshot. M-4's have magazines loaded with thirty tracer rounds rather than their normal ball ammo. The order of the engagement was to use any weapon that burns to beat back the enemy and the effort in assembling the required weaponry was a resounding success.

Due to the nature of the battle, too much of the world before them is in flames for the thermal ware to expose the much cooler bodies of humans. Their night vision goggles are largely unnecessary as well in the flaming illuminated world.

The quiet nature of their advance is unnerving to many of the soldiers. No attacks have been made against them throughout their movement in the Palisades area. As the troops continue their trek across this smoldering landscape, the only recipients of the flaming projectiles and streams of chemical fire thus far are the occasional animal that had survived the aerial bombardment and is startled out of the rubble by the passing men.

The first line of soldiers has reached a wooded area which separates them from the next objective, the Foxhall Crescent subdivision which lies adjacent to the university. Satellite data shows the majority of people are being held on a field and tennis courts to the southeast of their position.

Before advancing farther, one of the lieutenants radios to express concern over the lack of resistance.

"We haven't encountered any of the mutants."

"Drone imagery shows none in your area. We are unable to differentiate between mutant and non, but all living persons in the area still appear to be gathered around the courts and field at the school. We are unlocking your data stream so you should be receiving a still image of the coverage area as we are currently viewing."

"Roger that. I have it on my display. I'm shutting the display down, and we'll move through this wooded area to the next subdivision."

"Be advised, Lieutenant Morales, the final row of houses before reaching the campus field should be untouched or minimally damaged. The civilian population is too close to that location for us to use ordnance unless there is a major advance."

"Everyone continue the advance," Morales calls out over the com.

"Lieutenant, there's something wrong with this. We should have encountered something by now."

"This morning, these mutants were just kids, Watkins. It is possible they are scared of us and hiding at the school."

"Scared of us? You saw what they were doing to people on those videos. Why the hell would they be collecting all the regular people in the area around them unless they were going to be used as food?"

"Maybe they are kids that are afraid of the dark and want adults around for protection. Look, I don't know why we haven't run into any of them yet, but I'm not all gung-ho about running in there and burning them all up. My little brother is out there somewhere."

"Out here? In D.C.?"

"No, not here, but he's out in the country somewhere, and even if he did change, I bet he's afraid. I heard one of the higher ups mention these things were talking. If they're talking, then they didn't lose their minds when they changed. And if they didn't lose their minds…"

"Then they still have the minds of children."

"Exactly. Little kids that don't know what the fuck is going on any more than we do."

The advance through the trees and the rubble-strewn streets of the burning subdivision is as uneventful as the previous trek through the Palisades portion. No sightings, no movement, no fight.

"Lieutenant Morales, there is some movement going on in the crowd on the field. Advance another hundred yards and hold."

"Everyone, head up another hundred yards and hold position until we get word."

"Base, can you release live drone footage to me? It would be helpful to see what's going on up there myself.

"Base, this is Lieutenant Morales. Can you release live drone footage to me?"

"We are reading you, Lieutenant. That is a negative on the drone footage. You are to ascertain what you can and cannot make of the enemy through visuals alone."

"What the fuck is that about, Lieutenant? Why won't they let us see what's up ahead?"

The lieutenant shoots a look to Watkins to get him to shut up. Although they are right next to each other and Watkins whispered, it is still possible some of the other men nearby could have heard him. It doesn't help leading men into a battle if they think the higher-ups are hiding information and something is wrong.

"Lieutenant Morales, we are tasking a satellite to get a visual of the area. Has there been any rocket fire in your vicinity or any aircraft overhead?"

"Base, there has been no rocket fire or aircraft overhead since your ordnance stopped right before we cleared the wooded area."

"Just to be clear, Lieutenant, there have been no explosions in the air overhead?"

"Base, there hasn't been anything. The only thing I hear out here is the crackling of fire from what's left of these burning houses."

"Be advised the drones have been lost, Lieutenant. We have no more drone coverage of the area."

"Base, have the images been jammed or locked?"

"The drones have been lost. Something has impacted both drones and they have been knocked out of the sky. Do you have any visual of the enemy yet?"

Several flamethrowers shoot out at once toward a lone figure approaching the line of soldiers. The figure is a tall, pale woman wearing no clothes but carrying a strange object on her back.

A clear resonating voice echoes through the air. "Why have you destroyed our homes? Who is in charge here?"

The lieutenant grabs an amplifier and calls back to the woman. "We're here to free the people the mutants took hostage. Who are you?"

"Free the people? Aren't you here to kill us as well? I am one of the mutants you came for."

"What is your name?"

"My name is Amanda."

"Amanda, if you release the people you have at the university behind you and leave this area, there will be no need to for us to take aggressive action."

"The people at the school are our family. They are our friends and neighbors. We are protecting them and have been organizing our new community." Her voice grows in intensity and anger. "You have destroyed our homes! I lived in a house just beyond the woods that you made sure is no longer there. There is no safety for them in this wasteland you created."

"Will you release the people you are holding?"

"My mother does not want me to fight you, so I will give you the opportunity to leave. If you go now, you won't be punished for what you have done."

"Lady, I have four thousand men with me. You will release those people or we will. You don't want us to start killing you and your friends do you?"

"Four thousand men and you are in charge of them, correct?"

"If you're thinking of getting rid of me, it won't stop my men from completing this mission."

"I heard a woman speaking to you in your earpiece, can you still speak with her? Is she able to hear what is going on?"

When Amanda mentions his earpiece, he inadvertently puts his hand to his ear. *How could this woman hear the voice from base?*

"If you can speak to her, I want you to tell her everything you witness here tonight. I will save you for last so they understand exactly what they have done by sending you to destroy our homes."

The woman lowers her head and the strange object she was carrying on her back opens up and spreads out.

"She has wings!" Lieutenant Morales says as gunfire and flames erupt toward her.

Two pale white wings start beating at the air and lifting her into the sky as tracer rounds fly around and into her. As she flies away from the fiery onslaught, the men let out a cheer which is quickly extinguished by the entrance of the pale mutant army. The men on the front line are barely able to fire ten rounds before they are hit by a small group of mutants that speed out of the darkness at them.

"You have brought four thousand men to kill me and my family." Amanda's voice echoes through the night air above the din of gunshots and explosions. "Watch and report to your superiors what just twenty of my one hundred and forty brothers and sisters can do if we are provoked."

The mutant group run head on into the columns of liquid flame pouring on them. Covered in fire, the mutants pierce the line at one spot and toss bodies through the air in all directions. Once beyond the front line, the group split off from each other and head into two, then four, then eight different directions. They break up geometrically and spread out among the soldiers who are unable to use the flame throwers in the crowded field and are barely able to fire their ineffective rounds at their speeding attackers.

"Lieutenant Morales, what is happening, what do you see?"

The lieutenant relays his image of the destruction.

"I see fire. The mutants are using it against us. Fire doesn't affect them. I repeat, fire does not affect them or they are able to self-repair quicker than it does damage. Oh my God. They are using the flamethrowers."

"Are our men starting to win? What is happening?"

"The mutants. They are using the flamethrowers against us."

Just then, the lieutenant is slammed to the ground, and with a great rushing of wind, he is lifted into the air. Amanda has him and is flying him above the battlefield.

"I wanted you to see the fight from up here since I took out your little drones. It's beautiful isn't it?" she whispers into his ear. "Almost like fireworks on the Fourth of July. Tell them, tell the woman what you see."

"I see explosions and fire everywhere. The mutants are crushing the chemical tanks on our soldiers' backs and throwing them into the air before they explode in flames. I see one, no two mutants have taken flamethrower packs and are running around our men setting everyone on fire. The mutants are too fast and the fire isn't affecting them. Base, we have to retreat. Call in a retreat."

Amanda pulls the headset from Morales and speaks into the microphone as she continues to fly higher over the battlefield.

"You can order a retreat if you want. Most of your men are already running for their lives but none will make it. I will kill every single one of them for what you have done to my home."

Amanda replaces the headset on Morales and spins him around so he is facing her at the end of her outstretched arms.

"Please," Morales says in barely more than a whisper.

Amanda's reply is expressionless. The only sound she utters is the beating of her enormous wings as she releases him to fall into the flaming mass of men in the distance below.

Hundreds of miles from the battle, President Connelly listens to the fighting as it unfolds. Hands gripping tightly over the back of a chair, he watches a thermal satellite feed of the carnage.

"How much time has gone by?" Connelly asks.

"Twelve minutes, Mr. President."

"Do you think she can do it? We have four thousand men down there. Can she kill them all with only twenty other mutants?"

The room goes silent while they listen to Amanda's final words, and a few people shudder when they hear Morales say please followed by his long agonizing scream as he plummets hundreds of feet to his death.

"Can she kill all of our men out there?" Connelly yells.

"Sir, we can't get a visual of the mutants engaged in the battle due to their speed and the heat signature of all the fire. As you can see, there are individual heat signatures of fast-moving mutants surrounding the battlefield. No one will be able to escape that area. I'm afraid our men are trapped and at the mercy of the mutants at this point."

"I want our ships to unload everything they have on that area."

"But our men, sir. They could..."

"They could what? Be captured and used as food? You heard that monster. She said she would kill them all, and I agree our men won't make it out of there alive! I want those mutants killed. Order our ships to fire on that field and keep firing until we give them new coordinates or tell them to stop."

"Yes, sir."

The chief of staff gets on the phone to relay the president's orders while the rest remain glued to the lopsided destruction on the screens. Some hurried discussion followed by some angry orders into the receiver cause the assembly to turn their gaze to the secretary.

"Mr. President, our ships aren't responding."

"What? Is it the mutants? Are they blocking our communications?"

Walking swiftly over to the soldier running the satellite feeds, he gives him some coordinates to enter. Half of the screens blink to another scene of destruction. A ship engulfed in flames is rocking violently as it lists to one side. The hulls of two others are in the water as well.

"How many did we have out there?"

A bright flash causes the thermal image to white out. The picture returns to show the flaming ship now ripped in half from an explosion and it is sinking into the sea. The warm white heat outlines of human bodies can be seen swimming away from their former ocean posts. One by one, each of the heat outlines vanishes under the waves until the screen shows only the remnants of burning hulks.

"There were five vessels in that group, sir."

The lights blink out and the screens go blank. Distant gunfire and screams are heard in the school above them before any flashlights are able to be turned on.

"Mr. President, get behind us!" one of the men yells as they roughly force him into a corner of the shelter and crowd in front of him with weapons raised toward the door.

Shouting and gunfire continues its slow approach to the door of the shelter. They can hear the shots move across the hall above them as the president's men are killed or retreat back to the shelter. The echoing gunfire continues moving down the stairs, and the final few shots are given outside the door before them. The door slowly swings open, and Agent Carlisle moves into the light the remaining guards are shining at the doorway.

The words he utters sound vacant and robotic. "I have a message for you from Amanda."

Carlisle's body falls from the grip of the mutant that was holding him. The men guarding the president all begin shooting at the intruder, but the night is lost. A large hundred pound propane tank is tossed into the room with several unpinned grenades taped around it. The president and his men disappear in the rubble of their burning fortress when the tank explodes and the battle comes to an end.

CHAPTER TEN
OATH OF OFFICE

Colorado

Hurried footsteps run down the stairwell surrounding Secretary of Defense James Thomas. Three armed men in front of him lead the way as one of the four others pull him along forcefully in their exit from the building.

Only moments ago, Thomas was in a meeting with several other nations' defense ministers. Thomas' surprise when the men burst into the conference room was muted compared to the reaction of the other diplomats. The sensitive nature of their discussion had all of the men on edge and while Secretary Thomas was jolted for the first few seconds. He is familiar with the extraction techniques American military and government forces use to rescue officials.

He knows from his work with military and security personnel that the most difficult aspect of an extraction is the person being removed from danger. Too often the target being rescued would delay their movement by asking ridiculous questions or even fighting the rescuers out of shock or an overinflated sense of self-importance. If these men are here to get him, something is terribly wrong, and he isn't going to waste precious time demanding answers he knows he won't get until he is in relative safety.

He keeps his mouth shut as they run down the eight flights of stairs of the Grand Hyatt building and move along at the running pace the men who came to get him established. They push him into an open back door of one of the three black SUVs waiting on the sidewalk in front of the building.

As the vehicles begin to speed away, the secretary finally asks to be filled in by one of the men peering out the window next to him.

"What's going on? Is there just a threat or has there been an attack?"

"It's some kind of attack," the man says without turning to look at Secretary Thomas.

Before he has time to string another question together, the SUV skids to a halt, throwing the passengers forward.

"It's gonna hit!" the driver yells, pointing out the windshield.

The first SUV continues speeding along the road unaware of the danger approaching them. Spinning wildly, an airliner missing one wing crashes into a skyscraper in front of them and explodes. The debris remnants of the plane and building continue their destructive trajectory crashing through two other buildings and raining wreckage onto the roadway below.

Smoke from the burning tires of the first vehicle draw out behind it as it successfully breaks before ramming into the rubble.

"Do we know who's responsible for this attack yet?" Thomas yells as the SUV speeds backward and turns down a side street to head around the blocked area.

"No one is responsible," the man yells back to him, still not taking his eyes away from the window.

"If you knew terrorists were going to attack Denver, you must know who is doing it!"

"It's not terrorism and it's not just Denver." Finally turning away from the window, the secretary sees a look on the man's face he last remembered seeing in Vietnam. This man is wired like he is on the losing side of a firefight. "This is happening everywhere. Not just here in the U.S. but all over the world."

The vehicle swerves around some abandoned wrecked cars in the road, and the area of tall buildings gives way to a residential neighborhood. The area of houses is filled with more destruction like what the plane crash had caused. Finally taking closer notice of the world outside, the secretary witnesses bodies scattered along the sidewalks and roadways as well.

In front of them, a woman carrying a baby runs out of a house and into the street before the front of the two-story dwelling explodes out behind her. The woman didn't make it far enough and is knocked down by some of the debris from the house. She is alive, but injured and trying to move away from the creature that destroyed her home.

She is followed by what looks like a movie-set monster nearly as tall as the house it broke through. The behemoth creature is swinging its arms and swatting at a pale white naked woman holding onto its head and scratching at its eyes. Three other naked albino-looking people appear from the sides of the house and begin beating the creature, two use their fists and one is swinging at the monster with what looks like a small tree.

"What the hell is going on out there?" Secretary Thomas screams in disbelief at the scene unfolding before him.

The behemoth makes too much progress, and in its feverish defense against the albino nudists, it swings its arm and impacts the woman and child, knocking them several yards away where they land without further movement.

The pale woman riding the beast screams when she sees the escaping woman fall. She jumps down and rips a stop sign out of the ground, slamming the still-connected concrete base into the side of the behemoth's head. The concrete ball shatters on impact and causes the behemoth to stumble slightly. The woman turns her sign post weapon, takes the rigid metal pole, and shoves the end through the beast's skull. It falls to the street in front of the SUV and makes the ground shudder when it hits.

The pale lady makes an impossible leap to the woman and child that were hit and she picks them up into her arms. The screaming cry she utters over and over send chills down the secretary's back, and even though his military mind is able to remain neutral to what has transpired before him, the painful cry impacts him each time she yells it through her tears. "Mama!"

"Mr. Secretary, we have to go." His body shakes.

"Mama!"

"Mr. Secretary, you need to get up."

"Mama!"

"Mr. Secretary."

James Thomas opens his eyes to a man in an Air Force uniform.

"Secretary Thomas, you're needed in the front room. We have information from President Connelly's staff."

*

"I do solemnly swear that I will faithfully execute the Office of President of the United States, and will to the best of my ability, preserve, protect and defend the Constitution of the United States."

"Mr. President, what is our first course of action?"

"Never in my life did I believe anyone would call me President Thomas and never have I wanted this position. As the Secretary of Defense, I thought I had achieved the greatest calling of my life. I had the honor of protecting and defending our fellow citizens with the greatest military might the world has ever seen. Today, I see that might is useless. The equipment and structure we so desperately relied on is completely ineffective against our current enemy. In fact, I hesitate to use the word enemy at all and feel instead I should use the proper term for these mutants that they deserve."

"What is that, sir?"

"Citizens."

Expressions of shock and concern etch themselves on the faces of those gathered around their new leader. This man was the secretary of defense, the leading military man of the nation. What most were expecting was a declaration of how they would fight back and win against the mutants that have destroyed their nation and the world.

"Sir, I don't understand. How are we going to win? What are we going to do to fight back?"

James Thomas is an intimidating man. He stands six feet two inches, has a barrel chest, and arms the size of most men's legs. His expression when soft can be described only as stern. He rose to his rank not through the usual political kowtowing modern generals have to perform, but through action on the battlefield and leading his men to victory when their base in the Middle East was overrun by superior numbers.

His popularity and respect as a man that could get the job done led him to his positions of increased rank and his performance kept him there. This man of action, the people's hope of turning the tide against this new menace wants to call the monsters they are fighting "citizens."

"You heard me give the Oath of Office just now, correct?" The pause is greeted by nods from the confused group. "I would like any one of you to explain to me what our Constitution is supposed to protect. What is it designed to defend?

"Anyone?"

"The nation." "The country." "The land." are all offered in response.

"The constitution is there to protect the people. Our people. You may not like what I am going to say, but in my escape from Denver, I experienced these creatures first hand. These mutants were only children yesterday, and from all the reports I have heard, in many ways, they still are children."

"But we think they can read minds, sir! They will be able to absorb other people's experiences…"

"They can read our minds. Exactly! I would like any of you to tell me how we can successfully fight an opponent that can read our minds. An opponent who so far has shown no weakness to our weapons of war. And more than that, let us say we find a way to kill them and win, what then? Do we wait the next fifty to sixty years until the remnants of humanity dies out? Do we destroy these mutants and watch the human race go into extinction?

"And what of this nation? How does our government survive if there are no more children? Who will obey the laws or care about the next day if people understand that there is no hope for a future? I made an oath to protect and defend the U.S. Constitution and implied in that oath is the necessity that there is someone left to govern. Someone must be alive to govern or our way of life is truly at an end.

"Tonight at seven, I will address the nation the way former President Connelly advised he would. In that address, I will announce our surrender and advise our non-mutated citizens to attempt communicating with the mutant leadership of their area in order to come to some type of agreement that will keep everyone alive."

"How can you do this? You lead your men to victory! How can you just give up?"

"I am not giving up! I kept my men alive against an enemy that wanted us dead. These children do not want us dead. They didn't seek us out to attack us, they defended their territory when Connelly sent missiles and flamethrowers at them."

"But they killed millions of humans yesterday, and today they killed President Connelly."

"I know damn well what they've done. I also know what I've been told by our scientists. They say the attacks by the mutants are an uncontrolled response to their accelerated growth. These mutants, at least the pale white ones, have not continued with a wholesale slaughter of humanity which we all know they are perfectly capable of accomplishing.

"Yes, somehow they found the president who was several hundred miles away from the attack zone and killed him and that should be a warning to us against further acts of aggression. Tell me, have there been any further attacks by the mutants from the battle zone?"

"No, sir."

"And around the nation, has there been the same level of violence in the last six hours as there was during the initial outbreak? The answer is no. If we go into areas to try and clear them, the mutants will know, and while we may possibly find a way to kill some of them, we cannot win a war against an army that can kill four thousand soldiers with twenty men.

"What I want to do now is try to end the fighting and save as many American lives as possible. Is that understood?"

One of the men walks out of the room and slams the door. The others remain and wait for the president to continue.

"I want as much information as we have on what is happening before I go on air tonight. Check everything and give it to me. I want our satellites scouring the cities and towns for any images they can get. Send up every drone we have available. If the crowds of people gathered are being harmed or killed, we take a different approach, but right now, I am taking the mutant Amanda's word that they are protecting the people.

"If they are protecting them, find out what they are being protected from. We didn't know any of them could fly before attacking D.C. and now we know there are tall giants and troll-looking types as well. There may be other types of mutations out there that we don't know about and we need to know everything."

CHAPTER ELEVEN
DR. USACHOVA

Massachusetts

The cold artificial wind from the air conditioner kicks on with the timer, causing shivers to wake Dr. Usachova from her hard floor lumbering spot. Every part of her aches from sleeping on the cold tile. Scanning her immediate hiding place under the lab table is useless in the dark room and provides one clue to her safety. Most rooms and especially the labs like the one she is in are run on motion detecting lights to save on electricity, so outside of her barred hiding place, there has been no movement in the room for at least five minutes.

While comforting to some extent, she knows that there could be someone on the other side of the overturned table in front of her that is just sleeping the way she was or worse, waiting and remaining still. She also has to deal with exposing her own location to others in the building on this floor once she moves from her spot and the lights in the lab flicker to life. There is no way for her to move across the room at any level and not trigger them to come on.

Searching with her eyes through the crack between the table top above her and the one blocking her access to the room and providing her refuge, she wonders, *When did I fall asleep?* Her head is aching from the impact against the wall when Dr. Pashmun shoved her under the desk to safety. *I don't have my phone or I could check the time.* It could be day or night outside, and she wouldn't know from this room without a clock. The labs are largely in sub-levels under the building, and while this one is on the main floor, it is still completely shielded from the outside.

Taking a few deep breaths to build her resolve, she places her hands against the table preparing to shove her way to freedom. Her palms splay flat on the cold stainless steel table top in front of her, and she draws them back without giving the push she desires so greatly to make. Instead, she feels around on the floor and picks up a clipboard and some papers. Slowly, she slides one of the sheets through the opening and waves it back and forth between her fingers until the lights click on.

For a few seconds, there is only the continued sound of air being pushed through the vents overhead and the dull irritating buzz of the florescent bulbs as they warm to life. Then there is a distant, startling crash followed by the repeated thudding sound of impact against the reinforced window to the room she is in. The paper she released when she pulled her fingers back to safety floats to the ground and Dr. Usachova withdraws, pulling herself as tightly as possible into one corner of her impossibly small prison. Her legs are pulled to her chest, and her face is pressed into her knees while she wishes over and over the Baba Yaga would go away.

Seconds later but what seems like an eternity, the pounding on the window stops and a new sound echoes through the building. Voices. People are talking. *Oh my God! It must be the morning lab workers coming in for their shift.* Unable to find the will to move from her protected spot to yell a warning, the doctor squeezes her eyes shut and presses her hands to her ears to shield her mind from enduring more screams that are bound to come.

Even with her hands planted fiercely and painfully hard against her ears, the echoing scream of Baba Yaga's latest victim flows through the cracks between her fingers and assaults her eardrums. The screaming is followed by the loud and repeated popping sound of gunfire and the doctor opens her eyes and shoves hard against the table blocking her way, screaming for help the whole time.

"In here! I'm in here! Please help me!"

Tears burst from her eyes when she sees heavily armed men in black vests and helmets walk up to the lab window and scan the area. "We're looking for Dr. Usachova. Have you seen him?" the head soldier asks, not seeming to care if she is all right.

"I am Dr. Usachova. Doctor Tatyana Usachova." *You would have known that if you understood Russian last names,* she thinks to herself, angry that people still assume she is a man when looking for her. "Are you going to get me out of here?"

"First, you need to prove who you are. As much as we would like to rescue every person or pretty woman we run into, our orders are to rescue Dr. Usachova and anyone that he, or you, needs to complete your work."

A quick scan and three steps take the doctor to her overturned leather briefcase bag against the far wall. She hurriedly fumbles through her papers and fishes out her passport, then flattens it up against the glass for him to see. "If I was a man my last name would be Usachov, not Usachova," she tells him.

"Got anything to prove you're a doctor?"

"Listen, blyad, you are welcome to check this entire building and search each body you find to see if you come up with another person that has my name or you can get me the hell out of this building and somewhere safe that I might do some good."

"That doesn't help, ma'am."

"I don't work here! I only have a visitor pass. Nothing with my title on it...no wait." Reaching into her bag again, she pulls out a book and presses the cover against the glass. "Cosmic Rays and Solar Hibernation: How Solar Particulates Impact the Physical World by Dr. Tatyana Usachova."

"We got the doctor, men, let's get her to the trucks." He reaches for the door, but there's no handle only a digital keypad flashing the word *locked* in red letters. "I don't know the combination, ma'am, so you'll have to let yourself out if you can."

She steps on a pressure switch that is supposed to open the door for lab personnel when their hands are full and fortunately the door slides open. Had Dr. Pashmun pushed her into one of the lower level labs to keep her safe, the men would have had to shoot or blast their way thru the wall depending on which lab she was in. While the Environmental Quality Lab doesn't specialize in infectious diseases, it does work with many environmental toxins and handles some water or airborne diseases that the state deals with from time to time. This required them to build reinforced research labs that could lock personnel in or out depending on the emergency or spill.

The area has been quiet since the men shot the girl that destroyed the front office and forced her to flee. The men still form a protective circle around the doctor as they guide her to the front exit. She gasps as the men step over the body of a young man she spoke with just yesterday. He was a lab assistant and worked closely with Dr. Pashmun. His eyes are wide, and his mouth is stretched open as if his expression froze as he cried out in fear.

"Doctor, you need to keep moving. There is far worse than this outside, and I can't have you freeze each time you see a body."

The group bunches up at the main doors, peering out the glass to the streets beyond.

"That mutant we shot will be back and she might bring others. We have to move quickly when the vehicles come back around."

"Are they picking up someone else?"

"No, we have to keep the vehicles on the move or the mutants will converge on them. If we parked and left them out front, those things would have zeroed in on this place knowing we must have come in this building.

"We have been fortunate that the mutants have decreased their activity today. It won't be easy making it out of this area for us, but at least you won't have as difficult a time getting out."

"Aren't all of you coming with me?"

"I wish we could. Our job is to get you to a park seven blocks away where you'll be picked up by a Harrier that will take you to see the president."

"At the park? Is it some type of helicopter?"

"No, ma'am. We don't have enough helicopters left after yesterday, most of them were taken out during rescue operations. The Harrier is a jump jet that can land and take off vertically. You're lucky the Marines have some of their two-seat trainers in the area. These jets are the only things we have left that can come into tight spots to pick people up and get out before the fliers arrive.

"Here come the trucks, let's go!"

The group crowds into the assortment of trucks after shoving the doctor into the backseat of the first one and they drive off.

"What have you seen out there?" the man in charge asks the driver.

"They're all over the place, it looks like they're still gathering survivors. I think at least one of the behemoths is out there getting rid of the bodies. We drove back the way we came, and the streets were empty except for a few overturned cars."

"You didn't see what it was?"

"We didn't stop to check it out. When I saw the cars on their sides, I left that route and came back this direction."

"We've got one up ahead!" the front passenger yells when a red car flies out of a side street and collapses the face of the building it crashes into.

Instead of stopping to avoid the danger lurking around the corner, the lead truck Dr. Usachova is in speeds up and she grips her hand tightly into the leg of the man sitting next to her.

"Don't worry; if it's throwing cars, it's probably fighting the pale ones," the soldier tries to reassure her, but his words are meaningless until they breach the intersection and she can see the fight taking place as they speed past.

A giant creature is spinning around to face them. She sees pale naked men and women climbing all over it and hitting it. The image appears and vanishes so quickly, she isn't certain she has actually witnessed what took place.

"What was going on back there?"

"The pale mutants don't like those giant ones and that's a good thing for us. The big ones will eat anything they can grab and destroy everything in their path. The pale mutants only seem to attack humans right after they change. After they stop attacking, they work at collecting the remaining humans into groups."

"I need you to turn around."

All of the men, including the driver, turn to look at her in disbelief. The driver sideswipes a car on the side of the road and shakily regains control.

"Our orders are to get you to that plane, not a sightseeing tour of Hell."

"Look, if we can drive by that road again, maybe from a distance, it will help me figure out what's going on. I need some information, I need to observe those things if I'm going to give the president any useful information."

"I'm not turning us around, if she needs to see those things, you'll have to give her your phone, Critter."

"Damn it!" Pulling a phone out of his pocket, the soldier nicknamed Critter turns on the phone and hands it to the doctor. "I've been shooting videos of what's been going on out there. I've captured three different kinds of mutants so far. I don't want to see these videos on your own YouTube page, okay? Those videos are mine!"

"This idiot thinks he will get famous by uploading videos to his page. We keep telling him this shit is going on around the world and the internet is toast, but he won't believe us."

"You're all just jealous that I had the brains to record what's going on outside."

A deafening roar of engines over their heads announces the arrival of the Harrier jet. It lands a block in front of the trucks and the men quickly climb out to escort Dr. Usachova the final few yards to her escape. As she climbs up the side ladder into the cockpit, Critter yells to her one last time.

"Remember those videos are mine! I don't want to see them on your own page."

*

"Mr. President, this is Dr. Usachova."

"I hope you have information we can use."

She lowers her outstretched hand, realizing the president isn't going to shake it.

"Thank you for sending those soldiers to rescue me, Mr. President. I think I will be able to help."

"I hope so. You should realize a few things right off the bat. Ten men lost their lives to bring you safely here, and we haven't sent rescue parties out for anyone else. If the information you provide is useful, then I will extend my gratitude to you for coming."

"I... I understand. I do appreciate what it took to get me here, and I will help in any way I can."

"Well, why don't you start by telling me what we are dealing with and try to keep in mind that not all of the people assembled here are scientists. We need to know what this is and how we can deal with it." He stretches out his arm offering her a chair at a large table with seven other seated people. A large group of others are sitting at various other tables all with notebooks and awaiting her input.

She takes a seat and looks confidently around at the other people in the room. "First, you should know there is nothing we could have done to prevent this from happening and likewise, there is nothing we can do to change it. Everything occurring is due to two main influences beyond our control: solar winds and magnetic fields. Depending on how our survival as a species results, we happen to be alive at the right or wrong moment in time.

"As for the 'what' in what is happening. Some form of mutating radioactive cosmic particle is causing what has happened. What the particle is will take testing to determine, but its presence is evident with the blue hue to our sky.

"Mr. President, I need to know, are there any secure facilities or underground structures that have remained immune to the effects of the mutating particles?"

The president and several advisors look with uncertainty toward the assembled group in the room.

"I'm not asking you to disclose any secret locations to me, I just have to know if humans in any location you control have been spared the effects of this mutation. It is vital to understand if the particles are abated by soil, steel, concrete or any form of protective structure you are aware of."

One of the advisors in the room offers, "We haven't been able to determine that completely. There is no known location or base, above or below land or sea, that has not been affected. While we do have locations where no children are present, such as submarines or certain underground facilities, we have received information from certain underwater and underground locations that did have children mutate."

"Thank you. That means we are possibly dealing with a new subatomic particle which can travel through objects with little interference at the atomic level. The change in visual hue in the sky could be due to immensely heavy bombardment that is interacting with air particulates or it is interacting with the visual centers and processes of our brains causing us to see the sky as heavily blue. Either way, we are receiving intense bombardment of this unknown cosmic particle at the moment.

"Now, the why. Earth's magnetic field has been weakening quite rapidly over the last hundred years. Our magnetic field plays an important role in keeping out most cosmic radiation. In this case, however, even if it were still at full strength, it might be somewhat ineffective at preventing our bombardment from subatomic particles. Our Sun's magnetic field and solar output are in part to blame for this as well.

"The solar winds our Sun produces normally help clear the space around our planet of cosmic rays. So a weak magnetic field on both the Earth and the Sun, along with our particular position in the galaxy, are causing us to be bombarded by the particular cosmic particle that is causing these mutations.

"So you see, there is nothing we could have done or can do to change the outcome we are in. Unless you find some substance that these particles cannot penetrate, then we are at an impasse with protection from continued mutation. Our only other option, which is impossible, would be to strengthen the Sun or Earth's magnetic fields or change our planet's current position in the universe."

"Based on the presentation you gave the military previously, we were under the impression that some of the historical accounts of defenses against the mutants would work. Is it still your opinion that previous accounts of vampirism were the result of exposure to cosmic rays?"

Dr. Usachova's brow wrinkles and her eyes open wide in confusion.

"I am sorry, Mr. President. I made no claim of the sort. During my briefing to your military leadership, I spoke about historical data regarding mass extinctions and possible mutations in the past. I said nothing regarding recent history or fictional characters of literature."

The president slams his fist on the table and looks at General Gutfeld.

"Mr. President, if I may?" Dr. Usachova inquires trying to regain his attention. "I never mentioned vampirism specifically, but it is quite possible that what we regard as fantastical tales of creative or demented minds could have been factual accounts of previous mutations. If those events were real, then they were localized events, not global as we are currently dealing with. Perhaps small fluctuations in magnetic field strength allowed particles to enter smaller locales for brief times. This would have created the mutations and could easily have been explained in antiquity as connected to whatever natural events, religious beliefs, and animal behaviors they were familiar with at the time."

Clearly angry and yelling, "So why is nothing working against these mutants? President Connelly sent four thousand men to deal with a small group of these things and the fire they used just washed around their bodies. Video footage we recovered shows they are almost immune to it instead of it making them weak. Deploying garlic powders and sprays has also had no effect and neither has silver. Even the ones we thought we killed get up after resting for a short time. Their bodies are able to heal from any type of wound we give them. Nothing has worked to permanently stop them."

"I can only speculate based on the limited information I have."

"Speculate then."

"We are still being bombarded. The cosmic wind or cloud our planet has entered is still here. When it passes there may be another change in mutation. It could cause the mutations to revert, it could change their level of regeneration, it could cause them all to die. Unfortunately, without the ability to block bombardment of the particles, we cannot test what will happen when they are gone."

"How long will this last, this bombardment?"

"I don't know."

"Best guess then."

"Mr. President, it could last anywhere from one more hour to thousands of years. I don't know what particle we are dealing with. I don't know how extensively it is present in the location of space our planet or solar system are traveling through. I don't know how much affect the magnetic fields have on the particle. There are far too many unknowns to answer your question. This change could be with us for the remainder of humanities existence on the planet. As I have heard in your decisions, you understand that our race's current position on survival versus extinction is directly related to how we deal with the mutants. If I knew of some way to stop the mutations or the mutants, I would give it to you. All I can do now is offer my skills in researching it so we can hopefully find some answers."

The president rubs his hands over his face and through his hair in frustration. No longer angry, he looks up.

"I understand what you're saying and appreciate your offer to work with our scientists. Do your best to discover what this particle is and attempt in some way to measure it and tell us what else we have in store for our future.

He pauses and looks thoughtfully at Dr. Usachova. "I was actually hoping you would tell me I am wrong and give us something specific we could do to take our country back. With our collective understanding of science, I was hoping for... I was hoping for hope I guess."

"Sir, I will do whatever I can, to find out what is going on. Please don't blame science for not having the answers. Science is young. What we think of as modern science only started forming in the 1870's, and as recently as the 1950's, scientists were claiming future researchers would have little else left to discover. True science as we know it is barely older than most of the people in this room. We will figure this out. In the meantime, you need to continue doing what you have been to keep the human race alive in whatever form it currently takes."

CHAPTER TWELVE
HOW THE MIGHTY HAVE FALLEN

Undisclosed Location

My fellow Americans, with a heavy heart, I am addressing you tonight as your new president. Last night, after a coordinated effort to retake the Washington D.C. area from the mutants, President Connelly was killed.

The former president sent four thousand of our finest troops in to wrest control of the area and all information we have from that endeavor is a total loss of all the men and women that were in that battle. Our four thousand soldiers were destroyed by a force of only twenty of the vampire-like mutants. The capabilities of these vampires are too great, no weakness has been discovered, nor do we have an ability to stop them with any of the weaponry we currently have at our disposal. On top of the ineffectiveness of our modern weapons, none of the historical accounts of vampiric weakness to fire, garlic, silver or anything else has been accurate.

Our inability to defeat them on the battlefield has prompted me to issue this proclamation of the complete and total surrender of all government and military forces within and without the United States territories. All remaining military forces are ordered to stand down and cease attempts to eradicate the mutants. Do not engage them as it will result in greater innocent civilian casualties. I urge those Americans who remain free at this hour to avoid initiating any aggressive or combat stance against the vampires for two vital reasons.

First, there is no physical way to defeat them. There is no known method of modern weaponry that has any long-term effect on them. They heal too quickly, and in fact, when they are injured, they seek out human blood to replenish their systems, so causing injury to a vampire actually increases the danger to non-mutated humans in the area.

Second, and this is the primary factor in my decision today: However mutated these children have become, they are still our future. They are the future of humanity. Complete victory over the mutant population would result in the extinction of the human race. Even if we had a way to kill these vampires, which we do not, killing them would result in the removal of our species from the planet. That is extremely important for all of us to remember, not only now, but in the months and years ahead as we work to find some form of consensus under which we can co-exist.

The human race has had an evolutionary leap of what I consider the horrific kind. That does not remove the fact that it is still the human race we are dealing with. There is no guarantee that those children out there who have not yet mutated will not do so in the future. In fact, my scientists believe from information they have gathered, that puberty is the causative agent in this change and all young children will eventually mutate once they reach the age range of eight to twelve years.

This event is worldwide. No nation is exempt from the mutative effects of the cosmic particles causing the blue haze we see everywhere. There is no place from which we can seek aid, and there is no nation that has achieved any success against the mutants in battle. As horrific as these last thirty-three hours have been, for our survival, for the survival of the human race, we must find a way to work with the mutated children.

For those U.S. Naval Forces who are in the world's oceans tonight, I urge you to remain at sea for the foreseeable future. Return to the coasts of America if you are able, but do not return to our shores. You are the last remaining bastion of free humans on earth. Stay afloat and remain free. There may come a time when we find a way to defeat the mutants or discover a way to reverse the effects of their change. If that time should arrive, your ability to remain outside of the influence and control of our mutated children may be a deciding factor in any success we have.

*

As Americans, we aren't used to failure. There isn't or hasn't been until now a situation or event we couldn't overcome. The American motto is similar to that of the U.S. Marine Corps stating, *the difficult we will do today, the impossible will take a little while longer.* No task is considered undoable by those raised in this nation, yet today, the president has told us we have failed. The full might of the federal government and our military assets are incapable of dealing with this new form of humanity the blue haze has given us.

At least in this moment of failure, it is our own children that have managed to bring our nation to its knees. This truth of self-inflicted destruction offers no consolation to the millions of families that have lost loved ones in the last day and a half. Under normal circumstances, the president's address would have been a severe shock and blow to the psyche of the average citizen. Today, the shock of hearing about defeat is tempered by the fact that most of the nation's population is already surviving in groups rounded up by the dominant local vampires.

Very few Americans were outside of the cities and towns in which they lived, and so most Americans listened to the president in groups of several hundred to several thousand as they await instructions on how the new society they are going to live in will be structured.

In some cases, the humans are actually grateful to the vampire mutants for saving their lives from the rampaging troll-looking mutants that were destroying everything in their path. In all areas, people were witness to the vampire mutants protecting younger children and babies above all else. Those witnessed actions of small children being rescued and protected helped to assuage some of the fears and anxiety that the brutally violent encounters of the day had created.

CHAPTER THIRTEEN
REUNION

Oregon

A dragonfly darts erratically over a small tree-lined pond. Greg Cavanaugh's back is aching while sitting against the rough-barked tree. His legs are asleep, and his body is yearning to move. The discomfort he's feeling puts a smile on his face as he lightly runs his fingers through Evelyn's hair. She has broken through her sorrow over the loss of their baby and chose to join him away from the camp.

"I'm glad you came out here with me."

She is silent but grabs his hand and gives it a quick squeeze of acknowledgment.

"I didn't only want you to see the pond here, I needed to get away from all of the new additions that have been coming to the camp. You don't have to say anything yet, just having you come here with me is enough to let me know you're getting better. I am here for you as I have always been whenever you want to say something."

Greg continues silently watching the insects and occasional bird go about their business. The blue haze hasn't affected them, and the world seems oblivious to the problems people have. Two dragonflies begin to chase each other to and fro, causing Greg to chuckle inwardly.

"You should have seen this one man named Jordan, he came in yesterday. He arrived at noon with his parents, and when he saw all of the children at the camp, his eyes lit up."

"Is he a human?"

Startled for a second by her question, he continues trying not to make the reappearance of her voice such a contrast.

"No, he's one of them, but it's what he did that made the scene so bizarre. This Jordan is easily over six feet tall and has more muscles than you could believe. I mean he looks like a pro wrestler that forgot to get a tan. The best way I can describe him is just huge.

"So I'm watching him look around at everyone and he's watching all the young kids running and playing. One of the women walks up to his family and offers to show them where they can put their things to settle in and John, the vampire, walks up to this new guy and whispers something in his ear.

"Now, picture this. You know how big John is and he's whispering in Jordan's ear. Two humongous men in the middle of the forest having a private little chat. Jordan literally jumped up and down a few times then turned to his parents and asked them something. Guess what he said?"

She just looks up at him and smiles.

"He asked them, 'Can Johnny and I go play?'"

Evelyn sits up and turns to face Greg. "He did not."

"Yes, he did. Can you imagine it? I laughed out loud, I couldn't help myself and had to turn away. It is so strange seeing these…these children the way they are now. I hate calling them vampires even though I know that's what they are. I'm even getting used to their pale skin, but I can't seem to wrap my head around the fact that they are still mentally little kids in these giant, adult bodies.

"I found out later that they were both ten years old before this haze changed them. Somehow, they could sense they were a similar age and wanted to go play. They ended up playing some version of cops and robbers with some of the other vampires that looked like a movie running on fast forward. It's amazing how quick they are."

Evelyn reaches her hand out to Greg's neck and softly rubs the two small red holes he has just below his left ear. "Was it frightening when you were bitten?"

Nodding at first without saying a word, Greg grabs Evelyn's hand and presses it down on the bite at his neck.

"I was terrified, I thought I wouldn't survive. It was a girl named Sasha, I'm not sure if you met her or not. I didn't believe her when she said she wouldn't need much, just a little more than people give up when donating blood. I thought, *Sure, I've seen the movies, you're going to suck me dry.* I didn't say it out loud, but I know she felt my fear."

"Did anyone else have to give to others?"

"Not at that point. We were only here for three days, and she was the first whose hunger had returned. I was hoping they would be able to return to eating normal food, but when I heard from Cora that one of their vampires needed to feed, a part of me felt relieved. I stepped up and volunteered to be the first."

"You were afraid she would drain you, but you still volunteered. Was it because of me?"

"Yes, a part of it was. I won't lie and say things have been easy on me." With a bit of painful anger in his voice, Greg takes a deep breath and tries to continue without sending his wife back into her silent depression. "I know the pain you are feeling. We both lost our son and our baby. That is a pain we have both had to endure. On top of that for me, you hadn't left the tent since we arrived and you stopped speaking to me. I thought we were all going to die anyway and you seemed to have given up. I couldn't stand to watch you slowly waste away, not after losing Lloyd and the baby, and I wanted to be able to drift away and disappear the way our world has."

She nods and grips his hand but doesn't interrupt or make an effort to stop him.

"I also feel responsible for the others and know it is what I should have done. If I or anyone could survive one of the vampires drinking our blood, it would change everything. We would still have to fear them to a certain degree, but arrangements could be made to save humanity. I had to step up and be the representative people expect me to be. I have to be involved in this if we are going to find a way to live together in the future."

"I'm sorry I haven't spoken to you. I just needed time, thank you for giving it to me."

"At least you had that talk with Cora."

Shaking her head, her eyes show an honest innocence. "I didn't speak with her. When she came into the tent two days ago, she did all of the talking. I listened, but she didn't ask anything and I didn't give any replies.

"She sat there and spoke about her family and what life had been like up until the change. She told me how afraid she was that the others are all looking to her for guidance when she doesn't know what is going on. She basically told me everything she was going through and it was exactly what I was feeling. Looking back, I guess that's probably why she did it. I keep forgetting she can read minds. After she finished her stories, she left and I haven't seen her since."

"No one has seen her since that day, at least no one in the camp. All of the new arrivals have been sent here by her, and they say there is some type of reorganizing of where people live and zones of control. One of the new vampire children told me when Cora gets back, I'm supposed to speak with her about it."

A brief lull in the conversation is interrupted by the fluttering of wings overhead. High in the sky, a massive group of winged vampires floats overhead. From this distance, they look like large birds, but the pale wings followed by human legs give the outlines away for what they are.

"Speaking of Cora, I think that's her."

Cora's wings are another thing that make her stand out. Like everything that has happened in the past week, wing shape is something no one truly understands. Why some children got them and others didn't and why they aren't all the same. Except for Cora, all of the vampire wings they have seen so far look like giant bat or dragon wings. Cora's, while they are still all skin like the others, took the shape of bird's wings.

There is a layered and rounded look to them making it appear like they are covered with feathers until you get right next to them.

While the winged mutants fly above the camp in a slow circular motion, one tucks its wings and darts down to the group like a falcon diving to its prey. Landing between the trees only twenty feet away, Greg and Evelyn stand up. For a second, they see only this vampire's back and notice his wings are identical to Cora's.

When he turns to face them, Greg's eyes narrow and Evelyn leans on her husband for support. The winged vampire looks like Greg, yet with wings and pale skin.

"Mom…Dad?"

"Lloyd!"

CHAPTER FOURTEEN
THE MORNING LIGHT

Colorado

Heavy wings flap in the early morning air above a landscape of farms. The searcher is heading toward sorrow. A feeling of despondency woke him thirty minutes ago, and he realized the feeling was not his own.

Jared was struggling as all the others that have experienced The Shattering to come to terms with the new thoughts and emotions they could pick up from others. For some, it made them angry and violent. Others absorbed with empathy the feelings of their fellow changelings. It made them want to be better people than they had before. Jared is one of the good ones.

His wings beat slower as he brings himself down to land in front of a barn with sobbing emanating from inside.

Standing outside the door in a soft placating tone, Jared calls. "You should come out."

"I can't. You don't know what I've done."

"I know what you've done, and I know you couldn't stop it. The same thing is happening everywhere, all over the world. The same thing happened to me."

"But I killed them. I didn't mean to but I killed them."

Jared looks out at the penned-in field over the bodies of several cows to the remaining cattle huddled in the farthest corner. He can sense their fear, he could taste it when he opened his mouth to speak. The cattle aren't the ones this boy is mourning over, and as much as Jared wants to help, he knows it would be unwise to enter the barn. He must wait for this boy turned man to come out.

"If you come with me, you can be with others like us and we will work through our problems together. I don't want to leave you here all alone. Please, come out."

A large mass begins moving in the barn and approaches the door. The twelve-foot height of the opening is a few inches too short for the figure inside to exit. He has to duck down before entering the world being lit up by the morning sun.

Jared steps back as the creature leaves the building. He is a giant, but not like the others his group encountered so far. For one thing, this giant can speak well and has complex thoughts where the others had only strong emotional signals and limited vocabulary like that of a two year old. Another difference with this giant is his shape. He still looks like a human, a man, albeit a gigantic one standing over twelve feet high. The other giants encountered were taller than this one and became hugely massive around the middle, looking like misshapen, lumbering sumo wrestlers.

"Who are you?" the giant asks while wiping his eyes.

"I am Jared. I have assembled a group outside of Frederick and would like you to join us."

"I'm Carl." He turns and looks back into the barn and begins sobbing once again. "My parents… I didn't want to… I couldn't stop myself." His tears flow with force as he drops to his knees. In between the sobs, Carl continues. "I don't think I can be trusted around others. I don't know what I will do."

"The thirst is the strongest during the change. Once you gain your final form, it dies down."

"How do you know? What if I haven't finished changing?"

"Did you kill the cattle in that field?"

"Yes."

"You didn't kill them all. You stopped or were able to stop when your body replenished itself."

Carl looks to the bodies in the field and thinks for a moment. Returning his gaze to Jared, he notices something odd about the man.

"What is that on your back?"

Jared's wings spread out behind him and he flaps them twice before folding them up once more.

"I would rather have wings than be this tall." The small smile on his large face belies an innocence still present in Carl that Jared wishes he could regain.

"If you aren't sure you can control yourself, walk into that field and see if you can keep from attacking the cattle. If you don't have any strong urges, then you can come with us."

At that moment, Jared notices several fast-moving creatures in the distance heading toward them. He stands with uncertainty, and Jared can sense Carl's fear building.

"They are with me, Carl. They don't have wings but can run extremely fast. Please head into the field and see how you do around the cattle."

Carl gives a few uncertain glances back to the dust trails kicked up by the approaching runners and then steps out into the field, easily traipsing over the fence like it was a small log in his way.

As Carl makes his way to the cows, the approaching group of mutants arrive and gather around Jared. Holding his hand up, he stops his assembled fighters. Each of them are carrying some form of weapon. Four are holding rotor blades removed from the tail of a helicopter, and the others are armed with posts and bars removed from street signs or construction areas.

"Lower your weapons," Jared tells them all. "We won't need to kill this one. He isn't like the others."

"How many different mutations are out there?" a pale woman asks to herself more than to the others.

The ground shakes slightly as Carl runs back toward them with a huge grin on his face. He jumps over the fence and lands before the group in a youthful manner and looks at the new faces around him.

"I didn't want to attack the cows. They even stink like regular cows again, not that sweet smell they had yesterday." Not skipping a beat, Carl continues to ramble in excitement. "You're all so pale. Were you this white before you changed?"

"No, we all looked smaller and had normal color yesterday. I am twelve and I looked like a twelve year old. How old are you?"

"I'm nine."

"Have you encountered any other changers? Or any regular people?"

"No. I haven't left the farm," he says sadly, returning his gaze to the barn. "I don't know what I should do."

"Carl, I have the ability to absorb people's thoughts and feelings, some of the others have that ability as well to some degree. Are you able to sense anything more than you did yesterday? Do you feel any differently...other than your size of course."

"Um...what does absorb mean?"

"I can read people's minds if I touch them. Absorb means I see what they are thinking and their thoughts and memories become my own. Almost like I experienced them. I was twelve yesterday, but I have seen and felt things through regular adult minds that have made me older. Do you have anything like that?"

"I'm sorry. I don't feel any different today than I did yesterday. I can't read your mind." He kicks at the dirt nervously but then takes a step back when he looks at the others more closely. "Does that mean you won't take me with you? Is that why they are carrying weapons? You're not going to hurt me, are you?"

Jared flicks his hand in a slight motion, not noticed by Carl and the assembled group drop their weapons to the ground in unison.

"We aren't going to hurt you, but we haven't encountered anyone like you before. There are others that changed and they kill everything. They are taller than everyone else the same way you are, but they are round in the middle as well, like their insides are blowing up. They look as wide as they are tall and are extremely muscular. They are dangerous, and I was afraid you were one of them when I came here."

"They kill everything like I did to my parents?"

"They don't stop killing the way you were able to. They kill everything and everyone they come into contact with including us." His arms motion to the other mutants.

"You are welcome to join us, but first we will help you bury your parents."

"Thank you. I didn't know what I should do."

CHAPTER FIFTEEN
NEW WORLD ORDER

Cheyenne, Wyoming

A heavy prattle of raindrops fall on the muddy ground outside the open doorway. The day and sky are as dreary as the mood of the group being relocated to this human internment camp. All humans are being rounded up and placed into camps of various sizes in which the vampires can keep track of them.

Overlords or protectors, what regular humans call the vampires in their charge, depends largely upon the behavior of those that run the camps. This particular camp is being setup on Francis E. Warren Air Force Base just outside of Cheyenne, Wyoming.

Sitting hunched over in a chair, hands on his face and speaking in muffled tones through his palms, the president says, "I am the last President of the United States. Do you know how that feels? Do you have any idea what it does to me every time you address me as Mr. President? I have the small comfort of not having been elected and was thrust into this position. But my first day on the job, I declared our complete surrender. I didn't even try like President Connelly did."

"You didn't have to surrender, sir."

"Like hell I didn't! If we kept fighting, they would have killed us all and you know it."

"That is exactly my point, sir. That is why I keep addressing you as Mr. President. You made the decision to place the lives of the American people above your own self-interest. You saw what we were facing and rightfully had our armed forces stand down against the threat we have no chance of defeating."

"So why do I feel like a failure?"

"Because this isn't a success. Unfortunately, not every correct decision ends in victory. We are alive right now, and millions of Americans are also alive because you surrendered. Sir, like you, I wish that the circumstances were different, but this is what we have. I think we should be thankful they brought us here to Wyoming and took us out of the Denver area."

"Thankful!?" Standing up with clenched fists, he stares at his secretary.

"She's right, James." The president's chief advisor stands in the doorway with several other people waiting to enter behind him. "We need to come in and discuss what is still to come."

President Thomas nods and waves his hand in a gesture for them all to enter. They wipe mud from their shoes, shake umbrellas, and remove wet jackets before sitting down in the small equipment storage room.

Two Secret Service Agents that were silently standing in opposite corners of the room head for the door to wait outside.

"Terry, Hendrickson, wait, stay in here. There's no point in your going out into that storm and getting sick. Stay inside and have a seat. I doubt anyone will be able to get past the vampires to attack me today."

Oddly, even though the members of government have been scattered throughout the U.S. and any meaningful form of representation ended, the vampires are making quite a show of protecting President Thomas. They have allocated ten vampires to surround this building as presidential protection while the base and adjacent city of Cheyenne is thoroughly searched. Once the search is completed, they have been assured the president and his staff will be assigned specific houses and buildings to reside in. It took only twenty vampires to defeat the four thousand troops that went into Washington D.C. so this show of protection is either overblown or there is a concern that the president might be attacked by other vampires.

"Mr. President, may we begin?"

President Thomas and the others sit on stools around an oil-stained shop table that has been cleared of tools.

"The first thing we need to deal with is population attrition. We estimate forty-three million people have died in the past week.

"Nearly twenty-eight million adolescents went through the change on the first day, taking the human population down below three hundred million. Approximately twenty-seven million people were killed the first day in attacks by the newly changed children. It is grim, but we are fortunate that not all of those that became vampires killed humans when they mutated. Many used multiple sources of blood for replenishment or were the arch-type vampires and only fed on other vampires, thus limiting the number of deaths. We project the deaths caused directly from vampire attacks account for around sixteen million people, not including those people lost due to aircraft, car or other vehicular accidents due to The Shattering.

"The two other groups that have cost us lives are the behemoths and giants. They have added significantly to our losses. The behemoths are the large mountain-troll-looking creatures that grow in size each time they consume a human or mutant. There has been no successful communication between the behemoths and either humans or vampires. They are one hundred percent committed to the destruction of anyone and anything in their vicinity, and the vampires have taken to killing them on sight. The death toll associated with their activity is about eleven million, fewer than deaths caused by the vampires, but there are far fewer children that became behemoths as well. Perhaps only one million children became the behemoths and possibly fewer than that."

"And they caused that many lives to be lost?"

"Yes. Our information is not complete due to the broken state our nation is in, but the numbers we have compiled in communications with others around the country coincide with what we have been given by the vampires. The giants caused the least destruction but still account for two million deaths. They have limited vocabulary and interact awkwardly according to information from the vampires, but they are not violent once they are replenished after mutating.

"We have lost an additional sixteen million people in the past week due mainly to losses of the elderly or others that were dependent on continual medical care or varying degrees of life support. A small percentage of those sixteen million would be caused by children that have gone through The Shattering after those that changed on the first day, but those losses account for less than fifty thousand. That brings us to the total lives lost of forty-three million."

"Do you know why children mutated differently yet?"

"Not yet, but Dr. Usachova is working on it. She has nearly as many vampire guards as you do, sir, so they view her information as a valuable resource as well as we do. She told me she is being given access to everything she needs for her research and will let us know what she finds out as long as communications between groups remains possible.

"We also understand the possibility that they are keeping her secure on the chance she discovers some weakness to their condition. We have given her codes to use if she feels threatened or has information for us that she is unable to directly convey. Unfortunately, with many of them being able to read minds, I don't know how safe or secret anything she discovers would be."

"So she could discover a way we could beat them and they will know before we do. Fine, what's next?"

"I haven't finished with population attrition yet, sir. Unfortunately, forty-three million deaths is the number today. We can expect one or two million more people to die every week for the foreseeable future if things remain stable. There will be continued issues with health, stress, and age-related deaths. The relocations are hard on many people as is the lack of electricity around the nation.

"The problem we are facing is leadership and knowledge among the vampires. Before this event happened, most normal adults had no clue how to go about feeding themselves without running to a grocery store and their clueless children, the vampires, are now in charge of us all. Right now, the vampires are scavenging supplies from all the stores and warehouses in the country. With the loss of continued production of goods, we will be looking at mass starvation occurring within a few months at the most, especially in the larger cities. Rationing has to be put in place immediately, and word must be sent throughout the nation if possible."

"How many do you think we will lose?"

"In addition to the lack of food, I have to mention we are heading into the fall and winter seasons."

"How many?"

"Best case scenario, by spring, seventy-five million dead. Medium case, two hundred million dead."

"Medium case! What the hell is the worst case?"

"I'm afraid the worst case is complete extinction of all non-mutated human life. But we don't anticipate the worst-case situation occurring within the next year unless there is some type of war or other escalation."

"So you believe up to two hundred million more Americans could die by next spring?"

"Yes, sir. I'm afraid with no electricity for heat and no food production, a majority of the nation's population will die. What we are looking at is a near return of society to that of the eighteen hundreds. Our modern food gathering and production capabilities rely on fuel and electric power to gather and process. Those systems are all currently shut down. Once we are through the winter, we could return to the agrarian ways of the past, but even if our people were given the mobility to plant and harvest crops or raise livestock, most of them don't have the skills necessary to survive a farming lifestyle.

"I believe you should expect loss of life numbers to equal that of our scenarios regarding an electromagnetic pulse attack. Many of those were in the range of eighty to ninety percent death toll with an EMP attack on U.S. soil alone. We are facing a similar circumstance with our being confined the way we are."

The new Director of Intelligence, Bradley Hoskins, speaks up. "Sir, if I may?"

"Go ahead, Bradley."

"There is something more happening here than we know about. You have ten vampire guards outside this building alone and my men have counted close to a hundred around this base. They are not taking shelter from the weather, but regardless how superhuman they are, the elements still affect them. The rain and cold still bother them, but they are staying at their posts and I believe it is all to protect you, sir. If they are guarding you this way because they respect your position, then you have the influence necessary to make requests to have people return to work in needed occupations.

"It is in their interest to keep as many of us humans alive as possible. Their answer to a simple request to have people return to work in necessary industries will tell us everything we need to know about the real situation we are in. I just hope they say yes."

"What do you believe our situation is if they say no?"

Everybody but the president shifts in their seats. Several heads around the table bow down and more than a few frowns appear on the faces of the advisors.

"Sir, we all know they don't need such a show of strength against us humans. All of these guards are to defend you against other mutants, other vampires. What I believe, what we are afraid of, is escalating territorial disputes among the mutants. There are millions of children around this nation that for the first time have unprecedented power. Think back to when you were twelve or thirteen. If you were a regular middle school kid one day and the next you had the superpowers of someone in a comic book, what would you want to do?"

"I was a Superman fan, so if I had his powers, I'd want to kick the ass of every bully and troublemaker I could find."

"And if there are superheroes, there will be supervillains as well. We saw that with what happened in Washington D.C."

CHAPTER SIXTEEN
MAKE AMERICA GREAT AGAIN

Oregon

A light fog floats over the grassy ground of a clearing in the McDonald-Dunn Forest north of Corvallis. Cora is waiting at the edge of the woods with Lloyd and two other winged vampires.

"I can hear someone coming."

A lone vampire speeds through the trees approaching their location and bursts into the clearing, barely slowing her immense speed before turning abruptly to face the group she is heading toward. Running right at them with no indication she will stop, the others listen more intently to the forest for others that may be approaching and all four prepare to take flight. At the last possible moment, the woman freezes her legs movement causing her to slide sideways to a stop in front of the small assembly. A Cheshire grin bursts open on her face.

"I'm so happy you asked me to meet you here."

"Cora, this is Erica. Erica, this is Cora, Lloyd, and Ruben."

"You should be careful approaching people like that." The frown on Cora's face, as well as her stance, lets Erica know she almost started a fight with the people she was hoping could help her and her family.

"I'm sorry for that. I still get excited about what I can do. I wasn't trying to start anything."

"I understand that, but things are getting more serious than you can imagine. You do know what we may be headed into correct?"

"Actually, no, I don't really know what you want. Brian only told me he wanted me to travel around Corvallis and get an idea about how the humans and vampires are dealing with each other. I already told him it wasn't going to be easy because of the Clark brothers."

"Please tell them what you know; this will help us decide what we can do to help your friends and family."

Erica loosely flops to the ground and crosses her legs in a childlike manner.

"The Clark brothers are twins and they control the city. They have wings like you do, but I don't know what their actual powers are other than being mean. They travel around the city and make sure all of us that have changed keep the humans from getting out of line. I think they were bad kids in school and were used to getting in trouble, because when they

92

talk to people, they sound like a parent yelling at their kid for doing something bad.

"There are other vampires with wings like you guys, and I heard one of them saying they had a few hundred in their group. I'm not really sure the exact amount of fliers there are, though. They don't spend time with us runners and don't treat us very nicely. I know there are two thousand eighty-five runners. They told me that the day I changed."

"Are all of the runners and fliers willingly working with the brothers or are they being controlled somehow?"

"I know there are some that don't get along with them, but they still do what they're told. Someone let me know one of the brothers killed a few of the other vampires for disagreeing with them, and it made everyone fall in line. I have no way of finding out how many are with them or against them without someone telling on me."

"What about your parents and friends? What is their situation?"

The girl in the woman's body looks up at Cora and shakes her head.

"You don't know where your parents are?"

"I know where they are. I don't know what that word 'situation' means."

Cora kneels down and smiles. "We need to know how your parents are being treated and where they are. Are they still living in your old house?"

"Oh, I get it. No, my parents and brother are kept in a building along with some of the other families of the runners. All over the city, the family members of those like us are kept together, and the people without any changed family are kept in other places. Once I changed, they were moved. I was told it was for their protection, but I could tell the girl who told me was lying. I think they keep them together to keep us in line like when my mom would threaten to take away my favorite dolls if I was bad."

"Thank you, Erica."

Frowning, Cora stands and looks at the others. "Corvallis sounds worse than Albany. It will be tougher with two arch-vampires in charge. What are your thoughts?"

"I wanted you to meet Erica because I think you have the greatest chance of helping the people in this area. Listening to her give more details, though, I don't know what can be done if they are willing to kill other vampires to keep everyone around them in line."

Cora looks briefly back at the girl still sitting on the ground watching them. "I know what can be done. I know what will have to be done to get rid of the brothers, but if we go down this path, where does it end?"

Lloyd looks at Cora and smiles softly before frowning and turning his gaze on Erica. "You seemed upset when you mentioned the regular people. How are they treating the humans?"

"I want you to know I can't do anything about it. I asked a few times and said it wasn't right, but they kept telling me to be quiet so the brothers don't find out. They don't like it when people question how they treat the others. *It's our time to run the planet, their time is over.* That's what they make us say at the events."

"What events?"

"They hold fights between groups of humans. They make them fight each other and the losers are drained. One man tried to protest and refused to fight so they broke his bones and then pulled him apart. I have nightmares about it. I know we all did awful things the first day we changed, but that was when we couldn't control what we were doing. Now they are hurting and killing people for fun. This isn't how I want the world to be. I want things back like they were before, I want to go home with my parents."

"I think that's part of your answer, Cora. If we go down this path, where does it end? If we don't go down this path, where does it end?"

Ruben and Brian nod and Cora turns away from Erica to face the others.

"If we do this, it will end up being a war. Those brothers are the type of people that will fight to the death, and I bet the same will happen with the one controlling Albany. We'll have to gather everyone together to survive the kind of battle it's likely to be but I think it's a fight we should have. I don't want to leave humans to be tortured, and I'm not going to leave these child-minded vampires to be controlled by psychopaths either. So we should start by clearing out the area around Salem and move outward from there as we gather more like-minded vampires."

"I have an idea where we can get weapons for the fight."

"Guns can't kill us, dork!" Ruben punches Lloyd on the shoulder and smiles at Cora trying to get her attention.

"The bullets won't kill us, but they will slow us down. You can bet that after we start taking down the vampires that control their own areas, word will spread. The vampires in the cities we are heading to next will grab whatever weapons they can find to fight back. We can't expect to fly into an area with just our bare hands and our strength and survive against equally strong opponents that also happen to be filling us full of bullets.

"I also wasn't thinking about guns. I think we should get some swords to try them out, they might work out better for us in the long run. My friends and I did a lot of fighting with blades when we were members of SCA and did historical re-enactments."

"What the hell is SCA? He is a dork, Cora. Are you sure you shouldn't be hanging out with me instead?"

In a show of solidarity, Cora wraps her arm through Lloyd's and grabs his hand. "SCA is the Society for Creative Anachronism, and I happen to like the fact that Lloyd did more with his time than play videogames before the change. I also prefer him looking at me in the eyes over you always staring at my breasts."

*

No blood is on the ground, but bodies lay everywhere. Hundreds of vampires are huddled together in fear on Kinder Field in the middle of Albany, Oregon. Overhead, flashes of white flesh dart through the sky firing bullets at each other from armory liberated firearms. More vampires run up and cower together with the others already on the field.

The sounds of bullets fade as shells fall from the sky along with bodies. What many are learning in this early battle is their ammunition runs out far sooner than the battle runs its course. The fight is turning to one of brute force. Punching, scratching, wrestling, and ultimately biting, which leads to death.

A spent body falls from the sky, its severed arms, legs, and wings loosely wave as they are all pulled by gravity to the earth. Impacting several yards from the vampires trying to shield themselves from the horrors of this new reality, it causes a collective shudder through the huddled mass. The head lands last, bouncing off the torso to which it was once attached. When it lolls to the side, the fearful group sees the face of the arch-vampire that had so severely controlled and threatened them over the time since the change occurred.

The battle rages on in the streets and sky of the city, but five winged vampires, with weapons from the past, descend and land by the body and parts of fallen Dmitri, the boss of this region. Two of the five descend on the parts that lie before them, draining them of blood and bringing that vampires fight to its ultimate end. The shivering group of running and winged vampires trying to avoid taking sides or participate in this battle are the objective of the other three that landed by Dmitri's body.

"I understand you were children just a short while ago. I realize also that many of your parents shielded you from the violence the world has to offer and would not let you even watch movies or read books that presented the realities and dangers of life. Shielding you from the truth was a mistake." The woman speaking spreads her feathered-looking wings out before them in a manner that is both terrifying and comforting. She looks poised to attack, but her actions feel as though she wishes to embrace the small crowd before her.

"Because of The Shattering that changed us and the evil actions of people like the one that controlled this city, your childhood is over now. All of our childhoods ended that first day, and this is what the world is now. You do not want to fight, and that lets me know you have decent hearts. You had good parents that loved you or love you still, and I must ask you this, where are they now?

"We are fighting the vampires who worked with Dmitri and will torture and kill your families if they have the chance. Are you going to kneel here in the grass and cry like little children while the world around you burns and gets destroyed by monsters like him?" She points her arm and a wing to the body of the fallen.

"Will you stay here and do nothing while your parents are out there and need your help? Your friends, neighbors, brothers, and sisters are locked up in buildings as we speak and need your help to achieve their freedom. You know who the bad ones are. You know where the innocent are locked up. You know better than any who needs to be stopped in this city and how to help those that need it the most.

"Stand up and fight with us. Fight to free the people of this city. Fight to free yourselves from the evil deeds Dmitri forced you to commit in order to survive. It will be difficult. It will be terrifying, but your loved ones need you. We need you to be able to right the wrongs that were committed here. Join us and be the people your parents hoped you would become."

One by one, the huddled masses start peeling off from the crowd in the field and run into the city to fight. Cora, Lloyd and the three others that led their new army into Albany beat their wings and lift from the ground to rejoin the fight as well.

The staccato rattle of gunfire is diminishing all over the city. More from the lack of planning than the spreading news of Dmitri's death. The choices these changed children have made are firmly ingrained in their minds, and they won't easily switch to liking humanity simply because a small battle is being won. The allies of Dmitri will fight to the death or try to escape. There is no common ground that can be reached with Cora and her soldiers. There is no pretending to switch sides while hiding true intentions with the mind-reading capabilities of some vampires.

The war going on in the sky and ground around Albany is truly savage. Empty firearms are discarded all over the streets and building tops and the fighters are using whatever weapons they can pick up and use against their opponents. Concrete blocks are thrown, pulled up street signs are swung, manhole covers are smashed down over heads and all with the intended result of slowing the enemy enough to grab them and get in a lethal bite so their blood can be drained. The ground around the city is littered with the drained and discarded bodies of the fallen.

Victory's progress is with Cora's troops. The former controllers of the city are realizing they are losing and many run or fly to the south attempting to escape. Their pursuers are too far behind to easily catch them and Cora calls them back before they get out of earshot.

"Let them go, we know where they are headed."

"If we don't catch them, we'll have to fight them again in Corvallis."

"And if they reach Corvallis with news of their loss, it might demoralize the Clark brothers."

An explosion on one of the streets below has collapsed a building and set two others on fire. The group flies down to investigate and find the charred remains of a dozen soldiers. Limbs and torsos are burnt, scattered, and still moving in the rubble around the blast zone.

In an urgent and frustrated tone, Cora calls her nearby soldiers to help. "Gather the body parts and bring them to me. I will tell you which ones to drain and which should be pieced back together."

*

"How soon can we move out to Corvallis?" Cora looks at the leaders of her new army which has gathered for discussion now that the battle is over.

"We could go in another hour, but we should wait until tomorrow. It will be dark soon and most of us don't know the layout of Corvallis. I am still getting used to my enhanced night vision so I'm sure others are as well. We don't need to put ourselves at a disadvantage going into a new place." Lloyd looks at Cora with concern. "There is also an issue with our numbers. We freed more vampires from control here than we lost in battle, but we could still end up with fewer fighters moving on to Corvallis. This isn't what most of us want to be doing and the brutality of it all is putting some of the kids into shock."

"I'll be able to do something about that." Cora stands and puts her hand on Lloyd's shoulder. "Finish with this meeting and begin gathering whatever ammunition you can find for the next fight. I would like to move against the brothers tomorrow. We will need to find more swords, you were right to bring them. The firearms are largely useless and the ammo runs out too quickly."

"If we start using swords, you have to work on your thought-transfer ability. It takes a long time to learn swordplay the traditional way and would be much quicker to implant sword fighting skills into people's minds."

She smiles at him and walks off, touching two other vampires that also have her abilities as she walks out of the gathering. The two she touched follow, with the silent remaining members watching them leave.

"I've seen the kids that are in shock, will she really be able to help them?"

"Cora gained some interesting powers with her change and she is still developing them. She has an influencing power that lets her affect emotions and behaviors. It's the same thing Dmitri was using to keep people under his thumb here and probably what the brothers are using in Corvallis. The good news for us is the strength of the influence is relative to our individual desire. If we fly into an enemy city, the vampires controlling that territory can't take over our minds and force us to join them because we don't want to hurt the humans. Our goals are opposite.

"That is also the reason there is no capture or trading sides in this war. If a vampire we are fighting wants to enslave humans but decides to join us to save his own life in a battle, they would be easily turned in the next city's fight and couldn't be trusted at any time in between."

"How many next cities do you think there will be, Lloyd?" The innocent and honest question is one that is on all of their minds.

Lloyd looks around at the group and all eyes are fixed on him. He takes a moment to think and thoughtfully nods his head.

"I was born and raised here in Oregon, in Springfield, actually. I had a great life, better than most. My dad was in politics and was popular. We had money and I got to do almost anything I wanted. It is a privilege to be my parents' son. One thing they told me above all else, I had to give back for the things I had and hoped one day I could go into politics like my dad. I want to help people. I want to do what we are doing now, I want to free them. The problem we have is figuring out where our responsibilities end?

"My goal is to make my family, my friends, and the people of my state safe. To do that, I can't just clear out the Oregon coastal cities or free the people within our state boundaries. With each city we free, there will be two more that are still enslaved. I think what we are doing is going to continue until we have lost our battle, or we have cleared our nation of the evil our world contains. We are going to have to go town to town, city to city, until we have freed every last man, woman, and child within our country. Even then, we might have to do more.

"There is no magic barrier between our country and Canada or Mexico. We will have to push on until we decide we would rather take a human life than save it. Right now, I am in it to make America great again. After that, I will be in it to keep her great."

CHAPTER SEVENTEEN
THE FUTURE

Oregon

After a heartfelt but brief reunion, Lloyd walks with his parents to the campsite where the other winged vampires are beginning to land. Something is different in this arrival. There is a buzzing energy felt throughout the camp and everyone is gathering in the center to hear what's happening.

When the final flyers have landed, they organize themselves around Lloyd in what looks like a military order of protection. This group is regimental in their behavior and stance, and it makes the hair stand up on Greg's neck even though the one they are protecting is his son. Greg and Evelyn step into the crowd and wait to hear what their son is about to say.

"I can sense your fear and have to say that some of it is warranted. You don't have to fear us, but there are those like us that you should fear. Cora has been traveling around the Willamette Valley gathering us together and organizing us for what is to come.

"The devastation and death humanity has endured up to this point may only be the beginning if the wrong group of mutants ends up in control. While Cora, myself and a great many of the other vampires out there know we can coexist with non-mutated humans, there are those that want to enslave you in pens like animals and drain you dry for food.

"Because of this, we have been organizing humans into protection zones that we can control to ensure the human race isn't wiped out of existence. These zones will be guarded by those of us that are trusted and can protect you from capture in the coming war."

Murmurs begin throughout the camp at the mention of war and protection zones.

"How close is this war?" a voice calls out.

"Zones of protection sounds like internment camps to me," another person calls.

Lloyd raises his hand, stretches out his wings and causes his voice to unnaturally amplify. "I said your fears were warranted, but we are not the enemy. I only have a short time here before I must move on. Allow me to tell you what I know and you can ask your questions when I am done."

The grumbling has subsided but the fear of the people has increased with his show of strength.

"Just as not every human is good, the same can be said of your children. Some of us have become the purest form of evil. They have a lust for power and domination. They have chosen to keep humans as slaves and play toys in blood sports. One of you asked how close this war is, it is here and going on right now. Cora and her forces have cleared the area around the Salem/Keizer area. There are current battles going on in Eugene and Portland as we speak.

"I will be joining the Southern Forces later, and once we clear that area, we will move back in this direction and help in the fight to clear the Portland/Vancouver area if it isn't already in our control. The ultimate goal is to increase our numbers through victories, and we will eventually be able to have a group head south to secure the region to the California border. Right now is the time to act while those with evil intentions are still disorganized. Their greed and lust for power is keeping them fragmented and fighting one another, while our desire to keep humanity safe is allowing us to join forces and work together.

"We will need your help in organizing zones of control and will rely on humans to govern themselves with minimal input from us other than protection and food gathering. As we clear areas up and down the coast, we will then begin to move eastward in the hope that we will be able to eradicate this threat from our shores, east to west and north to south. This will take at a minimum a few months and could possibly last into a year or longer, depending on the level of organized resistance we receive as we move farther east.

"That is all I have to say. What questions do you have?"

"Why should we stay in zones of control? After you've cleared an area, why can't we return to our normal homes and live there?"

"Our hope is that most of you will be able to return to your homes, as that is the most natural way to set up the control zones. It will be best if people are living in areas and around other people that they know. For those of you at this campsite, it is a bit more difficult. We have to make sure the area you lived in before The Shattering is safe and under our control before you can return.

"There will be instances where your homes or communities may no longer exist due to the destruction of houses and areas that have occurred because of fighting or unchecked fires. Another issue with returning home is there are still unchanged children in the world. It is believed that The Shattering occurs during puberty, and as you are all well aware, that is the most dangerous time for human contact with those like us.

"Over the next few months, if things remain as they are now, there will be more children that go through the mutation and some of those children will agree with our enemy that you should be enslaved. Keeping our zones of control smaller, with about three to four thousand, will allow people to better know when a threat is among you.

"There is also the final possibility that there may be losses on our part or incursions from the enemy into our territory, and it will be easier to evacuate and protect you if there are specific foot soldiers assigned to smaller groups. Very few winged vampires like myself will remain in an area once it is cleared, we will be needed on the front lines which will make you vulnerable."

"What if I want to join in the fight?"

Lloyd smiles and nods his head.

"I would welcome you to join us, but that would be a death sentence, and even if it were only my decision, I couldn't in good conscience allow it. There is no way for one of you to kill one of us, at least no way that we know of at this point. If some way for you to harm us becomes known, we will welcome your assistance in the fight."

"That's not true! When we were escaping Eugene, we killed a few by shooting them in the head."

"I am afraid you are wrong. Each side in this war has liberated firearms from armories and used them during our skirmishes and bullets are only a means to slow each other down. I have been hit over three hundred times so far, and the longer the battle lasts, the quicker I heal. The only way to kill a vampire is to drain them of their blood. Draining our enemies' blood gives us increased strength and regeneration so we can keep fighting, but this regeneration works for those we fight as well.

"With the speed and strength we have, there is nothing a human could do on the new battlefields but be crushed and killed in the onslaught or captured by the enemy and used as fodder to distract us."

"I can drive a tank," one of the men calls back in defiance.

Lloyd clasps his hands together in front of his mouth and makes a strange howling call into the air. Several seconds later, the ground begins to quake, and a rumbling noise is heard moving through the trees toward them. Out from the trees run five men and one woman who stop before the crowd and hover over them.

"These giants are some of our soldiers." The crowed peers up at them with an awed anticipation. "These five are big but not the tallest we have found. So far, the largest we've encountered stand fourteen feet high. It only takes two of them to tip a tank over. Four of them can pick up and toss a tank over twenty yards. If you still aren't impressed, look at Peter."

Lloyd points to a winged vampire standing in the defensive line. He has one normal arm and the other looks shrunken and burnt.

"Peter was shot by a tank projectile, and it tore him in half."

Peter removes his shirt to show that his chest looks shrunken and burnt in the center as well.

"Even with his body ripped in pieces, he was able to pull himself together and begin to heal. Our regenerative abilities are amazing. His one arm was lost because one of our enemies drained it of blood before he could get it back, but as you see, a new arm is growing in its place. So I am sorry, there is no way for you to help us that won't get you killed, and that is a chance we aren't willing to take with the future of humanity."

"I thought you were the future of humanity."

"We don't know what our place in the future is yet. Right now, we are a bunch of children that are learning for the first time what our parents sacrificed to keep us safe, and we aren't going to squander the lives that you gave us by allowing such evil to exist in this world. The greatest gift any of you could give us in this ongoing fight are your memories. As many of you know, some of our winged vampires like Cora can absorb your thoughts and memories. If you have tactical or military experience, those experiences of yours could help us win the battles that lay ahead."

CHAPTER EIGHTEEN
THE LONG ROAD AHEAD

Oregon

Greg and Evelyn Cavanaugh help each other hang clothes on a line strung between trees in a clearing by their camp. This small community of people have worked together with minimal difficulty over the past few weeks. There are the common strains that occur whenever groups are forced to live together, but most of the issues were attributed to boredom and frustration and quickly subsided. This camping trip doesn't have the jovial feel of an excursion from reality, however. All of the people here realize they are, in some form, captives of the vampires who control this area.

While pinning one of the few remaining shirts, a gust of wind hits Evelyn from behind. With her son off at war, the silent arrival of an arch-vampire is a dreaded event for Evelyn. Each winged entrance fills her with a shivering fear that the worst news is being delivered by some unknown face. Her sense of foreboding is eased by the large grin on Greg's face, and she quickly turns to see her son approaching them.

"Lloyd!" Her running embrace of him would have caused them both to fall over had he not gone through The Shattering. "I wish you would tell us how you are doing more often."

"Phones aren't working anymore, Mom, but I'm here now. Dad, can you back me up on this one?"

Patting his son on the shoulder, Greg gives Lloyd a smile while shaking his head. "I'm sorry, son, your mother is right. There have been vampires from your group coming through here for the last five days leaving messages with our prison guards. You could have sent word with any of the travelers that you were okay."

"Why do you call them that? You know those vampires we leave here are for your protection."

"Protection or not, we aren't able to leave this place and are kept here against our will. Now stop changing the subject and explain to your mother why you haven't given word about how you've been."

"I'm sorry. I thought I was coming back with the first wave heading to the north but something came up." Shrugging his shoulders and sheepishly hanging his head. "I'll let you know how I'm doing more often."

Evelyn grabs her son and gives him another crushing hug. "We already thought we lost you once, Lloyd. Knowing you are out there fighting a war is too much to take without you sending us word or hearing how you are. You're gone for days or weeks at a time, and I don't even know if you're still alive."

"I know, Mom, I'm sorry."

She gives him another hug.

"Enough of that now, are you going to be here long? Are you hungry?"

The awkwardness of her question hangs in the air. He doesn't eat regular food anymore, but it is a mother's prerogative to inquire about how her children's stomachs are doing.

"I don't know how long we will be here, a few days, maybe a week. We've cleared Oregon to the southern border and are regrouping here to figure out our next move. The Angel wanted to speak with someone at Willamette University, and I'm trying to figure out a better way to fight our opponents."

"The Angel, who is that?"

"Um, Cora is The Angel." He blushes a little and points up to her in a group of vampires hovering a thousand feet above them. "Something happened during a night battle we had and I said, I mean everyone said, she looked like an angel. She is incredible out there. You should see the things she is able to do."

"I understand what you mean. Even I think she looks like an angel when she flies, and I know it isn't just her wings or the pheromones she says she releases." Evelyn looks at her son with a huge motherly grin, thinking she knows what his term for her probably means. Greg looks on without registering the possibility. "There is a magnetism about her, a purity that everyone is drawn toward."

The assembly above them breaks up, and they watch Cora spiral down from the sky readying to land in front of them. She reaches out for Lloyd right before she sets her feet down and when they take each other's hands, it appears as though he is helping her down from a tall platform. Taking a few steps closer to his parents, Cora and Lloyd don't let go of each other's hands.

"Lloyd tells us he is calling you *The Angel* now. Does this have anything to do with you two holding hands?" Greg gets a giant grin of mischief as the two pull their hands apart quickly and both blush.

"Thanks, Dad!"

"I keep telling everyone they should just call me Cora, Mr. Cavanaugh. It is sweet when Lloyd calls me Angel, but it's a little embarrassing since our troops and some of the people we rescued started calling me that also. I'm not used to so much attention."

"Well, the name certainly is fitting." Evelyn grabs hold of Cora's hands. "Don't let Greg embarrass you like that, it's just what fathers do. You do look like an angel, and I think you are a perfect girlfriend for my son."

"Thank you, Evelyn. Please excuse me, I have to go see my parents and let them know I'm all right. Lloyd, I'll be leaving for the city after I see my parents, could you gather everyone for a discussion here this evening?"

Lloyd nods. Cora smiles and moves away from them in a running blur to find her family.

*

The vampires are assembled in a clearing by the campground waiting for Cora to return. Relieved family members are gathered around their returned warriors, knowing the time for them to be together is short. Other people from the wooded shelter are arriving as well in anticipation of news about the outside world.

Lloyd steps to the center to begin. "Many of you here, including my own parents, have asked how things are going and what we are dealing with. My father told me I should be honest, so I will be. This might be hard for some of the younger children to hear." He waits a moment to see if anyone wants to take their kids away but no one moves.

"The fighting we have engaged in so far is brutal and unforgiving. There is no surrender in this war of mutants. Each individual has made up their mind on what kind of world they wish to live in. As we have expanded our territory, we have so far encountered as many bad mutants controlling territories as good ones. We are also having to fight the behemoths that are still out there."

"What are behemoths?" someone calls out.

"Those are what we originally called mountain trolls. Unlike those of us that have become vampires or giants, the trolls continue to grow when they... when they eat someone. We have encountered some that are twenty-five feet tall and nearly half as wide. For some reason, they have remained as aggressive and bent on destruction as they were on the first day they changed.

"They are difficult to kill but are largely mindless in their behavior and lash out at anything that moves. The greatest danger on the battlefield for us is mutants like me, other vampires. They have our strength, our determination, and our ability to heal. The fight to capture Newport was particularly difficult and bloody. Both sides had major military hardware in the fight, and while the bombs and bullets can't kill us, they still cause pain and damage us when the explosion is large enough."

Several mothers and fathers give gasps when Lloyd mentions explosions.

"Is that how my son was killed?" George King is standing with his arms around his crying wife in the crowd.

"I'm sorry, George, hasn't someone spoken to you about your son yet?"

"No. No one has, but we knew he must be gone when he didn't come back with the rest of you. I have to know what happened, Lloyd." Grabbing his wife tighter, he added, "We have to know."

Turning to his soldiers, Lloyd calls out, "Does someone know what happened to Phillip? I sent him here right after we lost George's son and his squad."

One of the winged soldiers steps up to him and whispers in his ear.

"Your son was killed in an attack at Newport along with the eleven other members of his own squad and another fourteen soldiers from different squads. We were attacked by humans using tanks and artillery against us as a decoy. They were being controlled by Michael, an arch-vampire that claimed the Newport area. We were trying to stop the humans without killing them and that extra effort on our part enabled Michael and his soldiers to catch us while we were distracted. Our compassion is what enabled Michael to succeed in killing so many of us, in killing your son.

"I apologize to you and your wife that you are finding out only now and in such a manner. The boy I sent back to let you know was found murdered on our return trip here. Michael must have had some soldiers in the forests behind us expecting us to disperse and run. They would have been ready for any of us leaving the main battlefield. Phillip was a capable soldier, but I shouldn't have sent him on his own."

Tears flow down George's face, and he turns away from Lloyd without a word. Holding up his wife, they walk through the parting crowd back toward the campsite. Lloyd stands there silent with his head slightly lowered as the couple leave.

Lifting his head back up and taking a deep breath, Lloyd wipes tears from his own face and returns to his task.

"The fighting hasn't been easy, and we expect it will get worse rather than better as we gain territory and increase the size of our army. We have lost a lot of good people, and as difficult as that conversation just was, you should all prepare for the possibility that some or all of us won't return at some point. Those of you in this campsite are fortunate that only one of the children from this area have been lost. I have had to inform many people in different parts of our state about the losses we have had.

"It has taken three weeks to capture all of the Oregon coastline, and we are mobilizing to move north through Washington and into Canada. We are also moving east to capture the rest of the Washington and Oregon cities and towns. With each area we free from oppressive vampires, we are encountering new problems we have to deal with, and I need help from my parents and the rest of you adults to figure out what to do about it."

Once again, the people of the camp are reminded that the pale people with adult bodies were all just young teenagers a few weeks ago. With their own children, they instinctively know that their eyes are lying to them. With the vampires they didn't know before the change, it is too difficult for their minds to unwrap the illusion The Shattering created with its change.

"Are you having to fight everywhere you go?" someone asks.

"No, some of the towns are controlled by human-friendly mutants like us. They just want things to return to as normal a situation as possible. But often in the larger cities, that isn't the case. With so many children that mutated at the same time in such close quarters, the bad ones always seem able to gain control through coercion and threats. Many of the decent vampires end up leaving. They move to the outskirts of cities or suburbs with their families and other humans they can rescue.

"Sometimes, they are killed outright by those that want to enslave humans. I'm afraid in many areas, as we gain control over more cities and towns, the decent vampires and their families will be murdered by the bad. Right now, what the enemy vampires may view as uneasy alliances with friendly mutants will be seen as more of a threat as we approach.

"One of the issues I need your help with is in dealing with aggressive humans that we've freed. The territories held by the enemy vampires are usually run with brute force and the humans held in those areas are often put through various levels of abuse, neglect, or even torture. We have had many people fighting against our changes in areas we have freed. Sometimes they attack us directly. They say we are no different than the other monsters that controlled them before, and they won't be tricked by our attempts to be nice.

"You'll continue to have that sort of problem as long as you force people to stay in containment zones," Greg tells his son.

"I know what you're saying, Dad, but I don't think freeing people to go wherever they want will work either. The attacks against us are more of an annoyance than anything else, but we aren't the real victims in the attacks. The people that are really angry with how the vampires treated them are attacking other humans. Our wounds heal faster than we can scratch at them, the real casualties of the violence are the people working with us to secure their towns. The ones helping out and pitching in so we can all rebuild our lives.

"Right now, we are able to keep track of the agitators but I'm afraid of what could happen if we give everyone complete mobility to go from town to town. I think those humans that are angry will organize and specifically target all the humans that are working with us. I don't understand what they think they will gain by killing other humans?"

"What are you doing with the families of the enemy vampires you have to kill, son?"

"What do you mean? We aren't doing anything with them."

"That might be a big part of your problem. If an opposing group of vampires came in here and killed you and your men and then claimed we were free, how do you think I would respond to anyone that worked with them?"

"I guess you'd be pissed off." Lloyd's eyes go wide with uttering a curse word in front of his parents. "Sorry, Mom and Dad, I didn't mean to swear."

Ignoring his son's apology, he continues. "Lloyd, if some strange mutant came in here and touched a hair on your head, your mother and I would be more than pissed off at them and anyone that was helping them. You aren't just running around freeing humans from their oppressors, Lloyd. Some of the people you think you are freeing will have more power before you kill the vampires they are related to. In this world, parents are under the protection of their evil children just as we are under yours, and you are taking that away. You are dealing with power, politics, and family, and it isn't going to be easy figuring out what to do with those people."

"Not all of the troublemakers are family or friends of the vampires we killed, but I think you're right that they feel they lost something when we moved through to free everyone."

"That's another problem in your thinking," a man calls out. "You may be going from town to town getting rid of the vampires you claim are being bad or evil, but you aren't returning anything to normal. I believe you when you say you are stopping the bad guys, but as long as you keep us in containment zones, all you are doing is changing management on a bad situation. Prisoners don't care how nice the guards at the prison are."

"This isn't a prison, the towns aren't prisons!" His irritation breaks through in a frustrated tone.

"Maybe to you and your family, but this is a prison to me. I'm John Rutledge, and I'm the man that flew your parents and several others out here from Eugene. You may think we have things great here, but I've spent most of my life being able to hop in my car or plane and go anywhere I like, whenever I like. You and your vampire buddies have kept us 'locked up' in the woods for nearly a month. When is it going to end?"

"I should have said something about this earlier. We were planning on moving everyone out of the woods and into Salem in the next two days."

"I don't want to go from a wooded prison to a concrete one! I want to go back to my life and be able to travel wherever I want."

Lloyd looks at his father pleadingly while several other voices rise up expressing the same frustrations.

"Everyone!" Greg calls out. "Everyone, listen up!" He walks out to stand next to his son.

"I agree this isn't the situation any of us want to be in. I am also sick of being in the woods and want to return home, but my son is just a teenager and so are the rest of his people fighting on our behalf. They came here for advice and we are giving it to them. We won't solve anything if this meeting turns into a mob demanding immediate action.

"I think the zones of control are a bad idea, and we will all work to have them eliminated and have our real freedoms returned. I will offer myself as a liaison between vampires and humans in order to work through any issues that come up once we have mobility again. Let's just remember there is a war being fought out there right now and the only safe area we could travel to at this point is the Oregon coastline.

"John, I know you want to find out what is going on with your own family beyond our borders, so let's all work together and give them the best information we can so they can win back our country."

"Thanks, Dad," he whispers as Greg walks back to stand by his wife.

"Zones of control are a bad thing. I get that now." Several chuckles emerge from the crowd. "I'm sorry, I didn't think of it the way you put it, but I'm glad you're letting me know how you feel. We'll do what we can to make sure you are free to travel in the areas we control."

"The next big issue we are dealing with is food. Being stuck here in the woods, you may not know how devastated the world outside has become. All aspects of our easy access lifestyles have disappeared. Groceries stores are no longer being stocked and goods are no longer being produced. We can't fill up massive carts of our favorite foods that have been shipped in from around the world." Turning to look at his mom, "I can no longer neglectfully throw away a third of the food I had on my plate like I did as a child. That was when I knew you would always keep me fed and free from hunger.

"Every morsel of food must now be cherished and protected so it can be eaten by you humans. Currently, almost every human out there is completely dependent on us to provide whatever food items we can scavenge for them. There are some cases where people living in out of the way properties and farms have managed to remain independent from vampire control but those cases are rare.

"In the areas we have cleared so far, we are preparing to allow people to return to farms and orchards to grow and gather what they can. Unfortunately, in a world without electricity and modern food packaging, many of the items pulled from the ground, from trees, or culled from herds must be eaten immediately or it will all rot.

"We may be the current rulers of this world, but most of us still have the mentality of children. We know nothing about food production and storage. On top of that, like many of you, most of the remaining adults were city dwellers before the change and didn't have direct farming or gardening experience. Most of us only know things can be grown but have little clue as to how to properly do it. Here in the free territories, the most valuable members of the new society will be farmers and those with any type of skill in animal or plant production."

"How about fishing?" a man calls from the crowd. "I'm no good with plants, but I've worked the Alaskan fishing and crabbing boats. There's a lot of food out in the ocean for us."

"Yes, fishing will be great as well. Thank you, that is what we need, ideas! Ultimately, we need tactical knowhow. We need some ideas on how to properly protect the human areas or how to leave those areas and allow you to protect yourselves without the risk of destruction. And we need everyone that has the ability to hunt, grow, or fish for food to tell us how, where, and what to do."

*

"We have a choice to make about the direction we should head," Lloyd offers to the large group while they await the arrival of Cora. "Now that we control Oregon and Washington, we can move east fairly easily and keep gaining ground. If we do that, it's likely that we won't run into major resistance until we're halfway across the country in Minneapolis. That will give us territory, but not bodies.

"We could head south into California until we get to the Mexico border, but there will most likely be fierce resistance in the heavily populated areas. We could have heavy losses, but we could potentially free many more people. What do you think we should do?"

A booming voice sounds from the sky above them. "Hitler." Large white flapping wings beat heavily, lowering Cora into the middle of the assembled group. "Hitler was obsessed with territory during WWII. He valued capturing land and many believe his misunderstanding of that point was the saving grace for society."

"Hitler?"

"Yes, I just absorbed a history professor's thoughts. Hitler could have captured Moscow and dealt a terrible blow to the Russian people's morale. Instead of the capital, Hitler wanted territory and thinking it mattered, was capturing tons of farmland. Hitler's forces ended up spread out defending empty fields and tiny villages instead of capturing the capital and population centers and it cost him his fight on the eastern front. We have to move south and free the cities that are held by dominating vampires. We will free as many people as we can before winter arrives. The land doesn't matter if we don't free the people who can live on it."

CHAPTER NINETEEN
INSURRECTION

Oregon

Senator Cavanaugh presses his hands against the small of his back trying to push the aching out of his muscles in an unsuccessful stretch. Rolling his head from side to side, he works his cramped neck free of the stiffness he has created with hours of hunching over the paperwork he is reviewing. In a final fit of exhaustion, he stands and walks to the windowed wall of his office and looks out at the Willamette University campus.

Eighty-three days have passed since The Shattering Event occurred, fifty-eight days since he and his group left their impromptu home in the woods and returned to the newly secured city in hopes of finding some form of government in charge.

The secret shelter under Ford Hall on the university campus was intact when they arrived but devoid of any government officials of any meaningful rank. None of the state or federal designated persons of vital importance are here. They weren't able to make it past the behemoths at the Salem airport or the few streets beyond it. Seventeen DHS officers and some of their families, a few law clerks, eight secretaries, and thirty-six college students were here when the Cavanaughs arrived. The college students gained entry when the officer in charge managed to pull their group into the shelter before he was killed by a mutant and the shelter was sealed.

The vampire army led by Cora and Lloyd have now secured all of the territory north of Portland and into Vancouver British Columbia and have retaken all of Oregon and most of Washington state except for Spokane. Spokane has a particularly nasty group of vampire soldiers holding the city and surrounding towns. They also have some heavy armaments and aircraft from Fairchild Air Force base just outside the city.

The military weaponry still isn't able to cause irreversible damage, but the tanks, cannons, and larger caliber weapons are a nuisance. The greater worry is the difficulty in stopping the humans being forced to fight while trying not to kill them. In the case of the Fairchild base, there is a vampire in charge of the area that is able to manipulate the minds of the human population. She will be able to have the human pilots from the base fly missions against those who want freedom.

Before moving in, the Northern Army is waiting for reinforcements from the Southern Army that spent the last two weeks securing the Sacramento, San Francisco, and San Jose cities in California.

Many of the early cities taken in California have required minimal fighting. The vampires in control of those areas either agreed with the idea to free humanity and rebuild society or they fled. Hearing of the strength and success of The Angel's army, some of the slave-minded vampires left the west coast and headed east in search of allies with whom they could build an opposing force.

All of those problems and issues are things Greg Cavanaugh has no control or influence over, but they still occupy his mind because his young son is a general on the front line in that war. The larger issue that is causing Greg's unease is what he must decide to do about rebelling humans.

In many of the cities and towns that have been freed by the vampire's, humans are fighting back and causing various levels of destruction. It was hoped rather than believed that the people would get along better once they were again free to travel. This hope has not materialized.

In efforts to minimize animosity, human-run governments were established immediately to deal with security, health, and all other necessities people require. Greg's role, as the highest-ranking survivor of the apocalypse, is leader of all freed humans until elections can be managed.

The humans who are fighting back are no longer attacking the vampires who remain to guard the towns, they are attacking and killing the humans that are working with the vampires or the government.

Several of the flyers on Greg's desk that were found posted in an area of Portland state, "Kill the traitors that are helping the vampires enslave us." "All mutant enablers must die."

Some part of him understands the sentiment of the people frustrated at the occupation of the cities by the vampires. People are angry that their lives have been destroyed by this mutation event. The nation was filled with people who believed themselves to be important. They had positions of prominence in modern society such as lawyers, engineers, architects, and the many professional classes that no longer exist with society's new standstill.

They are also justifiably angry at the tremendous loss of life and destruction that has occurred at the hands of the mutants. It is rare to find a town or city that doesn't have large sections of city blocks destroyed. There are many places that were brought down by fires, crashing planes, rampaging behemoths, or some other destructive power related to the mutants activities. Those destroyed city streets are where people are trying to survive and rebuild what they have lost. Even just the mindset of having to survive instead of being able to live is demoralizing, and people naturally seek a way to lash out in anger.

The mutants are the obvious target for retribution, but their immunity from harm and need for human blood after injury taught people to stop attacking the vampires. So humans are once again their own worst enemy and are rising up against their fellow survivors to fight and kill over real and perceived injustices.

Greg Cavanaugh's dilemma is what he can do about humans that are inciting riots and killing people that are working with the vampires. There are minimal resources available now and no prisons or jails are functioning as a result. Whatever decision he makes will be carried out in every city and town that is freed from enemy vampires. It will be the law until his son's armies are stopped, or they find a higher ranking official that can take over the decision-making process and the blame for the results.

"Mr. Cavanaugh, you need to make a decision." The group of human emissaries from various towns arrived to get help for the violence they are dealing with. "We have to allow our people to remain in control of their own towns and cities, but we can't have humans killing each other the way they have been. Our police forces are not equipped to deal with some of the new tactics being used. There was a suicide bomber that destroyed a food distribution center this morning. It would be one thing if they were trying to kill the vampires or even us officials, but they are attacking the weakest and most innocent of the people that are seeking help."

"The people you are dealing with, the leaders directing the violence, will mostly come from the families and friends of the vampires that were killed to free those areas from brutal control. It is a problem we have seen from the beginning, but I haven't found a peaceful way to deal with what's happening. Are you positive there is no way to set up some type of prison system where we can keep those people?"

"I'm sorry, sir, there isn't. We have places we could put these people, many of the jails and prisons are intact, but holding facilities aren't the problem. The food supply chain is destroyed. Manufacturing is rare and won't be able to come back online until the vampires free vast areas. We have no access to the facilities necessary for the production of electricity.

"The mutants are only able to gather a limited amount of supplies for us humans and to have them create an extra supply line to keep an incarcerated population fed will just make the general populace more angry. You can imagine what people would think if the vampires are supplying food to people in prison camps while the rest of the populace is struggling to find food on their own."

Silence fills the room for a moment, and Representative Cavanaugh's expression doesn't change. "Bring them in."

Three mutants walk in when the assistant opens the door.

"Have you made a decision?"

"I have. The general population is the priority for food and supplies. In all areas we control, the people will be allowed to be as free and in control of their own lives as possible. Mutants will help to find supplies and fix infrastructure where needed but with other items are to help only when humans need it to survive or have specifically requested help as we have already planned.

"Those people that are instigating violence and are killing or destroying property will be captured and incarcerated in central holding facilities away from civilian populations as soon as the food supply situation is organized to the point that there are no shortages for the general population."

The three exchange glances.

"You know the projections for that aren't good. With each new city we free, there is a tremendous strain added to the already scant supply of food. It could be months before we have food supplies stable enough to house prisoners anywhere. What do we do with them until then?"

"Until that time, you must kill them. When you take over a city, round up the family members and friends of the vampires that had humans enslaved and have one of the arch-vampires that can read minds search their intentions. Anyone that has sympathy for the evil mutants must be considered a potential combatant from now on, and all of those that will act on their resentments must be stopped before they can cause their destruction.

"I know many of the people fighting back might be under the misguided belief that they are freedom fighters or patriots, but make no mistake that they are the enemy of everything this nation and our constitution stands for. They claim to be fighting against all enemies, foreign and domestic, but where was their spirit to fight back while other vampires enslaved them? They conveniently found their outrage after the violent tyrants were killed. Today's rebels were yesterday's leeches, sucking on the fat of our nations oppressors.

"From now on and until we can re-establish a prison system, humans and vampires will be treated equally on the battlefield. No vampire is allowed to remain alive if they are in favor of enslaving humanity and from now on, no human will remain alive if they will act out in revenge over their loss of power after the general populace is freed.

"Send word to all of our soldiers that they must work with our police to make sure the criminals currently out there are found and eliminated. Immediately! No further loss of innocent life or disruption to supply lines or centers will be tolerated. And don't do this behind a veil of secrecy either. You tell the people who you are executing and exactly what their crimes of disruption were. The sentence for acting out against humanities freedom and survival is death."

CHAPTER TWENTY
FIRST SNOW

Salt Lake City, Utah

The first approach is never easy in a battle. Being on the front lines during this vampire war is no exception. Thousands who follow The Angel run and fly with their swords held high toward the opposing troops assembled at the city's edge.

The soldiers guarding this territory are organized and regimented. It is a rarity in the fights they have had so far and not a welcome sight in a battle they all hoped would be a quick and easy one.

"You will not take my city," the leader's voice booms from the flying wall before them. "Stop your troops and go home."

Cora's soldiers press on.

"Free your humans and we can end this war," Cora calls back.

The great distance between the army is closing fast.

"The humans had their time. We will treat them well, but they belong to us. It is no longer their planet to rule."

Uncertainty begins to spread in Cora's ranks as they approach their targets. Their enemies are standing and flying at attention with arms behind their backs. No weapons have been seen and no bullets have been sent at The Angel's rushing forces.

"I do not wish to harm fellow vampires. Call a stop to your advance and leave our city."

"We will leave when the people are free."

Seconds before impact, the defending soldiers bring their arms forward and present shields and sledgehammers. The defending forces of Salt Lake were able to take advantage of two manufacturing foundries to supply their weapons. Before the blue haze arrived, the facilities made construction tools and military armor plating. The strength of the mutants allows them to use the large two-inch-thick metal plates as shields and swing the heavy hammers with ease.

The edges of the battle line make contact before the center. Ringing resounds along the line as metal strikes metal with swords hitting shields. Hammers swing back in return, crushing chests and skulls, causing limp bodies to fall to the ground to begin their healing process.

In the center, another force impacts Cora's soldiers. An invisible blast pushes out from a single spot, throwing The Angel's fighters away from the front line. The blast radiates out along the line from center to end until

Cora's fighters have all been pushed back by twenty feet. The Salt Lake forces move forward but do not break ranks to engage. The fighters retain their line and move over the fallen vampires, leaving them on the ground as they pass.

With the next impact, the line returns twenty feet again. More soldiers fall, and no ground is gained.

*

The battle for Salt Lake City has been a brutal stalemate. For two days, fighting has raged as Cora's forces attempt to free this territory. The Interstate 80 corridor through this part of the Rocky Mountains lies on the city's eastern edge.

The controller of Salt Lake has two main powers they have detected so far: telekinetic push and power sharing. She can force things away, and she is able to share her gift with others. She has been able to create invisible walls to keep Cora's army from entering the city.

The constant yet miniscule shifting of the front line is demoralizing to troops on both sides of the fight. The Angel's army is battered and exhausted. Even with the quick healing of physical wounds, a healed battlefield injury does nothing to protect the wounds a mind endures in war. For months, the battles have waged across the western United States. With each victory, the army has gained new followers, new mutants to join the ranks in the efforts to free humanity.

With each victory also came the emotional turmoil of seeing new friends and allies die. In this battle, the former children fighting in it are witness to the ultimate futility and depression a conflict can produce when neither side is able to gain an advantage over the other.

Brian flies up and nods to Cora.

The plan for the final assault begins taking place. The ground troops and fliers begin to spread out and up instead of advance. In all previous attempts to go around or over the front line, the defending leader would use her power of force to knock the advance back. This time, The Angel's forces are posing less of a threat as they continue spreading out. The winged vampires are the key. Cora has four times as many arch-vampires as her opponent and is now having her troops fly higher into the sky than ever. They are forcing the defenders to stretch their defensive line in return.

Confusion and then laughter spread among the Salt Lake forces when Cora's forces reveal the weapons they chose for this stage. Firearms are aimed but not yet fired by every other winged soldier of Cora's line. As ineffective as those weapons are, it is the assortment of other items that cause the laughter. Hands are holding flares, hastily made torches, and bows of various styles with flaming arrows and bolts.

"Are you getting desperate? Is this the best the famed Angel has in her arsenal?"

The only reply is a rumbling sound in the distance behind The Angel on the frontline. Cora chose to keep the giants out of most battles. They don't have the ability to heal the way vampires do, so she uses them only when necessary or when they insist because they have been prevented from helping for so long. In this moment, they are necessary. Each giant is carrying the final stage of this fight.

Industrial and manufacturing centers are great places to find or make weapons for war. In this particular battle, the problem is being able to advance through the line. The way to open this defensive formation is on its way. It is a simple design of four basic parts; industrial strength glue, lawnmower blades, propane tanks, and fire.

Thousands of lawnmower blades have been glued to hundreds of propane tanks. The blades will increase the shrapnel that will rip through bodies when the tanks explode. The Angel's vampires are carrying twenty-pound tanks, and the approaching giants are running up with one-hundred and five-hundred-pound tanks. A loud whistle is emitted and in unison the tanks are all propelled at the currently impenetrable wall.

The force with which the giants are able to launch their large tanks causes the enemy line to break before any explosive damage even occurs. Bodies are smashed out of their place in formation by the impact. Then come the bullets and the flame. The explosions destroy the defending leader's army, and she is knocked unconscious by a blast as well. Half of her soldiers lay in pieces on the earth below, the other half are in dazed confusion or shock from the explosive concussions they've received.

*

"Why wouldn't you give up?" Cora yells into the enemy leader's face while she is being held down. "You said you weren't going to hurt the humans, why wouldn't you let them be free?"

"We have no one to set free. Our humans are all dead, only a few children remain."

"You killed them all?"

She struggles to be released but is unable to move against so many bodies restraining her. Even her telekinetic gift is weakened. She was drawing energy from her fellow vampires to increase its power.

"Many of them killed themselves. When the blue haze arrived and we first started mutating, a large number of the families here committed suicide. As the weeks went on, the humans gave up and continued to find ways to die. There was nothing we could do." Her eyes dart to every face around her and her eyes blink while telling her tale.

Cora grabs a part of their captives exposed wing and stands, drawing her sword. "Drain her."

None of Cora's soldier's comply, so she quickly slices the vampire's head away from her shoulders. Blinking and stunned, the vampires surrounding Cora shake their heads.

"She was using her powers on you. Their humans are alive and in the basements of many of the buildings here." Cora spins around, directing her thoughts to the assembly, working to remove the cobwebs of confusion and distrust the powerful arch-vampire attempted to fix in place.

*

With little training and less preparation, Cora has pushed her army from one town to the next, hoping to free the entire U.S. by winter. It is an impossible goal.

"I thought we could do it."

"We can't push them any farther, Cora. They need time to absorb what it is their friends are dying for or they'll all give up or worse, they could be slaughtered in the next fight."

"I thought the vampire controlling Salt Lake might be something different. I was beginning to doubt we were doing the right thing, but when I read her thoughts, she was just like the others. Just another bitter person that had a pampered life before the change and was consumed by a petty belief that the world owes them something. She tortured humans and used them in games like so many of the others have."

"You need time to rest as well, Cora. We will run into more problems as we head east. Word has spread about what we are doing, and the vampires are preparing for the battles now."

White flakes leisurely float to the ground around the winners of the battle for western Utah. For twelve days, The Angel's forces have fought with their enemy to capture the towns and cities along the Interstate 15 corridor. Cora is standing at the foot of the Rocky Mountains on the edge of Salt Lake City, staring at the rock wall blocking her progress with a hateful eye.

Lloyd puts his hand on her shoulder. "We've done all we can for this year."

"I know you're right, but I hate to think of all those people beyond the mountains at the mercy of the enemy through the winter."

"I don't like it either, but that doesn't change what can and can't be done. Winter is here and everyone will be needed to gather food and supplies to keep the humans alive and warm through the colder months.

"You especially need to help the soldiers. Use your powers to calm their minds and ease the pain of what they've been through. I can sense

how close some of them are to giving up. We can't lose sight of our current responsibilities on the way to our goals."

"You're starting to sound like my father."

"I'll take that as a compliment. Now please, we have to help prepare people for the months ahead."

"Okay, you have Brian start working on our soldiers, and I will deal with the giants this time. They'll be on body detail, so I will stay and help them."

Lloyd gives Cora a quick kiss and flies off through the thickening flurries.

The tragedies of war that can't be healed with medicine require time. Sometimes it takes years and intense therapy, other times it takes a simple thank you from a person being saved. All instances are specific to the individual that had the trauma, and the success of treatment is as varied as the individuals receiving it.

Like having greater success on the battlefield during war, the vampires have an edge on healing shock and trauma. Cora and the arch-vampires like her have increased their skills of entering the minds of the wounded to massage away the difficulties.

In the early stages of the war, she could only send feelings of warmth or relaxation but not make a tremendous change in how her soldiers perceived the fighting and destruction. Now she can go in and dull the memory of a good friend's death and strengthen their feelings of the joyful memories they had instead. It is also possible to erase the bad images completely, but that was rejected by their group as something they thought the bad ones would do. Memories of experiences are what make us individuals rather than a collective hive.

The job she and the giants have today is to pick up and prepare the bodies of the dead for funeral services before burning. They attempted burial at first, but the increasing numbers of fatalities prevent them from being able to continue the practice.

The numbers of the dead continued to rise as the armies move east, not only because of greater resistance and violence on the part of defending vampires, but also because of time. As time continues to ebb away from the first day of The Shattering, an increasing number of humans die from starvation and disease.

The slave-owning class of vampires the army is defeating show little respect or concern for the wellbeing of the humans in their charge, and on many occasions, buildings full of corpses have been discovered. Why they were sealed inside structures and allowed to starve, no one was ever able to find out. The hope is the acts are caused by negligence and not out of evil malice, but the end result is the same.

CHAPTER TWENTY-ONE
CHRISTMAS DAY

Medford, Oregon

The smell of cooked ham permeates the house and smiling faces are shared all around. Christmas carols are being hummed by some in the gathering and hugs are given to the children who have just arrived. The several families in attendance are celebrating the safe return of their children from the war.

The people at the compound were largely spared the troubles of internment because of the isolated nature of the ranch. Being offset in the wooded hills made the area an unnecessary target of the arch-vampires controlling the Medford and Grants Pass regions. It also helped having so many children among the families mutate during The Shattering.

It was the children turned vampires that helped their parents escape the destruction of their cities and homes and make it to the survival training center in the hills.

"Eddie, come here and take a picture with us." Simone smiles while waving him over, his attention previously fixed on the food being brought to the table.

Simone is standing in front of the newly decorated Douglas fir tree they cut down and brought in a few days ago. William and Amelia are standing in front while Benjamin is cradled in his mother's arms. Eddie walks over to join his six favorite people for the holiday picture.

"Hannah, Olivia, you'll have to put your wings down or we won't be able to see the tree."

The camera flash blinds them all.

"Arthur, Donald, we should get pictures of everyone."

"Not right now," Patricia Langford chides the group. "The ham is on the table and I want you over here to enjoy it. We can take pictures when we're done."

*

Twin Falls, Idaho

Tables are filled in the Twin Falls High School auditorium. Various families from around the city mingle and chat while others eat the shared community meal. An assortment of stews, breads, and mixed vegetables are being served from the cafeteria line.

Individual families are celebrating Christmas in their homes with returned soldiers from the war effort. The fighting has ceased for some time, but the efforts to stockpile and distribute food have been continuous, keeping their loved ones away. The gathering in the auditorium is for the families of the fallen. The people here lost family in the fight to free them.

Twin Falls has a disproportionate number of losses in the war. Their children turned vampires were being killed long before Cora's army arrived. The particular skills of the arch-vampire controlling this area were cruelty and distrust. Instead of only abusing humans, he liked to turn vampires under his control against each other to fight to the death for his entertainment. He trusted no one, so there was no ideology or level of loyalty that he cared for. The good were pitted against the bad, the loyal against the openly rebellious. All were forced to fight and all were killed that were drawn into his all-encompassing form of mind control.

The meeting is somber, but the people are still happy to be alive and grateful to have the chance to once more live a free and unmolested life.

*

Tulsa, Oklahoma

A small house on Seventh Street is packed with people. Revelers are on the lawn outside, playing music too loudly and singing in the falling snow. Fire barrels are burning around the yard and have small groups crowded around them to soak up the warmth. The revelry is active but is tainted with malice rather than joy.

"The house is almost full. We're just waiting on Danny; he went through the change today so he's bringing his mother."

"We've got a big crowd together. I'm glad we decided to hold off the trials until Christmas, it gets old doing this every week."

"I know. It's like Dave expects us to enjoy spending time with them or something. I don't know why we don't just get rid of them all right now."

"Right, idiot, and what are you going to eat then?"

Danny walks up the street with his mother. Her clothes are filthy and hanging from her skeletal frame. Families with children about to change are given extra rations, but Danny's parents took only a small portion of what they were given and had their son eat the rest of their food.

When Danny changed, his father was too weak to withstand the amount of blood drained by his son. His heart gave out, killing him. His mother is the unfortunate one; she survived Danny's change.

Reaching the door to the house, she turns to Danny and wipes tears from her eyes and then his.

"You do what I told you, Danny, you do what you must to survive. There was no choice for me or your father. You are the last of us."

She turns and walks through the open door. Danny shuts and locks it behind her.

"That's the last one, everyone get in line, get formed up."

The mutants that changed over the previous two weeks are gathered in six rows of four in front of Dave, the leader of this city.

"You've all gone through the change and you're almost one of us. Say the pledge."

"I pledge myself to my new family, the family of the strong. We are the rulers of the Earth. The ones chosen for the future. Humanity was a curse to the planet and we are the cure. With our offering today, we reject our false family of the past and take our place in the real family of our future."

"Welcome to the family." Dave looks at the vampires before him and touches each of their minds with his own. "Now light it up."

The assembly splits up. The fire barrels are picked up and tossed against the house containing the new vampires' families. Fathers, mothers, as well as any brothers and sisters too old to change.

This horrific ritual is normally carried out every week for Dave to form a controlling bond over the minds of the new vampires in his territory. Any new mutant must participate in killing their old family to remove any connection to humanity they once had.

The story always told is that Dave was an orphan that was passed around from one state home to another. The truth is, his mom and dad were one of the few married couples on his street before the change. His only friend, Sydney, knows the truth, but also knows to never say anything about it to anyone.

The smoke from the burning house fills the sky, turning the falling flakes black and gray.

*

Columbus, Ohio

"We found him out here this morning. He must have made his group come out in the night to try catching some fish."

Three hundred human statues are frozen along the bank of the Scioto River. Some have fishing rods still in hand, the lines locked in place in the now frozen holes.

"He said he was tired of his people being hungry but didn't tell me what he would do."

"Damn it! He's only nine years old. You are supposed to be responsible for what the younger vampires do. You need to teach these kids it's dangerous to go outside in the cold, especially at night. He tried helping them, and they were all either too scared or too stupid to tell him they needed to stay warm."

"What should I do?"

"Take him inside and thaw him out. When he wakes up, bring him out here and show him what he did. The fishing was a good idea, but he should have told us about it so we could have kept everyone safe. I don't want to make everyone's Christmas even more miserable so let's wait until tomorrow to let the others know.

"Once we do tell the others, we should start bringing all the humans and vampires in our area through here to see how many people died. Once we've explained the danger to everyone, then we can figure out a way to fish on the river without anyone else dying."

"I don't think we'll be able to catch enough fish to keep everyone alive."

"Do you have a better idea? The humans have gone through all of the other supplies and are eating the dog and cat food. It's only Christmas, and we have at least three months of winter left. Every fish we catch might save another life. It's better than them eating the alternative."

"Rats?"

"Each other."

*

The intentions of the vampires controlling the nation are varied, but the outcomes are largely the same. Even the vampires that care for the humans cannot make food sprout from the frozen ground. They are constrained by the territories they control and often end up with the same shortages when they fight with others to gain access to supplies.

The basic principle is that a large population kills. The more humans there are within a geographic area, the lower the chance of survival becomes. Cities beyond the freed territories are death traps. Starving masses are dropping dead in the frigid shelters they huddle together in.

The southern states have the decided advantage of more moderate weather, moderate but not warm. As in years past, multiple cold fronts have passed from the arctic to reach as far south as Louisiana and Florida. The freezing temperatures are taking almost as many lives as starvation.

CHAPTER TWENTY-TWO
LOST SOULS

Colorado

A thunderous roar like the galloping of a thousand hooves echoes over the ground. Through the air, the rippling sound of loose sails fluttering in a strong wind join the chorus of running feet down below.

Over forty thousand runners are matched by six thousand of their winged brothers and sisters in the sky. Dirt, branches, and leaves are kicked up like dust billowing behind a speeding truck on an unpaved road. The breadth of the attacking line causes the appearance of an approaching sandstorm to the onlookers outside the city.

The flying soldiers, led by The Angel, tuck their wings behind them and begin their spiral approach. Targeting their progress are the exploding rounds of bullets and cannon fire. Flying projectiles tear into many of the speeding mutants advancing on their targets on the ground.

Screams of fear from the human inhabitants of the city echo loudly in the ears and minds of the sensitive mutants. The fear of the people urge the attackers on even more.

Hundreds of bodies fall from the sky as they absorb the incoming barrage from the ground, but Cora urges them forward. Seconds later, the foot soldiers arrive at the frontline of military armaments guarding this zone of control.

While running, the pale fury open fire with weapons of their own again procured from military installations. The battle for Denver begins, and like all others before, it will only end when one side is completely drained of blood. Cora's soldiers on the ground toss the enemy combatants and equipment through the air. Alongside the vampire troops are the giants she has collected from their displaced and empty homes around the west.

As terrifying and deadly as the fighting inevitably is, the giants demanded to be included in the first war of the spring season. Their talents of strength are often utilized for reconstruction projects, but many of them feel most at home on the battlefield. Several of her strongest pick up an Abrams tank and toss it away, taking out two others in its trajectory. The humans in the tanks that were forced to fight are an unfortunate casualty in this war.

With the aerial bombardment against The Angel's air forces thwarted by her ground troop's success, the rest of her army is able to lay siege directly on the buildings containing the frightened and screaming humans.

The buildings are on fire. She sends her thoughts to the others. *We have to save them!*

"You know it's a trap," Brian calls out from her left.

We can't let them die that way. We came here to free these people, not let them be burned alive in front of us. We are going to kill the vampires willing to do this to people, and I will fight until we win or I die.

"Here they come!"

From around the backs of the flaming buildings, the Denver's air force defenders finally take flight. Gun barrels flashing from underneath wings, the defenders of the city know they have to stop The Angel's advancing army here on the front line or the entire city will fall. With the flaming towers and screaming lives at their backs, they unload all of the bullets they have to weaken the attack of the flying mutants.

Cora's forces do not fire back. Their bullet trajectories would continue beyond their intended targets and into the burning buildings. None of them want to risk killing even more humans than necessary to win this battle. Unfortunately, from what Cora is able to sense, thousands of the surviving humans have been forced into the burning skyscrapers they are approaching. The people they came to save are trapped in the buildings the defenders set aflame.

Cora and the others leave their guns strapped tightly to their bodies as they spin in for the final few hundred feet of the attack. Repeated thanks have been given to Lloyd after various battles for his decision and insistence on using swords.

To the defenders of Denver, the weapons The Angel's forces use are still a secret. Word spread across The Rockies about the advance of an army freeing humans, but no mention of their choice of weapons reached the ears of those over here. Lloyd's selection of weekend entertainment provides the perfect weapon they need to fight their mutant brethren in close quarters, a weapon their foe in this battle do not possess.

Each winged fighter draws out a sword which they hold before them in their spinning approach. The blinking flashes of light reflecting off the blades from the sun help disorient the mutants Cora and her soldiers are targeting. They successfully fly through the enemy line with blades swinging freely and furiously at the opponents they came to destroy.

Mutant grabbing mutant in collisions in the sky. Bones snap on impact, wings break or are severed from their owners by slashing blades. Above all else, teeth are plunged into the necks and bodies of enemies on both sides of the battlefield. Each bite causing death and regeneration alike.

The Angel flashes through the aerial battleground, freezing many of her opponents in the air before her with a raised hand and a psychic directive for them to stop. She then severs their heads or wings in order for her ground troops to drain the blood from the fallen bodies once they land. Her goal, as always, is to make it to the flaming buildings and save as many of the humans in this territory as she can.

One building is completely engulfed in fire. The screams of the dying inside are heart-wrenching, but there is nothing she or her soldiers can do for them any longer. What she can accomplish is helping those in one of the other three buildings.

Cora flies to the ground and picks up a large industrial garbage dumpster as deftly as if it were a small cardboard box. Flying to a large pond across the road from the flames, she scoops her container full of water and tosses the water into the air.

Lloyd calls to his lieutenants, "Fly to The Angel. We have to help her."

They begin circling the building and beat their wings to force the falling water into the open windows to douse the flames.

Dozens of others join her with metal dumpsters or other scavenged containers of their own. They unite in her efforts at making an artificial waterfall flowing into the flames of the buildings while the others continue their fight around them. Many of the flying saviors are killed while distracted by trying to put out the flames as well as some that are tossing water into the air with Cora, but they are quickly replaced by others that move in to assist in the rescue.

The enemy army defending the Denver territory is losing. The Angel's ground troops have finally reached the buildings where Cora and her fliers have been battling equally against the flames and attackers. Some of the runners begin clawing their way up the sides of the burning buildings and reaching through windows to toss humans out to be safely caught below. Others are speedily climbing their way up to the top floors where they jump out into the air to catch a flying enemy soldier and bring them down.

The carnage is terrific and terrible. This is the most vicious yet one-sided battle many of the fighters have been in so far. With no swords or blades on the opposing forces side, The Angel's troops are making incredible progress in breaking through and destroying defenses. The streets and rooftops below the current combatants is slick with blood, a telltale sign of warfare that has been absent before now. It seems the bodies of the enemy are being chopped apart and fall from the sky so rapidly that the freedom forces are finding it difficult to drain the bodies of their blood. They are instead bleeding out on the ground until someone drains them or they piece enough of themselves together to attempt fleeing.

The tactics by the enemy have also changed dramatically. Outside of using trained humans to man military weaponry, at no point before now did enemy mutants threaten or consider to use their human captives as fodder to stop the advance of The Angel's army. This time, the forces of Denver chose to burn the humans alive, knowing the pained cries of the trapped men, women and children would distract and disorient The Angel's forces during the battle.

The front line has been broken, but the defenders are fighting ferociously to kill The Angel's forces and stop their advance. Many troops are able to break through the line completely and move their fight into the streets and skies beyond the cities edge while attempting to win the Denver territory.

Out of the six-hundred sixty-thousand people that populated the city before The Shattering Event, there are believed to be only sixty-five thousand humans left alive today. The brutal winter and lack of food have taken their toll. How many humans manage to survive the destructive battle going on around them is unknown. If the mutants holding this area continue to set fire to the buildings the humans are housed in, there could be losses of a third or more of those few that survived the starvation of winter.

In a last ditch push to save Denver from The Angel's forces, Rafael, the general controlling the territory, sends new mentally binding instructions to many of his remaining winged troops. *Bring her down. Target The Angel, I want her dead.*

Flanked on all sides, in front and back, above and below, The Angel, her generals, and her lieutenants hover in the air and wait for the incoming attack. Many of her soldiers fly high above them and drop their swords to Cora's surrounded group. Half of Rafael's remaining flying soldiers have their attention locked on to the white-winged beauty. Beating her wings high above the carnage below, her painted white armor is stained in red from the slashes her sword produced against her enemy.

It is Rafael's fault for not being a student of history and not being a general that leads his soldiers in combat. Any observer could see the death his people were flying into, but he was no longer there to witness it. He is flying off to secure his own safety now that he has given the order for his vampires to continue their attack.

With outstretched arms, The Angel and her surrounding vampires start spinning in the sky. With a sword in each hand, their spins increase and the intensifying velocity makes the blades sing as they cut through the air. The soldiers flying into them are firing their guns, but the bullet impacts are having no effect. The Angel's forces are so gorged with the blood of their enemies that their regeneration against the small projectile fire is near instant.

Rafael's soldiers want to stop their progress, some twitch slightly as they attempt to turn and fly away, but his control over them is too strong and his command is final. They continue to fly into the spinning blades of death the Angel and her mutants have created. The first group to reach the blades are carved into halves and quarters. The severed parts fall to the waiting soldiers below who will drain them and end the threat of Rafael's group. A second wave attempt to fight through the line and get at her, but even with the blades held fast without the spinning motion, they are cut down in seconds.

To show her power over Rafael, Cora does something none of the other arch-vampires have the ability to do. She sends him the vision from her own eyes of the final vampire he sent at her, the blade she holds coming down and cleaving the arch-vampire in two. She forces her sight into his mind and makes him watch as the body falls to the ground, cutting off the vision in the end with one powerful and hate filled thought to pummel his mind. *You are next!*

The power of The Angel's message is so strong it ends Rafael's mental control of his forces defending the city. The remaining soldiers on his side are finally able to choose their course of action. A few choose to change sides and fight on the side of The Angel's army, a few, but not many.

Rafael exerts his will on the soldiers during battle, and his power is stronger than many other vampires that were defeated in previous conflicts. Unlike others, Rafael can control minds, even if his goals don't match those of his followers. If the battle were not so physically devastating to his troops, he would have been able to draw on their strength to begin controlling the minds of The Angel's forces.

In this case, even though he could have, Rafael didn't need to struggle against competing views while running the Denver territory because many of the vampires friendly to humans left when they took the president to Wyoming for safety. The forces that remain on Rafael's side are largely of the mindset that their evolutionary leap of mutation has put them in the driver's seat of the future. The non-mutated human race is there to be nothing more than a food source that can be treated in any manner necessary.

Some of Rafael's loyal winged forces remain to fight for the city while most follow him as he flees the area.

With the numbers on her side, gaining control of the city should be an easy task at this point. Even with some remnants of Rafael's group remaining to fight, they are so incredibly outnumbered the complete battle should be over shortly.

Should be an easy task, is turned into a could have been when Rafael's final weapon is released.

The Angel spent her time bringing into her fold as many like-minded vampires and giants as she could find to free the remaining humans from their slavery and internment. Rafael spent his time collecting behemoths and penning them up in buildings and parking garages. Their naturally destructive nature due to their size and relative lack of control have been fostered in some way by Rafael and his soldiers to make them lash out even more violently at everything that moves.

Once freed from their prisons, the behemoths spread out and begin to destroy all that they see. In attempts to break in and get at the screaming souls inside, several buildings where the humans have been corralled are brought crashing down around and on top of the humans and their destroyers. Taller and much wider than the giants on The Angel's side, the behemoths are able to prolong the battle several more hours and enable more of Rafael's troops to make their escape than Cora would have liked.

*

In the end, the death toll is in the tens of thousands and many more human lives lost than there should have been. Even though they had a limited fighting role in the battle, because Rafael used the lives of humans to distract The Angel's army, nearly thirty thousand people were brutally killed in fires or building collapses. Many more humans that survived through the deadly winter and this battle will soon die due to injuries sustained during the fighting and rescue. It is difficult to contemplate the evil actions that placed innocent lives into buildings so they could burn. The difficulty is compounded when considering they were concocted by a vampire who was not so long ago a simple thirteen-year-old boy.

CHAPTER TWENTY-THREE
INTERNMENT ZONE #758

Wyoming

Quick splashes are made by the small feet quickly crossing the muddy yard. Julie Moore is rushing to let President Thomas know he has a visitor.

"Mr. President, she's here."

"Who is here?"

"It's the one they call The Angel."

"Great, some bleach-skinned mutant that wants to take even more away from us? Maybe you should speak with her if you are so excited about it."

"Mr. President, you have to speak with her, she is here specifically to see you."

"Why do you still call me that? We have no country left. There are no free people to serve and I have no power."

"She calls you that because that is who you are, Mr. President." The pale winged woman speaks to him standing in the doorway to President Thomas' room.

The beauty of the vampire the people call The Angel has not been exaggerated. She stands tall at 6 feet 6 inches with her head nearly touching the door frames top. She is wearing all white, which in contrast gives her skin a warmer pink color, and she has a friendlier feel than the vampires that like to wear dark colors or black. President James Thomas is taken aback by what his mind can only identify as magnificence.

The Angel smiles at the president. "May I come in?"

James stands and looks from his aid back to the winged beauty and hesitates before squaring his shoulders and standing taller than he has for months. "This isn't my property, it is controlled by the mutants of this area. I cannot deny you entry if you wish it."

"And I am asking your permission still."

"Then come in…"

"Cora, you can call me Cora."

"Come in, Cora, and have a seat."

President Thomas sits in a chair and motions to a comfortable loveseat for Cora to sit. She walks over, spreads her wings out and slowly lowers herself to the cushions. Her wings then flutter and fold up behind her over the back of the small sofa.

"I don't mean to make a show of my wings, sir. I have been told it is intimidating to some. I cannot sit down comfortably otherwise, I hope you understand."

*

Word has spread of The Angel's arrival and the residents of this internment area are gathering outside the president's building by the hundreds.

"I heard she has come to kill him," one person whispers.

"They are trying to take away the last person that means something to us," another person says quite loudly.

*

"President Thomas, you believe you no longer have power and that your position is a meaningless one. You should not give up, I am here specifically because you are wrong. You were not elected by the people but you are still the president and the citizens of this nation look to you for council and guidance. The weekly addresses you have been giving to your internment group have also been broadcast to hundreds of other zones and areas around the country.

"They are powerful, have meaning, and have given the people of this nation hope. In fact, there is a great uprising occurring right now, and your words have helped to encourage the people to rise up and begin fighting back against the mutants who hold humans as slaves."

"Have they now? And you are here to stop me, I suppose?"

"That is what the people gathering outside believe. You should take a look. There are three thousand people in this internment zone and almost all of them are gathering around this building right now. They believe I am here to kill you. Their loyalty and concern for you is undeniable."

"If you are here to prevent me from speaking to my people, I won't stop. I will continue giving them hope, and we will continue trying to find a way to defeat the mutants so the human race can be free! If you want to stop me and my message, then you'll have to kill me and then you'll have to kill all of the people that have heard what I have to say. What will that do for your food supply then?"

"If I wanted to stop you, I wouldn't have set up generator systems or ordered power stations to be brought back online to support the broadcasting of your speeches. I wanted to speak with you because there is a difficulty with the uprisings I did not foresee. There are inevitable casualties in any war but I wasn't prepared for the tactics used by my enemy. In our fight to control Denver, more than fifty thousand lives were lost, nearly fifteen thousand of those were mutants."

Thomas lifts his head, eyes wide at her words. Looking from Julie back to Cora he smiles. "Mutant deaths? So someone has figured out your weakness, the people are fighting back!"

"The people loyal to you and this nation have been fighting back, but there hasn't been a discovery of any weakness humans can use against the mutants. Aren't you concerned over the human lives lost, Mr. President? I am here specifically because it has gotten so out of control. In the battle for Denver, over thirty-five thousand humans lost their lives, and I need your help to figure out how to prevent that from happening again."

"Your vampire friends and even some humans might call you The Angel, but to me, you are nothing but a demon. You enslaved humanity the first chance you got and now you are upset that the people are rising up and killing your precious mutant friends? Well, get used to it. We will continue to fight you to the end. Even I will willingly die to get rid of your menace and free my people from your control."

"I have to apologize, sir; I am reminded that you are not aware of what has been going on during the battles or why I am here. You did hear what I said about your speeches, correct? Aren't you curious to know why I had them broadcast to other camps?"

"Damn it, woman. Tell me what you want! If you're here to kill me, then get it over with. I'm not going to stop trying to free our people and will continue to give them hope in any way I can."

Her expression doesn't have the malice he believes it should for the task he thinks she has arrived to complete.

"Why are you here?"

"My soldiers and I are here to set you free. I understand your disbelief, but I assure you I am not here to stop you from speaking or to kill you. I am here to let you go. With all of my questions, I have been trying to gather a better understanding of your character by observing your thoughts during our talk.

"I am not only here for your freedom, I am here because I need your help. It is not the humans that have been rising up to free humanity. It has been my soldiers and I.

"We have been re-taking cities, and in our last major battle in Denver, the enemy commander, a vampire named Rafael used tactics we were not prepared for. He set buildings filled with humans on fire and let loose dozens of the behemoth creatures which brought down many more buildings.

"During the previous battles, no one used humans as shields or distractions, but now with the change in tactics, I need your assistance in preparing the humans we can reach for the difficulties which lie ahead.

They need to understand that there is a vampire army out there that is fighting for their release. The population is in all-out war and regular humans are in the crossfire."

A few seconds of silence are broken by a light sniffling sound. Julie Moore is wiping tears from her cheek. "Is it really over? Does this mean I can see my daughter?"

"Miss Moore, I doubt she's telling us the truth. If she were here... If you were planning on freeing people, why wouldn't you have come to me first? If you say my speeches are having such an effect out there, why wouldn't you include the president in the planning of battles?"

"We had to fight our way here from Oregon. We have freed the entire western coast from the Rockies to the Pacific Ocean. Our advance was stopped by the winter. We had to choose between heading over The Rockies and continuing the fight, or spend the winter finding food to feed the people we had already freed.

"I made trips over the mountains throughout the winter to determine where we should strike first and Denver had the strongest psychic vampire presence I could detect. Once the spring arrived, we attacked the city with as many forces we could spare from along the coast. As with all previous battles, we freed the humans who weren't killed during the fight. We have spent the last two weeks moving more forces across the mountains for our expansion east.

"I knew you were being held here and I wanted to speak with you, but the humans in your zone are better fed than many in the surrounding areas, so we moved through other towns and cities to help before arriving here."

"How long have you been fighting this war?" His calm tone has a hint of continued skepticism.

"We had our first fight against other vampires about three weeks after The Shattering event. I didn't know if we could win that first fight but we had to try. For the next few battles, I wasn't sure how many of my kind wanted things to return to how they were before. Many of us believed there could be no going back because of the things we did to others when we changed.

"The fourth battle taught me more than anything that it doesn't matter how close we can get to pre-change normal, we cannot let the country remain as it is right now. I will not allow humans to be used as cattle and have their intelligence and greatness bred out of them. None of the soldiers who follow me will allow humans to be harmed.

"This world cannot be populated by a might-makes-right mentality where we are in charge solely because of our strength. I was only twelve years old a few months ago, and while I can absorb peoples' thoughts, those of us without wings largely have the insights of teenagers and pre-teens. We are an army of children and are ruling a world we have not earned the right to be in charge of. I need your help to take it back."

"What can I do?"

"I will tell you what I know and what exactly I need from you in a moment, but we should go up to your speech platform on the roof. Your people outside need to hear what I have to say as well so they will calm down from their agitated state before they do something that will get them hurt."

"We have limited electricity here as you know, we'll have to take the stairs."

"That is fine."

"It's dark in there, Miss...Miss Angel," Julie stammers nervously.

"Just call me Cora."

"It's pitch black in there, Cora. Would you like a lantern?"

"I won't need one, you will have yours, but even without them, I can see in the dark."

Cora stands before Julie, preventing her from leaving the room. "I don't know who your daughter is, Miss Moore. If you will allow me to touch you, I might be able to see if she is among our group."

Julie places her hand into Cora's and thinks of her daughter.

"I'm afraid I haven't met her yet. Did she live in this area?"

"No, she was in Arkansas with her father and grandparents when the blue haze arrived. I haven't heard anything since before that day."

"Was her autism developmental?"

"I didn't..."

"I can see her in your thoughts, Miss Moore. I will search for her so you might be reunited, but you should understand she did not become what you think of as a vampire during the change. Any base genetic variance from standard human cells created different mutations during The Shattering."

Julie snatches her hand back from Cora and looks at her with squinted and piercing eyes. "You don't sound like a child to me. You don't know anything about my daughter. She was a normal little girl."

"I am speaking about cellular changes only. There is a scientist we found in Denver that we have been speaking with in trying to understand the changes. She worked with President Thomas briefly after he was sworn in. I am passing on what I learned from her. I didn't mean to upset you."

Turning to leave the room, Julie grabs The Angel by the arm. "Please, I need to know, what would she have become?"

"She will be a giant based on our understanding of the change."

"Not one of the behemoths?"

"No, not a behemoth. Those mutations were are caused by genetic trisomy disorders."

The cold concrete stairwell echoes with footsteps as the group ascends to the roof. The view from the top is a concerning one for James Thomas. The people of his camp are gathered in the streets below, shouting back at the pale mutants that have encircled them. Thousands of humans are surrounded by nearly as many mutants on the ground.

The truly intimidating vision is the sky above them. As many as a hundred of the winged mutants are circling the air overhead.

"Why have you brought so many mutants with you?"

"I told you, Mr. President, we are at war. What you see down there is simply my personal guard. From north to south, I currently have over three million mutants on my side."

The enormity of the situation is not lost on the president. He watched the D.C. Battlefield coverage before he was sworn in and has reviewed the footage countless times since. Four thousand trained U.S. soldiers were killed in minutes, and in that fight, they only faced twenty mutants. *If she has that many vampires in her army, she might be telling the truth; there is no reason for a mutant army to be so large to fight the humans.*

Stepping up to the microphone, the president waves to his people on the ground. "Please calm down everyone. People! Citizens!" he yells into his microphone. "Calm yourselves. I am not being harmed and the vampires' presence here is nothing to be feared."

The shoving has ceased and people are paying attention to what the president is saying.

"I am still being informed about the events going on, so please allow me a few minutes to hear everything the vampires have come here to say."

Raising her hand and pointing, Cora directs the president's attention to an approaching mutant in the distance. He is carrying someone in his arms, and he shoots past several birds at a speed that makes the smaller winged creatures appear to be struggling through the air by comparison.

The direct course to their position on the roof causes James to adjust his footing to leap away if necessary. It doesn't seem possible the incoming vampire can stop in time with his velocity. His wings flap up in a breaking fashion, and he indeed floats softly to the gravel surface of the roof placing his passenger on the ground. A gaunt version of the woman he knew smiles at President Thomas.

"It's good to see you, Mr. President."

"Dr. Usachova, that was quite an entrance, it's good to see you as well. I never expected I'd get to see you again."

"Did Cora tell you what's going on? Did she tell you what she has planned?"

Turning to Cora and looking at the masses of mutants above and below them, he understands. "You really are at war with other mutants, aren't you?"

"Yes, Mr. President, we are at war with other mutants. With your help, we are going to take our country back and set our people free."

"What do you need with us then?" His question is filled with anger. He knows the history of warfare and the use of pawns and disposable units on battlefields quite well. "I won't help you convince my people to be cannon fodder for some fight with mutants we can't survive."

"James!"

The voice from the president's past admonishes his accusation. Turning around, James sees his sister has been brought to him and her husband is landing as well.

"You need to hear what she has been doing, James. Stop being so argumentative."

Cora places her hand on the president's shoulder. "I know you regret your first decision to surrender to the mutants, but it was the only decision you could make and still keep your people alive. We haven't treated you properly, and in efforts to protect you, the vampires that brought you from Denver have kept you in internment zones. For all of these months, it is the only way they knew how to keep humanity alive, we nearly did the same thing on the west coast."

In a softer tone, he repeats his previous question, "So what do you need us for?"

"If you will allow me to speak to your people, I can let everyone know."

He nods and steps up to the microphone. "My fellow citizens, I have been informed by the vampire you heard of called The Angel that her forces are here to free us. They claim they are fighting a war on our behalf. Please continue to remain calm and give her a few moments to address all of us."

Stepping back from the rooftop platform, he looks at Cora with sincere eyes. "I want to believe you, but we have been in this situation for some time. Are you honestly here to free us?"

"I am." She steps to the platform and looks down to the crowd.

"This information will be difficult for many of you to believe, but what I am going to tell you is the truth. The vampires I have brought with me today are part of my army. We have been fighting with other vampires to remove from power those that chose to treat humans with brutality. We have freed humans living in the western states beyond The

Rockies and are now here to continue the war to free the rest of the nation.

"Humans in the states we have liberated are able to travel freely, control their own governments and are working to restore society. We are encountering difficulties with the humans we free, however, and I came here to ask the president, to ask you all, for your help moving forward.

"I have an army of young teenagers and with my powers, while I am able to guide them through the difficulties of war to a certain degree, they need something more. We all need something greater to think about or aim toward. It is fine for them to rally around me as The Angel and our common goal of freeing humanity, but I need an ultimate goal to give them. I have to provide the incentive needed to have my soldiers continue this war and free the whole nation.

"They need to know that when we have succeeded and the humans are all freed, there will be some form of society in which we can all live together. The western states have been organized and run by Representative Cavanaugh of Oregon. What he has accomplished over the mountains should work out here as well, but I need you and your president's authority to bring the humans out here and in the rest of the nation together." Turning to the president but still speaking into the microphone, "I need you to unite the humans in some form of acceptance of us."

"All of those mutants out there are children who need to learn how to grow up and be proper adults. They still need to be taught how to interact with others and how to be responsible citizens. We are freeing you from this camp and allowing free travel of all humans in the territories we control. I hope some of you will find it within yourselves to overcome the difficulties my kind has caused and choose to interact with the children that still desperately need your guidance."

The crowd is stunned and silent until a voice shouts out a question. "You are really ending the camp system?"

"Not just the camp system, everything. You are all free to go anywhere you choose within the states and territories we control."

A cheer erupts from the crowd and people begin leaving the assembly in different directions. Some begin running past vampires with no set destination in mind, just moving to show they can.

President Thomas walks after her as she leaves the platform.

"I still can't believe you are ending the camp system."

"We end it everywhere we have succeeded. This isn't what any of us want."

"If no one wants it, then why did you have to go to war?"

Cora gets briefly agitated, but in less than a second, her piercing stare and pursed lips soften. Her expression turns to a slight frown and her head nods slightly.

"That isn't what I meant. Of course that is why we are at war. There are some that want things to remain as they are now. Some would have far more control over the normal human population than you have experienced. There have been thoughts and talk of creating holding facilities and breeding factories where they can force humans to reproduce. The children would be raised as mindless meat, taught to appreciate being used for food and slaughtered before they mutate. We are fighting to stop those that would do such things."

Having considered all possibilities for humanity over the last few months, he takes the shocking information in stride.

"Before I agree to work on encouraging humans to work with the vampires that free them, I need some assurances from you. How do I know the vampires you have defeated will remain defeated? How are you holding the enemy you have captured, and what guarantee can you give that they won't escape and enslave us or put us back into zones?"

"Mr. President, my people can read minds. There is no capture or surrender on our battlefields, no changing minds or perspectives. You are either for the enslavement of mankind or for freedom. The only living vampires that have been defeated are those that have escaped for the time being. Our fight is to the death."

CHAPTER TWENTY-FOUR
PREPARATIONS

Undisclosed Location

In the weeks following President Thomas' meeting with The Angel, humanity's role in the world is shifting once more. Zones of control are being dismantled in the newly freed states and human beings are regaining the ability to freely travel.

With the U.S. and the world having been out of normal production mode over the winter, some infrastructure is damaged or destroyed, and the food stocks are extremely low in some areas and wiped out in others. Millions of people are dependent upon the supplies the mutants are able to scavenge for them. The uneasy alliance of children turned murderers, turned slave masters, turned providers of food, and drinkers of blood has worked well in the western states. The humans and vampires must see if the system they developed can continue to work as they move farther east. What little food there is must be stretched between more and more humans as territory is captured and people are freed.

A video message prepared by the president was sent by winged messenger to every city and territory. The audio portion is being broadcast over all frequencies in each state that The Angel's forces control.

*

My fellow Americans, my fellow human beings. We are at a crossroads to the future existence of our species. The struggles and difficulties we have endured so far are not yet over. Most of you listening to me now have been freed by The Angel's forces. My appreciation for the actions that set us free are great, but I must first address our previous conditions.

Some of you know better than most the cruelty and violence humanity's children are capable of committing. You were held in territories by vampires that saw humans as nothing more than a nuisance race worthy of life only as a source of food. You understand what must be done and why we must do it, but there is a segment of the freed population that is unaware of the destruction and loss of life that occurred.

Myself and many others were more fortunate. We were not mistreated by the mutants but were kept in isolation in internment camps. Our loss of freedom made us believe we were being wronged. I must address first, specifically those people like me who did not know of the true atrocities being committed against humankind.

We were kept confined by the children we loved and cared for. We were kept captive by those to which I provided an unconditional surrender to so many months ago. They claim they were acting for our benefit in the best way they knew how to keep us safe, fed, and warm through the long winter. Whatever form of discomfort, hardship, or pain you have experienced in this time, my choice to have you cease all aggressive actions against the vampires bears as much responsibility for your difficulties as do the decisions of the vampires and giants among us. It is up to each of you, my fellow Americans, in how you wish to spend the rest of your days.

Many have expressed to me, you would have preferred to fight and die in the early days of this change than to accept enslavement by the mutants in exchange for life. Now you have the freedom to fight them if you wish. You are not obligated by any agreement to remain cordial or work with the vampires in any form to secure your future. I ask before you choose your course, you watch and listen to what the mutants that have detained us for so long have sacrificed to secure your current release.

The sounds and brutal images of mutant battles are played on the screens in each zone. The president narrates his address over the video images of the fighting.

While we were sitting in our homes and buildings, feeling sorry for ourselves, our children were fighting a war on our behalf. While we were angry at the ease in which we gave up our freedom to these mutants we once called our sons or daughters, they were losing their lives on battlefields we knew nothing about so that they could free the rest of us from brutal and tortured slavery.

While many of us were brooding and complaining about the conditions the vampires kept us in and the paltry food they provided to keep us alive, boys and girls no older than age fourteen were losing their lives to prevent us from being controlled by an evil element of the mutant kind.

Images of starved and skeletal humans being freed from filthy camps are displayed.

There are vampires in this world that seek to keep humanity enslaved and rule over us with a brutal hand. Those that I despised recently have shown me how much I have to be thankful for, how much we all have to be thankful for.

The video ends in a heroically scripted fashion, showing vampires pulling humans from burning buildings to their safety. Another group of vampires fights off attempts by their enemy to reach a human that is running from the scene while carrying an American flag.

When I saw this scene with the man and our flag, I turned to the vampires showing me the footage and I scoffed at them. I have witnessed many forms of propaganda in my life, but this was blatant and false, I told them. To that, they introduced me to the man in that video who survived the encounter. His name is Jeffrey Warren, and he was a Boy Scout troop leader before the world fell apart. The vampires that fought to protect him were members of his troop that joined the battle so they could try and save his life. Several of them gave their lives to protect his.

In their youthful innocence, they told me they put in that particular footage because it looked "cool" and it showed what the battle really meant to them.

Now you have seen what they have been doing for us in these past months. While you are still welcome to take whatever actions you think you must against those who held us in camps, I ask one thing of you. If you really want to express your frustrations and grievances against an enemy that wishes us harm, join us in the fight to free our remaining citizens who right now remain in captivity.

I will not gloss over the fact that there is no way for humans to defeat a vampire directly. They are using our deadliest weapons against each other with little harm or consequence. The only way we can help the vampires who are fighting to free our kind is to provide them with the one thing they need from us. They need our blood.

The mutants have a tremendous army and have pushed the vampires who wish to enslave us farther east. Battle lines have been drawn from Winnipeg in Canada down to Houston, Texas. Plans have been made to move eastward from that front line until every human and vampire between the Pacific and Atlantic Ocean is free. Free from enslavement and the threat of death by a group of individuals that wish to turn us into cattle.

To win the freedom of our fellow humans and defeat the threat to our lives that the evil vampires pose, I am asking you to join the almost seven million vampires and giants that have assembled along the front line in preparation to do war on our behalf. Move east with us and do what we as Americans were born and raised for. We were put on this Earth to fight for what is right and just in this world. We were put here to show all who attempt to knock us down how freedom can be challenged, but it cannot be extinguished. We need to join the fight with our children to secure the promise of humanities future. We will fight for our nation's independence, and we will win.

*

The movement east is unprecedented. Millions of humans and vampires traveling at once all in an effort to save the world from the shared threat the vampires in the east pose. In the past seven days, twenty-three million bodies ran, drove, flew or were carried to the front lines of a new approaching war. Without the help of the humans west of The Rockies who survived the winter in freedom, the war could not successfully continue. The people currently being freed from most cities and towns have been starved to such an extent many do not have the strength or health necessary to donate even a small amount of blood to a vampire before battle.

*

President Thomas is reunited with his military advisors and surrounded by chemists, engineers, doctors, physicists and every manner of scientific specialist that could be found. Tucked away in the halls of NORAD's Cheyenne Mountain Complex, they are all working on the problem of the vampiric telepathy that is causing the losses during battles to be so extreme.

Two days are remaining before The Angel and her generals plan to lead the first charge. Cora's mother opens the door to Julie Moore, the president's advisor.

"We found something. They would like to see Cora for testing."

"Thank you, Miss Moore. She's sleeping right now, why don't you come in while I wake her?"

Walking into the small room, Julie smiles sadly. "I'm sorry for this. I know it must be difficult for you."

"I have been crying a lot lately. As powerful as my daughter has become, I know it makes her the ultimate target in any battle. I..." Tanya sits heavily on a stool and leans against the counter. "I never imagined any of this. I mean, of course no one did, who could have, but I mean if the world stayed the same, there was never a thought that my daughter would join the military or go to war. I expected her to go to college, get a career, meet a nice man and get married one day. I didn't even get to send her off on a first date or have her turn into a teenager that hates her mother's rules.

"This whole situation is so... I can't even think of a word it's so bad."

"The president and the military men that saved me keep calling it FUBAR..."

Tanya chuckles. "I guess that will have to do, even if it doesn't express my motherly longing to have my little girl back."

"I miss you too, Mom."

Tanya and Julie jump at the sound of Cora's voice from a second doorway.

"Julie came to get you, sweetheart. They have something they would like to test on you."

Cora walks up to her mother and pulls her into a standing embrace, wrapping not just her arms, but her wings around her mother as well. She smiles at her mom, lets her go, and walks out the door with Julie.

CHAPTER TWENTY-FIVE
THE ROCKET'S RED GLARE

Mutant Casualty list

Winnipeg - 33,428
Minneapolis - 48,352
Chicago - 62,171
St. Louis - 37,421
Nashville - 42,951
New Orleans - 51,384

The video message screen crackles with the presidential address on the progress of the war. His tone has softened considerably from the anger-filled frustration born of enslavement. No longer are the pale mutants that fight for humanity referred to as monsters, even though that is still what they are. The term monster is used solely for the enemy. The enemy troops that torture and kill as many humans under their charge as possible rather than allow them to be freed in battle.

The Angel's troops and the human supporting army have advanced beyond the Mississippi River's boundary line, and the final stage of pushing across the country is at hand. Rafael and his soldiers take their humans and drain them completely before a battle to gain a blood superiority in the fight. Those fighting for freedom drink from their humans as well, but on this side of the battle, the humans are volunteers and no one is drained to the death. It is considered the same as donating blood and is often no more in amount.

"As our children have advanced across our nation, taking back territory and freeing what humans their evil counterparts have left alive, they have done so at tremendous cost. More than a quarter of a million of our children have given their lives while we have advanced the front line. The tactics of the enemy grow more vicious and desperate as our army continues east.

"The Angel has returned from her battles in Mexico and will be leading our largest force yet to take back Richmond. The enemy general, Rafael, is there and has assembled an army of Three hundred thousand in an attempt to prevent the loss of the southern territory. It is imperative to emerge victorious in this battle. Doing so will push Rafael and his forces back to the Washington D.C. area.

"I have been advised that a new ally from South America has joined us, and we will start seeing them among the groups of vampires and giants as they move through the territory in the next day or so. Please try to remain calm at the appearance of the new mutant forms. They are joining us in battle to fight for their own version of independence, and we should welcome all that wish to fight for the cause of freedom.

"For those that are in line to donate blood before the battle begins, please remember to eat and drink to capacity the night before so your blood will be rich and our victory will be sure. Thank you, and may the light of freedom once again shine from sea to shining sea."

*

Rafael's soldiers adopted the tactics of The Angel's army after the battle of Denver. Stores and shops across the U.S. were scoured for whatever medieval weaponry could be found. The remaining living farrier's and blacksmiths were collected to produce the swords and hammers to be used as the weapons of choice on modern battlefields.

Some firearms are still used but sparingly since bullets do so little damage to a mutant body, especially after being satiated from drinking an enemy's blood. The giants carry large hammers and can crush skulls and bodies of vampires, preventing them from reconstituting quickly. The vampires carry swords and axes and cleave their way through battle lines with parts and pieces being picked up and drained by any opposing vampire.

"This battle will be different in many ways," Cora calls out to over two thousand captains and generals that have converged to lead the assembled army. "Rafael will be leading this fight personally. He has grown stronger and is getting assistance from Amanda. I haven't been able to see into her mind to discover her powers yet, so we know she is powerful. Rafael's gift is control. You will have to use every ounce of your abilities to prevent him from gaining control over the minds of the vampires and giants fighting under you.

"I'm assuming Amanda must have a power similar to mine. She is able to keep me from reading not only her mind, but has been preventing me from seeing their planning as well. This inability to read their minds will cost us, but you have already had to deal with these issues while I was fighting in Mexico and pushed into South America.

"We have a new ally that will be joining us in the fight. We have various groups of these mutants joining us, but they are not native to the North American territory, so we have had little interaction with them. What I found out when I headed south is these creatures have kept the human population safe and prevented the vampires in their regions from choosing the path of enslavement. I wish we had their assistance in the earlier stages of our war.

"You should know they have limited vocal abilities and speak mainly in Spanish when they have something to say. If you have any questions, please direct them through vampires like myself that have the ability to read minds or to anyone that may speak Spanish."

Cora shoots into the air with three strong beats of her wings and signals to Lloyd on the ground to have the new army enter. A small howl is heard from the buildings behind him, and a dusty cloud bursts forth and rushes over the field to the assembly area.

In seconds, the assembled group Cora was speaking to is surrounded by the new mutant army. They move incredibly fast, and at times, seem like blurs of motion, even for the vampires' enhanced vision. The creatures stand in varying heights ranging from three to six feet tall. They are covered in hair, have long tails, and snouts full of vicious-looking teeth.

"These new soldiers are able to fight without having their minds taken over and controlled by arch-vampires. They are faster than us and can use their tails and legs as well as we can use our arms. They will help to keep us alive if Rafael gains control over large portions of our army. Use the next few days to coordinate with the other mind-reading troop leaders to place the werewolves within your divisions."

"What are they? I mean what were they?" Turning to one of the werewolves standing next to him, the vampire smiles oddly. "No offense intended."

The hairy wolf-like face turns to him, grins, and gives a peculiar howl. He is six feet tall, covered in black hair, and is muscle bound. "I Mantled Howler. We wish free."

"They were monkeys," Cora states to the crowd. "Their similar DNA caused them to mutate in much the same way we did. They, of course, look like werewolves to us. Compared to where they began, they have gained tremendous levels of intelligence during their mutation, and they are seeking a place in society with the rest of us once our lands are free. I have agreed to their autonomy, and they have agreed to fight to free humanity and stop Rafael."

*

Fifty miles from the Richmond city limits, four hundred and eighteen thousand vampires, giants and werewolves set up camp under the southern stars in anticipation of the coming morning's battle. The humid summer air buzzes with insects and the busy sounds of swords being sharpened.

The human volunteers that will be providing the vampire soldiers with blood are already set up between the fighters and the city which is their goal. Normally, the human's camp farther back from the front lines, but the president convinced Cora and her army to allow the humans to be a bit closer to harm's way. *Any advantage we can give you will help free us all.*

The scientists working in NORAD developed an electronic helmet which blocks the ability of arch-vampires to read the wearer's mind. They are setting up production facilities and hope to produce enough for the entire army. So far only a limited number have been produced.

While Rafael and Amanda, the woman helping him, cannot gain control over the vampires who wear the helmets, it also prevents Cora from looking into James Thomas' mind. The president chose to fit himself and his advisors with some of the first caps produced. Cora's desire to know what the president is thinking becomes an urgent necessity with the illumination of the night sky.

The shrieking terror of thousands of rockets flying overhead echoes through the woods and hills. Movement from the front lines causes all the mutants to grab their weapons and prepare to fight.

Humans, tens of thousands of humans, run through the woods and line up in front of the mutants in preparation to have some of their blood consumed.

President Thomas walks up to Cora and offers her a serious smile. "I told you earlier, anything we can do to give you an advantage."

"But what have you done?" she cries back at him.

"We have sent rockets to destroy all of the humans they are holding captive in the Richmond area. In the morning before the attack, they would have killed them all anyway. They would have drained their blood and been better fighters against you as a result. Take your army and destroy Rafael now while they are disorganized."

"How could you?" Her eyes are welling up with tears. "We are trying to save humanity not destroy it!"

"This is war, Cora. If you want to save lives, then get your army moving and don't let those lives lost out there be in vain."

The roar of thundering feet usher forth from the camp as the giants and werewolves head off to battle. The vampire soldiers run among the humans standing in line and drink before speeding off in a blur to the night time battlefield.

Lloyd grabs Cora's arm and pulls her around, her hateful glare torn from the president's face.

"War is what they're good at, Cora. There is a reason you wanted the help of adults after the battle for Denver. He told me about his plan to do this, and I thought it was a good one. We only saved a thousand humans in the last battle, and it isn't worth letting Rafael have so much blood before a fight."

She wrenches her hand away from Lloyd in protest and anger and points her finger at the president. "We'll discuss this when I get back." Flapping her large wings behind her, she flies into the night sky followed by her winged guard. The cacophony of feet, rockets, and wings display an auditory example of a rush to war that no one could mistake.

The city of Richmond is in flames. The rockets stop falling just before the first of The Angel's army reach the city boundary. Rafael's soldiers are in disarray from their human slaves being killed before their blood could be consumed. Many of them are running away from the front line, attempting to escape before Rafael is able to reorganize them with his mind. Then, the werewolves arrive and begin tearing his soldiers to pieces. None of them have seen or battled the werewolves before, and at first, they are overwhelmed by their appearance.

Rafael can see the destruction through the eyes of those he controls. He can feel their fear.

He shakes his head not believing what his soldiers are fighting. *These new creatures look like wolves and can drain the blood of vampires just as easily as I can. And they are fast.* He tries leaping his mind connection ahead from soldier to soldier before it is ripped apart and drained, and his thought jumping barely stays ahead of the new army's advance. He tries time and again to gain purchase to control the minds of the werewolves destroying his vampires but is unable to grasp their thoughts.

The giants arrive at the battlefield, swinging their enormous hammers and crushing all enemies in their path. With their arrival, The Angel's vampires won't be far behind. They will run through the field of severed and crushed bodies consuming every ounce of blood they can find. It is the same tactic his soldiers successfully used several times as well before they lost their alliance with the giants.

Rafael orders his winged vampires into the fight, and his ground troops start to push back against the raging horde before them. His soldiers are holding the line, but The Angel's winged troops haven't yet arrived, when they do, the battle will turn, and he will lose this city as well.

He grips his hands in fury and prepares to start giving the kill code. He developed his powers of control over others to the point that he can program vampires in his power to fight to the death. He discovered a vampire given the kill code will become twice as effective in battle and has helped him destroy large swaths of The Angel's troops in previous fights.

Before he sends out the code, a calming voice enters his mind. "Pull them back."

He looks to the sky and sees The Angel's winged forces approaching.

"The battle is lost, pull my people back. Amanda is with me, we will stop them in Washington."

His mind whirls through his soldiers as he calculates. He grabs the minds of nearly a thousand soldiers at a time and gives the kill code. Over and over, he reaches out until nearly twenty thousand of his troops are fighting to the death. He orders the rest to retreat to Washington D.C.

The city of Richmond roars with flame in the humid night air. A weather-beaten American flag still waves from the pole atop the capital building, the Virginia state flag can be seen just below it.

With so many soldiers given the death code, the violence and death of the battle will be prolonged. Cora orders her winged soldiers into the bloody fray and she turns around to leave the city. Her people know what to do, and without Rafael in the area, she can focus her attention on the president and what he did to the human captives of Richmond.

CHAPTER TWENTY-SIX
CHANGING FORTUNES

Virginia

Cora drops from the sky and impacts the ground like a meteor crashing to earth. She is ten feet away from President Thomas. When she stands, her strained face has sharp angled features, making her look more like a monstrous demon than a friend. Her hands are still holding her sword and dagger, and she looks ready to pounce on the president and cut him in half.

Defiantly, President Thomas stands his ground and faces her with head high and back straight. He isn't sure at all that she won't end his life for his murder of so many innocents in this battle. He is ready for her and still considers his actions a necessary evil to keep the human race alive.

"You can be angry with me all you want, but what I did saved thousands of lives."

"You have no right to make such a decision."

"I have the only right! I am the president of this nation. I have to make the choices that will allow this nation and its people to continue to exist or allow ourselves to be wiped from history as an afterthought. I don't care that you are upset with what I did, I did it to save lives, not to make you happy."

"The people will hear about what you did tonight."

"Only if we ultimately win."

Cora begins pacing in front of him.

"This isn't a game, Cora. All of our lives are on the line. If this war is lost, we don't go to little camps where we silently live out the rest of our lives. If you and your soldiers lose, we will be rounded up and killed. You, your giants, us humans, we will all be slaughtered and eaten. If you want to play nice, then you will lose. Those people I killed were considered casualties in this war long before I sent the rockets at them. If you wanted them to live, then you should have chosen not to fight this war."

"Even if I can see the logic of it, you're hiding something. This just doesn't seem like something you would do. What else aren't you telling me?

President Thomas rubs his hand over the digital skull cap.

"Yes, your cap is working. I can't read your mind. Now tell me what is going on."

"A large section of your northern force lost the battle for Washington. They captured Pittsburg, and because they only had a few extra hours to make it to the capital, your generals decided to have them push east, hoping they could cause the enemy to fracture. They believed they would have a chance to cut off Rafael's eventual escape from Richmond by taking the capital. The problem is the enemy have another controller besides Rafael, someone we didn't know about."

"You obviously don't mean Amanda."

"No. It is another male, but we barely know anything about him. What we do know is he is more powerful than Rafael and Amanda. In fact, it is possible he is more powerful than you as well."

The implication of this isn't lost on Cora. Through every battle since Denver, they have had the continuous fear of having Rafael take control of their soldiers' minds and turn the tide against those fighting for freedom. Once The Angel's army passed the Mississippi River, Amanda began showing up in conflicts and used her mind-reading powers to anticipate maneuvers and redirect fighters during engagements. If the enemy has another controller that is even more powerful than Rafael, the level of the war entered a new stage of desperation.

"You understand now that the victories we have had so far aren't as significant as we may have believed. This whole time, with all of our battles and wins, we could have been doing the work of the enemy. The eastern vampires were probably more fractured and battling each other for supremacy. We only considered them united because Rafael and Amanda kept showing up to lead the battles. By clearing city after city and taking down who we considered enemy generals of a united front, we could have been destroying our enemies enemy for them."

"How many did we lose?"

"I have called for your southern border army to come reinforce us, they should be here from Texas tomorrow."

"How many did we lose?"

"Two hundred and eighty thousand."

Cora's expression falters and softens. Her anger fades away, and she returns to the beautiful woman that people enjoy being around. She lowers herself to the ground where she sits and puts her head in her hands.

"How could we lose so many? That's more…"

"Yes, that is more than we lost in the last six battles combined. Your troops were still running for their lives when I sent the rockets into Richmond. Unfortunately, no arch-vampires escaped to safety. Whoever they have as their controller, he turned at least third of your troops against us all at once and gave them what you call a kill code.

"Over four hundred thousand of your troops converged on Pittsburgh and they took it easily. Three hundred thousand moved on to Washington where they encountered the new arch-vampire. It's fortunate that the whole army didn't move on to the capital together. If they did, it's likely all of them would have been destroyed. We at least have the hundred thousand remaining that stayed in Pittsburgh as well as the twenty thousand that made it back from the capital alive.

"I am willing to support your call in pulling whatever troops you need from around the nation. It will cost a tremendous amount of human lives if we pull them away from their jobs in the free territories, but there will be no human left if we don't win. There is only one alternative we have to sending a million or more soldiers into a battle to defeat this vampire. I'm not even sure you could win if a million went with you to fight."

"So this new vampire is the reason you killed the humans?"

"No. I planned on sending in the missiles before I heard about our losses. As wrong as my decision was on one level, using the missiles and killing the enslaved humans helped your army to have such a swift victory.

"Satellite imagery tells us the missiles also stopped the enemy in the capital from pursuing your army back into Pittsburgh. As soon as the missiles struck in Richmond, the D.C. forces pursuing your northern troops turned back. We don't have enough of these digital caps for all of the soldiers to wear, and they are the only thing that can save all of your people from the kind of mind-control ability the new vampire has. We have to take measures that are potentially more brutal to win this war, but they will save lives, and we are going to have to carry them out soon."

The president removes his cap, allowing Cora access to his mind for a brief moment. A short time later, a man carrying a suitcase handcuffed to his arm walks up to President James Thomas.

"Nuclear war? Are you serious? You want to use nuclear bombs to wipe out our enemy?"

"You tell me there is another way. Our scientists have studied your regenerative capabilities. Nothing we do can kill you vampires and nothing you can do will stop this man that is more powerful than Rafael. If we lose this war, we lose the planet. A nuclear blast will vaporize blood, tissue and bone. Even a vampire won't be able to regenerate from that, not from ash."

"And you expect their army to stay still and let you bomb them to oblivion?"

"We don't need to kill all the vampires, only Amanda, Rafael, this new man, and anyone like them that can use mind control and want to subjugate the human race. We need to be able to take them out, and the only way I know how is with the use of nuclear weapons.

"To your point about them staying still and waiting to be bombed, for that, I need something from you that I don't want to ask of you. I am a military man by nature and training, and I have been successful at figuring out every possible way to save the most lives. In this instance, without any effective weapons other than yourselves, I am limited in that I must trade good lives for bad rather than just cost our enemy their lives.

"I need you to have your army move into Washington D.C. It won't do us any good if we fire a missile and when it lands, the enemy is hundreds of miles away."

"How will we get clear of the blast zone?"

The president pauses and gives Cora a serious and stern look. "You won't be able to." The people in the area go silent.

"The digital caps will allow you to get in close to this new threat without having your minds taken over and turned against the rest of us. Unfortunately, as you know, we have only produced a small number more than the two thousand you and your commanders already have. Someone will need to be in Washington to verify that the targets are in the city so we can send in the bomb.

"Anyone that you send in should know the risks and probabilities. If they do somehow make it out of the blast zone, the radiation might still kill them. We don't know what effect radiation will have on your kinds' mutated cells, we haven't had the time to test for that yet."

Cora's mother and father walk up, along with her brothers and sisters. She reads their minds and knows they have been told about the president's plan.

"Do you think this is something I should do?"

Cora's father, Robert, walks up to her and puts his arms around her. "I don't think you should do it, but I think it is something that has to be done. You and the president have a chance to end the war, at least here on our soil. If we didn't lose almost the entire northern army today, I would say forget it.

"You have been winning all the battles and taking back the land, but this new mutant is someone you haven't encountered yet. I know you don't have the numbers here to withstand a vampire that can capture the minds of more than a hundred thousand troops. One final battle, one final sacrifice could end the war. Choose some generals to lead your army into the capital and set the people free."

Cora turns her gaze back to the president. "You want this to happen today, don't you?"

"We have to move on them while they are in Washington D.C. and before they decide to move on us. This new bastard can even avoid fighting us altogether and still win the war. If he moves west across the territories you have already freed, he will be able to capture or co-opt every mind he comes into contact with all the way to the ocean."

"You are willing to destroy Washington D.C.?"

"The English took our capital once before. Yes, it is a symbol of this nation, but symbols are meaningless without having people around to remember what they stood for."

"I'll fly back into Richmond and organize the push to D.C. I will have our troops start to move as soon as the Richmond area is cleared of the kill-code vampires. After that, we can make it to the capital in two hours if we don't run into resistance along the way. Will you be ready?"

"I have the codes with me already and two submarines are in the Chesapeake Bay. It will take no more than five minutes from launch to detonation. I would prefer it if you don't go with your soldiers into that battle."

"You and I both know my presence will be necessary to keep their three most powerful leaders in one spot. I don't want to do this, but I am willing to do it to end this war, and I'm trusting you to keep my family safe."

"The only way I can promise that is if you win this war. I would like you to do one extra thing. Ten seconds before the bomb is set to explode, you will hear a series of three loud beeps in your helmet. When you hear them, take your helmet off and let them read your mind. I want those bastards to know what is coming."

CHAPTER TWENTY-SEVEN
THE LAST FLIGHT

Virginia

Thirty miles outside of Washington D.C., Cora looks over at Lloyd and smiles. She only took the winged vampires that have protective helmets with her. The full army has been ordered to remain in Richmond. Two thousand vampire soldiers are flying together in formation, and each of them know the final outcome of this battle has already been determined.

A strange sound approaches the group from Chesapeake Bay and coming in high over the water are an assortment of military planes.

Crackling in her helmet's earpiece, she hears, "Angel of the mutant army, this is Marine Corps Captain Ethan Black. President Thomas let us know there was a fight going on in the capital today, and we thought we would join you. We know what you're up against and all of the pilots have protective helmets on. We have a mixed group of F-35's and few Air Force A-10 Warthogs with us. While we can't stop the enemy, we figure we can help slow them down a little so you can do what you need to finish the job."

"Captain Black, I hope the president gave you the full details of the operation."

"We know the plan, ma'am, and are with you to the end."

"Then it's good to have you with us."

Cora looks over at Lloyd, smiles at him and flies closer to grab his hand briefly before beating her wings again in a rush forward.

"There are so few of us. This feels like when we started attacking Los Angeles."

"It feels wrong leaving everyone else behind."

"I'm scared, Lloyd." The wind rolls her tears quickly off her face.

"I'm scared too."

*

President Thomas is watching on a screen as a swarm of green dots progress toward a red blinking circle. The simple display of unit progression is the best to view the aerial battle groups headway. Other screens show live satellite feeds of various military units all stationary in this offensive. One image is assigned to specifically follow The Angel.

"Is everything progressing?"

"Yes, sir. The bird is ready and will arrive at its nest within five minutes after you give confirmation to launch. The Angel's army will arrive at their target in forty seconds at current speeds."

Thomas turns to Doctor Usachova. "Are you sure this will work? It's a hell of a sacrifice if you're wrong."

"Mr. President, it will work, my calculations aren't wrong."

"And if they are?"

"Then we will all die."

*

The view over the city before them is bizarre in comparison to the previous battles they have endured. Instead of facing the thousands of arch-vampires flying above Washington D.C. with an overwhelming force in the air and on the ground, The Angel is having to go in undermanned and with no hope of winning. The winged enemy, which look to be twenty thousand strong, are in a massive wall formation. There is a thick cluster of soldiers in the middle, around what is hoped to be the goal of this offensive, three leaders of the enemy.

Twenty thousand winged enemy soldiers is a much better prospect than the battle against forty or fifty thousand they were expecting. Rafael escaped the Richmond area with almost this many fliers, and they all thought Amanda or the new leader would have had their own winged troops to add to this fight. There is a faint amount of relief at the smaller size of the enemy force, but it is still an overwhelming number for them to face with only two thousand helmeted fighters among them.

The ground is the opposite of the sky in multitudes of fighters. The leaders of this area clearly favor ground troops over their winged counterparts. Probably due to the level of mind control needed to keep the winged arch-vampires in line. It looks like a swarm of locusts consuming the earth below. The streets and buildings are concealed by the bodies of wingless vampires. The shapes of the towering structures are barely recognizable underneath the moving mass. Not even the sides of buildings are free from the mutants as they are clinging to every spot making the city look overgrown with human-shaped vines.

"I am offended that you bring so few to fight me. You cannot win against my army." The unified phrase echoes out from the crowd on the ground. "I control all of the vampires here and will soon control you as well, Angel."

Cora presses a button on her helmet. "Verbal confirmation the enemy leader is in Washington, still awaiting visual."

The arch-vampires with The Angel continue to fly forward without hesitation. Swords at their sides, they are prepared for the bloody yet hopeless task at hand. A visible ripple in the enemy defensive line occurs.

It is a shudder of mind-controlling energy that starts from the center of the flying cluster of vampires and rolls through the troops on the ground until it extends past the area The Angel's troops have already flown.

The helmets worn by The Angel's soldiers do their jobs and keep her large assembly intact against the enemy's psychic powers.

The block, wall, and cluster formations vampire armies use during battles are near perfect defensive forms against attackers with swords and hammers. Like ancient defenders of the past who locked shields to stop an enemies advance, the arch-vampires in the air over Washington are clustered together to prevent The Angel's army from breaching their line. With only The Angel and her two thousand swords, her advance and attempt to breach the line to visually confirm the enemy leaders are present would fail. Even if the enemy forces movements are slightly slowed due to the mind control keeping them in check, The Angel's soldiers would be destroyed against the large numbers of defenders. In this battle, they have something more.

Only a few other mutant battles utilized modern military aircraft and none of those attacks were attended by Rafael or his cohorts. The military jets complete a circular path to come up behind their allies in this engagement and let fly their missiles. Rocket after rocket bursts away from the planes toward the defensive wall formations which are their targets. The leaders hiding behind the layered formation must be getting anxious. Two more mind-controlling ripples erupt from the flying enemy cluster before some of the missiles impact with the dispersing group and explode. Large clusters of vampires are damaged beyond their ability to instantly repair, and their bodies and limbs fall from the sky by the thousands.

"I see them!" Lloyd yells "They're with the president's son."

"President Thomas' son?"

"No, President Foster. I met his son, Adam, in Washington after my dad was elected. Everyone thought he died with the president on the first day of The Shattering." Pressing the button on his own helmet, "Visual identification confirmed. Rafael, Amanda, and new enemy leader all at the battle in D.C. It is President Foster's son, Adam."

One long tone sounds in their helmets signifying receipt of confirmation, and now they must fight and wait.

Having no opposing army of runners to battle, Adam releases control over his ground troops in order to focus all of his energy in attempting to once again gain power over the minds of The Angel's incoming fliers and the humans or mutants flying the jets. The physical reaction from his mental ripple is still noticeable, even though he and his troops are flying erratically to avoid the incoming spray of bullets from the machine guns on the aircraft.

"I can't get into their minds!" he yells out in frustration and fear. "I don't know what's happening. She must have brought her most powerful soldiers! Amanda, try to read their minds."

Released from their mental subjugation by Adam, the ground troops are free to choose which side they want to be on in this war and begin to fight among themselves. Even in the air, some of the vampires supposedly sided with Adam begin to take flight away from the approaching soldiers before he regains dominance over their minds and brings them in line to battle on his behalf.

Amanda searches for a way into the minds of The Angel's vampires while holding up Rafael. A large piece of shrapnel broke his wing, and they are both waiting for it to heal. "I can't get into their heads, something is blocking me."

The jets circle and fly by the reforming defensive line again, strafing Adam's warriors and sending missiles at them the entire time. Adam's fear and mental control are getting huge swathes of his arch-vampires blown out of the sky. They keep trying to disperse to avoid being hit, and Adam keeps pulling them back into formation to block the missile and bullet paths to himself.

A signal is given for The Angel's forces to halt their forward progress and wait. They are close enough to begin their assaults, but they are still massively outnumbered even though thousands of the original enemy group are no longer remaining. The enemies, who are now absent, have flown or fallen to the ground with injuries from the bullets and exploding missiles. If they aren't engaged by ground troops that turned against Adam, those vampires will eventually heal and return to the fight.

There is still a hesitation on the part of Adam to directly engage his troops with The Angel's forces. His fear of having to fight The Angel and her army continues to prevent him from sending his soldiers out and away from him to freely battle her. This is a costly mistake that is allowing the circling aircraft to repeatedly attack his bunched-up protectors.

"Enough!" Adam yells and hundreds of his soldiers split away from the group and fly directly at the oncoming jets. The first several attacks result exactly as all witnessing it imagine they would: the swords of Adam's warriors bounce off the glass canopies of the jets.

Adam and his entire force wall begin moving forward to engage The Angel and her hovering group. His massive formation moves in one large block forcing The Angel's soldiers to form their own defensive wall.

Another jet flies through on its run, and an explosion then black smoke burst from its side as the vampire attacking that plane is pulled through the engine. The same explosion of gore occurs with the next two jets to fly by signifying the engines are the intended targets to bring the planes down.

Adams forces continue forward. He still has a six to one advantage over The Angel's group with twelve thousand of his soldiers remaining, but he is still moving in slowly to maintain the defensive formation in front of him. Even though he has unrivaled psychic power on this battlefield, it is useless against his current foe, and that unnerves him more than he wishes it did. In his experience, psychic power can only be defeated by greater psychic power, yet none of his troops have been taken from him by The Angel's forces. *Her troops must have tremendous blocking capabilities.*

Adam knows the history of The Angel and her tactical abilities have propelled her across the entire U.S. in an amazingly brief time. Adam's power doesn't include the ability to read minds, but Amanda was able to share memories from other vampires with him. He was shown battles The Angel had fought in and won. Through those memories, he gained the knowledge of how vampires on both sides have been fighting during the war but watching another's memory is no substitute for personal experience.

The last fighting Adam participated in was aboard Air Force One nearly a year ago, and that was against humans. In every encounter he has had since that time, he has used his gifts to make other vampires and humans fight for him.

The jets continue to make their runs and a few of the aircraft are taken out each time they pass.

"Captain Black, this is The Angel. You've done what you can for us, we're moving in."

"Roger that, Angel. We'll stay in the area and help if we can."

"You picked the wrong day to go to war, Adam," Cora calls in a taunt "I can see in your cowardly eyes you've never been in a real fight before." Moving slightly ahead of the others, she smiles at Lloyd then turns back to face their objective. "Attack!"

The call to begin is followed by Cora rushing forward, wings beating in a direct line at the hole through which she can see Adam's face. The soldiers of his line are directed to group together, and they line up in four tight rows to guard the terrified boy. His fear-filled control over them once again gets his soldiers killed. Even Amanda and Rafael are kept frozen at Adam's side to ensure he has their fighting experience near him if someone should break through.

Seconds from impact with the enemy, The Angel changes direction and shoots left, raking her sword across the throats of the unprepared vampires in the line. Lloyd and the others strike in similar fashion and sever many limbs with their abrupt direction changes. The defensive wall breaks up and forces are finally allowed to begin peeling off. They are now being directed in different manners by Rafael and Amanda as well as Adam. The pulling and twisting of Adam's soldiers helps The Angel's forces, but they are losing vampires in the fight as well.

The Angel's soldiers split into multiple teams and unite into flying boxes. The boxes are formations of twenty-four vampires with four soldiers fighting in each of the six sides of a box. They moved in close to Adam's defensive wall before forming into boxes to prevent Adam's vampires from gaining a speeding charge to breach the sides. It is an effective defensive structure that would be more potent if they brought shields, but The Angel's fighters are still able to kill many of the vampires which surround them.

Unfortunately, skill is only able to take combatants so far in battle. In this open-air battlefield without any physical obstructions to hide behind or maneuver around, the overwhelming number of soldiers Adam has on his side is winning the fight for him.

The Angel's forces are falling one by one. Many of the cubes are collapsing, and her soldiers drained or severely damaged bodies continue plummeting to the Earth.

Lloyd calls out, "All units push for square sum and Denver spiral."

Without being able to read minds or send thoughts because of their helmets, the verbal orders have to be called out. The fortunate aspect is their enemy has no clue what Lloyd meant with his orders. The Angel's forces begin to ascend in the sky and move together as they continue their fight to survive. They pick up velocity, making it difficult for the attacking forces to swing their swords and remain in line for the fight. Adam, Rafael, and Amanda stop following at ten thousand feet and watch as their soldiers pursue the diminishing numbers they need to kill in order to win this fight.

The square sum order is achieved at fifteen thousand feet and most of The Angel's remaining troops form one gigantic box formation which stops rising and begins to fall with the force of gravity. The Angel and a small group work separately from the box formation and head directly at Adam in a spiral attack like they used in Denver. They spin with their swords out in front aiming at the group defending the three leaders.

"I've had enough of this!" Amanda yells at Adam. "It must be those stupid helmets they're wearing. Order your idiots to stop cutting off their heads and grab their helmets instead. Make The Angel and her guards kill each other!"

Thousands of vampires pursue The Angel's groups in their speeding drop and nearly as many remain with Adam for his defense. With all attention focused on The Angel, the mutants neglect to watch the aircraft that they believed had ended their engagement earlier. Four jets fire missiles and then fly into the mass of vampires pursuing their allies back to the Earth. Three A-10's fly through Adam's group at the same time, the pilots open up their guns seconds before impact. The bullets, jet impacts, and explosions cause thousands more bodies to fall from the sky out Adam's groups.

The Angel flies directly at Adam, beheading two of his guards and reaching out to slice him in the stomach as she passes. The fight has reached the leaders and the protective helmets are starting to be pulled from The Angel's remaining fighters.

The Angel, Lloyd, Brian and twenty others are fighting furiously in the center of the enemy cluster. They are slashing their way through to get at Adam as well as trying to keep their helmets from being removed. Lloyd watches his own soldiers, who are now being controlled by Adam, as they begin to surround his group in preparation to fight.

Three beeps ring in their ears. The Angel takes off her digital cap and smiles at the three they came here to fight.

Amanda screams with the image of approaching death she sees in The Angel's mind and begins to fly away, but Adam pulls her back with his mind. Slapping her hand on Adam's head, she yells, "Look at her thoughts, she's killed us all!"

Adam is jolted by the image and loses his controlling grasp of the other vampire's minds but is able to angrily issue a verbal command. "Let's make her pay." The entire focus in the seconds they have left is to make The Angel suffer for what she has done.

"You won't touch her!"

Lloyd cuts through the disoriented vampires in front of him and grabs Rafael who still seems dazed in fear from the image of the bomb he received. Lloyd sinks his teeth into his enemy's neck and drains him. Amanda flies to help Rafael escape from Lloyd's embrace, but his body is already drained and falling when she reaches the pair. Lloyd stabs his sword through Amanda's neck and tosses her away and into Cora's awaiting sword. Adam approaches Lloyd from behind.

Cora watches Adam advancing on Lloyd while she struggles with Amanda and yells for Lloyd to turn around. Cora sees a bright flash and her vision goes black. A sharp pain is burning through her head, and she has the sensation of falling before her thoughts disappear with her vision.

CHAPTER TWENTY-EIGHT
AFTERMATH

Virginia

Wearily opening her eyes, Cora turns her head to see wires and a red tube connected to her arm. She feels exhausted. Every inch of her aches in some form, and the small movements she is making just to lift and turn her head cause deep pain.

A nurse steps into her line of sight.

"Where am I, what happened?"

The nurse just smiles and nods while holding up her index finger.

"Please, tell me what's going on."

The nurse doesn't say anything, she only holds up her palm and walks out the door.

Letting her head rest back on the pillow, she stares at the ceiling tiles above her.

*

"Good morning, Cora. The nurse just came and let me know you were awake. Are you feeling all right? Can you speak or do you need to go back to sleep again?"

Slightly disoriented and looking toward the sound, "Dr. Usachova? How long have I been here? Why wouldn't the nurse tell me anything?"

"I'm afraid that wasn't her choice. Your nurse is no longer able to speak, she had her tongue removed by one of her captors. She was freed from Washington D.C. after your battle. She is getting your parents right now; they are sleeping in one of the rooms on the next floor down."

"I'm sorry, I didn't know."

"Don't be sorry, Cora, you saved her life. She is grateful she has the honor of looking after The Angel."

"Can you please tell me what happened? Why am I still alive, wasn't the bomb supposed to vaporize me? How long have I been here? Where are the others?"

"Don't get yourself worked up, I will answer all of your questions. You have been here for three days. The president did use a nuclear bomb, but not in the way he originally intended, and you are alive because your cells can completely regenerate."

Robert and Tanya walk into the room and walk up to the bed on each side and hold her hands.

"Your father and I are so proud of you, Cora. You saved us all. The whole country is talking about it. Your final battle gave us back our lives."

Shaking her head and blinking, Cora looks at her parents and smiles but looks at Dr. Usachova with a pleading expression. "I don't know what happened. Please, I was fighting with Amanda when Adam was grabbing Lloyd, and then I felt a pain in my head. I saw a bright light and everything was gone."

Smiling, Dr. Usachova sits next to Cora's bed. "We discovered something sensitive about your brains after you left with your soldiers. One of the electronic helmets we produced to block the psychic waves malfunctioned in the testing facility. It disabled an arch-vampire that was working there. A small EMP was released when it short circuited and he blacked out."

"EMP?"

"Electromagnetic pulse. The helmets use an electromagnetic shield that keeps psychic waves from penetrating the brain. Normally, the shield is contained, but a helmet was defective, and we discovered we could use the electromagnetic pulse from a nuclear bomb to knock out the enemy forces. The higher the psychic ability of the vampire, the greater the impact that would be felt.

"The president ordered all ground troops to enter the battle thirty minutes after you left. They weren't happy that you went without them, and I understand a few of the faster soldiers made it to D.C. shortly after the bomb had been detonated high above the atmosphere. A large number of the soldiers you were fighting against had turned hostile to their own group when Adam was knocked out, and when their forces combined with ours, the enemy was totally wiped out."

"Even Adam?"

"Yes. Adam's body was returned to us along with Amanda's and Rafael's. There were a few others that were considered leaders in their organization, but those three were the most powerful, with Adam at the top. One of your ground generals made sure they were all completely drained before they were taken from the battlefield."

"What about Lloyd? Adam grabbed him before I blacked out."

As is typical with terrible news, the expressions on the faces she knows and trust show the answer before the information is provided.

"I'm afraid Lloyd didn't make it. His body was found drained near Adam's, but we weren't sure exactly what happened to him until now.

"Radar showed your group was fighting at ten thousand feet when the bomb detonated in the atmosphere. You and the other arch-vampires had quite a fall after you blacked out. You were found in a ball with your arms, legs, and wings wrapped around yourself on the ground, did you do that before you passed out?"

"No, I was still fighting Amanda when I blacked out."

"It probably doesn't mean anything, the vampires that picked you up just mentioned how unusual it was. No other body that fell to the ground did that. I need to get back to the president so I'll leave you alone with your parents." Gently grabbing her hand, she said, "I'm truly sorry about Lloyd, Cora, I know he meant a lot to you."

CHAPTER TWENTY-NINE
LOSS AND RENEWAL

Oregon

A tall woman stands solemnly on a driveway, staring at the large house up the path. Rain pours around her and thunder cracks overhead as she contemplates her approach. If she wanted, she could read the minds of the people in the house to determine if now was the right time, but she knows no time will ever be right with the pain they have endured.

Cora closes her eyes and moves herself toward the inevitable pain of the encounter. The cold rain rolls itself down her body as she moves. After knocking on the door, she finally opens her eyes and waits.

"Hello?"

"Hello. I am here to see Mr. and Mrs. Cavanaugh."

The man at the door speaks into his radio announcing the guest. Touching his ear, he tells her, "Please come in, they will be with you shortly."

Walking down the hall from the rear of the house, the Cavanaughs fix eyes on Cora before she is able to make it through the entryway. The smiles are bittersweet, the expressions on all sides are torn. Each of the parties is filled with happiness and anguish with the reunion.

"I'm sorry I didn't call. I'm sorry I didn't come sooner. I wanted too, I…"

Evelyn walks up and pulls Cora into a tearful embrace.

*

On the patio, Greg, Evelyn and Cora sit together watching the rain drip from the patio roofs edge.

"I remember springtime being more beautiful," Cora tells Lloyds parents softly. "I remember everything being more beautiful before the change."

Evelyn and Greg just sit silently as Cora begins to cry again.

"I miss him. I know you miss him as well, but I miss him so much. I keep expecting him to show up again, to just be there by my side. I don't know what I'm supposed to do anymore."

"I won't pretend it is easy for us that Lloyd is gone, but his father and I had to deal with his loss before. When I thought he was gone the first time, I also lost our baby, it nearly took my will to live. After you found him and sent him to us in the forest, Greg and I decided to cherish every extra moment we were given with him. We chose to hold dear to those times, but we knew there was the greatest possibility that he would be gone soon because of the war.

"We had to deal with the families that would hear about their sons and daughters being killed in the fighting while you and Lloyd were…well, while you were out saving the world. Nothing I can tell you will take away the pain, Cora, but I can tell you how much you meant to our son.

"He loved you. As much as Greg and I love each other, our son loved you, and he dedicated himself to keeping you safe above all else. He loved you, and he believed in what he was fighting for.

"Those facts don't take away our loss, but they help me when I think of how my child, the boy I raised, how he chose to live the short time he spent away from us. So many people have lost their lives because of this forsaken blue haze, at least my son was able to die for something he believed in. He lost his life in a manner that he chose rather than being one of the faceless millions that tragically lost everything without understanding why.

"Our son loved you, and I know you loved him as well."

"I still love him."

"All I could ask for my son was what you gave him, Cora. You gave him happiness. Thank you." Evelyn stands up but motions for Cora and her husband to remain seated. "I have something for you to take with you, I found it when we returned to our house. It's something Lloyd made for you. Please sit and talk with Greg, I'll be back shortly."

They both watch as she walks into the house and leans against the counter inside briefly to cry before heading around the corner and out of sight.

"I am sorry it took so long for me to come speak with you."

"I understand. Evelyn and I both understand. We know you and Lloyd were close, and it isn't easy for you to have to see us after his loss. I would like to know, were you near him when he died?"

Fresh tears flow down her cheeks as she looks Greg in the eyes and nods silently.

"Please tell me what happened. I don't have to know the details, I just want to know what happened. I need to know how he died."

Taking a deep breath, looking up and away from his intent gaze, she tells him the story with five heart-wrenching words. "He sacrificed himself for me.

"I don't know how much of this information you already know, but my parents knew before we went into that last battle and they were able to say their goodbyes. We were told by the president that he was planning on using a nuclear bomb on the capital. Lloyd, myself, and our soldiers were there to ensure their lead arch-vampire, Adam, was there along with

Rafael and Amanda. We were told the bomb was going to destroy the area and us with it and that was the only way to end the threat our enemy posed.

"Lloyd and I both believed we would not make it out of Washington D.C. alive, but we were hopeful that we wouldn't feel anything in the nuclear blast. While we were fighting, all three came after me. They hoped they could tear me apart and make me suffer when they found out about the incoming bomb. Lloyd broke through and took them all on. He knew we only had seconds before the bomb went off and it would all be over. He didn't want me to suffer at their hands before we all perished. He didn't give up and give himself to them, he fought until the end. He just didn't want to let them hurt me.

"He managed to kill Rafael and threw Amanda to me right before Adam must have grabbed him from behind. I was fighting with Amanda when the bomb went off. I remember an excruciating pain in my head, my vision went black and I fell. I woke up three days later in a field hospital.

"Dr. Usachova told the president after we had left that the EMP from a high-altitude nuclear explosion would disrupt the psychic abilities of all the arch-vampires. The president never wanted to have all of us die, that's why he changed the order of the D.C. area annihilation to an EMP burst. I was knocked out by the blast and fell. Adams ground troops were already fighting each other when he released his control over them. Then our ground troops arrived and joined the battle. They killed the enemy soldiers and gathered up the bodies of our friends and brought them to safety.

"For a while, I thought the president had betrayed us again, and I blamed him for Lloyd's death. He shouldn't have sacrificed himself for me, and I was thinking we didn't even have to be there! I wanted to believe that, but there was no other way. Rafael, Amanda, and Adam wouldn't have stayed in the area if we both didn't show up to the battle, they were too smart for that."

Leaning against the doorway, Evelyn speaks. "A part of me is resentful that you were able to be with him at the end when I wasn't. As a mother, I've always wanted to keep him from harm, but he wasn't the kind of boy, the kind of man, to walk away from things that needed to be taken care of. I know his death was difficult for you to witness, but it gives me peace to know he wasn't alone when he died."

Walking up to the table, Evelyn places something into Cora's hand.

"He carved this angel pendant out of glass. He told us after he made it that you glow like the sun and are truly an Angel. I never knew my boy to be poetic, but it was a beautiful image of how he sees you."

"I imagine you don't know why everyone calls me The Angel; it isn't because of the relationship Lloyd and I shared. I usually only do this during battle, but let me show you."

Greg and Evelyn look at each other with perplexed expressions.

Cora stands up and spreads her wings. Her arms reach out toward the pair in a welcoming motion, and she begins to glow. Her skin emits a pale luster of white as if the color of her pale skin is floating off into the air around her. The depth and brightness of the glow increases until it is a bright beacon of light the Cavanaughs have to squint their eyes against.

Cora's voice when she speaks sounds echoed and distant as if she is across some vast space. "I first discovered this power during a night battle when some humans were trying to escape. They could not see in the dark, and I gave them my light and called to them in order to guide them to safety."

Her emanating light diminishes and her echoing voice returns to the soothing, delicate tone of the woman who first arrived. The husband and wife, as well as two agents that approached to investigate the bright light source, stand in awe at what they witnessed.

"I had no idea. You truly are an angel, Cora. Why haven't you let the people see this? Seeing your gift would help those humans that still have doubts about the mutants come to terms with all that has happened."

"I'm not so sure. It seems every time a new power of ours is revealed, it increases fear rather than calming people. You know me, so my light isn't a potential threat in your mind."

The pair nod their understanding while Cora returns to her seat.

"There is one more thing you have to know about my relationship with Lloyd. It is another reason I was afraid to meet with you before now. Earlier, I wasn't ready to face a backlash from you if you were upset with me over his death, but it's something you have a right to know as his parents.

"Lloyd and I, well, I'm pregnant."

CHAPTER THIRTY
FIRST REMEMBRANCE DAY

Link-In Break

Link-In Reinitiated

Washington D.C.

"We are just moments away from President Thomas addressing the nation for our first annual Remembrance Day celebration. The crowd is an excited and eclectic mix of the new form of humanity we all share. Vampires, giants, and werewolves are mixed in the crowd along with human civilians and soldiers. There is even a group of the pilots that took part in the final battle up on the stage with The Angel and her generals."

"This is an exciting time indeed, Jennifer. People all across the nation are waiting to see the president walk out of the White House for the first time since its liberation."

A roar of excitement drowns out the reporters as the president makes his way out of the White House and onto the stage built before the crowd.

"My fellow Americans…"

The cheer let loose by the throng prevents President Thomas from continuing. He nods his head and claps his hands while also gesturing to one of the American Flags behind him on the stage.

"My fellow Americans, it is with great pleasure that I can once again address you as the President of These UNITED States."

The crowd starts cheering in unison *U.S.A.! U.S.A.!*

"Twelve months ago, our world was torn apart by the arrival of this blue haze which blankets the Earth. The Shattering Event we all endured was followed by the most unspeakable horrors we could have imagined. The lives we lost that first day were tremendous, but we managed to survive.

"Then came our captivity at the hands of those we once cared for. I personally felt I betrayed all of you by ordering our surrender. Only time and several battles later would prove what I suspected, that there was nothing we could do against this new threat we faced from our children. Even with this level of defeat and humiliation, we still found the will to survive.

"Little did we know in the isolation of our camps that these mutants, the vampires, giants, and werewolves were fighting on our behalf.

Fighting to free us from the oppression that this rapid change in humanity created. When The Angel…"

The crowd roars in excitement again when he points to her on the stage.

"When The Angel arrived at my camp in Wyoming, I believed she was there to kill me for the weekly addresses I was giving. Little did I know that she had been fighting brutal battles for many months just to free our people, to free our nation. When she arrived and told me she needed my help, I thought we had finally found a way to hurt or kill their kind and she wanted me to put humanity back in line.

"To this day, I am still amazed at the truth of what the vampires did for us. And on this first Remembrance Day and every one going forth, we should remember how far we came. That with all their strength, power, and ability to keep humanity as slaves for all eternity, the vampires chose to rise up and lead the other mutants in a fight for our freedom. They chose to become the people we all wished we could be. The people that would work to bring hope and freedom to all of humanity when the easiest course would be to do nothing and keep the control they gained with their physical and psychic superiority.

"Many of you do not yet know the exact details of the battle that freed us all. I will give you the details now. The final battle to free North America occurred over this spot on September 2nd, just one month and two days ago.

"A new enemy vampire leader had shown an ability to destroy entire armies of friendly mutants. On September 1st, our enemy led by this new mutant, killed almost three hundred thousand vampires of the Northern Army." He pauses to let the people absorb the depth of the loss. "Three hundred thousand of The Angel's forces were lost in one battle, on one day, in the fight to return to us our freedom.

"The following day, at my request, The Angel and her generals came here, to Washington D.C. for a final battle to lure the enemy's most powerful leaders to this spot. The only way we believed possible to defeat the psychic powers of this new enemy leader was with a nuclear weapon. The soldiers we sent into battle believed this would be their final assault, and they did not expect to survive. They were prepared to be obliterated in a nuclear blast that I had arranged to occur over this very location."

The crowd is silent, the only sounds are the flags behind the president lightly rustling in the breeze.

"I want you to know the details so you can understand this was not just another victory that you heard about. It was not just some other horrific battle where our troops planned to fight valiantly and believed they could have survived if they won. This was a one-way ticket, and they volunteered to come and fight for us all. The planned nuclear blast was our final hope to remove the greatest threat of the mind-controlling vampires that wanted to keep us enslaved. The vampires and pilots you see on this stage with me today, came to Washington believing their sacrifice could return our country to us."

The crowd is still in hushed anticipation of his words, but now the reporters in the background are making feverish calls to their offices about this new information the president is releasing.

"These human pilots flew in from their aircraft carriers in the Atlantic to help our mutant soldiers by slowing down the enemies advance with their bullets and missiles. They also knew the fiery end that Washington D.C. was supposed to become. Fortunately, the sacrifice these fine mutants and pilots were willing to make last month was not necessary. In the final minutes before the missile was set to destroy everything..." The president turns to a woman on the stage and light-heartedly offers "...and I mean literally in the final minutes. After the missile had already been launched, we received word from Dr. Tatyana Usachova here, that the same missile could be detonated high above the Earth's atmosphere and the resulting electromagnetic blast would disable the brains of the highly sensitive mutants and render them unconscious.

"So you knew they fought for your freedom but did not know of their willingness to face such a destructive end to secure it for you. That willingness by them to sacrifice their lives in battle, to reunite this nation, is one of the things we are here to celebrate. This is not just a Remembrance Day of October 3rd when the blue haze arrived, this is a remembrance of how much was sacrificed to bring us back from the edge of extinction. Their sacrifice was greater than you have all been made aware until now, and I felt it appropriate that you knew the true level of their love for you, their love for us all as human beings.

"Some of us are Giants..."

Many loud screams echo from the crowd.

"Some of us are vampires..."

The vampires and humans all cheer.

"And some of us are humans or even our new mutated friends, the werewolves. We are all part of the future and celebrate October 3rd as Remembrance Day. The day we can stand here in a united front of defiance against the tyranny of oppression brought about by a genetic disruption of nobody's choosing. Let us continue moving forward from this day on, remembering those we loved and those we lost. Let us remember all that we fought for together to move beyond the suffering and regain our collective dignity and freedom once more."

U.S.A.! U.S.A! U.S.A.!

CHAPTER THIRTY-ONE
THE DAY AFTER

Washington D.C.

"My fellow Americans, Citizens of Canada, Mexico, and all of our sister and brother nations of South America. I address you today on a serious matter that some of you knew would eventually come and a matter which we can no longer in good conscience ignore.

"Through great trial and tribulation, through the overwhelming loss of life, The Angel's vampire army's managed to return to us our freedom. They prevailed, and we have lived together as one this last month beginning to rebuild the lives and society which we lost.

"While we proclaimed the 3rd of October as our Remembrance Day to remind us what we have in common and must fight for, there is a tremendous battle which still lies ahead of us. We are not a race of beings residing solely on the continents of North and South America. We are humans, vampires, giants, and werewolves living on the planet Earth, and there is still a segment of humanity enduring enslavement in the rest of the world.

"Just as in times past, it once again falls to us to be the arbiters of freedom, not because we choose to bring war to those that think differently than we do, but because we know the true and natural condition of man is free. We cannot in good conscience pretend to enjoy the freedom we have here while our fellow humans remain enslaved.

"Aside from knowing we must go because it is the right and just course of action, the outcomes of the wars in Europe, Asia, and Africa will ultimately impact us all. As we know from our time dealing with our own brutal oppressors, if we leave them unchallenged, the vampire enemy that is intent on dominating humankind will eventually exhaust their supply of human slaves. They will fight to expand the territories which they control and move against the free society we have created. They will not stop until they have enslaved the entire world.

"This past month, we have been able to selfishly avoid looking to Europe and Africa's troubles because we were only recently freed and required a short time to heal and explore our own society's new burdens. We have our freedom and an end to our war now, and while our time of peace has been far too brief, it is the right time to continue this fight. Now is the time to move, before we force those enslaved people across our oceans to endure another brutal winter without hope. It is time for our armed forces to travel by ship to Europe. In two weeks, the first ships will sail, and the first planes will fly with The Angel's troops to begin working to assist those friends of ours in England. We have heard some of them managed to establish a safe zone for their human citizens in the English Isles."

*

"Preparations for the upcoming war in Europe are well under way, sir. The departing mutant armies we can spare are gathered along the shores of the northeast states. The remaining numbers are being distributed along the west and east coasts to defend against possible invasion."

"What about the unrest?"

The general pauses and breathes in before continuing. "The unrest is nationwide. With the mutants removed from their controlling positions, we are likely going to see more of it. The easiest solution would be for us to delay going to Europe and return the mutants to a policing role until we can re-establish human governments and police forces."

"You want the vampires to retake control of our nation?"

"No, sir. It isn't what I want to happen, it is only the quickest solution to the problems with the unrest. Millions of people out there are finally able to appreciate the destruction we have endured because of The Shattering and this war. Labeling the other day as Remembrance Day was a good start, but more will need to be done to keep people in line, particularly while industry comes back on-line and some form of economy is formed."

The president grits his teeth and looks at the general. "I appreciate what the mutants have done for us but none of us should forget we were freed by The Angel's army and not our own. I don't like having millions of soldiers on our shores that aren't directly loyal to our government, no matter how friendly they may be. When can they be sent to Europe?"

"As soon as you give the order they can be on their way. In five days, we will have all of the satellites re-tasked and aerial reconnaissance set up, but that is for our benefit, not theirs."

"I think the people are as uneasy about how our victory was achieved, as I am. What we need is a distraction, something to keep the people occupied, to keep them involved in helping themselves and this country while it heals. I think we should prepare people for national elections. I will announce my intention to resign the presidency."

"Sir, with all due respect, the people need you right now. You are the only official of substance that we haven't lost, and there are two years remaining in the presidential term."

"I appreciate your confidence, and in part, I am counting on it for the future elections. However, I have not yet been elected to lead our people.

This is not the time for me to remain in this position. However correct I feel my decisions were for the nation, I am as responsible as the vampires are for our internment over last winter. I am part of the division from which our nation needs to heal, and I will not stay here and continue our peoples' suffering out of some misguided belief that I have earned my place and title.

"There are many men and women around this nation that did their part to inspire and protect the people around them. Many of the uprisings are a result of our citizens continuing to feel powerless. Having elections is the best way I know to give our people the control over their lives that they want and deserve. It won't be easy, but I want a new election to take place before the New Year. The next president should be able to take office on January 20th."

*

"My fellow Americans, together we have endured the worst disaster in recorded history. We all continue to deal with the immeasurable losses we have had in our own personal ways. It is my opinion that to help in that recovery, I should step down from my current position as president and take up another role more suited to my military background and training. Without a living vice-president or active congress, I will remain in this post only as long as it takes for the citizens of our nation to hold elections and establish a legitimately elected governing body. It has been my greatest honor in serving you in our time of conflict and helping to guide us through the final battles to restore freedom to our shores.

"It is no longer the time for a military man to lead our great nation. In this time of healing and recovery, we need a person who is elected by the people, not a man that was promoted to this post through catastrophe."

CHAPTER THIRTY-TWO
THE SUN WILL COME OUT TOMORROW

11:22AM
Massachusetts

The Angel is standing at the edge of a four-story building in Boston, overlooking thousands of mutant troops preparing to board military ships bound for Europe. Some modern weaponry is being taken along, but the primary weapons of these soldiers are hanging at their sides in the rudimentary scabbards designed to hold their swords.

The crowd hushes to silence as she raises her arms and prepares to speak.

"I want to let…" Her words hang, echoing in the air as she looks beyond the enormous throng and into the glimmering ocean past the shores edge. A rippling effect like a heat mirage on a desert highway is floating over the distant waves and moving toward the mutants assembled in the area.

The crowd turns to watch the approaching undulation in the air which stretches across the horizon. The brightness of the morning increases with the ripples advance until an awareness of what is happening enters the minds of those who will be affected.

The blue haze which brought The Shattering is dissipating. The unfiltered sun is shining brightly across the ocean as the haze disappears. The approaching sun is welcomed by some, but many in the crowd start running from the shore in fear.

The Angel remains on the rooftop, waiting for the leading edge of sunshine to reach the scattering mutants on the ground below.

"Cora, should we leave?"

"I have to see what will happen when the haze is gone. We might be able to change back to the children we were before."

"Or we could be burned alive! You do know what sunlight is supposed to do to vampires, right?"

Her look of longing for a return to normality becomes a tense anticipation mixed with fear. Only seconds to wait before the sun hits the mutants on the ground that are trying desperately to squeeze into the buildings which surround them.

A fearful shiver runs down The Angel's back as the bare sunlight reaches her friends and compatriots still on the shore. Screams echo through the air as skin bursts into flame in the unfiltered light of day. Giants and werewolves work to lift cars and other large objects to shield the vampires near them from the direct rays of the sun.

The Shattering has ended.

*

"Mr. President, we're under attack!"

"What? Where?"

"I'm getting reports of vampires being destroyed all along the east coast. I think all of the troops preparing to leave for Europe have been destroyed."

"My God! The Angel was with those troops. Are the European mutants doing this? Is this some new power we haven't heard about yet?"

Bradley Hoskins, the Director of Intelligence, runs into the room. "It isn't an attack, Mr. President, the blue haze is gone. It is dissipating nationwide. From what I'm gathering so far, the giants and werewolves are unaffected but the vampires...well, it appears they are catching fire in the sun."

"So the history books were right. Do you know what this means, Hoskins?"

"The mutants will have weaknesses, sir."

"Yes, that means humans might be able to kill the vampires. I'm afraid with the current level of unrest in the nation, that likely means another war."

"It might not lead to that, sir. If you were to reconsider your resignation, give the nation time to work through this new occurrence. If you leave the people to throw together a hasty election while the vampires go into hiding from the sun, it could cause everything to boil over and explode."

"Get Dr. Usachova in here. I want to know what she knows."

*

Walking along the fifth-floor hallway of the downtown Boston Hilton, Cora smiles weakly at her fellow vampires as they huddle in fear from the sun outside. Some of the rooms have been opened for those seeking refuge, but many are too frightened of the sun to venture into rooms with large windows, even if they are blocked by heavy curtains.

Cora's wings are blistered and the skin on them is black. Her dress is partially burnt away where the sun touched her before she made it to safety indoors.

"How many do you think we've lost?"

"There's no way to tell so far. I can feel my body start to repair itself but far slower than it did before. How many of us survive this morning's exposure might depend on how long the sunlight reached their bodies. I wasn't out for long, but I'm not sure how well I would be healing if my injuries were worse."

*

"Mr. President."

"Dr. Usachova. We never seem to meet under better circumstances."

"I think it's the nature of our chosen professions. Science and politics aren't good bedfellows."

President Thomas' mouth is pulled back in tight thin line showing the strain he is under.

"I need to address the nation shortly to let them know what is going on. Please tell me what's happening out there."

"I can't tell you anything more than you could see out your own window, sir. The blue haze has gone as quickly as it arrived. The children that mutated have not reverted back to their original form, and from what I have heard, the vampires can now be mortally wounded by sunlight if they remain in it for too long. Everything else you probably want to know I will have to utilize tests to find out."

"What about our future? What happens to the children that haven't hit puberty yet? What do you believe will happen to them?"

"I am quite certain the children that have already been born will still go through The Shattering once they reach puberty. The greater unknown is what will happen to those that are conceived from this day forward. The mutation particle from the blue haze affected us all, not just the children. Even with our uncertainty, there is a high probability that any future generations of humans will still mutate in some form at puberty."

"And you can test for that as well?"

"The test for that is time, Mr. President. Now we must wait to see what will happen. In a week or two, we will find out if children entering puberty continue to mutate or not. For future generations of those not yet conceived, we will have to wait ten to twelve years for those children to enter puberty."

"And what are the odds for that?"

"As I said, Mr. President, there is a high probability of continued mutation. I still believe we are the last of what we consider non-mutated human kind. All future generations will change in some way due to what the blue haze did to our genetic make-up. May I ask, are you still going to retire from the presidency?"

"It was a selfish decision based on the vampires going to Europe and our nation ready to move on and heal its wounds. With this new difficulty thrown into the mix, I don't believe I can step down. Our country is already filled with protests and frustration, but people are hesitant to act on their anger because both humankind and mutants had lost a great deal.

With this new ability to kill vampires and their army not leaving our shores, I'm afraid for what our nation's immediate future will be."

*

"My fellow Americans, as most of you are aware, earlier today the blue haze which caused The Shattering dissipated. My scientists tell me the haze is most likely gone for good. While this is welcome news, the changes caused to our genetic codes remain. It is the belief of our brightest scientists that even with the haze gone, mutations are likely to continue among our children. There is even a high probability that future generations of children born after the blue haze will also go through The Shattering. The warning you should take from my words is this: the mutants of our nation are still its future and what they become is what our human race will be for the rest of our time on this planet.

"Because of this turn of events, The Angel's army will no longer be able to head to Europe and Africa to assist in freeing the human populations on those continents. We do not have the necessary equipment to safely ship or fly the millions of soldiers the war would require under the cover of darkness. Instead, we will need to turn to ourselves and work together in this time of change to forge our nation in the image we wish it to become.

"In two hours, the sun will set on the east coast enabling our vampire soldiers to come out of their places of hiding. I have spoken to The Angel, and she stated the desire of her troops is to return to their homes. This will be a mass of movement across our nation over the next week as many of them are on opposite coasts from where they began. I do not know what changes, if any, will accompany them as a result of the haze being gone.

"What I will say is all humans should remain indoors after sundown and allow the vampires free travel to return to their homes. Those of you who have grievances against their kind, remember: the vampires remaining on our shores are those that fought to free you from enslavement, they are not the ones that abused you.

"Any of you that have homes which can be used as shelters for the vampires, please mark them in some way. During their travels as dawn approaches, the vampires will need to hide from the sun. Please put some type of identifying sign or flag outside your residence so they know they can safely take shelter with you. This will help prevent the vampires from disturbing those people that wish to remain unbothered.

"We will work through the coming difficulties together over the next weeks and months. Due to this unforeseen event, I am rescinding my decision to resign and will instead work through the remainder of the two years of the current presidential term. I believed at the moment I made my decision that we had made it through our most trying times together, and my resignation would help the nation move on and heal. It is not appropriate for me to relinquish my responsibilities as your commander-in-chief when there is such uncertainty created by this new event.

"Please remain strong and vigilant in the days and weeks to come. The tasks we have laid out for ourselves have not been altered by the new circumstances. We will continue to repair and rebuild the infrastructure which we lost over this past year. Electricity, water, and phone systems will continue to be expanded as we work together to get them back online. All citizens who have occupations that have not yet been revived, I urge you to offer your services to your local government in any way to help our critical services be restored."

CHAPTER THIRTY-THREE
THE HUNGER

Two Months Post Haze
Washington D.C.

"We are going to have to form a unity government." President Thomas is addressing a mixed meeting of his advisors and mutant leaders as well. "Cora, as the leader of the mutant army, you are the obvious voice of vampires and the other mutants. They know you and trust you. Also, most of the remaining humans appreciate what you have done for us. Even with that level of familiarity or appreciation, it doesn't mean this will be easy."

"I don't understand what will be difficult about it. We have different needs than you humans do and should therefore have our own voices in government."

"Your ages are one problem. You should have your own voices, but legally you are still adolescents. The oldest of your kind is maybe fourteen. That, of course, is just a legal hurdle which we can remedy easily through congress. The greater difficulty is with what your kind now represent or at least what you supposedly represent." The president looks over at Dr. Usachova and frowns. "The people are beginning to understand what we have known since The Shattering Event first occurred: humanity is about to become extinct. We will now be working on legislation and governance with a new race that will replace us on this planet, and it isn't something people will continue to accept gracefully."

"There won't be problems caused by the vampires, Mr. President. You saw during our return to our homes after the haze vanished that there were no incidents caused by our kind. We just want life to return to normal. We want things back the way they were before."

President Thomas sits down with an exhausted and morose expression which Cora doesn't understand.

"Dr. Usachova, tell her."

"Cora, I have studied every possible way humans and vampires could coexist, but I always arrive at one ultimate result that cannot be avoided. Based on observed cellular changes, it is believed that every human child born from this point on will mutate during puberty. There will no longer be a human race as we know it."

"Yes, you have said so before."

"But the long-term implications of this are what you need to understand. You and the other arch-vampires feed on other vampires, but most of your kind feed on humans. Eventually, the food source of the majority of vampires will become extinct. Before that happens, the shortages will cause the regular vampires to fight over a diminishing food supply. There will be wars and a high probability that your kind will once again choose to enslave humans to ensure there is some form of human blood for them to eat. We will die out no matter what is done, but you will have to enslave us to ensure your kind do not also become extinct."

"But humans don't live forever, the rest of you will die out in seventy or eighty years. So are you telling me no matter what we do, we will all starve to death in the end?"

"That is something we have to research and figure out a way to avoid if we can. The time for normal humans is over. For those not yet born, the only non-mutated portion of a person's life is before they hit puberty. From what I understand, vampires do not currently drink from children, but when the human population starts dying off, that will become one of the only sources of non-mutated blood to use.

"The problem with that is even if you enslave humanity right now and force us into breeding programs, the numbers of human children you would need to feed on is greater than the numbers that can be conceived. There are only three possibilities we have figured out so far for your continued survival. Our first option is clones. We can begin growing human clones with the hope that the blood from them will sustain the regular class of vampires. Our second option is to attempt genetic manipulation of some other animal species to develop a suitable human blood alternative.

"The third option is what you must do for yourselves." Dr. Usachova blushes slightly at the thought. "Cora, your vampires need to start having children. I know you are all young, but your bodies are physically capable, and we need to find out if there is any hope for humanity to live on in your form. If you and the other vampires are incapable of having children, then the time of humanity is truly over. However, if you are still physically able to become pregnant and give birth, your own offspring might be the source of your survival."

President Thomas speaks up from his chair. "As you now understand, all of our options are based on your ability to reproduce. If your kind cannot produce children, then all hope for the future is lost and all of humanity's desire to help you will fade away. Every living being, human or mutant, will devolve into a self-serving struggle of the last living humans on the planet. There would be uncontrolled chaos as people lose hope and the will to live. The whole point of civilization is to ensure the survival of future generations. You need to do your part in proving to the people that we are struggling for a purpose greater than ourselves. You need to give us proof that there is a future with your kind."

The Angel looks at her fellow mutant representatives and back to the president with a perplexed expression on her face before bursting out in laughter. The tension built by the doctor and the president's words washes away as the assembled group all begin to laugh or chuckle in some form of release.

"You should have removed your caps so I could read your minds, it would have made this a lot less awkward." Cora smiles softly. "This is an area some of the mutants have spoken about with their parents, but I see now it is a matter of national importance as well.

"This past year has been a difficult one on those of us that mutated. It was not just our bodies that grew the days we endured Shatterbones, our hormones surged as well. The world was filled with teenagers who suddenly had adult bodies, and we were forced in many instances to be without clothes until we could find items that fit our new shapes or appendages." Her wings lift behind her in response. "Things have happened between many of us; they are private moments, but I can tell you there is hope for human kind. I will personally work with Dr. Usachova so she can record the progress of my own pregnancy. Lloyd and I conceived a child over three months ago, and I believe the gestation period for mutant pregnancies will be different than that of regular humans; it will take longer to reach full term."

Dr. Usachova stands up in anger. "How could you keep this a secret from us, Cora? There are things that must be done, supplements that you must take to ensure your baby's health." Raising her voice almost to a shout, "You were pregnant and fighting in a war? And you almost left again to fight in Europe, how could you be so reckless!"

"Please calm down, Doctor. This was a private matter that I discussed with my family. You are aware my mother is a nurse, and you should know my powers give me the ability to self-monitor my baby's health. I didn't know my pregnancy or any other would become a matter of national importance, but I will let my fellow vampires know the significance of what it currently means."

CHAPTER THIRTY-FOUR
FRIEND AND FOE

Three Months Post Haze
Washington D.C.

"Mr. President, this is our chance to get rid of the mutants. They are weak, and we have the weaponry to eliminate them for good."

"How many times do people have to tell you everyone's genetic structure has changed?"

"They are lying to you, Mr. President. That Usachova woman is being controlled by the mutants. They are manipulating her thoughts to tell you what you want to hear. Our genes may have been altered, and they may not have. The scientists I've spoken with all believe the children conceived from this point on will be born normal now that the haze is gone. They will be born and grow up like us. Real humans!"

"Bradley, we have been through a lot of things together. I accepted your premise that we had to kill the civilians in Richmond to win that battle, it made sense and it worked. I agreed with your idea to use a nuke against the enemy in Washington…"

"And if you did what I told you to do and blown those monsters to hell in that battle, we wouldn't have this problem now. You could have eliminated all of the arch-vampire leaders, and now we could do what we want with the rest of them."

"There was no one hundred percent guarantee the bomb would destroy all the enemy vampires and then we would have been facing other new threats without The Angel to direct her forces."

"But we've won the war now and we can finally eliminate them."

"Are you listening to yourself? These are the nation's children you are talking about, they are our future. Are you really suggesting we should kill every child that was born before the blue haze?"

"No, Mr. President. I want you to kill every child that was born before or during the blue haze. In fact, my information suggests we should end the term of any current pregnancy. Only those children that are conceived from this moment on should be considered viable."

"Bradley, I want you to tell me where you are."

"Why, so you can send one of your mutant controllers out to get me? The joint chiefs agree with me. The Chinese and Koreans have already begun purging their lands of mutants and children; if we don't do it as well, we will lose everything."

"The Chinese and Koreans have been enslaved from day one by vampires. They haven't had the opportunity for freedom or the choice to work with their mutants before. Don't confuse the Chinese people's actions of revenge with the correct course for all of humanity. Of course they would use the new weakness of the vampires against them. I would have as well if the haze lifted before our people were freed by The Angel."

"The Angel? Listen to what you call her, and tell me she isn't controlling your mind. She is no angel, Mr. President. That woman and her kind are demons and must be eliminated."

"I will give you one more chance to come in and discuss this face to face."

"I'm not coming in, James. I think your unwillingness to deal with the mutants as the threat that they are shows you are under their control. I will not follow the orders of a president whose mind is being manipulated by those pale freaks."

"Bradley, you're fired."

"I don't recognize your authority to fire me, your mind has been compromised."

The line goes dead, and President Thomas looks around the room at the assembled advisors.

"Admiral Pembroke, you are my new director of intelligence."

"Thank you, sir."

"First question, what can he do?"

"He has access to all surviving military personnel; names and current addresses. He will know their dispositions and whether they are someone he can trust and count on."

"Can't we block his access to our databases?"

The admiral motions to one of his aids, "Get it done; have Bradley Hoskins locked out of everything." The man leaves and Pembroke looks at the president while shaking his head. "Bradley didn't do this on a whim, Mr. President. We can lock him out of our systems, but he likely already has all of the information he needs. If I were him, I would have compiled all of those lists before I discussed the issue with you. He knew what you would say, that's why he did it over the phone."

"Bring The Angel in here, let's see what she has to say about this."

"Before we bring her in, Mr. President, may I have a word with you privately?"

Taking a deep breath and rubbing his forehead, he nods. "Everyone, give us a few minutes."

"Mr. President, this will sound harsh, but we should consider some of what Hoskins was saying. There is still a great deal of animosity among the general populace over what the mutants put us through this past year. We missed an opportunity to weaken the power structure of the vampires in particular. I'm not suggesting we do anything to directly harm them, but it might not be a bad thing to allow the people to get some form of revenge against the mutants for what they've been put through."

"The ones working with us aren't the bad ones. They fought and died to free us."

"We have some continuing problems that make me question how honestly they have been working with us. From day one of this freakish calamity, the Navy has been losing ships. At first, we thought other nations might be sinking our vessels in retaliation. Perhaps because they believed we were responsible for the haze and mutations. But our ships continued to disappear over this past year. The vessels that went missing didn't have children on board who could mutate, they didn't approach any shores, and they took no aggressive actions against the vampires.

"Several of the groups that disappeared were anchored or adrift in deep waters to conserve fuel and were no threat to any of the mutants. In fact, the arch-vampires would have been the only ones able to reach them and would have had to make quite the effort to fly out to where our ships were located. They must have seen them as quite a threat to carry out the attacks that sunk them. You should ask The Angel how innocent she and her mutants are regarding our missing vessels.

"Another area you must consider is about the things the mutants did before the war. They may have fought these battles to free us, but they still have the blood of millions of humans on their hands from the first day of The Shattering. If it were a human, if a human murdered someone and then went on to save others, wouldn't we still require that person to be held accountable for his crimes?"

"What could we do to hold them accountable?"

"Let the people work through their hatred of the mutants. We could let the people rise up in certain circumstances. Let them take out their aggressions, and then after a time, arrest the people that commit crimes against the vampires. The human populace will gain sympathy for the mutants for what happens to them, and we get some criminals that are itching to cause problems off the street. It is something you should consider. Our nation is hanging together by a thread right now, we need a win in the human corner for once."

"I'll consider it. Now have everyone come back in and send for The Angel as well."

*

The Angel and her people listen to a recording of the call.

"What do you have to say about this, Cora? Is there any truth to what Bradley was saying? Is Dr. Usachova being manipulated by you and your kind? Are any of us?"

"I think there is some mind control happening, Mr. President."

"What!" Admiral Pembroke stands up and takes a step toward her in anger before being knocked back into his chair by her wing.

"I am not manipulating anyone. You need to relax, Admiral, if you want the longevity of your position to last more than today. What I meant is I believe a mutant might be controlling Mr. Hoskins. Someone must be tipping his personal prejudices to the breaking point. I sensed that his thoughts were his own, but they were twisted somehow while he was speaking. He never would have disrespected you like that without manipulation, Mr. President, no matter how greatly he felt about our kind."

"Perhaps he is reacting to vampires eradicating our peaceful Navy."

Head cocked to the side, The Angel's expression belies curiosity then becomes one of concern. "I don't know anything about problems with the Navy. What has been happening?"

"We have a large number of ships and their crews missing."

"How long have they been going missing?"

"They started sinking or being destroyed on the first day of The Shattering, and the disappearances have continued throughout the war. Two days ago, we lost another cruiser, and a submarine failed to make contact a week earlier."

"Were they close to shore?"

"No, all in deep waters as agreed. They remained away from our shores and made no attempts to attack mutants."

"Only vampires could make it out that far, but none of my people have attacked those vessels; we consider them our allies. I will check into it but still do not believe Mr. Hoskins was influenced by the missing ships or he would have mentioned them."

"Explain to me why a vampire would manipulate Hoskins to have him suggest we start killing other vampires?"

"We must have missed someone during the war. There may still be vampires out there that want humanity enslaved but with enslaving you being off the table because of our victory, the next probable step would be to start a war between us to make us want to enslave or kill you. There is a tremendous level of animosity by humans growing against us in the country, so it doesn't take great skill to push someone like Mr. Hoskins over the edge."

Looking directly at the president, she continues. "Even now, there is no way for humans to fight a war with vampires and win. We are weak but even with our vulnerabilities, we could remove humans as a threat within four weeks if we wanted. We would sustain losses but could wipe out your kind within a month if we tried. If the plans Mr. Hoskins are being pushed toward succeed, all of humanity could end up enslaved again or more likely, dead."

"And you can assure us you aren't manipulating our thoughts like Bradley suggested?"

"I can't assure you of anything, Mr. President. My vampires and I are not doing any manipulation, but my saying so will do nothing to change your personal level of trust in me. If I was manipulating you, I would still tell you I wasn't.

"The digital caps you and your men continue to wear are still working. I can no longer read your thoughts without physically touching you as I mentioned before, and I have no information that other vampires have greater powers than myself since the blue haze is gone.

"May I offer a suggestion for security?"

"Yes, please."

"I imagine you do not keep your caps on all the time, and there could be other persons that have been manipulated the way Mr. Hoskins was. They could be manipulated when they take off their caps to sleep or bathe. This will require a great deal of trust on your part, but I would like to scan the minds of every one of the people in your administration to ensure there are no spies or assassins among the people you trust."

The second the last words leave The Angel's lips, a Secret Service agent steps through the doorway and draws his pistol on the president. The arm holding the firearm is severed by the quick blade of The Angel's personal guard. The one bullet the agent fires flies wide with his arms awkward descent to the ground. The bullet hits Cora in the chest, and she scratches the wound lightly as if she has an itch. The bullet seems to work itself backward out of the hole and falls, bouncing on the table when her body finishes healing the wound.

The armless, bleeding man is now barely visible under a pile of fellow agents that are holding him down.

"He is wearing a digital cap, Mr. President. You should have your people check that his is functional, and I implore you to let us check the rest of your staff for others that might have been manipulated."

"Check him first. See if you can look in his mind and find out who is behind this."

She removes the digital cap from the wounded agent and places her hand on his forehead.

"I can see who it is, but I haven't met him yet. This agent doesn't know anything about the mutant that altered his thoughts. It happened a few days ago while he was at the store with his wife. I know this man just tried to kill you, Mr. President, but he wasn't in control of his actions. Please keep that in mind when dealing with him. If there is nothing more you need from me, I am going to the store where he was shopping to see if I can pick up a trail of the vampire responsible for doing this."

"What about checking my other people?"

"Brian will stay and do it. Brian, look into this man's thoughts and see if you can find the mutant that took control of him." While Brian leans over the wounded agent, The Angel shakes the president's hand.

"Brian can't see all thoughts, but is adept at spotting deception. He will be able to clear the rest of your personnel. You should change your protocols immediately and never allow one of your people to return to your side without first being scanned for altered thoughts."

"I've got him," Brian says while standing up. "When you get to the store, speak with the manager. I believe her memory was altered to erase the stores video of the event."

"Thank you, Brian."

CHAPTER THIRTY-FIVE
BETRAYAL

Four Months Post Haze
Undisclosed Location

The smoldering wreckage of two city blocks brings Cora to her knees.

"How many people were killed?"

"Ninety-seven vampires and their families were registered in the buildings when the fires started. Three hundred and eighty-eight lives altogether."

"And you're sure it was arson?"

"The fire started in the morning, just after sunrise. Gasoline trucks were apparently brought in, and the grounds around the buildings were soaked with fuel. When it was lit, the sun prevented the vampires from leaving, and the fire ensured that none of the humans were able to escape.

"Our fire departments tried to put out the fires, but the size of the blaze and amount of accelerant used made the fire too strong. It engulfed the buildings too quickly for my people to have any effect. I'm sorry this happened in my city, Cora. I hope this doesn't cause difficulties between vampires and humans."

The man steps back from the look of fury expressed in his direction.

"This is the sixteenth fire I have been witness to in the last two days, Mr. Clyburn, and I'm afraid it will have a major impact in our relations. This is happening nationwide, and we won't stand by and allow vampires and their families to be executed in their sleep. This is your community, and you need to find out who is responsible for this terrorism or my people will have to do something about it."

*

"The humans will continue to kill us! We have to do something about it."

The Angel and twenty arch-vampires are meeting in Washington D.C. The escalating violence against their kind is forcing their hand. In the past month, organized cases of arson have been increasing, and over three thousand vampires and their friends or family have been killed.

The mystery vampire, named Kevin, that had influenced the president's director of intelligence and a Secret Service agent was found, but ended up being a dead end. Instead of uncovering a conspiracy to turn humans and vampires against each other, Kevin had been on a crusade of revenge against President Thomas. Kevin was orphaned shortly after the president declared humanities surrender early in the war, and he was only trying to have the president killed by using already existing tensions.

"There aren't enough vampires like us to find the people responsible. Even if we gathered everyone we know that can read minds, there would be less than five hundred of us. How would we go house to house and search the minds of millions of humans in the few hours that the sun is down?"

"We put them all together," a voice calmly states in the silence of her question. "We tried to be nice, we tried to do the right thing, but it isn't working. You all know it isn't working. The attacks against us are increasing. Each time a group of us is killed, it emboldens more humans to try their hand at killing vampires."

"Brian? I can't believe you are suggesting this. You were with me from the beginning. You were the one that suggested to me and Lloyd that we should fight to free the people."

"And I am now telling you I was wrong." His tone is sad yet defiant. "The human race is going extinct. The president knows this. All of his advisors have told us so in our meetings with them. Why should we allow them to kill us off when they are dying out? They know their days are numbered and are trying to take us down with their sinking ship."

"We can't just enslave them. I will not live in a society that treats humans as cattle or pets. If that is what you have in mind, then it will mean war." Her stance and the tightened grip on her sword tells the group the seriousness of her statement more than her commanding tone.

"I don't want slaves, Cora. None of us do. I want to sleep during the day without fearing for my family's lives. I don't want the people I care about slaughtered simply because they love me and won't leave my side to join some anti-vampire human brigade. I don't think we should enslave the humans, I think we should kick them out."

"Kick them out? Kick them out of what, the country?"

"Yes. We should remove them from part of it. We should claim certain territories for vampires and expel non-family humans. Only allow those people with a vampire relative or with children that can still turn remain in our chosen territory and kick everyone else out of our lands."

"There are a lot of humans that won't want to leave. Many have families that lived in the same states and towns for generations."

"And those are exactly the kind of people that are burning the buildings around us and killing us all. In their minds, this is their planet, it is their state or their town, and they are defending their territory against us invading vampires. I have read some of their minds, and I know you have too. It doesn't matter that we come from the same towns or even have distant relatives in common in some cases. They see us as an aberration that must be destroyed. Our only two choices remaining are to kill them or move them somewhere else before they kill us."

"We could move."

"We could move where? No matter where we decide to go, the end result is the same. Humans are everywhere, and we have to remove them from the territory we choose as our own. Their willingness to relocate will determine their survival."

The Angel stands and gazes at the assembled group. She is searching each mind as she looks for the best possible answer as they sit quietly and wait. Unlike some, her psychic abilities have grown since the blue haze departed. She is able to peer into minds from quite a distance now when she chooses. For her interactions with the president and other humans, she still places a hand on individuals to give them the impression she needs physical contact to read their thoughts. It has helped assuage some of their fears of privacy.

The Angel stretches her wings and nods her head. "It feels wrong, but I know you are right. We saved the humans lives and set them free, we have earned a right to have a territory of our own where we won't have to live in fear. If we don't do this, it will only be a short matter of time before even I am pushed to the breaking point and start seeking revenge for the vampires they have killed.

"The coasts of our nation would be most suitable locations for humans to survive in comfort. They will have access to fishing, ample farmlands, and we can move the nation's cattle stocks closer to the coastal states as well to ensure they have enough food to provide for themselves. We could take the heartland and spread out from there as their numbers continue to diminish over time."

"And what do we do about a food supply?" another voice asks.

"Dr. Usachova and other scientists are working on cloning programs that will grow human tissue and blood in laboratories. We should ensure the technical expertise necessary for such work is absorbed and transferred to as many of us as possible. Moving humans out of the territory we claim or allowing them to stay will do nothing to help us with long-term survival. The doctor explained to me a day will come when humans will be gone, and the only humans the runners can find to drink from would be our own children before they mutate. There won't be enough children born which will lead to the potential for starvation as well as war and conflict among ourselves. It is better that we live separately from the humans now and put all of our energy toward cloning research and development."

*

"Where the hell is she? Where are her people?"

"Mr. President, I'm not sure what you expect."

"The vampires are starting to kill civilians, and she is their damned leader! I expect her to keep me informed of what is happening. Has anyone heard anything from them?"

"All of the vampires left Washington after the biggest fire in Wichita over a week ago. No one has had direct contact with them except for the police and firefighters on the scenes of the latest attacks."

"How many humans have been killed?"

"Not nearly as many as the vampires, sir."

"How many?"

"One hundred and twelve as of the second attack last night. I should remind you that nearly ten thousand humans and vampires have been killed in the fire bombings of their homes. You know their response to those murders has been expected."

"What I expected was some information, to be kept in the loop. That's what I was expecting."

And I was expecting you to address the nation condemning the attacks against my people.

The Angel's voice echoes in the president's mind as if it was shouted in the room, yet she is nowhere to be seen.

"Did you hear that?" he asks his secretary.

"Hear what, sir?"

Turning to the others in the room, "Did any of you hear that?"

The looks returned to him cause him to question his own sanity.

You aren't going crazy, Mr. President. I am just outside and would like to come in.

"Mr. President, The Angel is out on the White House lawn."

"Don't call her that! Her name is Cora. Let her in, but I want everyone to stay and hear what she has to say for the actions of her people."

Bewildered expressions are shared at his anger for the leader of the vampires.

"You no longer want to call my vampires your people or the nation's children, I see," the Angel says as she walks through the doors. "Is that why you said nothing to the nation to condemn the attacks against my vampires?"

"I spoke to people to remain calm and not act out of anger or revenge."

"You said nothing!" The Angel's voice explodes with force through the room. Her anger turns her words into a physical manifestation which tweaks the nerve endings of everyone present. They recoil in pain and fear from the assault; the Secret Service agents draw their weapons against her, but she raises her hand and silently forces them to drop their firearms to the ground.

"For weeks, my people have been slaughtered in their sleep by humans, and you said nothing about how it was evil. You said nothing about bringing those that were doing the killings to justice. You said nothing that would make a difference in the minds that chose to do us harm and in your empty rhetoric, I saw that you, too, are bitter and angry that your race will go extinct and ours will live on.

"Me and my vampires could do exactly what you fear, we could enslave you. We could murder you out of some misguided belief in revenge the way you have done to us, but we aren't the evil ones. We won't stand idly by while innocent lives are being destroyed as you and your people have. We will take action that will ensure the continued survival of human and mutant kind."

The president raises his hand to block the bright light The Angel is beginning to emit. "What are you going to do?"

"We are splitting up the nation."

President Thomas drops heavily into his chair and The Angel's light begins to diminish.

"Vampires will be moving to the center of the country and removing humans to the coasts. We will no longer allow your kind to murder us or our families. Any human that remains in the central states will do so only with our authorization, they will be subject to our rule, and anyone that attempts to fight us will be killed."

"You can't split up this nation!"

"You are the one that has split up this nation, Mr. President. You have allowed humans to slaughter my people and their families. It has taken every bit of my power and influence to prevent a wholesale extermination of the humans in the areas in which we were attacked. You are fortunate there are more examples of your betrayal from the past. I was able to draw on them so my vampires don't feel they are being specifically targeted because of our mutation."

"What examples are those?"

"We aren't just the nation's children anymore. Lloyd died for you! I chose to fight for you, and in Washington, I chose to die for you and all of the humans in order to keep you safe, to give you another chance to live. Me, my vampires, and the other mutants are the veterans of our nation's most recent war and our government and people have a long history of betraying its veterans.

"I gave my soldiers examples of how the Vietnam veterans were spit on and allowed to starve, homeless in the streets. They were able to read and watch examples of how veterans were left to die by injury or suicide because the V.A. did nothing for them. And now we have a 'President' that allows us, the veterans that sacrificed their lives to free this nation, to be burned in their sleep without so much as a statement of solidarity from their commander-in-chief.

"What do you have to say for yourself? Tell these people why you wouldn't condemn the attacks."

"I didn't realize I hadn't condemned what was going on. It truly didn't occur to me." He reflexively touches the digital cap on his head while he speaks.

"And yet you were ready to make a national speech tonight to condemn my people for the counter-attack that killed only a hundred humans. That should tell you everything you need to know about your level of concern for us.

"Go ahead and make your appearance on television tonight. Go tell your people that the personal failings of their president has led to the fracturing of our once great nation. Tell them how your inaction has allowed ten thousand of the people that freed humanity from the bonds of slavery to be murdered. Here is a list of the states we will be taking as our own. Tell your humans they are no longer welcome to remain there and to get out!"

The paper containing the list slowly drifts to the table as The Angel's body has already left the room. The people remaining are shaken by the encounter, some are visibly pale as a result of the energy she was emitting. There is no doubt that her words were sincere and her meaning was clear. On the paper laying in front of the president, two simple sentences are written above the list of states.

All humans with no vampire family connections are ordered to leave the states listed below. Failure to leave the area will result in removal by force or death.

Montana
Wyoming
Colorado
North Dakota
South Dakota
Nebraska
Kansas
Minnesota
Iowa
Missouri
Wisconsin
Illinois
Michigan

and Indiana

The coastal states will be the allowed human territory as those are the regions which are best suited for your survival. Any further actions against vampires or their families will be dealt with immediately and harshly.

Cora Taylor

*

"You know he was lying right?" The Angel's guard asks as they fly away.

"I knew weeks ago that the president was advised to let our people be slaughtered for national unity. Their digital caps no longer work against my ability to read their minds."

"Did you let them kill our people? Were you able to stop this from happening?"

"No, there wasn't anything I could have done to change the outcome. The president isn't directing the attacks against us, none of his people are. What's happening out there is the real manifestation of humans' hatred against our kind. The only thing I could have done was force the president to declare outrage against the attacks, but the attacks would have continued. I was hoping the president would come around and show his support for us, but that didn't happen. The humans are tired of sharing their cities and towns with mutants and what we are doing now is the best solution for all, although I am sure they won't see it that way at first. We have to separate our races so that each may live out their lives in some form of peace."

"About our future, isn't it dangerous placing all vampires in one specific region? They could target us all without fear of harming humankind."

"We have made plans for that."

*

"Mr. President, The Angel might have given us the perfect opportunity to remove the mutants as a threat," Admiral Pembroke suggests after the vampire delegation has left. "If we allow them to remove humans from the central U.S. and only have mutants and those loyal to them in that area, we won't have to worry about human casualties if we attack."

"Attack with what?" he snaps back at his director of intelligence. "We don't have anything that will affect them."

"We have nukes, sir. Nuclear weapons can take them out."

Three secret service agents and the admiral's secretary draw their weapons and fire at the admiral's head, killing him. In unison, the four men speak with a pre-programmed message.

197

"We have anticipated the possibility of you choosing to use nuclear weapons and have taken steps to ensure this choice of action is not carried out. Any recommendation of nuclear weapons against the mutants will result in death. Any attempts to use nuclear weapons against us will result in the wholesale slaughter of the human race. The choice is yours, live in peace or die."

The four men drop their weapons and begin looking around the room unsure of what they have done or how they moved from their original positions.

CHAPTER THIRTY-SIX
ANNIHILATION

Six Months Post Haze
Washington D.C.

Tensions are strung to their breaking point as the crowd makes a path for President Thomas to enter the situation room.

"How long has this been taking place?"

"The video feeds started this morning. The mutants wanted us to see it, so they unlocked the satellite channels. I know you have resigned, but we felt we should bring you back to the White House to see what is taking place."

The video screens in the room have images from multiple sources. Satellite coverage is showing bloodshed in multiple cities and news footage is being broadcast as well. The footage in every screen and from all angles is showing vampires killing humans. Their heads are being cut or ripped from their torsos, and the bodies are being allowed to bleed out.

"How many people are they killing?"

"From what we can tell, they are killing every human that is too old to mutate. It is a complete slaughter of humankind."

"Is this retaliation for something a human group did?"

"This isn't retaliation, sir. As you can see, they are letting the blood spill. We received word the mutants have perfected a blood-cloning system and are removing humans as the only obstacle and threat they have."

"How long do we have before they make it here?"

"I don't understand, sir?"

"Damn it! Look at the screens, they're killing all of us! How long before they reach Washington?"

"I'm sorry, sir, I thought someone told you, these feeds are from Europe."

"Is any of it on our shores yet?"

"No sir, none of this is happening here yet. The resettlement of humans from the interior states is nearly completed, and while there are continued instances of resistance, they are put down quickly and quite harshly by the vampires. There will likely be several million casualties once the process is complete."

"Have you heard anything from The Angel?"

"No sir, nothing from her directly. We only get the news broadcasts they show as warnings of what is done to those who attack them. Perhaps if you sent word to the vampires, they might respond. We have been trying to communicate daily and have had no reply."

"I can't. I'm the one that caused all of this. She knew I was lying when I told her I didn't know I wasn't defending them. Did you know that? She knew from the first day Pembroke suggested it that I wasn't going to defend them."

"We know, sir; that might be why you are the only one that can open a discussion with them. You made it a point to remind us constantly that the mutants are only children. Their silence could be nothing more than anger at you for your betrayal."

"What could I say?"

"You could apologize. It is impossibly simple, sir, but I think an apology is all Cora and her people want. It won't change the situation our nation is in, but it could help prevent what is happening in Europe from coming over here."

"What about Asia and Africa, how are they holding up?"

"Asia is a dead continent. As you know, all of the Asian territories rose up to destroy their mutants once the haze dissipated. Communications went dark so we didn't hear the result, but satellite scans show few signs of life remaining. Whole cities were burned to the ground to prevent vampires from having places of refuge from the sun. At night, the remaining mutants worked to destroy what was left of the humans. I'm sure the animosity was amplified by the fact that the mind-controlling mutants in those areas were dominated by those who favored enslaving humans.

"Africa is in the stone age. The cities are gone as well, but the humans seem to have won the war in most parts of the continent. How long they survive is anyone's guess since they murdered all of their children to prevent future mutations from occurring."

"So that only leaves North and South America?"

"Yes. The Canadians are splitting up along similar lines as ourselves, humans to the coasts and mutants to the interior. Central and South America have been largely kept in check by their werewolf populations. They have protected the vampires during the day which blocked humans from starting the fires and the bloodshed we experienced after the haze."

"Does The Angel or her people know about the blood substitute?"

"I doubt there are many things we know of which she isn't also aware. Before Dr. Usachova left to live with the vampires, she told me The Angel's powers increased after the haze, and she wasn't sure what her limits were or if she had any."

Despite the engrossing nature of the European footage on the screens before them, while looking around, the sound has been muted from the feeds and all eyes seem in transfixed attention to the discussion between former President Thomas and President Harlow.

Nodding his head at the suggestion, "Do you know how I can contact her?"

Before Harlow is able to respond, the phone at the conference table begins to ring. President Harlow looks at James and shrugs. "It's probably for you. We really don't know the extent of her powers."

Hesitantly, James Thomas picks up the phone. "Hello?"

"Hello, President Thomas."

"Hello, Cora. Are you aware of what is happening in Europe?"

"I know what they are doing, and it is unfortunate. We gave our allies in Europe the process requirements for cloning human blood, and they have determined their own path forward. Only England is handling the situation in the same manner we have currently chosen."

"I'm sorry for not supporting your people, Cora. I know my decisions were wrong. I want to thank you for not making the rest of humanity suffer for my mistakes."

"I am aware it causes uncertainty for humans that my kind have such powers and abilities. I hope once our territories are more clearly defined we can begin working together as separate groups. I always had the personal belief that regardless of the form it takes, we share the long-term goal of the continued survival of the human race."

"I am no longer the president, but I will do what I can as a representative to work between our two groups for continued cooperation and understanding."

"Thank you, President Thomas. You should contact Representative Cavanaugh from the New Oregon Territory. He has some ideas about what might work for our two groups to help the children in your territories that endure Shatterbones. Things can be done to prevent them from becoming problems for you."

CHAPTER THIRTY-SEVEN
OUR FUTURE

Seven Months Post Haze
Oregon Territory

The floor is littered with bodies. The difficulty of making it across the large room without stepping on someone's arm or tripping over a torso is compounded by the darkness. Holding a small flashlight, Cora's father traverses the treacherous landscape in a desperate attempt to get to the bathroom.

Cora delivered her baby, Grace, earlier. The timing of her delivery and the sun rising trapped her personal guard as well as those friends that came by to support her. The sun shutters were closed to seal the home's windows, and the vampires eventually fell asleep in the living room.

Robert and his wife, Tanya, are spending the day in the downstairs office while Cora is sleeping in their room with her baby. The birth was a joyous affair with Grace being a healthy and extremely vocal baby girl.

Giving him a small shock, the door opens when he reaches for the handle and he receives a smile from Dr. Usachova.

"I'm sorry, Mr. Taylor, I didn't mean to startle you."

"It's fine. I forgot there were other people in the house that weren't asleep."

"Could I speak with you and your wife after you're done?"

"Sure. Just head into the office; Tanya is awake and I'll be there shortly."

Laughter greets Robert's ears as he opens the door. His wife and the doctor are having some sort of entertaining discussion.

"Did you check on the kids?"

"Yes, they're still playing outside. Claw Water and the others are with them."

"Claw Water." Tanya shakes her head. "I was barely willing to let my children play with a stranger's dog before The Shattering, and now they are being protected by werewolves. What happened to our world?"

Patting her leg as he sits down, he smiles. "I still don't trust most people's pets. I think the fact they were monkeys helps, but being able to speak with them makes the greatest difference to me. I need the ability to communicate to build trust."

The doctor smiles at their interaction and takes their words as everything else she hears into her overall understanding of what is happening. All things in this new world are data and she no longer leaves her research mode.

"I wanted to speak with you about Grace, the rest of your children, and what I have been able to discover these last few months."

"Is everything okay?" The apprehensive look on the new grandparent's faces betray the high level of their concern.

"Don't worry, your children are fine, and I'm sure Grace is as well. They are all healthy, but there are some physiological changes we discovered, and we have to check Grace to see what variance she may have. There is obviously a difference in genetic orientation between humans and the vampires. Vampire gestation is forty-eight weeks, not forty like regular humans for example.

"Longevity is one of the areas we are studying. We need DNA samples from you, your children, and Grace. What we are hoping to discover or determine is if changes have been written into the genetic code to alter lifespan."

"You think the vampires might live forever?"

"It is a possibility based on tales from history."

"Of course, we'll give you anything you need for your research. When do you think you will have an answer?"

"That is the difficult part of research. What I am looking at are the ends of chromosomes called telomeres. They slowly diminish over time as the cells of the body replicate, and it is believed they are the reason people grow old. Unfortunately, it will take at least ten years to make any measurable determination of telomere length."

"Hell, in ten years we'll probably be able to see with our own eyes if they are going to live forever."

"Yes, well there is a chance that the vampires won't appear to age externally but will still be aging at the cellular level. That is why research and data are so important as opposed to observation…"

A buzzer on the desk rings.

"Three vehicles have stopped at the fence, armed humans are riding on the outside of two of them."

Now it is Dr. Usachova's turn to look alarmed, but Robert and Tanya seem relieved at the news.

Smiling, Tanya presses the intercom button. "We'll be right out."

"You should come with us, Tatyana; it's probably Grace's other grandparents."

*

Smiles, hugs, and surprised looks are shared by the Taylors when Greg and Evelyn Cavanaugh exit their vehicle carrying a new baby of their own.

"This is Lilly." Smiling, Evelyn holds her tiny infant for the assembly to see.

"I didn't even know you were pregnant! Did you?" Robert questions his wife who shakes her head in reply.

"She was a surprise for us as well." Greg smiles proudly. "There were so many things happening at the time, Evelyn didn't realize how she was feeling was due to a pregnancy and not the haze going away."

"So you became pregnant before the haze lifted?"

"Evelyn, Greg, this is Dr. Usachova. She used to…"

"Work for the president. Yes, I'm familiar with the name. Hello, I'm glad to finally meet you." Greg's handshake is enthusiastic to say the least.

"Greg has been wanting to meet with you to discuss research proposals on how to deal with future mutations in human territories," Evelyn offers. "Greg was in congress representing Oregon and is running for governor of the new Oregon Territory."

"I would be happy to speak with you. Anything we can do to minimize problems would be helpful."

A scream of pain from the side of the house has humans and werewolves running across the yard. Rounding the corner, Robert and Tanya are faced with a heartbreaking horror of their daughter, Elizabeth, writhing on the ground in agony. Her bones are snapping and her skin is distorting in unnatural angles as their support structures break.

"Claw Water, please get her inside. She can't be in the sunlight once the change is complete." Turning to Dr. Usachova and Greg Cavanaugh, "If you want to work together to minimize problems, figure out a way to keep the children safe when they change during the day. There has to be some type of test that tells us when the change is going to happen."

CHAPTER THIRTY-EIGHT
SHATTER RESEARCH CENTER FOUR

Nine Years Post Haze
Washington State

Evelyn is filled with motherly anxiety. In the seven years that the program has been in operation, there have been few fatalities. Few fatalities but still some, so not a perfect track record. All she can think when looking at Lilly is that her daughter is diminutive in scale compared to other girls her age. She is only four feet tall and fifty-five pounds. Of course, Evelyn is only five feet tall herself so she shouldn't expect her daughter to be at the same height as other children her age, at least that is what the doctors always tell her.

Your daughter will hit her true growth potential once she reaches puberty. Doctor Gregory kept reminding her over these last few weeks. Still, she is so small that the person she will be paired up with could pick her up and break her in half if they want. But she has been assured that isn't how any of the fatalities occurred. There were genetic anomalies in the children that prevented their pubescent change from completing its cycle, it caused them to grow weak and the adults they were paired with took the opportunity to kill them.

She is worried that Lilly might be one of those few because of her size but her genetic make-up is normal. If she didn't test normal, Lilly would not have been allowed to stay at home with her parents for the extra year. Most girls are taken to institutes at age seven and boys at eight. They arrive two years before they are supposed to hit puberty. The only exceptions are children like Lilly who have exceptionally wealthy parents and can afford the medical screens four times a day and security staff.

Evelyn stares at Lilly who is sitting across from her in the limousine. Lilly looks up from what she is reading and smiles at her mother briefly before seeming to return to her book. The ride is lonely and quiet without her husband, and she turns her gaze to one of the security vehicles driving beside the limo and the machine gun mounted soldier riding in the back.

"Are you okay, Mom?"

The soft voice of her daughter pulls her back to the present and away from her fears for a moment.

"I'm just going to miss you, sweetie."

"And you're afraid I'm going to get hurt?"

"Yes. I'm afraid for you."

Evelyn begins to cry.

"I'm afraid too, Mom. I've watched the videos and I know what to expect, but I'm still nervous that the person they'll pair me with will hurt me. That's why dad didn't come."

"No, Lilly," her mom says with an attempt at being sincere. "Your father is our territorial governor, he had to go to Washington today."

"I love you, Mom, but you and Dad need to coordinate your lies better. I'm almost nine, and he tells me a lot of things that he sees at the institutions. He tells me things you wish he would keep from me."

"What did he tell you?"

"He told me he's seen too many children turn with their puberty guides and couldn't bear to watch me go through it. Last night, he told me he loved me and that he made sure everything was in place for my arrival, but he couldn't come with and asked me to forgive him."

Evelyn is quiet for a moment, just nodding at what her daughter told her.

Puberty guides is the term used for criminals that are sentenced to be locked in rooms with children before they are about to mutate. The system was set up to control unwanted deaths or destruction in the human territories resulting from a child reaching puberty and going through The Shattering. Usually, only the largest and strongest individuals are paired with the children to ensure enough blood is present right after the change.

"Your father is in charge of institute oversight. He has seen things that…well, your father is a good man and loves you very much. As strong as he is, he has two weaknesses, you and me."

Lilly smiles.

"He isn't afraid you will get hurt or he would be with us. He wants to remember you as his little girl."

"He promised he would pick me up from the institution when Shatterbones is done."

"Please don't use that word, Lilly." Evelyn shivers as memories of her first exposure to the change at puberty are brought back. It unnerves her that today's children have adopted the term Shatterbones to describe what they will be going through.

Try as she might to remain composed for her daughter, Evelyn starts shivering and tears begin to stream from her eyes.

Forgetting her seatbelt, Lilly tries to stand up to cross to her mother's seat and give her a hug. "I'm sorry," she says before the seatbelt alarm rings auto-locking the limousines breaks and sending the security team into action.

The two security trucks next to the limo break and the teams jump out. Before Evelyn can protest, she is pulled from the car and Doctor Gregory is next to Lilly checking her blood.

Evelyn walks up to Sergeant Conner and slaps him in the face.

"Did I press my button?"

"No, ma'am."

"No, I didn't! You told me your men were trained. If they can't follow simple instructions, how am I supposed to feel safe?"

"Your husband changed our orders, ma'am."

Evelyn lowers her head, realizing she made the mistake. Of course her husband would do something like that. She should have rechecked with Conner after they left the house. She regains her anger and looks back at the sergeant.

"I don't care if my husband is the governor. Right now, you are transporting a mother and her child. She was only trying to give me a hug, that's what triggered the breaks and the alarm. Doctor Gregory will remain in the limo with us for the rest of the trip, and if my button isn't pressed, you will not let your men touch me. Do you understand?"

"Yes ma'am. It won't happen again, ma'am."

Evelyn walks back to the car where the doctor nods his approval before she gets back inside. This time, Lilly's eyes are filled with tears.

"I'm so sorry, Lilly. You know what they told you about staying seated while the car is moving."

Evelyn gives her daughter a long hug, and the journey continues once Doctor Gregory enters the cabin and sits next to Lilly.

*

The security trucks and limousine stop outside the main gate. Large black letters attached to the white wall proclaim *Washington Shatter Research Center 4*. Doctor Gregory checks Lilly's blood one more time before he steps out to begin the check in procedure.

This institute is a new facility. It was finished three years ago and started taking its first adolescents a year later. Most institutes are remodeled prisons, but this one is completely new and was designed in part as a research facility and also as a more comfortable place for the region's wealthiest children to spend The Shattering years.

"You're lucky to be here, Lilly. I've seen the pictures of the other institutes, and while they do their best to make the children comfortable, there is only so much interaction that can take place once you children are introduced to your puberty guides. Your room will be the same size as the one at our house."

"Do they make the guide stay in the room with me once Shatterbones...once The Shattering begins?"

"I don't think they would be able to take the guide out."

"They have to leave eventually, don't they? I mean, I don't want them sleeping in the room with me."

Evelyn shudders and closes her eyes knowing the videos they prepared for children are happy versions of what really takes place. The scripted movies are designed to give the children going to the institutes some understanding of what is in store, but not enough information to frighten them. Lilly doesn't understand that she won't want her guide to leave her side once The Shattering begins.

"They will remove your guide if he isn't to your liking."

Doctor Gregory returns to the car and asks Evelyn to step out.

"Lilly, your mom and I will have to walk in while the institute doctors check the vehicle and drive it in. Do you need anything?"

"Will you go far?"

"No, we will be walking right outside the car and you can see your mother through the window."

"Okay. Can I get one more hug?"

Evelyn steps forward to hug Lilly one last time, but the doctor puts his hand out and shakes his head. Evelyn slaps his hand out of the way and gives him that special look reserved for men when they do something extremely stupid. She leans in and gives her daughter one last hug. When she closes the car door, Lilly watches as her mom's finger starts wagging in the doctor's face. The lights surrounding the institute click on to illuminate the scene as dusk approaches.

*

Evelyn and Doctor Steiner are walking through a pale white corridor to the viewing room which overlooks Lilly's room.

"I am amazed you and your husband were able to keep Lilly with you for so long. Her tests show she could begin her cycle at any time."

"Doctor Gregory was doing her monitoring."

"Samuel Gregory?"

"Yes. He made the test, so we felt he would ensure us the most time before she had to be taken away from us."

Doctor Steiner wants to ignore her remark but isn't able to. He hears the same complaint from parents every day. It isn't his fault children are taken away from their parents and locked away for three to four years. But this is Evelyn Cavanaugh, her husband is the territorial governor and is in charge of overseeing these operations nationwide. She should know better.

Stopping in the hall and resting his hand on a door handle he says, "You do understand that I'm not taking your child from you. It's the law. The law your husband helped pass and is overseeing."

"I don't have time to play nice, Doctor Steiner. You know who my husband is, but right now, I am just like every other mother that brings her child into this house of torture. I want you to allow me to vent my frustrations and fears. If you can't do that for me, then find someone that can."

"I'm sorry, Mrs. Cavanaugh." The door is quickly opened. "This is your daughter's viewing room."

The room is a simple affair. Like the rest of the institute, everything is white. There is a desk that looks more like a control board in a music recording studio and a microphone hanging just above it. Three chairs are close to the angled viewing glass that looks into the room below.

Evelyn walks over and sees her daughter sitting on a bed, fifteen feet below the glass.

"Can she see me?"

"No. This is one-way glass."

"So there's a mirror on the other side?"

"Oh no. The earlier institutes tried that and it didn't end well. We have a non-reflective covering on the other side. You can speak to her through the microphone if you want. Her puberty guide is being put in place behind that far wall right now."

"Is it that time already?"

"Yes, I'm afraid so."

Evelyn grabs the microphone, and Doctor Steiner hits a button on the desk next to it.

"Lilly, can you hear me? It's Mom."

"Mom, hi, yes I can hear you. Where are you?"

Doctor Steiner pushes the button again quickly.

"You can tell her you see her, but don't tell her we're above her. It could complicate things."

"Mom? Are you still there?"

"Yes, I'm here sweetie. I can see you. How do you like your room?"

"How do you think, Mom? There's nothing in here but the bed and a toilet. When will I get my stuff to decorate?"

"You'll get your things soon," she lies. "The doctor tells me they are about to introduce your guide to you. I will talk to you for as long as you want, okay?"

"Okay, Mom."

"Mrs. Cavanaugh, we just received the digital file on your family's medical history, but there isn't much available in it."

"Our medical records have been classified. We want our privacy."

"I understand, I simply have to verify that Lilly is your first child."

"Ouch!"

"What's wrong, Lilly?"

"My hand hurts."

Evelyn looks to her side and Doctor Steiner nods and mouths, *It's beginning.*

"Mrs. Cavanaugh, Lilly is your only child correct?"

Angrily looking at him for bringing up her painful past, "No! We had a son who died in the war."

The doctor presses several more buttons on the desk and looks into the room as the far wall begins to slide away revealing the man currently assigned to Lilly.

"He was killed by the mutants?" the doctor continues.

"Yes, he was."

Lilly sits on the bed and begins to rock back and forth, holding onto her stomach.

"But he wasn't a mutant himself, correct?"

Walking away from the viewing window and confronting the irritating man, "My son was Lloyd Cavanaugh, you idiot! He was Cora Taylor's second-in-command and the father of her child. Now will you leave me alone with these stupid questions so I can help my daughter?"

She attempts to return to the window, but Doctor Steiner violently grasps her wrist.

"Your son was an arch-vampire? You should have let us know. That's not what we are prepared for today!"

She pulls her arm away from him and looks back into the room when she hears a loud familiar snap and screams echoing from the room's sound system. The man she is paired with is huge. He is at least six feet five inches tall, muscle-bound, and heavily tattooed. He is pressing himself against the wall behind him. The expression of fear on his face makes Evelyn think that is how she would look standing on a skinny ledge of a tall building. Clinging to the wall behind her for dear life.

Doctor Steiner hits a red button and an alarm begins to sound. "Emergency in room seven, we have potential arch-type with human subject."

Looking down at her daughter, she can see her right forearm is broken. Several more snapping sounds followed by more of Lilly's screams of pain echo over the speakers. Evelyn watches in horror as her daughter's bones are breaking, her arms and fingers are beginning to jut awkwardly at various angles. The man in her room is still clinging to his wall standing twenty feet away from the bed where Lilly is writhing in agony.

"We aren't prepared for your daughter's transformation." Doctor Steinberg tells Evelyn after shutting off the microphone. "We are going to have to abandon the facility."

"What the hell are you talking about? I'm not going anywhere!"

Standing at the locked door and trying to pull it open, Steinberg screams at Evelyn. "Our facility isn't prepared for an arch-type transformation! They are supposed to occur in the wild! Your daughter won't accept her puberty guide because she will need to feed on a vampire and we only have humans at this facility!"

Evelyn tries not to hear him but the fear his words instill cause her to shiver. Her face glues itself to the scene below, tears are streaming from her eyes at having to witness her daughter's pain and being unable to help.

A panicked voice sounds over the intercom. "Doctor Steiner, security protocol delta has been activated."

Several loud pops resound from the speakers, and Lilly is thrashing and quivering on her bed. She exhales a long scream as the sound of breaking bones intensifies in both speed and amplitude.

"HELP ME!" the muscular man yells from inside Lilly's room. "You can't do this to me. It's not right!"

The man's screams of protest stop when they all hear the familiar crackling sound of bones as they all turn brittle and seem to disintegrate. Now the only sound coming from the room is a static, white noise. First, it is like gravel being poured onto tiles, then it fades into the sound of a carbonated drink being amplified.

There is one final snapping sound, and Evelyn watches her daughter's body elongate and begin to regain its shape. Lilly stands and stares, the man against the wall is silent. There are small smears of blood on the wall at his side. He was scratching his fingers against it in an effort to dig his way out but too afraid to turn his back on the girl. The Shattering is complete, and Lilly's eyes are now fixed in his direction.

The man gives one final scream as Lilly jumps at him. She is able to cover the twenty-foot distance in one leap.

Instead of attacking the man, Lilly throws him to the side and begins hammering at the wall he came through as the easiest point of exit from her captivity. With little productivity at opening the reinforced wall, Lilly spins her head around the room sniffing and scanning, looking for a way out. The man is cowering in a corner.

Finally, Lilly's eyes fixate on the one-way glass panels designed to look like a continuation of the wall and leaps from the floor. She smashes through the glass and lands in the room between her mother and the good doctor who has noticeably wet himself.

A few seconds of uncertainty pass between the trio. Evelyn attempts to step toward her daughter, but Lilly holds out her hand at arm's length to prevent the approach. The door to their room rips out of the wall from the outside and a group of familiar vampires rush in. Evelyn and the doctor are picked up and rushed away while Lilly, in a blur of speed, is lead by the hand out of the room after them.

One final scream is heard from Lilly's transformation room as it and the observation room above it are flooded with flaming chemicals designed to erase any problems or abnormal transformations that occur during The Shattering.

In the courtyard, Evelyn is lowered to the ground from the arms of her savior, and she grasps hold of her in a tearful hug.

"Where have you been? Why have you stayed away for so many years?"

Cora smiles at Evelyn. "I'm sorry. It isn't much of an excuse, but I have been busy." They both look briefly to the side and see Lilly feeding on one of the several extra vampires Cora brought with her. "I knew she was set to transform, and I went to your house earlier. That is where they told me you came here. I was surprised the doctors let you into the facility knowing Lloyd was an arch-type."

"They didn't know." Evelyn shakes her head and laughs weakly in shock. "We had our records sealed, and the history books usually refer to our son only as Lloyd. They didn't know we even had another child let alone Lloyd being a Cavanaugh."

"Will Lilly be okay?"

"She will be fine. They'll take her with them when they go. She should be ready to return to you in a day or two."

"Cora, please, I have to know, how is Grace?"

"See for yourself, she's behind you."

Turning around, there are four arch-vampires standing around eight-year-old Grace who smiles shyly at Evelyn.

"Hi, Grandma!" Cora places a hand on Evelyn's back to steady her against Grace's exuberant run and jump into her arms.

"I can't believe how big you've grown. I missed you so much."

"I missed you too, Grandma."

CHAPTER THIRTY-NINE
REUNION

Oregon Territory

Like times past, Cora is sitting with Greg and Evelyn Cavanaugh outside their home. Her daughter, Grace, is rolling around the yard with the Cavanaugh's Bulldog, Mr. Darcy. The pure joy of his slobbering antics and playful pouncing with the little girl is keeping them all enthralled.

An awkward arrangement of human guards and vampires is spread throughout the yard as well. The mixture is a representation of the importance that Greg and Cora have to their respective governments.

"I'm sorry I haven't sent Grace to see you for so long. We were traveling these last fourteen months."

"You are always welcome to visit us as well, Cora. We haven't seen you since shortly after Grace was born."

"It is still difficult for me…seeing you brings back too many thoughts of Lloyd. With Grace, she doesn't have the memories of her father, but you and Greg, your emotional connection to him make being around you almost more than I can bare. It isn't a mature or reasonable response, but I can't explain how out of control I feel when thinking of your son."

"How are you doing now?"

"I would have been here for you and Lilly no matter the difficulty to myself. Something is different, though, and I wish I had arrived years ago. I think your wounds over Lloyd healed somewhat after Lilly was born."

A welcome interruption of loud giggled laughter from Grace running between everyone followed by Mr. Darcy helps erase the encroaching sadness.

"Well, Cora, where were you and Grace traveling?"

"Europe, Asia, and all over the African continent. It was an amazing journey."

"You should have left Grace with us on a trip like that. Weren't you afraid of being attacked?"

"Oh no, not at all. That's what my guards have to worry about." A light chuckle receives a serious look of angry concern back from Evelyn.

"Believe me, I would never put Grace in harm's way. A lot has changed in those countries over the last nine years. You must know what has been happening over there."

Greg shakes his head.

"We haven't paid much attention to international matters over the last six years, and I'm not sure how accurate the information from before that time is. With the absence of living or free human populations, I was told by the president that vampires largely deal with relations overseas."

"We do, but I expected at least the regional governors would be kept informed."

The strain of differing political interests is present in Greg's stressed comments.

"I would appreciate knowing what is happening in the outside world, but understand my government's reluctance in giving the people depressing information which we have no control over changing."

"I'm sorry, I thought you would have known what was happening, but in the context of human survival rates, I do understand why my excitement over our travels wouldn't be shared. Would you like me to give you the recent news or fill you in about more?"

"Please tell us everything you know. I think it could help me understand the direction we will need to head regarding policy."

"Perhaps we should sit down." Cora smiles and lowers herself into a chair while waiting for the others to join her. "Those nations whose governments killed off their children as a defensive measure against future mutations, all fell into rebellion or chaos before the first year ended. The following two years devolved into endless war, criminal attack, or mass suicides resulting from the hopelessness felt by the populations. There was a blockade set up, and no mutants entered those human areas even after requests for assistance began.

"Magnús Sigmarsson, the President of the Unified Eurasian Mutant League, decreed back then that the humans created their situation and must figure out a way to solve their own crises without mutant help. Within three years, a majority of the remaining humans in those areas had died, that is why your government stopped regular communications. The loss of hope from the murder of all the children drove the people mad, as it should have!"

Inadvertently raising her voice and shouting the words in anger prompts Cora to blush and pause.

"I apologize. I know your government and you particularly were horrified by those nations' choices. It is still impossible for me to comprehend the decision to sacrifice their children in some vain attempt to help normal humans retain their position on the planet. Seeing Grace playing while we talk makes me feel the pain the fathers and mothers of those murdered children must have experienced. I can imagine what they went through when their children were taken from them to be...when they were taken away.

"Because the populations had dropped so dramatically, the new governments' humans established after the chaos were no more than regional tribes or fiefdoms. Technology was an afterthought. Medicine was non-existent and access to electricity disappeared. On the other side of the world, outside of England, no human territories have remaining technology. No one will trade with them for the necessary products to rebuild their infrastructure, and they simply don't have the population or willingness to do the necessary legwork to re-establish themselves.

"The only thing that comes out of their territory is the feeling of heartbreak and an occasional newly mutated child seeking asylum."

"Is there something our human government can do? How long do you think they have?"

"Your government has agreed not to interfere with any human affairs across the oceans. A treaty signed years ago provides that any attempt to offer assistance to the human tribes remaining on the Eurasian or African continents would imply agreement and solidarity with their decision to murder their own children. Attempting to help them would allow mutants to go to war with humans on our continents again. That kind of war would be brief."

"What about the vampire territories? From what I recall, most areas outside of England were slave-holding regions. Where is the moral equivalence in allowing slaves or keeping humans as cattle compared to sacrificing children during a war?"

Cora nods, eyes squinted with understanding. "It is a valid point, but we settled those differences years ago. I made the mistake after the North American division in giving the clone blood process to Europe. They used the availability of blood substitute as an excuse to execute the remaining humans under their control. Once the children of those humans mutated, they went to war with the vampires that murdered their parents.

"The unexpected rage of those new mutants propelled their strength to levels the unchallenged mutants of Europe had never experienced. I never had to go to war to rid those continents of the slave-minded vampires; their own brutality turned against them and ended their reign."

"There couldn't have been very many children that mutated after the haze was gone. How did they overcome a continent filled with and controlled by vampires like the ones you fought against?"

"Most of the arch-vampires saw their powers diminish after the haze dissipated. Without mind-controlling powers, all mutants were free to choose their own path and harming humans wasn't what they wanted in their future. Killing the remaining humans pushed the attitudes of the vampire populations against the slave-owning arch-vampires. There were about fifty newly mutated vampires that ran through all three continents and wiped out the remaining slave owners.

"Outside of the human-controlled territories, vampires and the remaining humans have been able to work together, or at least in a similar segregated fashion as we do in North America."

"So what took you traveling over there?"

"Elections and preparations for human resettlement and land reallocation. The human population has dropped significantly in most nations, so we will be relocating people to other areas where they can live in communities together."

"I imagine vampires will be moving into the areas which you clear of humans?"

"Yes, that is also the goal. Our numbers have been increasing while those of humans have been diminishing greatly."

"Isn't there something you can do to stop this, Cora? I understand what those people did to their own children was wrong, but fear makes people do irrational things. Can't you keep the people from being moved away from their homelands?"

Cora stands, walks over to Grace, picks her up and swiftly places her to stand in front of Greg and Evelyn. "Yesterday, this was what Lilly looked like. You would never lift a finger to harm Grace, and you would have never contemplated hurting Lilly. Even without looking into your minds, I know you would have endured any hardship or pain to protect your own child as would I.

"The people who chose to murder their nation's children are the same ones that would have been human slave owners had they mutated. Evil is written into some people's DNA and there is only one way to deal with that type of sickness. Eradication.

"I have the unique ability to do exactly what you asked. Last month, I was elected President of the United World Mutant States. Within human history, I am in actuality the first leader of the world outside of the non-mutated human territories. With all of the power and discretion that provides me, I would not lift a finger to help any of those evil monsters. They will be relocated to France, Ukraine, Vietnam and South Africa, and even in those regions, they will have more land than their sparse numbers will know what to do with."

Evelyn stands up and places a hand on Cora's arm. "What our governments do are not always the choice of the people. Please consider looking for parents or families that were wronged by the decisions to murder their children."

Tears are streaming down her cheeks. "I have checked, Evelyn. For fourteen months, we have been over there, and I scanned every bit of territory I could in between diplomatic meetings and events. They are all dead. The decent humans were all murdered or who they were as people was destroyed by the violence of the last decade. I searched for any innocent or trustworthy human that I could reach outside of our territories and they simply do not exist.

"I'm afraid the same thing will happen everywhere when the human numbers start to significantly drop off. People reached a turning point in their hope for survival when they realized nothing they do would return things to the way they once were."

CHAPTER FORTY
TELOMERE

Great Plains Territory

The arrival of the blue haze brought with it one change to the human condition which they have been unable to reverse. The technological advancements they created were all dependent upon an intricate and fragile distribution structure which allowed necessary products to be delivered anywhere in the world within twenty-four hours. That system came crashing to a halt when the children mutated and enslaved the world's adults. It will never recover.

In contrast, the speed and strength of vampires and other mutants allowed them to create a new infrastructure not reliant on roads, rails, and mechanical air travel. Delivery of goods between mutant areas rivals that of the pre-change world. One aspect of existence the children were not willing to give up was communications. Computer and phone research and development continued and was encouraged even in the backdrop of humanities enslavement and the war.

Dr. Tatyana Usachova chose to live in the mutant territories when they separated. Following the mutants was a requirement of her field of study, but she would have chosen the mutant territories anyway over having to work in research for the human government.

Tatyana works in one of the larger research and development labs in the mutant-held Plains Territory. Her area of study, while not as exciting and geared toward entertainment, has always been given priority. She continues to study the effects and changes the haze has caused.

"It's good to see you again, Cora."

Dr. Usachova is greeted with silence as The Angel and her daughter stand just inside the door of her lab.

"Oh please, Cora, don't stare at me like that, you're going to give me a complex."

"I'm sorry, Tatyana, I didn't mean to stare. I wasn't aware so much time has passed."

"It has only been five years I think, although I would have liked to see you sooner. Don't worry about how I look, the dramatic shift is in my personal grooming rather than a stark change that happened since you last saw me."

"I don't understand, what happened to your hair?"

The golden blonde of the doctor's hair has been replaced with a dull gray. There are noticeable lines by her eyes and some slight wrinkling of the skin on her neck.

"I am fifty-six years old, young lady. A few years ago, I decided to stop fighting the hands of time and gave up coloring my hair. I imagine hair coloring will eventually be only for entertainment for you lucky youngsters who don't age."

The doctor walks up and places a hand on The Angel's cheek and caresses it.

"Amazing. Your skin is still as soft as a newborn's." She steps back a few paces and adjusts her glasses. "You haven't aged at all either. Please excuse my excitement. It is one thing to see what is happening in my calculations and lab tests but quite another to see and touch a living example of immortality."

Cora smiles at the woman while she directs her daughter to a chair and gives her a book to read.

"I wanted to visit you sooner, but there were so many things to do."

"Yes, I heard. Congratulations, Madam President. Leader of the planet now, how quickly things change in this new world of ours."

"I'm just the president of the mutant territories."

"Please, I'm on your side, Cora. I know better than most the hopeless condition of humankind. Our days are few and waning fast, this is the dawn of your time. You are the president of the only society that truly matters anymore and you know it." Her smile is genuine and warm. "I am glad you came to see me. There is something you particularly will need to address as the new president: overpopulation.

"You mutants are repopulating almost as fast as we are dying out. I know the effects of Shatterbones causes tremendous strain on your bodies, but as you know with Grace, it isn't only your muscles and bones that go through significant changes. Your kind mutate during and because of puberty, which causes your hormones to surge and has resulted in an unprecedented rise in population growth.

"As you recall, we were able to eliminate the behemoth mutations by testing for trisomy disorders in gestation so they won't be at issue. This problem of overpopulation also isn't a concern among the giant or werewolf populations because they are aging normally. It is something specific to you vampires which you will need to address immediately, or your population growth will lead to conflict over resources and possibly future wars.

"You need to find a way to slow down the amount of children vampires are having. Without killing each other on battlefields, I am concerned that none of you will die. You must understand what would happen to any species that continually produces children and no one ages or dies after they mutate. It is an exponential growth pattern that cannot continue without disastrous results.

"I have been studying the genetic make-up of vampires to look for anomalies, but even in looking at your chromosomes telomeres, not enough time has passed for any noticeable change to have occurred."

Cora looks at the doctor with a blank expression, still seemingly fixated on the gray color of her hair.

"Damn it, Cora, just read my mind already. I love your self-restraint, but sometimes you make it so difficult for me to explain things to you."

Cora searches the research in Usachova's mind without going into her personal thoughts. The doctor has always been a trusted friend to The Angel and the mutants. She vowed to give the doctor the only gift of value she felt she could offer: privacy.

"So telomeres determine lifespan?"

"Yes, they deteriorate in all living beings; however, I have mixed results in detecting any changes in mutants. Unfortunately, it will take another ten years before I am able to make a more concrete determination of whether you will live forever or are only aging at an extremely slow level.

"Cora, you need to prepare yourself and the others. I am getting old and so are your parents. You must make sure you visit them often and avoid surrounding yourself with only those that look young forever. It would be a greater tragedy than you realize if your perpetual youth allows you to lose track of time and miss the passing of a loved one."

CHAPTER FORTY-ONE
THE NATURE OF MAN IS WAR

Twenty-One Years Post Haze
Europe

In the years since The Shattering Event ended, the absence of man's dependence on technology has helped the quality of the air the most. The night is a comfortable fifty-eight degrees Fahrenheit and the sky is clear for miles.

Industrial pollutants no longer fill city skies with brown filth that must be blown away by winds or washed out of the sky by a decent rain. In this modern time, the only pollutant one would normally find to bar being able to see for miles and miles is the smoke from an occasional fire from accident or nature. Tonight, visual acuity is unparalleled.

Flying high above Spain, Cora, her four siblings, and their children, all watch the events occurring on the ground several miles below them. Without a cloud in the sky and the moon high and full, they are all able to see the blurred movements of the mutants on the streets below and those in the air around them. The giants are conspicuously absent as they have decided to remain neutral during this conflict.

Alejandro Salazar runs with blurring speed among the soldiers battling in the streets of Madrid. Heads are removed and upper torsos separate from their lower halves everywhere he runs with his blades. He moves with a graceful ease through the carnage around him until two axes from each side of the narrow roadway cleave him into thirds.

Vampire conflicts have increased this past year. Aggressions acted out on jealousies over the most favored land tracts and arguments of favoritism by this arch-vampire or another.

The pettiness of humanity failed to mutate away like our ability to endure sunlight. How cruel life seems to be.

The words are directed to The Angel's mind from another group of arch-vampires. They are nearly a mile away, also flying high above the battlefield. Like Cora's family, the other small group is hovering amidst the chaotic battle surrounding them with no threat being made in their direction or any notice to their presence at all.

Swords are slashing and bodies are falling mere feet from The Angel, but she is not involved in this fight. She has brought her family to witness what the future of mutated humanity has to offer if steps aren't taken to help guide them out of their personal grievances.

With the help of the ones she loves, they created a mental barrier around themselves, rendering them invisible to the fighting hordes around them. The vampire that spoke through The Angel's mind must have similar powers to her own to be able to observe the battle without becoming involved.

This bloodshed has more to do with us than what they claim outwardly; we need to meet and discuss this issue, The Angel responds in thought.

Seeing enough of this senseless fighting, Cora signals to her family she is ready to leave, and they fly higher toward the stars to clear the large open air fighting arena. One final thought she sends to her friends still below. *Gather those with our powers that are likeminded, we will meet in Odessa in one month.*

Odessa is human territory.

Yes, but they have no electricity and are all nearly gone now. They won't be concerned with our arrival, even if they discover we are there, which I doubt. We must meet in a place that the others wouldn't think to go, my suggestions won't be welcomed by them.

*

It is a miserable night for travel but the best circumstances for stealth. The supercell storm over Ukraine is bleeding rain through the sky as if the world's rivers have taken flight. The new moon is unnecessarily blanketing the area above the clouds in blackness, yet the few inches of visibility blink into blinding brightness with each of the many lighting flashes that occur.

Landing on the runway of Odessa's long-abandoned international airport, several families are carrying wounded participants who were unable to make it through the lightning storm without being struck.

"You picked a hell of a night to meet like this," Viktor Kalinich exclaims.

Representing the Russian territories, Viktor smiles with his arms outstretched while he remains standing in the heavy downpour. The others are gathered near him, but under the roof of a partially collapsed airplane hangar.

"I didn't think this area had such severe weather," one of the Indian representatives mentions while rubbing the large smoldering burn hole in their stomach. "I thought that lightning bolt was going to kill me."

The Angel smiles at the gathering of thirty arch-vampire families from around the globe. "I am sorry to put you through such a treacherous journey. I didn't want prying eyes to interrupt our meeting, so I asked my daughter Grace to enhance the weather for us."

"That's impossible!" Viktor booms with laughter as he walks out of the rain. "Your daughter was born after the haze."

"She was born after the haze but was conceived before it left the Earth. I am aware that no mutant conceived after the haze has had psychic powers; that is the main reason I wanted to meet with all of you."

"I am calling bullshit. No vampire can control the weather, and no vampire born after the haze has had powers."

Knowing her daughter's spirit, The Angel steps away from Viktor as do the rest of Grace's relatives. Seconds later, the hangar is lit up with a brilliant flash as a lightning bolt arcs under the roof and strikes Viktor in his backside, throwing him across the room.

Screaming in pain and holding onto his butt, most of the people in attendance stand in silent shock while the others who are more familiar with Grace, smile or laugh at Viktor's misfortune.

"Why would you hit me there? I won't be able to sit for a week now."

"I didn't want to hurt your wings," is the soft reply she gives with her diminutive voice.

"How have you managed to keep her powers a secret? The others already consider our abilities to be reckless and possibly dangerous; they won't like knowing she has such a capacity to manipulate nature."

"The others won't know." The fierceness of Cora's angered words impacts each of the vampires physically. They all recoil a few steps as if she slammed their heads with a hammer.

"You fear my daughter's strength. The wingless vampires fear arch-vampires. The winged vampires without psychic gifts fear our collective abilities. Fear and jealousy are what these new battles are all about. All of you here represent the best of what The Shattering Event had to offer. You all have powers of varying degrees, and yet you chose to use them to fight for freedom instead of enslavement. You picked the path of greatest resistance by believing human and mutant kind should rise or fall of their own accord and based on their own decisions.

"Even with your benevolence, the other vampires grow jealous and suspicious of our abilities. They are beginning to think they should kill us because we can influence situations and outcomes in ways they cannot.

"The wars they are fighting now over land and prestige will turn toward ridding the Earth of the people standing in this room within the next year. We must take action now, or we will be hunted down and exterminated."

Sophie Morgan of the English Territory steps forward. "What do you know that makes the others a danger? I was with you over Madrid. Many of us are able to create protective areas around ourselves preventing other vampires from even noticing us let alone being able to cause us harm."

"There are thirty families here, yet there are forty-two more that were not invited by any of us. Each of you knows why they were not chosen to attend. They have been using their powers to influence runners and fliers to fight in efforts to gain lands and riches. So none of us like or appreciate the judgment of those who weren't invited. Their powers have also diminished after the haze, and they have family members who have no powers at all. I understand that some of their abilities continue to wane as the years pass, just as some of ours have grown. I think their diminishing ability to influence others is the cause of their lust to increase territorial holdings.

"They are the ultimate threat to us, not the average runner or flier whom we can block. Those families with remaining strengths will move to eliminate us one at a time until we are all gone. They don't like the fact that they will eventually have no powers and are not willing to allow us to remain alive while we have ours."

"Are you suggesting we go to war?"

"I am suggesting we are already at war. They are currently thinking about coming after us but have not yet declared or organized a plan to do so. What I recommend is a two-part strategy, both of which go against the ideals of non-interference which we have strived for.

"First, we turn the soldiers against their masters. The warring arch-vampires have been using them to claim territory. They have chosen to waste the lives of decent vampires for selfish means, and we can manipulate the thoughts of those soldiers to go after the ones sending them to war.

"This means we can make efforts to kill them now, or we must continually scan the remaining arch-vampire families for their intentions. Orders to have them killed will be issued if they are deciding to come after us. Either way, we are reinforcing the fear which they already have; we are using our powers to eliminate them.

"In the larger scheme of things, until this point in time, we have left them alone while we should have intervened earlier. We have allowed them to do things that were agreed by all mutants would not be tolerated. Controlling other vampires to use in battle is justification enough to put them to death. In part, I blame myself for retiring from the presidency too soon. I should have remained longer to ensure our new society was better established."

"To that point, Cora, the president is obviously not here, so I assume we will we go after him and his family? He is the one that has allowed these conflicts to go on unchallenged."

"His family is participating in the conflicts. They are manipulating others to act as controllers on their behalf. His family's powers did not diminish after the haze and that makes him more dangerous than all of the others. I will be dealing with him soon, and I want all of you to remain far away from him and his ability to scan thoughts."

"If we are taking out the president, this means treason against the United Mutant Government."

"Yes, it does." Nodding, she looks at all in attendance for confirmation of agreement.

"So what is the second part of your strategy? I hope it does not involve more lightning," Viktor says to laughter as he continues to rub his backside in pain.

"The next part of my plan is to begin altering records of psychic abilities. It won't matter how many opposing vampires we eliminate if the knowledge of our powers remains. Those born in the future will be just as likely to become jealous or envious of what we can do. That jealousy will keep the threat against us alive in some form or at a minimum, encourage conflicts among the lower classes.

"We have to slowly scrub the history and memory of our abilities from all records and minds."

"I don't understand why we should bother. Won't our powers die with us?"

"You are still thinking in linear terms of human lives. My body has not aged in twenty years, and Dr. Usachova claims that not only are our cells perpetually regenerated, but the length of the telomeres on our chromosomes does not decrease. That means we could possibly be the first generation to live forever. Unless we are killed in battle or by some force that destroys the planet, we should prepare to be here for a long time after our normal human counterparts have died."

"What the hell will that do to us if no one ever dies?"

"I'm sorry, I wasn't clear. Only those that were born or conceived while the blue haze was present have perpetual telomeres. Those conceived later, their telomere regions are diminishing more rapidly than normal. We will find out the exact lifespan of the rest of our kind in the next twenty to thirty years. However short or long their lives are, we will remain. Continued knowledge of our abilities will forever be a source of strife among them and danger for us."

CHAPTER FORTY-TWO
MOONLIGHT SWIM

China

The Angel lands in front of a broken statue in the overgrown grass of the circular grounds of Sun Yat Sen Memorial Park. Her brothers and sisters land next to her. It is 5:30AM and uncomfortably close to sunrise to still be traveling. Victoria Harbor looks beautiful in the scant light of pre-dawn, even with the eerie backdrop and surroundings of the decaying and abandoned city of Hong Kong.

"I remember pictures of this city when I was younger. It was beautiful, especially at night with the buildings all lit up. It's a shame no one has chosen to revitalize this area yet."

"I plan on rebuilding this area once certain conspirators among our ranks are dealt with."

Augustin Kambanda, the current President of the United Mutant Government, lands in the park. Hundreds of wingless mutants run up and stand at attention behind him. The sky above the runners is filled with winged mutant guards circling in an orderly procession amidst the strengthening winds from the approaching storm. "Thank you for agreeing to meet me here away from the prying eyes of our brothers and sisters. I am surprised you brought your family with you as I am sure you know why I wanted to meet. At least you chose to leave your lovely Grace at home. I will deal with her shortly as well."

"You should have controlled your ambitions, Augustin. I will not allow you to continue waging this war you have secretly begun. You broke your oath of office and your pledge to all mutants when you began using your powers to influence others. Your petty lust for territory disgusts me."

"You act as if you didn't use your powers against your own. I learned in Rwanda long ago if you aren't gaining power, you are losing it. There is no static point of power." He laughs in his false and exaggerated manner making him seem even more unpleasant as the day creeps closer. The wind begins whipping fiercely and the mutants in the air, with their extraordinary strength, are struggling to remain in formation. A familiar yet silent face from the Odessa meeting three days ago breaks through the crowd and whispers into the president's ear.

"So your daughter is here somewhere? I imagine she can see us now. Well, let her witness what becomes of you when the sun rises. You will not be allowed to enter the safety of the city's structures."

The Angel smiles and winks at Augustin before removing a small bell from her pocket.

"Where did you get that?!" The veins in his forehead bulge through the skin with his furious glare.

"I found it in a schoolhouse in Rwanda. I understand from probing your mind during our earliest meetings that you had a difficult time with your teachers as a child and these simple bells have a particular meaning for you. I thought it only appropriate that I use this to signal your demise."

Rushing forward, President Kambanda is struck in the legs and wings by lightning from the storm clouds. The Angel and her sister, Elizabeth, step aside to allow his body to roll past them while the others around them stand still facing Kambanda's guards. Pulling a wad of paper out of the bell frees the clapper and The Angel rings it three times in the air.

While Augustin struggles to get up, The Angel's group begins running to the water. "Stop them! Don't let them get away, I want them dead!"

"You didn't think I would agree to meet with you without making plans of my own, did you?"

The condition of the water in the bay went unnoticed during the brief discussion the pair were having. All attention was placed on the turmoil in the sky and the approaching storm. The harbor had been quickly draining of water and now a wall of ocean is seconds from receiving The Angel and her family in their bid to escape the wrath of the presidential guard.

Looking behind himself to his troops that should have already passed him in their pursuit of the traitors, he sees they are in full battle with each other. A lone arch-vampire remains at Augustin's side as the towering tsunami continues its approach.

"You suggested Hong Kong as an ambush site, you have to help me out of here. I can't run or fly, I'll be killed in the water when the sun comes up."

"I'm sorry, Mr. President; I'm in it for the species, not for you. Telling you about the meeting in Odessa and coming to Hong Kong were The Angel's ideas, not mine."

The wave, now three hundred feet high, washes over the president and the assembled fighting soldiers on the ground as well as many in the air. Once the wave passes by, a new army arrives from below the depths; bizarre-looking creatures with flat gray skin and dolphin-like tails but arms, shoulders, and heads in a similar approximation to humans. Their faces have large protruding mouths with sharp tiny teeth, human eyes, and no visible nose or breathing holes.

This army of mermaids grab and pull the water-bound vampires either to safety or to their deaths. Each fate is dependent upon the individual's allegiance to The Angel or Augustin. The wounded President Kambanda is grabbed in the water by one of the mermaids. The swirling mass of water, dirt, and debris make it impossible for him to tell what direction he is traveling or how he will be rescued from the water with the sun about to rise.

A burning desperation hits him as his body begins convulsing for air. Almost ready to open his mouth and gulp in the mud-filled seawater, his head breaks the surface of the ocean. His raspy coughing breath fills his body with cool comfort as the oxygen hits his lungs and once again begins circulating through his system.

"I'm here! Someone come get me." His frantic shouts echo through the air grabbing the attention of the fighting vampires above him. "You have to hurry, the sun is about to rise."

Scores of arch-vampires loyal to the president disregard their opponents and fly down in an attempt to carry him to safety. They form a protective formation to allow a center vampire to grab the president while those on the periphery will act as defenders.

The remaining vampires in the sky take the warning as a sign to protect themselves from the approaching sun. They leave the battlefield, friend and foe together, to find shelter and live for at least one more day.

When the flying formation nears President Kambanda, he once again disappears below the water which has come alive with a thrashing tumult. The forty vampires seeking to save their leader are pulled from the air by arms reaching from the water or knocked out of the sky by breaching mermaids taking momentary flight.

Only ten are able to avoid the attacks from below. They turn, grouped together, to fly with their backs to the now rising sun and speed their way to find a building in which to hide. Flames ignite on the wings and bodies of the few in the back, and a mere fifty yards lay between them and a teetering wreck of former skyscraper that seems more a house of cards than a survivable shelter, but it is the closest chance they have to live on.

Terrifying screams of torture emanate from behind them, and the group turns their heads to look as they continue to fly. The mermaids are lifting the president and the other captured vampires out of the water to burn in the morning sun. Their heads and upper torsos are engulfed in flame.

The final progress to safety is blocked by a twenty-foot-wide wall of water that bursts from the harbors depths at the edge of the concrete dock.

A gargantuan head, torso, and arms appear before them as the water falls away. The hands of this titan clap together, smashing the group of fleeing vampires between his palms. As his body continues its fall back into the water below, he throws the crumpled remnants of his captured foe to the mermaids swimming in wait.

Gravity slams the titan's body back to his watery home, and the tail which is his lower torso flails up into the air before he brings it slapping down with tremendous force to speed him on his way. The mutated whales and dolphins had chosen their side after years of watching the activities of their terrestrial counterparts.

Arch-vampires, with all of their capabilities and powers, are unable to pierce the thoughts or minds of non-human mutants. For some reason, the ocean-based mutants have no such difficulty. Even without the capacity to directly communicate, they developed the ability to sense intent. This skill taught them to avoid the remaining humans that live along the world's coastlines for the last twenty years, and it prevented them from interfering with the affairs of other mutants until today. The war efforts of Augustin Kambanda would have eventually harmed the marine life of the world, and that is not something they will allow.

*

United States
Great Plains Territory

"When did it happen?"

"Two days ago while we were in Hong Kong."

The main scientific research lab in the central plains of the United States has been shut down. The buildings are intact, but the personnel have all been killed. Piles of human and vampiric ash are next to the main entrance where their bodies were either set ablaze or caught fire with the rising sun.

"Only one vampire has been found alive," a guard addresses The Angel who just arrived. "He is inside and in a catatonic state. He is repeating your name once every hour and says nothing else."

"Was he a scientist here?"

"No, he is Kambanda's head guard, the one that came out of Rwanda with him."

"Bring him to me."

"Ma'am, Kambanda had tremendous powers but we don't know exactly what his abilities were. I don't recommend touching this vampire to read his mind, it could be a trap."

"Thank you. Bring him here."

The captured vampire stares blankly into the air until he sees Cora in front of the crowd he is approaching. He grins broadly at her and laughs when he is dropped to the ground a few feet from her.

"Did you like the gift I left you?"

With a shaking head and shrugging, "I don't know what you're talking about, what gift?"

He stands with wide eyes and points to a large billboard. Its white front is covered with large dark smudges but contains no discernible message.

"You're giving me a dirty billboard?"

"That was for The Angel to see," the man shouts angrily. "Why did you take it down?"

Whispering into The Angel's ear is one of the first to arrive at the scene when they heard about the attack, "We brought her down, ma'am. We know you had a particular affection for her and didn't want you to see her treated in such a way."

"I was the one that did it. Augustin ordered me to come here in case he failed to kill you. We killed all of your precious humans and the traitor vampires that work with them, but I saved Dr. Usachova 'til the end. I planned on having it go on for days, I wanted you to see her final moment. Every six hours, I did something new. First, I ripped her hands from her arms, then her feet. When I snapped her leg in half, her body couldn't take it anymore and she died. I nailed her to the board for you to see when you arrived."

The vampires around The Angel begin to retreat away from her when she begins to glow. It is a pulsing white light that emanates from her skin and grows brighter with each beating flash. The black grounds under the night sky first begin to look as the though the moon is full and rising. The Angel's clothes burn away as the light and heat she is emitting intensifies.

The heat is causing the ground beneath her feet to smolder before the grass suddenly catches fire. Her soldiers and friends continue their retreat from the growing hatred she is directing at the now-kneeling soldier who killed her friend. With a final intense flash, the blinding light she is producing sets the skin of her enemy on fire and a piercing scream from her knocks his body to the ground and bursts his chest open. His body writhes in agony attempting to regenerate until it is finally reduced to ash and she allows her light to diminish.

No vampire remains within two hundred yards of The Angel as a result of her light. She turns where she stands and views the fear etched on the faces of her vampires in the distance. Some of them begin to approach, and she reads that their intentions are to put out the many fires she ignited on the buildings and around the grounds.

"Let the billboard burn. I want it gone."

*

"Mom, are you okay?"

Grace is standing in the doorway to Dr. Usachova's former lab. Cora is leaning over a computer screen, tears streaming from her eyes.

"She warned me this would happen. Ten years ago, she told me we had to do something about how many children the vampires were having or we would end up fighting each other. I didn't do anything and now she's dead."

"I'm sorry." Her daughter's comforting hand rubs the enlarged muscles just above her wings.

"She left her report for me. It's actually the report for us all, the one I mentioned in Odessa." Wiping her eyes, she tries to smile for Grace. "Things will be different in the future, Grace. Tatyana found the answers she was looking for."

"What does this mean for the future?"

"It means more changes are in store for us all." Standing up with a new resolve, Cora places her hands firmly around Grace's shoulders in a hug. "I don't know about you, but I want to go see your grandparents. What do you think?"

Her beaming smile gives the only answer necessary.

CHAPTER FORTY-THREE
A FAMILY AFFAIR

Oregon

"What happened to you, Robert? Your hair is all white," Greg Cavanaugh badgers his old friend.

"I'm sure you would have white hair to if you had any left. Did Evelyn say you would look more handsome if you shaved it or did it all fall out?"

"It all fell out you, old coot. I may not have my hair anymore, but at least now I'm not the only one that looks like he's pregnant with twins."

Both men laugh and rub their protruding stomachs while their wives look on and shake their heads.

"Our men will never grow up." Evelyn and Tanya look at each other smile and say in unison. "And we love them for it."

Lilly, Grace, and Cora share their own embrace and reunion in the living room. The Cavanaughs no longer hold positions in government and have no need for their own security. The Angel's guards chose to remain outside during this reunion.

"Look at you girls." Evelyn walks up to the youthful trio with arms outstretched. "I am so jealous. You look like three eighteen-year-old friends, just out of high school. If I didn't already know your secret, I would demand you give me your plastic surgeon's name."

The smiles and greetings go on for a while before a lull in the conversation prompts Evelyn to bring up the elephant in the room.

"We are thrilled for the visit, Cora. Especially to see your parents again, but what's going on? I've never seen your guard leave your side and now they let you come in here alone and seem almost uneasy around you."

"I heard it's because of something that happened in China and later at the research lab a few days ago." Lilly hops in her usual playful manner. Cora and Grace give her a surprised look. "Oh come on, you don't think something like that can happen without everyone talking about it do you?" Turning to the humans sitting together on the couch, Lilly continues her tale in a faux-shocked tone of gossip.

"Apparently, that unassuming little mutant over there, my best friend, Grace, has the power to control the elements. Rumor has it that she can

232

create storms, control lightning, and even helped defeat our former president by summoning a six-hundred-foot tsunami!"

"It was three hundred feet," Grace interjects and Lilly continues without taking notice of the interruption.

"But the real scandal is what Cora did. We all knew she had the power to emit light and that is how she gained her famed title "The Angel." But what no one knew until that infamous event at the science lab is The Angel now has the power to summon the light of the sun. She emitted a light so powerful that her vampire guard was forced to retreat. Her light was so immense that she burnt an enemy vampire to ash as well set nearby buildings on fire."

"Cora, is this true?" her mom asks with concern.

"Yes, it's true. My powers have been increasing."

Lilly grabs Cora and Grace around the necks in a playful hug and pulls them together.

"While most arch-vampires have seen their powers diminish and no one born post haze has any psychic powers at all, these two little devils have seen their powers grow to incredible heights. It has the other vampires a little freaked to say the least."

"You don't seem bothered by what they can do."

"I'm not bothered because I can do this."

Lilly's body slowly fades from view between her two friends. Then in a blink, Cora and Grace vanish as well. The spot around the three continue to disappear, and the vanishing act continues until the entire house is invisible. The only thing remaining in sight are the four humans sitting on invisible sofas in the middle of a yard surrounded by The Angel's vampire guards.

The guards take notice that the house is gone, and one runs toward the four visible humans and breaks through a wall to reach them.

The house and three vampires reappear around the foot soldier that is covered in broken drywall and dust from his unconventional entrance into the home.

"I'm so sorry," he says, stammering, "I thought the house wasn't here...I mean I didn't see it anymore...what just happened?"

The heads of two more guards pop into view, looking through the new hole in the wall their friend just created. Lilly has to bend over because she is laughing so hard.

"It wasn't your fault, Tony," The Angel says in a calm tone and guiding him back to the opening. "I'm going to step outside and calm everyone down. I'll be back in a moment."

*

233

"Are your new powers why you brought us all together?" Greg asks when Cora returns.

"They are only part of the problem. I learned something new from Dr. Usachova's files when we were at the lab."

"I really like that woman. How is she doing?"

"She was killed by President Kambanda's men. I brought you to be together here because I think you are in danger. I don't know how many vampires he had on his side or what his powers of persuasion were, but I can't take a chance that someone is still out there that can act on his behalf.

"We are facing two potential issues in the future. The first is our powers. They are already creating fear and distrust among our own kind. I think the best way we can prevent future wars and bloodshed is to erase the existence of them."

"I wouldn't want to get rid of my powers even if I could," Lilly counters.

"No, erase our powers from the records. It will take a great deal of time to get to every item that mentions our special abilities, but we need to alter them to make it seem like everything we accomplished was done through common physical means. If what Dr. Usachova indicated in her research is true, we will have all the time we need.

"Mom, Dad, she thinks we will live forever. Not all mutants, though; only the ones born before the haze left. Those born after will have shortened life spans and might only reach thirty years old."

"What?" Evelyn stands in shock and looks at her daughter.

"I meant those conceived before the haze disappeared, not born. Lilly is fine, I saw her records at the lab. All of the vampires conceived after the haze will begin dying in the next ten to twenty years. The rest of us might remain alive until we are killed by another vampire or in some cataclysm that destroys everything."

"So you're afraid we might be killed, everyone else is going to die, and you need to erase everyone's memories or they might get jealous and kill you. Anything else?"

"Thanks, Dad."

Tanya hits her husband's arm and shakes her head.

"What? It's not like we haven't been in danger from day one when this stupid mutation stuff started. We'll be fine, we always are. If things end up bad for us this time, I'm fine with it. Look at us all. I have the love of my life, great kids that are healthy and successful, and I've lived to have a pot belly and a head full of white hair. What more could I want?

"By the way, Cora, while you're out saving the world and ending the next inevitable war, you need to get your brothers and sisters to stop by more often. I know you have them running all over the globe taking care of all sorts of things for you. It would be nice if you would write your mom and dad into your to-do lists every once in a while."

Pulling her parents into a hug. "I will, I promise."

CHAPTER FORTY-FOUR
MORTALITY

Thirty Years Post Haze
Heartland Territory

"Cora, you need to get up, something has happened!"

The fear she feels permeating the building causes her to shiver. A lone guard is standing at the foot of her bed, forehead drenched in sweat, sword in hand, and eyes darting around the empty room.

"They're dead. Bobby, Jody, Wildcat and Yung! I tried waking them up but they're dead."

"Did you check the security footage?"

"Brinkley is checking it now, but I didn't find any signs of forced entry and the werewolves say no one arrived during the day."

She climbs out of bed and steps into a gown, pulling it up and then fastening it closed above her wings in the back.

"Take me to their bodies."

"I checked them for bites and didn't find anything. I think it might have been gas."

Feeling each body, she confirms what she could sense when walking into the room. There are no brainwaves, diminishing cellular activity, no warmth. She turns and places a calming hand on Nick's shoulder.

"We weren't attacked, it was just their time."

Brinkley runs into the room also in a panic. "There was nothing on the security footage and we're getting calls and messages from all over the country. What happened here is happening everywhere, vampires have been killed in their sleep by something."

"Brinkley, calm down. They weren't murdered, they died in their sleep. This is what I have been warning might happen, only it's occurring sooner than expected. The mutation shortened life spans."

"But they were only thirty! I'm twenty-nine. Does this mean we only have thirty years to live?"

The same panic and disorientation spreads itself across the globe with the setting of the sun and the arrival of nightfall revealing scores of vampires who passed away as they slept during the day. Everyone that died was at the young age of thirty. Each death recorded was connected to someone believed conceived on the first day after the haze left. The following day reveals a second vampire group of thousands that will no longer wake from slumber.

Shock turns to sorrow as the world's mutants and humans mourn the loss of their brothers and sisters, sons and daughters. A new horror is unleashed upon the humans of the world in parents having to witness the deaths of their children before them. These deaths are not the meaningful or senseless losses in a war or skirmish, they are the empty reminder that we are all the slaves to our genetic codes. The new written code is one that gives the children born after the haze unlimited youth in never-ending regeneration but a sharply abridged life span.

*

Two hundred arch-vampires are gathered at one of the new dome construction sites. The giant domes are entrances to the new underground cities that are being constructed. Living underground will enable future vampires to extend their productive hours beyond the limiting factors of the sun. The Angel and those like her have shunned the idea of retreating underground and are concerned what changes might occur if vampires no longer come out into the open world at night.

The Angel stands to address the group. "The tragedy of mass deaths we are experiencing is a small benefit to our efforts toward concealing our powers. As we continue to remove the records of the feats we are able to perform, so too will the deaths of the later born remove mention of them.

"We should begin the next phase of record removal and start altering the memories of our powerless arch-type and wingless vampire friends. Begin implanting hints and suggestions that they might have imagined that they saw. Every step we take moves us farther away from the potential for war born out of jealousy.

"The reports on your screens show the birth versus death rate should stabilize over time. While telomeres after Shatterbones of successive generations are still smaller than normal, they are getting longer. This means post haze vampires should begin living longer than thirty years with each new generation removed from the haze.

CHAPTER FORTY-FIVE
HUMANITY

Forty Years Post Haze

Gray storm clouds roll in the sky overhead. Grace's two sons stand behind her, knowing she must work through her sadness and allow the storm to clear on its own. Evelyn leans on Lilly as she watches Cora bend over the casket one last time.

"I can't believe we are here again so soon."

"I couldn't alter his thoughts," Cora says returning to the others. "I knew what he was planning and tried to make him happy again. I tried altering his memories after we buried my mom, but nothing would work. He loved her so much.

"The mermaids found him in the ocean a few days ago. He was floating in that little canoe they would take in the pond behind their house. He must have asked someone to take it to the ocean for him and he just started paddling out to sea."

Lightning flashes outside and a downpour begins as the flood of Lilly's emotions burst forth. Her mother's parents are both dead and her remaining grandfather isn't doing well either.

"How is Greg?" Cora places a hand on Evelyn's knee.

"He's in the hospital or he would have been here. We were afraid it was his time when he woke up and said he was weak, but it turned out to be the flu. I don't know what I'll do when he's gone. I don't blame your father one bit for his decision."

"I don't blame him either. It's just difficult with all of the others dying as well."

"Have the scientists discovered a way to do anything about it yet?"

"Some say we lack the technology, others say our scientific understanding isn't great enough. Dr. Usachova knew what would happen years ago, she just didn't expect it to affect humans as well. It all boils down to the changes the haze made to our genes."

"It doesn't seem fair that humans aren't able to live past age seventy-five any longer. I'm not happy to know my time will be up soon, but I'm happy to know you will all live on."

*

Fifty-Seven Years Post Haze

"Today, we return to the earth, our final ancestor. The humans who gave us life and from which our form mutated, were a people much like ourselves. They had conflict and turmoil, bitterness and envy. But they also had love and empathy, compassion and fairness. They gave us life and provided for us when we were young, the way our children's children now provide for their own.

"This passing of Emily Young shall be written into the history books and should be remembered as the closing chapter to the most tumultuous time in our mutant history. The trials and troubles, war and bloodshed we witnessed and often caused while coming to terms with our new existence are now behind us.

"Pettiness and quarrel still abound but warfare is now, hopefully, a thing of the past. Let us allow our thirst for discovery and conquest to turn away from our Earthly home and instead work toward reaching for the stars as our human ancestors once successfully achieved.

"With the passing of Emily Young, the last human on Earth, our darkest hour as a race passes with her. From this day forth, we should look to the future and not be anchored to painful memories of the past.

Link-In Break

CHAPTER FORTY-SIX
LINK-IN ORIGIN

Oregon Territory
Three Hundred and Sixty-Eight Years Post Haze

Jeremy Gordon taps lightly on his console waiting for the sun to set. He fought hard for the right to get to do this interview, beating out many other writers at the Virtual Link-In. The mirrored screen on his windows block the ultra-violet rays from reaching his body and causing him harm. Even with the barrier, it is rare for anyone to venture out during the daylight for any event, let alone an interview.

Through the screen, he watches as the sun dips lower until the last light finally blinks out of view below the horizon. His door slides smoothly upward allowing the unfiltered air of the world in. Checking one final time that he has all of his equipment, he turns to face the glossy stone walls of the house before him. There is a small opening in the wall into which he must place his arm for a blood sample. It is the type of security he has witnessed in only two high-level government facilities, and he wasn't permitted to enter those locations. His reports were done outside those facilities. He grabs on to a small yellow handle which pulls his arm into the hole.

"Hello, Jeremy Gordon from World Link-In."

A small ringing tone is sounded and a seam appears in the smooth wall surface before it splits open with each side sliding away with a whisper, revealing the walkway to the front of the house. A beautiful young woman sits on a bench in the courtyard off the side of the path.

"Lloyd?"

"Excuse me?"

"I…I'm sorry. Welcome to my home, Mr. Gordon. You look a great deal like someone I once knew."

"Please just call me Jeremy, Miss…um Miss."

She laughs lightly in a soft tone that seems flirtatious. "You can call me Cora. I've had the same response from your predecessors in the past. In the early years after The Shattering Event, people used to interview me when we'd pass a milestone, but no one ever thought of how to address me before they arrived."

"I apologize, Cora."

"There's no need for that. I have been around long enough to know not to be offended by such trivial things." Standing up, she stretches her wings out behind her and gives them a shake before turning toward the house. "The people from the Government Sciences Institute will be here shortly, shall we go inside to set up for the interview? I have more comfortable furniture inside than this hard bench."

"If you don't mind, I will begin recording now. I prefer not to miss anything."

She smiles and nods before turning away. Jeremy watches her enter her house and is frozen in place, a chill hits his neck, and he suddenly feels like a fly being invited into the spider's web.

"You're welcome to come in, Jeremy. Your feeling of unease will diminish after we have gotten to know each other better. My making you feel that way is a side effect of the experiences I have had."

Stepping through the doorway, he looks around briefly before asking, "You can sense what I'm feeling?"

"I can do more than that, the rumored stories you have heard are true. Those vampires like myself that were around during The Shattering Event had special abilities, often psychic powers of varying degrees."

Jeremy chuckles, his journalistic tendency of doubt and disbelief kick in. "I would love to believe you, but I know you're just teasing me for some reason. That type of change, those types of abilities, would have been recorded. If the original arch-types had powers, I would know about it. I've studied everything available about the history of The Shattering Event and the early wars."

"You have read everything that is currently available, Jeremy. I must tell you that I can not only sense your feelings, but I can read your mind as well." She smiles softly and motions toward a seat for him before walking around a counter and lighting some incense and candles. "I know what I tell you is difficult to accept, especially with your depth of study on our history, but when the other group arrives, you will be able to see for yourself what happened so long ago."

Jeremy rolls his eyes slightly and begins rubbing his forehead as Cora walks to another chair. *I keep forgetting how old she is, that must be why she isn't making sense.*

In anger at his thought, Cora grabs the back of an oak chair with her hand and crushes it while fixing Jeremy with a fierce gaze. The utter terror her action engraves on his features forces a bellowing laughter to erupt from deep within her. It is a non-threatening heavy heartfelt laugh that she hasn't had in many decades.

Through fitful attempts to regain her composure, Cora motions again for Jeremy to sit on a soft cushioned chair across from a small sofa.

"I am sorry for laughing at your expense, but I must also thank you." She smiles, shaking her head. "I haven't had such a release in a very long time. I will give you this warning, however; your thoughts will be more insulting to me if you try to hide them. Yes, you do keep forgetting how old I am but NO, I am not mixed up, confused, or forgetful in the slightest. The problem with your not understanding me is on your end, I can assure you."

"Then perhaps you can explain it in more detail for me? I have seen old recordings of the past, and neither they nor the books or articles ever mention special powers other than explaining how and why rumors about them began. I have done more than just some brief homework to familiarize myself with you; I am a history buff and have extensively researched the past."

"Your current understanding of what happened so long ago and your known expertise on the subject is why I chose you among all the others to do this interview. As I mentioned, you have researched only the history that is currently available, that which has been allowed public access up until this point. Tonight, you will be recording the true history of The Shattering Event and everything that has occurred since. The history you have researched up to this point has been censored."

"No, that's not possible, we have free records; there are penalties for document tampering."

"There are penalties for it now, but there were none in place when I and others like myself scoured archives to remove mention of psychic abilities."

"But why? I mean if I even believe you, why would you do such a thing. You were the hero of the war, the leader of the early vampires, what would you have to hide?" Standing in frustration, Jeremy begins to pace. "Was this to hide something you did? How much of the past I know is a lie?"

"The past you know is a partial past that existed. I didn't hide the things I did, I only hid how I did them. But that deception ends tonight when the others arrive with the device I helped design. The government finally perfected my design for the genetic memory recording device. It is able to extract and record visual and auditory memories that are written into my genes."

"That doesn't sound possible."

"Almost any task is possible if given the right motivation for completion. But I know you are referring to degrading memories in brain synapse transmission. Through my powers, I have the ability to absorb people's memories. I have had this power since the first day I went through Shatterbones. I can experience a complete memory of events if I choose, and I spent many years during and after the war absorbing everything I could about events which I thought mattered.

"In understanding my own abilities, I realized all memories are permanently recorded into our genetic makeup. It isn't just simplified or repetitive task memories like those instinctual behaviors in animals. Every one of the things you have experienced from the time you were born has been recorded into your genetic code, and we now have a device that can retrieve those memories for others to see the way I can."

"What about my previous question: if you have nothing to hide, why did you edit historical records? Why did you hide your abilities?"

"Jealousy and fear, those are the reasons why. We had to keep our powers secret when we discovered those children born after The Shattering Event had no extra powers. There were already too many conflicts among ourselves as well as between us and the regular humans when they existed. We didn't want our extra abilities to create grievances among everyone else."

After pressing a button on a holographic screen, a tray rises up through the middle of the small table between their seats.

"Please sit back down and have a drink with me, Jeremy. I think if you search your own feelings, the fear you have at the moment in trying to accept what I am saying should help you understand why we wanted our powers hidden. Anything that varies from normal is automatically viewed with suspicion and fear; it is a standard survival response."

"Why do you keep referring to yourself as we when talking about your powers? Do you feel they are an entity beyond yourself?"

Again, she laughs out loud and smiles at him. "I'm not crazy although I can understand why you think I might be. When I say we, I am referring to many of the arch-vampires that first mutated when the blue haze arrived. There were thousands of us that had tremendous psychic powers. We all decided we had to keep our talents secret, especially when many vampires that had our talents began to lose them."

"Yes, fine." He mentions in a slightly agitated tone. "I understand why to a certain degree, but I can't imagine the how. There would be people that knew the truth. Something would have been entered into historical database that you would have missed."

"We had ample time to remove or alter all that we wanted, and we have the abilities to control others to do the tasks for us. There were many things written or otherwise recorded about our powers originally. Mountains of government records and experiments, depositions, articles, books. There was even a segment of the entertainment industry that celebrated or decried what we were capable of. All of those records were slowly changed over time. First, they were changed into suggestion and innuendo, then into comic expressions about what people conspired to attribute to arch-vampires. Then after several decades of people believing it was a silly conspiracy theory, we removed any references to our powers from the record completely.

"You can shake your head all you want, Jeremy, but I was there at the start. I felt and saw what it did to us, and I know what we became. We turned into the monsters our parents told us about in stories as children. That first year was a year of blood, and the first day… that was a day we nearly wiped ourselves from the Earth's existence.

"Try to understand, back then, we still had regular humans. That was three hundred and sixty-eight years ago. Before the blue haze arrived, we were all just normal humans. We were regular people bumbling about our lives, finding ways to add interest and excitement to the boring routines of our waking hours. I was twelve years old the day I went through Shatterbones. Twelve years old, and in less than a minute, I grew into the young woman you see sitting before you now. I haven't aged a day since then, at least not physically."

He pulls his recorder from his shirt pocket and places it on the table. "Okay. Let's say I accept your assertion that the history I studied and think I know is altered. You say a device can record and display the real history from your DNA. Why would you re-release an unaltered version of our history that you worked so hard to hide? Also, why would you need me to report on it when, as you claim, everyone will be able to just watch your own memories of the events?"

"You and everyone else will find out in two weeks why I want our real history known. Right now, few besides myself know the reason. As for your part in all of this, you are a buffer between the truth and the lie. Knowing what we really became, what powers we truly have will be almost as frightening to the current population as it was to ourselves and our parents so many years ago.

"Hearing and reading your words on the Virtual Link-In will allow people to go through their own levels of denial before my actual memory recordings are released. People need time to absorb shocking new details over a few day's time at a minimum to prevent serious societal problems from occurring."

A chime rings out. *Multiple visitors approaching. Three blocks to arrival.*

"Scan and verify identities. Defense readiness check."

Defenses verified on full. Bacterial signatures confirmed. Doctor Avila, his assistants, Darcie and Marcus, and Vice-President Dunson.

"You have a three-block perimeter scan with defenses?"

"I have a three-block perimeter warning area for calm times like this. The scanning and defensive area is much larger."

"But I thought there haven't been hostilities between vampires in over two hundred years, is that history altered as well?"

"It is correct. There has not been a war between or among us for two hundred and forty-six years to be exact. I never had problems with vampires after that time and even before then, I was rarely challenged. Many of these defenses are new, only a few years old in fact." She takes a small sip of red. "Remember your thoughts, Jeremy. If you have a question like that, you should ask it, or I will think you are being rude. I will ask it for you this time. Why do I need new defenses like the ones I have if I am not a crazy old lady that can't remember that the war is long over? Is that how you thought it?"

"Yes, um, that is my thought exactly."

"Let me say for now I am involved in a great deal of scientific and military research."

"You mean governmental research right? You said military. We haven't had a military in…"

"Yes, we haven't had a military in over a hundred years…on planet. We aren't certain what we will encounter as our people prepare to leave the solar system, so military weaponry for exploration is still necessary. While many of the things I have developed with them are for use off planet, I feel it prudent to have certain items installed around my home. You will be told or will discover many of the answers you want over the next few hours, Jeremy. Please excuse me for a moment, my other guests have arrived."

*

"Everything is prepared. I will insert the needle with your permission and we can begin the search."

Jeremy looks over the equipment being set up with curiosity. "How long does the extraction process take?"

"In experiments with this device, it has ranged from one to two hours. However, we have never attempted extraction from someone like The Angel or with genetic data so old."

"Will I be able to see your memories right away?"

"As soon as they have isolated the correct timeframe, you can plug in or you can wait until everything is completed. If you wait until completion, the process will be a quick transfer such as anything else from the Virtual Link-In."

"How do I know it won't be a fabrication? This machine could be anything, it could be a holographic or hallucinogenic fabricator."

"You will know the difference when you are exposed to the memories. It is an all-encompassing experience, taste, smell, and touch will all be present, not only sight and sound. You will be embedded in the memories as if they are your own. You must prepare yourself, many of her experiences could be terrifying for you.

"This is the first time we are able to detect and isolate memories embedded in the genetic code. For it to be a fabrication would require entering an altered record into her genes. That is a level of scientific knowledge or ability we are nowhere near at this point in time."

"Why can't you just retrieve it from her blood sample?"

"So many questions." Dr. Avila gives him a frustrated look.

"This is all being recorded, Doctor, I need it for my story."

"Yes, that's right. I'm not used to so much chattering from the subjects I usually deal with. Blood samples will not work. For some reason which we do not completely understand, memories tend to degrade immediately upon removal from a host's body."

"If they degrade when you remove them, doesn't that prove manipulation?"

"No, because of the personal or proprietary nature, it is more explained as a consequence of removing the sole power source. We can extract genetic memories in vivid detail while still circulating in the body. They don't alter upon removal but begin to lose clarity immediately.

"Okay, I have isolated the correct sequence, Mr. Gordon. You can enter now and witness it as it unfolds, or wait for the process to be completed."

"I've heard too many impossibilities at this point to wait any longer."

The Angel grabs his arm and expresses a concerned look. "It might be a bit overwhelming. Remember that you look exactly like Lloyd."

"I'll be fine."

Link-In Initiated

CHAPTER FORTY-SEVEN
ACCEPTING THE PAST

Link-In Break

Oregon Territory
Two hours later

"I need to stop for a moment." Jeremy Gordon removes his link-in adapter and stares in disbelief at the woman whose memories he just experienced. She smiles softly at him as he stands up and begins to pace, not wanting to accept what he has witnessed so far.

"I understand why you called me Lloyd earlier. I do look exactly like him. Are we related somehow?"

"You are a descendant of Lloyd Cavanaugh's cousin according to Dr. Avila's records. I had him look it up while you were in the link."

He smiles at her briefly before remembering his reason for being here.

"Let me see if I have this correct so far. After you went through Shatterbones, you could read minds, absorb memories, influence minds, and you can even glow?"

"My luminescence is not related to my psychic abilities, it is a result of the physical transformation I went through. But yes, I had all of the abilities you witnessed."

"And you still have those powers today?"

"Yes, I do. Many of the original arch-vampires have powers of some sort, although mine and Adam's were the strongest I recorded before The Shattering Event ended and the haze left our planet. To what point did you witness my memories?"

"The war had ended, and you were speaking with the Cavanaughs in their home. You just showed them your ability to emit light, you told them you're pregnant. We're going to have a baby!" His smile fades as quickly as it arrived. "I mean you and Lloyd were going to have a baby! Sorry, I didn't mean we, the memories are so vivid."

Cora's features strain. She is trying to smile against the sadness that is evident in her eyes. "That was right before we were heading to war in Europe. Now you know that the history you are familiar with has been altered. It might suit the needs for your article to go to relevant portions of my memories from that point on instead of a continuous timeline."

Looking at Dr. Avila, "Will that be possible?"

"Yes, just like the Link-In, you should be able to approach specific memory locations by asking questions in your mind. It will be more difficult to separate yourself from the vivid nature of her memories, but your thoughts can guide you to any location if you focus. You will be able to jump through time to specific memories which your mind believes are relevant."

"Okay, I'm ready to go back in."

Link-In Initiated

CHAPTER FORTY-SEVEN
REVISITING THE PAST

Link-In Break

One Hour Later
Oregon Territory

"Now you have seen the relevant moments of our unedited past. What do you think?"
Jeremy sits silently while wiping tears from his eyes. "I'm sorry for your losses. I've never felt anything so powerful before."
"They were heartbreaking times for those of us that don't age. The first ten decades after the haze were the most difficult to deal with. Our friends and children would die at such a young age. My own grandchildren, Grace's children, they didn't live past forty. At least each new generation after the haze added two years to their longevity. Your generation is supposed to live for a hundred years, the same length of time my parents' generation were supposed to reach originally."
Dr. Avila and his assistants begin packing up the equipment, and the vice-president stands up in a daze. Without a word, he turns and walks out of the room, stumbling over a step and steadying himself against a wall before disappearing from view.
"What happened to him?"
"He was in my memories as well. Each of you viewed the portions of my memories that are relevant to yourselves and what you needed to see to complete your work. You wanted to know about our history for your article, and because of your resemblance to Lloyd, my emotional attachment brought you into my personal store on a deeper level than the vice-president."
"What was he here to see?"
"He came to see both the past and the future."
"You can't possibly…"
"No, I cannot see the future. But I know what is coming, none-the-less. This technology I have surrounded myself with allowed me to see it. I was able to discover what is coming. Just over ten years ago, I had a research probe launched into space. With it, I was able to scan the galaxy to search for the Sanguis Particle that caused the haze and mutations. I wanted to know if or when our planet would be passing through another location with it."

"You've detected it, haven't you? That's why you have yourself surrounded by these defenses. That's why the vice-president was here and why he looked so shocked."

"In thirteen days, our planet will re-enter the main body of the Sanguis Particle cloud. What we traveled through three hundred and sixty-eight years ago was only a thin arm stretching away from the main body. Apparently, our planet passes through the cloud arms with some regularity, but we do not enter the main body as often. Now that we have the technology to detect what the particle is and compare it to the movement of our planet and solar system, our past makes far more sense."

"When was the last time we passed through the main cloud?"

"You look so much like Lloyd. You have no idea how comforting it is to look at you with everything else that is happening."

"Please tell me, when was the last time we went through the cloud?"

"We skirted along the edge of it at the end of the Cretaceous Period sixty-five million years ago. The last time we went through the center as we will this time was at the end of the Permian Era, two hundred and fifty million years ago.

"You know your history, Jeremy; that is why you were picked for this interview above all others. Those eras in Earth's history are known as the Cretaceous Extinction and Permian Extinction for a reason. We lost up to ninety percent of the planet's species the last time we went through this part of the cloud.

"You have the knowledge and skills necessary to explain the unexplainable and help the people become aware of what lies before us. We are headed into a long period of change in which anything could happen. What I went through as a child was just a preview. The haze was only here for a year, a little blip in the planet's history, and it caused the upheaval to which you were just witness.

"In two weeks, when the blue haze returns, it will be with our planet for the next ten thousand years."

THE END

CHECK OUT OTHER GREAT APOCALYPSE BOOKS

WHITE OUT
by Eric Dimbleby

An apocalyptic snowstorm sweeps the globe. Experts predict this freak storm will be "The New Ice Age." Electricity is gone, as are all forms of communication and road travel. As each member of a divided family tries to survive in their own way, they must deal with a snow-driven madness that has gripped the underlying evil in the hearts of men. In an epic struggle to get home and reunite, they will find that terror lies around every snow drift... and even in their very own backyard.

NIGHT PLAGUE
by Rowan Rook

Humankind will soon be extinct. A mysterious pandemic cut through two-thirds of the population in just four short years, and within another four, it will decimate everything – and everyone – left.
The last days are ticking by, relentless and ruthless, and the reclusive Mason Mild finds himself torn between a peaceful end and a brutal immortality. Between his hopeless, but comfortable days with his family, and something new...something violent and wild.
Have the fang marks above his heel dealt him an early demise or a second birth?

CHECK OUT OTHER GREAT APOCALYPSE BOOKS

THE DEAD FAMILIAR
by J.D. McKenna

In the twilight hours of a failing world, one man seeks to bring his loved ones to safety. Jack Hightower: Marine, barkeep, and doomsday prepper. He knows of the coming calamity, and on the final night of an old world he seeks a new beginning.

This is the story of that night, the tale of how Jack and his survivor's colony in the north came to be.

DOMINION
by Doug Goodman

Dominion has been taken from man. Now, six friends must cross an apocalyptic wasteland dominated by a hell's menagerie of mega-fauna. Their middle-class suburban skills are no longer applicable to the world they live in. To find a safe haven in this world they will need to develop a new set of survival skills and fight the mutated denizens of the animal kingdom for every step of their terrifying journey.

SEVEREDPRESS

twitter.com/severedpress

CHECK OUT OTHER GREAT APOCALYPSE BOOKS

XY
by D.S. Lillico

An iron fortress protected by automated gun turrets is the only world Elsie has ever known.

When tragedy strikes, Elsie is forced to leave the sanctuary of her home and out into a brutal new world. A post-apocalyptic wasteland filled with savage mutants.

Hunted and alone Elsie stumbles into the care of a giant named Punch, but the world is now full of worse things than giants. Cannibals are starving, bandits are roaming and war is coming.

Elsie's arrival plunges the new-world further into darkness... and is there really something hidden inside of her?

SANCTUARY
by Ian Page

Deeta Nakshband, a Connecticut physician is attacked by a local surgeon while on duty in the hospital. Her friend, Janelle Jefferson, has similar experiences in Miami. Both of them become aware of an increasingly violent world as acts of isolated brutality escalate into civil unrest. They grapple with their paranoia as family members and coworkers become dangerously unpredictable. Worldwide, military units go rogue, war begins in Korea and cities implode as people slaughter each other in the streets. Martial law is declared in an attempt to maintain order. People are arrested, detainment camps are set up and interrogations end with tragic consequences as modern civilization crumbles. Deeta and Janelle band together with family friends and coworkers to save each other and find sanctuary.

www.ingramcontent.com/pod-product-compliance
Lightning Source LLC
Chambersburg PA
CBHW020057180626
46812CB00006B/2368